CELLULOID ANGELS

ALSO BY ALICE DUNCAN

The Daisy Gumm Majesty Mystery Series

CELLULOID ANGELS

A MERCY ALLCUTT MYSTERY
BOOK 9

ALICE DUNCAN

ePublishingWorks!
love what you read.

September 2024
ISBN: 978-1-664457-654-0

ePublishing Works!
644 Shrewsbury Commons Ave
Ste 249
Shrewsbury PA 17361
United States of America
www.epublishingworks.com
Phone: 866-846-5123

ACKNOWLEDGMENTS

Thanks very much to Mimi Riser, who helped me figure out why everything happened. Thanks, also, to David Bedini. I wanted to make him a villain in this book, but he wimped out on me (not Dave, but the character in the book).

And Iris Evans, who is a wizard at almost everything, not only gave me a recipe for cold cream, but she sent some she'd made herself! It's great stuff, too.

Thanks are due, too, to the brave souls who read the unedited version of *Celluloid Angels*, Margaret Cronk and Sue Krekeler (the real one, not the one who works in the dentist's office). They may well be masochists, but I sure appreciate them.

You can't wait for inspiration. You have to go after it with a club.

JACK LONDON

ONE

"*It's a girl!*" I shrieked. Then, appalled by my behavior in an office setting, I slapped a hand over my mouth.

Ernie Templeton, P.I. (which stands for Private Investigator in case you wondered) leaped from his chair and ran to the door to his room, which led into mine. I'm his confidential secretary and my office basically serves as Ernie's reception area. He stood in the doorway and stared at me as if I'd gone mad.

After clearing my throat, I said to my brother-in-law who was on the other end of the telephone wire, "Sorry, Harvey. Didn't mean to scream." Then I peered at Ernie and tried to give an apologetic grin, which was difficult as I was smiling from ear to ear. "It's a girl," I said to Ernie. "Didn't mean to shout. Sorry."

"Figured that's what you were yelling about," said Ernie. He smiled, and I relaxed. "Please congratulate Harvey for me."

"Ernie offers his congratulations, Harvey," I told my brother-in-law.

"Have they chosen a name yet?" asked Ernie

"I don't know." I returned to the telephone mouthpiece. "Have you chosen a name yet? When can I see Chloe?" For the record, Chloe is my sister and a brand-new mother as of that morning.

"Come now if you can," said Harvey. I could hear the elation in his voice. "We're at Cedars of Lebanon. We're not sure about a name yet."

"I'm at work, but I'll come as soon as I can."

"I'll drive you," said Ernie from his office door. "Let's go now."

I gaped at my kind-hearted, if perennially casual, employer. "You mean it?"

He gave me a sarcastic squint. "Got anything else to do?" he asked.

The answer to that question was "no." So I told Harvey, "Ernie said he can drive us both there now. Is that okay? How's Chloe doing?"

"She's fine. Tired. The baby is gorgeous."

"Of course she is." Then I thought of something not-quite-so wonderful. "Um, have you telephoned Pasadena yet?"

Here's the thing about Pasadena. It's a lovely city. However, it was also the city in which Chloe's and my parents resided during the winter months. Our father had taken a train back to Boston a couple of weeks prior to this day, but Mother had remained in Pasadena in spite of her daughters' telling her she needn't. She'd told us she wanted to help with the baby. It was one of her more ludicrous statements. Mother, though, believed in herself and her powers. Both Chloe and I knew a good deal about her powers, but neither of us wanted them anywhere near Chloe and Harvey's precious baby.

"Not yet. I'm thinking maybe I'll call tomorrow or the next day. When Chloe's not so exhausted. Giving birth isn't much fun, I guess."

"I guess it isn't," I said, sounding almost as sarcastic as my boss. "You men have a lot to answer for, Harvey Nash. But yes, wait a few days before you call Mother. If there's anything guaranteed to upset a sick person—or even one recovering from childbirth—it's our mother."

"You said it," said Harvey. It sounded to me as if he was glad I'd confirmed him in his decision to wait to report the birth of his girl child to a woman who, while an actual mother, had never acted like one.

Our mother's name is Honoria Violet Chudleigh Allcutt unless you're either Chloe or me, in which case she's The Wrath of God. And if there's any other one person more unfit to care for a sick person or a new mother, I can't think of whom he or she might be. Lizzie Borden maybe.

"Anyhow, thanks, Harvey. I'm so glad Chloe and the baby are well. Ernie and I will be there as soon as we can be."

"Glad you're both coming. Chloe will be pleased," said Harvey. I know he meant it. Both Chloe and Harvey liked Ernie a lot.

So did I. In actual fact, Ernie and I had begun "seeing" each other after office hours for a few months by that day, which was January 29, 1927. I hung the mouthpiece on the receiver hook and breathed a happy sigh. "A little girl," I whispered. "How sweet."

"Harvey probably wanted a boy," said Ernie.

He would.

"Harvey said, and I believe him, that he didn't care if the child was a boy or a girl, as long as both the baby and Chloe got through the ordeal well, and they did."

"Just teasing you, kiddo," said Ernie. I hated when he called me "kiddo," but I didn't say anything. "Do you need to pack a bag or anything?"

"To visit Chloe and the baby at the hospital?" I asked, surprised.

"Oh. Yeah, I guess you won't be staying with the Nashes yet."

"Harvey isn't going to telephone Mother for another day or three. Maybe four," I told him.

"Wise man, Harvey." Ernie had met my parents.

"Exactly. When Mother arrives, Chloe might need me." I gazed at him pleadingly. "May I take a few days off to help my sister in her time of peril?"

"Sure. Take as many as you need. I've already talked to Dr. Clutter, and he said if you need to be gone for any length of time, Glynis O'Fannin can answer the telephone here."

"How nice! And how nice of you to think of it!" I said, delighted with my boss who could be quite considerate.

"Anything for you and Chloe, Mercy," said Ernie with a chuckle. "I'll get my hat and coat. You get your stuff and we can go. Where is this precious child?"

"Cedars of Lebanon. Do you know where that is?"

"Sure," said Ernie.

No surprise there. Ernie and Los Angeles knew each other well.

It wasn't more than five or six minutes later when we took the elevator from the third floor of the Figueroa Building, where Ernie and I worked, to the lobby. As ever, there sat my pal Lulu LaBelle at the reception desk. Although I'd had a month or so to get used to her "new" look, I admit to being somewhat startled to see Lulu in a pretty but subdued skirt and sweater combination. Not only was she wearing office-appropriate clothing these days, but she was also busily buffing her fingernails, which used to be vivid red talons.

When I'd first come to work for Ernie and up until about four weeks prior to this date, Lulu had been one of the brighter sights in Los Angeles. She'd worn eye-poppingly colorful clothing and could generally be found either painting or filing her fingernails as she sat at the reception desk waiting for the telephone to ring.

A misunderstanding with a fellow claiming to be a talent scout had shocked her into amending her clothing and makeup choices. She still had bottle-blond hair, but these days she no longer looked like a colorfully wrapped Christmas present. In fact, she and I had enjoyed ourselves tremendously going on shopping expeditions to various consignment shops in Chinatown and elsewhere to purchase her new and suitable office wear.

She glanced up from buffing her nails when she heard us depart from the elevator, and she smiled a lovely smile. Today's smile wasn't outlined in violent red, but a rather subdued pinkish color her new Tangee Natural Lipstick tinted her lips. "Hey there, you two," she said, waving her nail buffer at us. "Where are you going?"

"Cedars of Lebanon," I told Lulu, breaking into a celebratory run toward Lulu's reception desk. "Chloe had her baby!"

Lulu leaped up from her chair, squealed in delight and met me in the middle of the lobby where we gave each other a huge hug. "Boy or girl?"

"Girl," I said.

"Oh, how sweet," said Lulu, letting go of me and wiping a tear of happiness from her faintly powdered cheek. "Have they picked a name yet?"

As I wiped a tear from my own faintly powdered cheek, I said, "Not yet."

"Golly, you'd think they'd have thought of a name for a boy or a girl before now," said Lulu returning to her desk and sitting once more.

"I'd have thought so too" I said. "But not Chloe and Harvey. Chloe said she wanted to meet the baby first and then choose a suitable name based on its personality. Her personality."

"Do babies have personalities?" asked Ernie as he joined us at the reception desk.

"Don't know," said Lulu with a shrug.

"I don't either," I said. "I haven't been around many babies thus far in my life."

"Me neither," said Lulu. "I was only a kid when Rupert was born, so we kind of grew up together." Rupert Mullins, Lulu's younger brother, worked for a motion-picture set-designer named Francis Easthope. Lulu's last name was really Mullins, too, but she thought Lulu LaBelle would look better on the marquee of a picture-palace.

"Same here, sort of," I said. "Chloe's two years older than I am, but I don't remember either of us when we were babies."

"Please give Chloe and Harvey my best wishes," said Lulu wistfully. "And the nameless kid, too."

"Will do," I said.

Fortunately for Ernie and me, Mr. Buck, the custodian at the Figueroa Building (and husband of my own cook/housekeeper) always saved a parking spot for Ernie directly in front of the Figueroa Building. Therefore, we didn't have to walk for blocks in order to find Ernie's almost-new Packard-Six. When I'd first come to work for Ernie last July, he'd had an old dilapidated 1909 Studebaker. It was a real pleasure to ride in Ernie's Packard, primarily because his old Studebaker had been unsafe at any speed.

Traffic seemed to get worse with each passing minute in the City of Angels. According to Ernie, who read the *Los Angeles Times* every day, more and better street lighting was coming to Los Angeles soon. Made me happy. I worried about the poor traffic coppers who had to direct traffic at busy intersections, and those semaphore signals were difficult to see sometimes. But, again according to Ernie, electricity would soon be the order of the day, and L.A. would have actual traffic lights.

We arrived at Cedars of Lebanon at about ten a.m. As I popped into the gift shop off the lobby to buy Chloe a bouquet of flowers, Ernie asked at the reception desk where the maternity ward was. "We've got to walk upstairs to see the mother and baby," he told me. He also retrieved the floral arrangement from my arms, which was nice of him.

"Second floor?" I asked.

"Yup. Chloe's in a private room of course," Ernie said.

"Of course," I said. "Harvey's a big-time movie mogul. He can afford a private room." I waited for a couple of beats, but Ernie didn't mention how nice it must be to have been born to money. That's what he called it. What's more, he maintains that the moment I walked into his office looking for a job, he'd known I'd been born to money.

He might be right about his assertion, and he was certainly correct about my relative wealth. However, the fact that I was then looking for honest employment meant I was unlike most others in my economic and social sphere. By golly, I *knew* I'd fled from what many people would consider an ivory tower.

I'd come to the City of Angels in order to learn to live life as ordinary people live it. I wanted to find out first-hand the perils of poverty. Well, maybe not poverty; but I understood that other women actually *had* to work at jobs and live off the money they made at them. I now had a job, but I didn't need to depend on my earnings in order to live. I tried to do so, however, and sometimes actually did.

The sad truth was that women didn't make much money no

matter what they did for a living, and I remained peeved about it. My mother called me a Socialist. If being a Socialist means I believe women should receive the same wages men get for doing the same work, then I guess I am. But darn it *I* think the rules of the world should change. Wish I knew how to change them, but I don't. Therefore, I do my simple best by renting rooms in my massive home to deserving working women like Lulu.

When we got to Chloe's door, Ernie tapped lightly and we entered. Chloe was sitting up in her narrow hospital bed looking beautiful but tired.

Harvey was there, as was the aforementioned Mr. Francis East-hope, who worked for Harvey's studio. Another man occupied a corner of the room, but I didn't know his name.

"Mercy! Ernie!" said Chloe, smiling happily. "So glad you could come."

"Where is the new little Nashlet?" asked Ernie, searching the room, presumably for a baby.

"In the baby ward. You'll have to walk down the hall a little bit to see the babe," Harvey answered for her.

"She's beautiful," said a rapturous Chloe.

"She should be," I said as I walked to my sister's hospital bed to give her a hug and a kiss on the cheek. "She has a beautiful mother."

"She does indeed," said Mr. Easthope, who was one of the best-looking as well as one of the nicest men in the world.

"Oh, Mercy and Francis, you always make me feel so good," said Chloe in a shaky voice.

To my horror, I saw tears trickling down her alabaster cheeks. "Chloe! What's the matter? I didn't mean to make you cry! I'm so sorry."

"Don't be sorry, Mercy," said Harvey with a chuckle. "Chloe's just emotional right now."

"Harvey's right," said Chloe.

"Hormones," said Mr. Easthope, nodding as if he knew. I wasn't altogether sure what a hormone was and decided not to ask.

"Oh, and you two brought flowers!" cried Chloe, weeping some more.

Good grief. If I'd known Ernie and I would make Chloe cry, I'd have stayed away.

No, that's not true. I loved my sister; she was my best friend; and if she was in an emotional state, she deserved it. I'd read about childbirth, and it sounded to me as though God had made a big fat mistake when He'd created the female human body.

"Yeah," said Ernie, smiling knowingly at Chloe. I don't know what he knew that I didn't, but she perked up slightly. "Any vases around here?"

"Let me go to the nurses' station and ask for one," said the man I didn't know. He began walking to the door, but stopped before Ernie and held out a hand for Ernie to shake. "I'm Roderick Crowhurst, one of the Nash studio's attorneys."

"Oh Lord, Roddy and Ernie, I'm sorry!" said Harvey. "I didn't realize you two hadn't met before. Roderick Crowhurst, please allow me to introduce you to Ernest Templeton."

"Happy to meet you," said Ernie.

"And you," said Mr. Crowhurst. "And this is Mrs. Nash's sister? Did I get that part right?"

"Yes," I said, marching right up to Mr. Crowhurst and holding out my hand. "I'm Mercy Allcutt, Chloe's sister."

Harvey slapped a hand to his forehead. "I'm sorry, Mercy. The baby's got me all rattled."

"It's all right, Harvey," cooed Chloe from her bed. "We know you're usually the epitome of gentlemanliness."

"Yes," I agreed. "You are."

Mr. Crowhurst laughed and said, "I'll go get that vase now. Good to meet you both, Miss Allcutt and Mr. Templeton." He left the room.

"Honestly, I didn't know having a baby would be so exhausting," said Harvey. "I think my wits have completely deserted me."

This time it was Chloe who laughed. "*You* think it's exhausting? You should try pushing a six-pound baby through a space too small for it to fit!"

I don't know about anyone else, but I could feel a blush creep up my neck and invade my cheeks. I was trying *so* hard to fit into Los Angeles society, which was ever so much more modern and relaxed than that of Boston's Beacon Hill, yet I blushed at Chloe's description of childbirth. Sometimes I think there's no hope for me.

TWO

After Mr. Crowhurst came back with a vase filled with water and we fixed my arrangement in it, it looked pitifully small among the other floral tributes already there. Because Harvey Nash was one of the wealthiest and most successful studio executives in the entire United States, all the flicker folks wanted his approval. Therefore, they sent flowers.

With Harvey, flowers wouldn't do the trick. He had his feet solidly planted on the ground and his priorities correctly ordered. If you were professional, polite and did your job well, Harvey would approve of you; if you were lax at any one of those behaviors, he wouldn't. He didn't care for toadies. I, for one, liked him for it.

The four of us chatted for a few more minutes, and then Ernie said, "May we see the new baby Nash? You say there's a baby ward. Is that where we can see the kid?"

"Yes," said Chloe.

"I'll escort you," said Harvey.

"No, you stay here," Chloe said. "I don't want you to leave me."

"And I think I'll take off now," said Mr. Crowhurst. "This is a family occasion. I'm mighty happy for both of you though. It was a pleasure to meet you, Miss Allcutt, and you, Mr. Templeton."

"Likewise," said Ernie, holding out his hand again.

"Indeed," I said doing likewise.

Mr. Crowhurst shook my hand and then Ernie's, and offered Chloe and Harvey another couple of congratulations and shook Mr. Easthope's hand too before he left.

Harvey, who had been gazing lovingly at his wife, jerked as if he'd just remembered something and said, "Thanks for driving me, Roddy. Appreciate it."

"Happy to have helped," said Mr. Crowhurst, and he left the room.

"Where were you that you needed someone to drive you to the hospital?" I asked. Snoopy, wasn't I?

"Just out to breakfast," said Harvey. "We needed to discuss some of the problems we've been having on the set of our new epic flicker."

"I'm sorry you've been having problems," I said.

"Me too," said Harvey. "But I don't care about that now. I care about Chloe and our first child."

"As is only right and proper," I said, grinning at Harvey and then Chloe.

"Here," said Mr. Easthope. "I'll lead you to the baby viewing room. The nurses know who I am and whose baby I'll be there to see."

"Already having been there seventy or eighty times?" asked an amused Ernie.

"You've got it in one," said Mr. Easthope, also amused.

So Mr. Easthope turned left after leaving Chloe's room and we followed him down about half a city block's worth of hallway until we got to a place where several people already stood, staring through a huge glass window. When we arrived, some of the people shuffled sideways so we could maneuver ourselves into the crowd.

I've never seen so many babies in my entire life! Well, truth to tell, I hadn't seen many babies at all during my twenty-two years.

"There they are," said Mr. Easthope, nodding at one of the nurses behind the window.

A smile lit up her face, and I knew her heart was going pitty-pat.

Mr. Easthope had that effect on women. Little did they know that all their smiles and pitty-pats were for naught when it came to him. He wasn't—to put it mildly—a ladies' man. Mr. Easthope saved his affections for people of his own sex.

Are you shocked? Horrified? Disgusted? Well, nertz to you. I'd lived long enough among motion-picture people to know there were lots and lots of them like Mr. Easthope, and they couldn't help being what they were. Heck, my own personal boss, Mr. Ernest Templeton, was still a little standoffish with Mr. Easthope. Silly man. People like Mr. Easthope don't court rejection any more than do men whilst dealing with women—or women whilst dealing with men.

So just stop it, all right?

Sorry. Didn't mean to lecture.

Anyhow, as soon as the nurse realized Ernie and I were with Mr. Easthope, she rushed to one of the little cribs and lifted out a baby.

I was horrified. "Ernie," I whispered to my boss, "it looks like a baby bulldog!" I ran my gaze over other baby cribs. "They *all* look like baby bulldogs!"

Both Ernie and Mr. Easthope chuckled.

"None of them is especially beautiful," concurred Mr. Easthope softly. "But don't say that to Chloe or Harvey."

"Wouldn't dream of it," whispered Ernie, "even though Mercy's right."

"At least the one the nurse picked up has some hair," I muttered.

The nurse carried the infant to the window to better show off her armload of just-born human being. Honestly, I hadn't realized how ugly newborn babies were until that moment. As I mentioned before, my exposure to the newly born was, well, nil.

"She has a bright red face," I added. "And a flat nose. And is her head misshapen? What does that mean? And look at her left ear! It's bent over. Oh, Lord, Francis, she's not deformed or anything is she?"

"I asked a nurse about that," said Mr. Easthope. "She said sometimes babies lie in the womb at an odd angle, and it might take a few days before their heads assume the shape they're supposed to have. And her hair will probably fall out, too, according to the nurse."

"Good Lord," I whispered.

"Don't worry about it, Mercy," said Ernie. "When I lived in Chicago, I saw lots of newborns, and they all looked like baby bull-dogs at first. It'll take a while, but that kid will take on features that look human soon."

"I sure hope so," I said. When I glanced from the bundled babe to the nurse, I saw the nurse frowning at me. I must have looked as aghast as I felt. Therefore, I forced a huge smile for the nurse and nodded as if this were the happiest day of my life. Heck, for all I knew it might well be.

"They all look pretty much alike too, don't they?" said Mr. East-hope. "I guess God graced women with the emotional wherewithal to be blind to their own baby's relative ugliness. I expect the mothers of these children can even detect which one is theirs, too."

"Amazing," I said.

"What's amazing?" came Chloe's voice from down the hall a bit.

I whirled around and was relieved to see her too far away to have heard my comments about her bundle of joy. She clutched one of Harvey's arms and both of them all but glowed with joy.

"Are you supposed to be out and walking around?" I demanded, rushing up to her and trying to take an arm. Couldn't do it, because both of Chloe's arms were securely wrapped around one of Harvey's. She moved slowly, which only made sense.

"I'm fine," she assured me. "The doctor said I shouldn't do too much, but walking down the hall to see my daughter isn't too much."

"I should say not," said Mr. Easthope.

"My sister didn't have any trouble after either of her kids was born," said Ernie reassuringly.

"Good to know," said Harvey as if he meant it.

"They want to keep me here for ten days," said Chloe. "I don't *want* to stay here. I want to take our daughter home. Thanks to you and Francis, Mercy, she has about the most perfect baby nursery any child could want."

This, I say with no modesty at all, was the truth. I'd had the brilliant idea of having Mr. Easthope and an acquaintance of Ernie's and mine, Mr. Jerome Brentwood, paint the walls of the Nashes' baby's nursery with pictures out of storybooks. It was gorgeous, and I didn't blame Chloe for wanting her child sleeping in it as soon as possible.

"We can probably take you home before the mandatory ten-day sentence," said Harvey. "After all, I've already hired nurses for you and the babe."

Of course he had. Harvey was richer than Croesus, whoever he was. Some old Greek fellow, I think. I glanced at my boss to see if he had an isn't-it-nice-to-be-rich smirk on his face and was glad to see he didn't.

The truth, though, was that Harvey had hired two nurses and a nanny to help the new mother cope. Learning about these arrangements, the hospital gave in to Chloe and Harvey's wishes and allowed them to take their wee tot—as yet unnamed—home to their palatial mansion after a mere five days.

And this, even though Harvey had finally called Pasadena and Mother knew of the baby's birth. Mind you, if she'd merely congratulated the couple on producing a healthy baby girl, nobody would have minded. Our mother however, as noted above, intended to "help" Chloe through her first few weeks of motherhood. Not that she'd had much to do with either Chloe's or my infancy—or even childhood—except to scold and nag.

"But Harvey couldn't say no to her," Chloe said miserably to me over the telephone that night.

Ernie had come to dinner at my house, christened Mercy's Manor by Lulu LaBelle. Lulu, as noted earlier, rented an apartment from me in my lovely—and large—home on Los Angeles's Bunker Hill. I'd bought the place from Chloe and Harvey when they moved to Beverly Hills, which was becoming the preferred residential area of the so-called stars of the flickers.

The Nash Studio held a place of pride in the industry, and not just because it produced excellent movies. Harvey was also a Very Good Man who didn't take advantage of the folks who worked for him. Ernie, Lulu, and I had recently been involved in a case featuring a fellow of whom the same couldn't be said. In truth, that fellow had been a slimy slug of a human being. Now that Lulu was no longer considered a suspect in his demise, I was glad he was dead.

We'd finished another fine meal cooked for us by Mrs. Buck and had settled in various chairs and the sofa in the living room when the telephone in my office rang. I rose, headed toward my office and said, "Be right back. It's probably Chloe or Harvey. Maybe they've chosen a name."

"I hope it's not something ugly," said Lulu.

"Lulu!" cried the Puritanical Caroline Terry, also one of my tenants.

"But I *do* hope it's nothing ugly," said Lulu, sticking to her guns. "I mean, they might name the kid after some rich relative who has a name like Pansy or Hortense or Bertha. Heck, I have a cousin named Prunella."

"That is pretty bad," said Ernie.

"Prunella Nash?" said Sue Krekeler, the last of my tenants, with a chuckle. "I don't like it either."

I flapped a hand at the roomful of my friends and lifted the receiver. "Mercy's Manor, Mercy speaking," I said into the receiver.

"Mercy!" cried Chloe. "*Mother's* coming!"

"Oh dear," I said to my disconsolate sister. "I'm sorry."

"Ernie said you can come here to help me cope, right?" said a trifle more perky Chloe. "And you can stay while Mother's here?"

"Yes, he did. But Chloe, Mother hates me!"

"She hates everyone, Mercy, and I don't want her to aggravate the nurses and the nanny so much that they'll quit!"

"How can I stop her?" I asked. "I've never been able to stop her from doing anything."

"Maybe not, but you've prevented her from running your life," said Chloe. "All I'm asking for is some help, Mercy. Please?"

Feeling a sinking sensation begin to travel from my heart and down my body to my sensible shoes, I said feebly, "How long do you expect her to stay?"

"I don't know. For as long as she can, I expect."

"But, Chloe, I have a job! Ernie's being very generous in letting me visit you, but I doubt I can outlast our mother."

"But Mercy!" cried Chloe. "You *have* to!"

I cast a pleading glance from the telephone in my downstairs office to the people in the living room.

"You can have a couple of weeks," said a generous Ernie. "You know I have Glennie O'Fannin set to fill in for you."

Turning my attention back to my sister on the other end of the telephone wire, I said, "Ernie says I can stay for two weeks."

"But what if she's not *gone* by then?" sobbed Chloe. "You know Mother. She'll take as much as she can grab and cling on for dear life."

"But…"

"But nothing! *Please*, Mercy! This is supposed to be the happiest time in my life, and I'm terrified!" In a choking voice, she added, "I d-don't want that woman around my b-b-*baby*!"

Feeling almost as frustrated as my sister, I asked, "Can't Harvey hire a bodyguard or something?"

"Mercy! I can't have a bodyguard toss our mother into the street!"

"Don't know why not," I said sulkily. Then I relented, knowing she was correct. "Oh, I know you can't, Chloe. But I truly hate being anywhere near our mother."

"So do I," said Chloe. "But maybe you can bring Ernie with you!" She sounded so bright and cheery after her suggestion, I felt my eyes widen and my mouth fall open.

After closing my mouth with a clack of teeth, I said, "Mother would have an apoplectic fit and die on your drawing-room floor if she thought Ernie and I were a couple!"

"I know," said Chloe. "So see? It'd be perfect."

Because I wasn't sure if she was serious, I didn't speak for a second or two.

"Mercy?" said Chloe.

"I'm here. But as much as I'd like to have Ernie stay in your house while I'm there, you know Mother would pitch a fit."

"Hey!" said Ernie in the background. I heard my tenants Lulu LaBelle, Sue Krekeler, and Caroline Terry giggling.

"I don't care if she does," said Chloe.

"Yes you do. Anyhow, Ernie has a business to run."

"Bother his business!" My mind's eye pictured Chloe wiping a palm across her damp forehead. "I don't mean that. But can you come?" she pleaded.

"Of course. I'd love to stay with you for a while."

"As long as Mother stays?" she asked, still pleading.

"I don't know," I said, growling slightly.

"Mother can't stay *too* long," said Chloe, sounding more optimistic than certain.

"She'll stay until somebody makes her leave," I told my sister firmly. I knew this from personal experience. *Bitter* personal experience.

"Oh dear. But you're better at standing up to her than I am. Maybe you can tell her to leave when she's stayed too long."

"Five minutes with her is too long," I said.

"I know, but I'll have to let her stay for a week or so I suppose."

After mulling this over for a heartbeat or three, I said, "I suppose a week or two wouldn't be so bad. This is her first grandchild, after all."

"Good Lord, you're right!" Chloe cried as if I'd just stabbed her in the heart. "That means she'll want to stay *forever*!"

"Oh, Chloe, I'm so sorry. But listen, today is Thursday. How about I go to your place tomorrow after work. Then I can stay the weekend and we can see how things go after that. When is Mother coming?"

"Tonight!" My poor sister sounded as if she were about to begin sobbing.

"But you just came home from the hospital today!"

"I know, but she's coming tonight anyway. With any luck, Harvey can keep her away from the baby and me until you get here. Nanny Gibson is pretty strict, and I have nurses who will keep her away from us for the most part. I hope."

"I hope so too," I said.

"Tomorrow then," said a bleak-voiced Chloe.

"Tomorrow. Can't wait to see the baby again. May I bring Buttercup? She and Pepper get along well." Pepper was the Nashes' adorable spaniel. Buttercup was my adorable toy poodle.

"Mother will hate Pepper. She already hates Buttercup."

"True, so that part will work in our favor," I said, thinking our mother *must* have a breaking point when it came to overstaying her welcome. Not that either Chloe or I had as yet discovered it.

"I only wish," said Chloe miserably.

Darn our mother anyway! The old bat spread dismay and misery wherever she went. I hated to see her upsetting new-mother Chloe before she'd even entered the Nash home. I decided to change the subject.

"Have you decided on a name yet?"

"No. We're thinking about Florence Catherine, but I'm not sure."

Huh. I didn't much care for Florence Catherine, but it wasn't my kid so I didn't say so.

"Let's go over possible names when I get there," I suggested.

"That would be wonderful," said Chloe. "Thanks, Mercy. You're the only person I know who can handle Mother."

"I can't handle her," I told her. "I just won't let her bully me around is all."

"That's what I mean," said Chloe. "I don't know how to do that."

I heaved a sigh. "I'll give you lessons."

"Thanks, Mercy."

"Good night, Chloe. Kiss the baby for me."

"I shall. Thanks again."

"You're welcome. See you tomorrow."

We both hung up our telephones, and I turned to see my entire household, including Mr. and Mrs. Buck and Ernie, staring at me. Mr. Buck was not only the custodian at the Figueroa Building where Ernie, Lulu, and I worked, but he was also the fellow who kept my house and grounds repaired and planted. Mrs. Buck, his wife, was

28

my cook-housekeeper, as noted earlier. They were both worth their weight in gold, but I paid them by check.

"Your mother's going to stay at Chloe and Harvey's?" asked Ernie, his tone suitably solemn.

"Yes," I said upon another big sigh.

"Oh, how sweet," said Caroline.

The rest of us turned to stare upon her in horror.

Seeing our expressions, Caroline said, "What?"

Lulu LaBelle said, "You haven't met Mercy's mother, have you?"

"No," said Caroline.

"Consider yourself lucky," said Ernie.

"Oh," said Caroline.

"She's really awful, Caroline," said Sue. "She's kind of like a… a…a…."

"Hippopotamus," I said, helping her out. "An angry one."

"Yeah. One of those," said Sue.

"She's going to inflict herself on them tonight, too. Poor Chloe and Harvey," I said. "And Chloe just got home from the hospital this afternoon! I swear, I don't know how one woman can spread such misery and unhappiness without half trying."

"Guess it's an art," said Ernie. "Or maybe she went to harridan school."

"Oh my goodness," said Caroline, finally catching on.

THREE

Although he didn't intend to stay with me at my sister's home, Ernie was kind enough to drive me to Beverly Hills after work on Friday, which was the fifth of February. He carried my suitcase up the impressive steps to the Nashes' massive front door and I rang the bell. Buttercup capered up the staircase with her little stubby tail wagging. She knew this was where Pepper, the English toy spaniel I'd given Chloe and Harvey, lived. They were pals, Buttercup and Pepper.

"Nice place," said Ernie, jarring me out of my dread about confronting Mother.

I squinted at him to see if he was being caustic. As mentioned earlier, he often teased me because I "came from money," which isn't my fault. But he was only looking around at the lovely, if incredibly large, house, manicured lawns and impressive grounds with an approving—or perhaps an envious—smile.

"Yes," I said. "It is. Harvey and Chloe were going to build their own place, but then Velma Blackwood and Stanley Hastings divorced, and this place went on the market."

"Yeah. I remember. And you bought their place on Bunker Hill."

"Yes."

The door opened, so our conversation ended. The Nashes' maid, Molly Johnson, attempted to smile at us. "Good evening, Miss Mercy and Mr. Ernie," she said, her lips quivering.

I hurried inside the house. "Molly! What's the matter?"

"N-nothing," she said.

Behind me, Ernie said, "Your mother's here, Mercy. That's probably what the matter is. Right, Molly?"

Poor Molly cast a thankful look at Ernie and nodded. I'd venture to guess terror kept her from speaking.

Sure enough, majestic as the *Titanic* but unfortunately still on this side of the ocean's floor, my mother hove into view.

"Molly! Don't stand there with the door open. It's cold outside. And what is that *dog* doing here?"

"She just opened the door for us, Mother," I said in a voice as cold as the weather. "She's not holding the door open for any other reason. And Buttercup came with me to keep Chloe and the baby and Pepper company."

Mother huffed. "So you're here, are you, and you brought your dog? You would. Dogs are full of germs and shouldn't be allowed near babies. And is that Mr. Templeman with you?" She sounded scandalized.

"You know very well his name is Templeton, Mother. Not Templeman," I growled.

Ernie, who had about as much use for my mother as I did, stepped past the quaking Molly and held out his hand to Mother, knowing as he did so that Mother would be, if not scandalized, at least outraged. After all, *she*, as the female in the equation, was the one who should hold her hand out for *him* to shake. "How-do, Mrs. Allcutt. You have a beautiful granddaughter. Mercy and I went to see her and Chloe at the hospital."

After glaring at Ernie's hand for several seconds, Mother condescended to shake it. She said, "Yes, thank you. She is a lovely girl. I'm sure Harvey would have preferred a boy, but I suppose there's time for that."

"What a horrid thing to say!" I told my mother. "And Buttercup and Pepper are *not* germy!"

"Mercy! Ernie! So glad you're here!" Harvey hurried into the fabulous tiled entryway to greet Ernie and me. "Thank you, Molly. You needn't help here. I'll take Mercy's luggage." Bless his heart. His intervention probably saved my life. Mother reacted badly when people told her she did horrid things and/or told her she was wrong about something—and I'd just done both of those things.

"Glad to be here, Harvey," I said.

"Oh, and you brought Buttercup," Harvey said happily. "I'll bet she and Pepper will have great fun playing together."

"Humph!" said Mother, who believed in using servants for pretty much everything and also thought—as you might have noticed—that dogs were dirty.

So Harvey took my bag from Ernie, smiled ingratiatingly at my mother and said, "Come with me, you two. Chloe is dying to see you. We're both thrilled to have a baby girl."

Take *that*, Mother!

"Thanks, Harvey," said Ernie. He took my elbow and we, along with Buttercup, followed Harvey to the closet where guests were supposed to leave their coats and hats. Mother chuffed along behind us like an indignant freight train. As Ernie helped me off with my coat, hung it in the closet and then hung up his own coat, Harvey spoke to Mother.

"Mrs. Allcutt, why don't you rest in the drawing room for a few minutes? I'm sure Chloe and Mercy and Ernie would like some private time together."

"*Private* time? For goodness' sake, why? I should be with them to chaperone!"

"I'll be their chaperone," said Harvey. "Chloe is exhausted, and she's been looking forward to seeing Mercy all day. We won't take much time."

"I should be there to help," said Mother.

"She has two nurses and a nanny to help her, Mother," I said. "She doesn't need you."

"Mercedes Louise Allcutt! How *dare*—"

It surprised me to realize it, but I honestly *had* learned (more or less) how to deal with my mother. This amazing feat became obvious when I interrupted her. Interrupting anyone else would have been rude. "Don't Mercedes Louise me, Mother. I'm going to see my sister and her baby, and you can butt out."

I saw Mother's mouth flap open but didn't wait around to hear what else she had to scold me about. I'd sure handed her lots of fodder to chew on, and Ernie and I had only been inside the Nashes' home for about two minutes by then. "Lead on, Harvey," I said.

So Harvey, taking advantage, led on. He'd had an electric elevator installed. As it was directly off the entryway, he'd already pushed the button, so he opened the cage door and gestured for Ernie and me (only the other way around) and Buttercup to enter. We did.

"Oh, Lordy, Harvey," I said, when the door to the elevator closed. "How are you able to stand her?"

"I'm not," said Harvey, sounding fretful. "But it's only going to get worse. I *really* have to go to the studio on Monday because we're getting the set ready for *Helen of Troy*. It's going to be a huge epic saga and there have been a couple of snags, so I have to be involved. I'm glad you'll be here over the weekend. You're the only person I've met so far who can get that woman to shut up and behave."

"*I?*" I asked incredulously. "I can't make her do anything. I can interrupt her and tell her to stop riding roughshod over everyone, but she never does anything except scold me for it."

"Under the circumstances," said Ernie with a judicial air, "that might do almost as well. At least she won't be picking on Chloe, the nanny, the nurses and the baby all the time. She'll stick to you and let Chloe rest up."

"Golly thanks, Ernie. I thought you were my friend." I frowned at him.

Harvey chuckled. "I think Ernie has a good point, Mercy. If you harass her enough, maybe she'll decide Chloe, the baby and I aren't worth her time and go back to Boston."

"I doubt that'll happen," I said morosely. "But I promise I'll stay for as long as she's here." I cast a quick glance at my boss as the elevator shuddered to a stop. "As long as she leaves in two weeks."

"Stay as long as you need to, Mercy," said Ernie, kindness personified. "No new mother or tiny child should be subjected to your mother. I know Chloe's got nurses and a nanny, but I expect your mother will roll over them like a bulldozer. She's used to obedience from her servants. And her daughters."

"True," said Harvey upon a sigh. "Although the nanny, Mrs. Gibson, does pretty well in holding her own. One of the nurses isn't too shabby in that department either. The other one's a pushover."

"I'll do what I can," I said when Harvey opened the elevator door and we escaped its confines, which led to the second-floor hallway. We all heard a happy yip, and darned if Pepper didn't race down the hall, slide several feet before she reached us, and then leap upon Buttercup as if they were long-lost siblings reunited after a hideous war or something. We all laughed when the two pups took turns pursuing each other down the hallway, slipping and sliding on the well-polished wood.

From the elevator we didn't turn to our right, which took one on a little walk overlooking the Italian marble foyer where Mother stood glaring up. I'm sure she'd intended to use her glare on Harvey, Ernie, Buttercup, and me, but Harvey turned left into a huge upstairs sitting room. Doors leading to suites of rooms lined that room. I knew where Chloe and Harvey's suite was, so I aimed myself there. "I can't promise," I added, "that I won't shove her over the balcony onto your marble foyer."

"Dear God, please don't do that," said Harvey as if he were taking my words seriously. "We'd never get the bloodstains off those tiles."

"Oh very well," I said, stopping at a door and tapping lightly. "I'll shove her out of a window. How about if I do it over the rose garden. If the fall doesn't kill her, maybe she'll get stabbed to death by rose thorns."

"Mercy," said Ernie. "I know your mother is difficult, but sheesh."

"She's not merely difficult," I told Ernie. "If there's anyone calculated to make what should be a happy occasion totally miserable, it's she. She's a gorgon. A dragon. A hydra-headed monster."

"All righty then," said Ernie, giving up easily. As already noted, he'd met both of my parents before.

Harvey only laughed. "And if there's anyone able to quell her more outrageous actions, Mercy, it's you."

A nurse opened the door, at first appearing apprehensive. When she saw who waited outside, however, she beamed upon us and opened the door wider. "Mrs. Nash will be so pleased to see you, Miss Allcutt and..." She's never met Ernie.

Mr. Templeton," I said.

"Thanks Della," said Harvey, and he ushered Ernie and me into the main sitting room of the Nashes' suite.

"Mercy, is that you?" came Chloe's voice from a far bedroom.

"Yes, and Ernie's here too!" I called back. I ran to Chloe's room and found her sitting amongst light-blue satin pillows, looking gorgeous but pale. My sister is an ethereally beautiful woman. I've never resented her for it. Well, not much anyway. She had naturally blond hair that Lulu LaBelle could only achieve via a bottle, and the most spectacular blue eyes and dark eyelashes you can imagine. Her smile nearly split her face when she spied Ernie and me.

"I'm *so* glad you're here!" she said. I saw with horror tears glistening in her eyes. A couple even rolled down her porcelain cheeks.

"Chloe! Has Mother been tormenting you so much that she has you crying?" I raced to her bed, plunked myself down, nearly slipped off the satin bed cover, corrected my balance and hugged my sister.

"No," Chloe said with a sniffle. "She's tried, but so far Nanny Gibson and Nurse Hall have been able to hold her at bay. But they're polite to her. You're the only one who's ever given her as good as she gives." Her perfect nose wrinkled. "Did that makes sense?"

"Not altogether," I said a trifle troubled. My mother scared the living daylights out of me; why did all these people think I could stand up to her? I guess I actually had stood up to her a few times, but mostly over the telephone. To continue defying her in person was a much more perilous undertaking. In fact, I still felt quivers from our encounter mere moments ago.

The door to her bedroom opened and those of us who could whipped our heads around, expecting to espy Mother standing in the doorway. But thank the good Lord, the person standing there was a nurse in a pristine white uniform and crisp cap, carrying a little pink bundle.

"Oh!" cried Chloe, enraptured. "Please bring her here, Nanny Gibson. I want to introduce her to her Auntie Mercy and Uncle Ernie again."

Uncle Ernie? I didn't ask.

"Gladly, Mrs. Nash. You have a delightful and beautiful little girl here," said Nanny Gibson, carrying the pink bundle to Chloe. Once she deposited the babe in Chloe's arms, she discreetly left the room.

Harvey rushed up to the bed, and I finally slipped off the satin covers. Fortunately I landed on my feet and pretended my slippage had been done on purpose. Ernie, I noticed, still hovered near the doorway. I glanced at him and mouthed, "Coward."

He only nodded and mouthed, "Correct."

Even though Ernie was fond of his sister and she had safely delivered two children into the world, I guess he and babies hadn't had a lot to do with each other in his thirty-odd (some might say extremely odd) years of life.

"Come on over, Ernie," I encouraged. "She can't bite you. She doesn't even have any teeth yet."

"If you say so," said Ernie, sounding uneasy. "But if she starts crying, I'm out of here."

"She's a darling love," cooed Nanny Gibson. "She only cries when she wants her mommy or daddy."

How disgustingly sweet. I didn't say so.

"So have you chosen a name yet?" I asked in order to alleviate the prevailing stickiness.

"Not yet," said Chloe, holding her daughter in her arms and gazing down at her with adoring eyes.

It's probably a good thing parents are so bedazzled by their children when they're born, because when I looked at the same baby girl Chloe saw, I still discerned no particular beauty. She was only six days old, of course, which probably accounted for it. The first time I'd seen her right after her birth, she'd been bright pink and wrinkly. Her face was no longer as pink or wrinkled as it had been, but her eyes were sort of crinkled and closed, her little nose remained flattish and her mouth was all puckered up. What little hair there was on her head looked brownish.

"Aw, isn't she cute," said Ernie in a voice I didn't believe.

"She is," said Harvey, plainly not detecting insincerity in Ernie's comment.

"Have you at least been talking about names?" I asked, thinking the kid probably should be called something other than Baby soon.

"Mother wants us to name her Violet," said Chloe.

"Don't do it!" I cried, horrified. "She'll never let go of her if you give her one of her names."

"We won't," said Chloe.

"We're considering Adelaide," said Harvey.

Adelaide was Chloe's middle name. Her first name was Clovilla, so you can understand why she chose to call herself Chloe.

"No, we're not," said Chloe firmly. "Harvey's only teasing. And she won't be Mercedes or Louise either." She glanced up at Ernie. "Any good names in your family, Ernie?"

"My sister's name is Elizabeth. I like that name," said Ernie. "Or you could name her Ernestine." His smile was brilliant.

"We could," said Harvey, laughing, "but we won't. My mother's name is Rose. I think Rose is pretty."

"It's passable," said Chloe, her perfect brow wrinkling slightly. "But I don't care for Rose Nash. Maybe Rosalind? Rosalie? Rosalie Nash sounds nice."

"I like Diane and Esther," I said. "I think they're both lovely names."

"Esther Nash," said Harvey. "I like that."

"I kind of do as well," said Chloe. "Esther Rose Nash. That would work, and your mother is a lovely person too, Harvey, so it would honor her."

"What?" I asked. "You don't like Esther Honoria?"

If Chloe hadn't still been glowing from happiness, she'd probably have hit me for that one.

A loud knock came at the door. Mother didn't wait to be invited but barged into the room like a ship under sail, her stiff bombazine gown a tribute to her Boston heritage. She never let Boston down, even when it was a hundred degrees in Los Angeles and she was there too. As winter prevailed for the nonce, her dark gray bombazine didn't appear too outrageous.

"What's going on in here?" she demanded. "Clovilla, you should be resting, not entertaining all these people."

"I'm not entertaining them, Mother," said Chloe, feebly protesting.

"Indeed she's not," I told our overbearing mother, taking to my quaking heart everyone's belief in me. "In fact, we're entertaining *her*."

"Precisely," said Harvey.

"Yeah," said Ernie, undoubtedly because he knew the word "yeah" would make Mother cringe if she did such things as cringe.

She didn't. If our mother's middle name hadn't been Violet, it would have been Zeno. Probably should have been, as he was the founder of Stoicism. At least I think he was.

"We've been discussing names," said Harvey, doubtless because he saw the outraged glance Mother shot at me and was trying to prevent her from pouncing on me and pounding me to a pulp. Actually, she wouldn't have done that, either, but she might have "Mercedes Louise'd" me to death.

"Violet is the perfect name for that darling child," said Mother, marching over to the bed. As I stood at the bed's head, Harvey stood right next to Chloe, Nanny Gibson stood like a solid oak tree on the other side of the bed, Ernie stood at its foot and none of us moved, she had to maneuver her bulk to get close to her older daughter. She shot everyone in her way withering glances, but we didn't wither. Nor did we move.

"Her name isn't going to be Violet, Mother," I told her, my voice firm in spite of my perilously positioned heart, which had taken to hammering and was about to dislodge itself and plummet into my stomach if not my shoes.

"I don't know why not," said Mother. "Or Alberta, to honor your father."

"Harvey has parents too, don't forget," I said. Then I forced myself not to shut my eyes or cower.

After shooting me a hateful glare, Mother said, "Yes, well, that's so. A name from your side, Chloe, and a name from your side, Harvey, would be quite appropriate."

"Appropriate has nothing to do with naming this adorable little tot," I said stoutly. I hoped nobody could see my death grip on the bed post.

"Don't be nonsensical, Mercedes Louise. A baby's name carries family traditions. Or," she amended, scowling at me, "it should." With a sniff, she added, "Although I don't know what your child will be thinking, growing up in that room with paintings all over the walls. I've never seen such a thing!"

"I certainly hope not," I said, finding it easier to stand my ground on this subject if on no other. "That room was painstakingly created by Mr. Easthope and Mr. Brentwood."

"That's right," said Harvey. "It was Mercy's idea, and the two gentlemen carried it out to perfection."

"I might have known that disgraceful notion came from you, Mercedes Louise."

Before I could tell her not to call me Mercedes Louise, Nanny Gibson took over the conversation. "It's time for Mrs. Nash to be alone with her baby now," said Nanny Gibson loudly. "If everyone will please leave the room. Mr. Nash, would you mind fetching Nurse Hall? She's in the nursery with Nurse Morgan."

"Happy to," Harvey said.

"I see no reason for me to leave my daughter's bedside," said Mother, again outraged.

"I do," I told her. What's more, I took not only my life but her arm in one of my hands. "Chloe needs peace now. And Harvey and the baby. She doesn't need you to loom over her and tell her how to do things."

"*Loom!* I would *never*—"

"Yeah," said Ernie. "You loom really well."

And darned if he didn't take her other arm. The two of us fairly dragged her out of Chloe's room. Harvey thanked us both later.

Ernie stayed for dinner that night, even though Mother loomed over the dinner table too. I hated to see him go, but I don't think he was sorry to get out of Mother's orbit.

Didn't blame him, but I sure missed him.

FOUR

The rest of that weekend was horrid, although Harvey and I, the nurses and Nanny Gibson, all conspired to keep Mother away from Chloe and the darling child who was, as yet, anonymous. Mother kept mooting Alberta, Violet, Georgina—Chloe's and my awful brother is named George—Henrietta and Bernice, because they were family names.

I wasn't surprised she didn't suggest Agatha, even though Great-Aunt Agatha had left me a large fortune. Agatha had been rather eccentric, and Mother had been offended when she left money to *me* and not my ghastly brother George.

On Monday morning, I almost asked Harvey if I could go to the studio with him just to get away from Mother, who seemed determined to order people around. I was exhausted from not obeying her and from attempting to protect everyone else from her. But I couldn't leave my poor sister, the servants, the two nurses, and the nanny to deal with her on their own. Unfortunately, everyone seemed to be correct in that I was the only one who could stand up to her and overturn her edicts. I didn't escape unscathed. I felt as if someone had been at me with a bullwhip.

And to think my rebellious streak started when I took typewriting and shorthand classes at Boston's YWCA. Compared to what I was dealing with now, those rebellions, which scared the wits out of me at the time, seemed infinitesimal.

I must say it's not pleasant to be loathed by one's own mother but Chloe, the servants, the nanny, and the nurses made up for it by thanking me every three or four minutes on Monday. I almost cried with relief when Harvey came home from the set early that day.

"Part of the scaffolding collapsed," he said, shaking his head glumly. "Fortunately, no one was seriously hurt, but it could have been a calamity," he said as I greeted him in the Italian-tiled entrance hall.

"I'm sorry," I told him. "I never even think about the sets in the flickers."

"I have to think about this one, because it's going to be a huge movie. Gigantic production with a cast of thousands."

"Good heavens," I said, awed.

"Maybe more like hundreds," he said, chuckling. "But that scaffolding collapse has me baffled." He glanced around and lowered his voice. "Where's your mother. She's not with Chloe and the baby is she?"

"No," I told him proudly. "I managed to keep her away from Chloe and your nameless child for most of the day."

"Bless you, Mercy. But Molly usually takes my hat and coat at the front door."

"Mother has commandeered Molly and Julie to move furniture around in the den."

"She *what*? That's my home office. It's where I work!"

"I know, Harvey," I said apologetically. "But it was your den or Chloe's sanity."

"Good point. I'm going upstairs to see my wife and baby. Pretend I'm not here for a while, will you?"

"I'm about to expire from exhaustion, Harvey Nash. Keeping my mother from Chloe and the child is a full-time job, and I prefer working for Ernie."

"I'm really sorry, Mercy." I could tell he meant it. "But I don't know what to do about your mother."

"How about telling her to leave your lovely home and go back to Boston?" I suggested.

Harvey stared at me as if I'd lost my mind. "I can't do that!"

"Don't know why not," I muttered.

"She's Chloe's mother!" said Harvey, shocked.

"She's my mother too, and I'm about to send her packing. But I'd need you or Chloe to back me up. She won't go away just because I tell her to."

"Hell," said Harvey, who wasn't given to swearing, being a gentleman through and through. "Maybe you can drum up a plague raging rampant through Los Angeles. Would that send her away?"

"Lordy, no. That would only make her camp out at Chloe's door. I don't know how to get rid of her, but I'll keep thinking."

"Thanks, Mercy. I don't know what we'd do without you."

"I don't either," I told him in perfect candor.

When Harvey started up the massive staircase to the second floor, the telephone rang. It really echoed in that marbled hall. He paused and started to come down the stairs again, but I said, "I'll get it."

"If it's the studio, I'll probably have to take it," he said.

"I'll let you know if they need you."

"Thanks, Mercy."

I picked up the receiver and Harvey hovered halfway up the staircase. "Nash residence," I said.

A tinny voice at the end of the wire said, "Trunk call from Boston for Mrs. Albert Allcutt."

I put my hand over the mouthpiece and told Harvey, "It's for Mother. From Father."

Harvey let his head fall back and I'm pretty sure I heard him thanking God for small favors before I again spoke into the mouthpiece. "Mrs. Allcutt is in another part of the house. Would you like me to find her now or have her—"

My father's voice interrupted me. His voice sounded kind of tinny too, but it was a deeper tin. Maybe copper. Or lead. "Mercedes Louise, is that you? Why are you answering the telephone?"

Instantly my hackles rose. It was their accustomed position since

I'd arrived at the Nash castle and began dealing with Mother. "Mother is bossing the servants around in another room, Father. Do you want me to fetch her, or do you want her to telephone you back?"

"How dare you speak of your mother—"

This time I interrupted him. "Hold the wire. I'll get her." And I laid the receiver on the glossy table in the center of the room and strode over to a small room under the staircase. There I found a row of buttons, each one connected to a speaking tube. I lifted the tube marked "Den" and pressed the button.

Molly, who sounded as if she were in tears, spoke into the tube in the den. "M-Mr. Nash's room," she said.

"Oh, Molly," I said in a voice oozing sympathy. "I'm sorry you have to deal with Mother. But Father's on the telephone, and he claims he needs to talk to her."

"Thank you, Miss Allcutt," Molly said fervently. I heard her turn and speak to Mother. Then I heard Mother stomp to the speaking tube.

"What is it, Mercedes Louise?"

"Father is on the telephone. He says he needs to speak to you."

"The telephone?" said Mother as if she'd never heard of such a device. "From Boston?" It would seem she'd not heard about transcontinental telephone calls either.

"Yes. There's an extension right in Harvey's den, so you can speak to him there," I told her.

"Hmph," said she. Then, I presume, she turned around. I heard her order all the servants out of the room. Then she marched to Harvey's desk, where the telephone sat.

Therefore, I replaced the speaking tube and scooted myself back out to the entryway and picked up the receiver. Placing my hand over its mouthpiece, I listened for all I was worth. I figured my parents were both so awful they didn't deserve not to be eavesdropped upon.

"What is it, Albert?" snapped Mother. "Why are you telephoning all the way from Boston?" She sounded as if she disapproved. Then again, she almost always did, so it was difficult to judge.

"It's George," said Father, also sounding as if he disapproved.

George! My sainted brother who could do no wrong? Whatever could *he* be up to that would provoke a long-distance trunk telephone call? Transcontinental telephone calls were expensive, and my parents didn't waste money except on themselves.

"You need to get back here as soon as you can," Father said.

"And why is that?" Mother didn't like being ordered to do things. She preferred doing the ordering.

"He's taken up with a chorus girl from the Ziegfeld Follies and is drinking alcohol by the barrel."

"*George?*"

It was the first time in my life I heard my mother shriek.

"Yes. George," barked Father. "Don't yell into the 'phone, Honoria. You sound like a fishwife."

"George has taken up with a *chorus* girl?" Mother lowered her voice, but probably only because she didn't want anyone else in the house to hear this conversation. Tut tut. "And he's *drinking?*"

"Like a fish."

"How could you allow him to do such things?" asked Mother.

It was a good question. I could hardly credit this tale myself. My parents' children didn't disobey them. Well, except for me, but I was the only exception and I only did it for a little while when I lived with them. Otherwise, in one of their homes, I was meek as a lamb.

"Because we both left him alone when we bought that house in Pasadena!" snarled Father. "The idiot got himself enmeshed in low company and alcohol. Why, he's even been going to the *Cotton Club!*"

Mother's shocked intake of breath almost sucked me through the wire and into the den.

"He's dancing to jazz music, drinking, spending money on that strumpet and is becoming an absolute disgrace to the Allcutt name! He's going to be arrested if this keeps up, Honoria. He's still doing his job at the bank, but his evenings are being frittered away on That Woman and Jazz." You could hear the capital letters at the beginnings of each of those words. Well, I could. You couldn't, because you weren't there eavesdropping.

"I shall come home immediately," said Mother.

"Good. If anyone is able to straighten him out, you can. He was already out of control by the time I arrived in Boston."

"Together we shall prevail," said my mother, sounding noble.

For a second or two, I almost felt sorry for George; but only for a second. George was a slab off the old block of granite. He deserved no sympathy from me. He'd been almost as obnoxious in voicing his condemnation of my move to Los Angeles as had my parents. He deserved to suffer.

"Excellent," said Father. "Let me know when your train is scheduled to arrive."

"I shall. *Please* attempt to talk sense into George until I can get there."

"I've been attempting little else for two weeks now," said Father, outraged at his son for once instead of me. Neither of my parents was ever outraged at Chloe, because she was always nice to them.

As soon as I heard my mother hang up the telephone in the den, I did likewise in the entry hall and made a mad dash up the staircase to Chloe's door. I tapped lightly, then opened the door and sidled in. I didn't want to interrupt anything too intimate, but Chloe had recently given birth, and I didn't think a whole lot of intimacy could be accomplished for a while yet.

Harvey had pulled up a chair to Chloe's bed, and he was in the process of rubbing noses with his baby girl. Chloe looked upon this display with such a sappy expression on her face, that I'd have snickered in derision had I seen it in the flickers. From my sister, brother-in-law, and niece, the picture thus created was charming.

Mother and father—the baby's, not Chloe's and mine—glanced at the door when they heard me come in. I fairly danced over to the bed.

"What the heck are you smiling about?" asked Chloe. "Did Mother die or something?"

"No, but she's going back to Boston!"

" *What?*" smote my ears in so loud a duet from Chloe and Harvey that the baby began fussing.

So, as Harvey lifted the baby to his shoulder and patted her gently on the back to calm her nerves, I told them both the story of George's disgrace and downfall.

"A Ziegfeld girl?" said Chloe, fascinated.

"And booze!" I said, chortling.

"And here I always thought your brother was a stuffed shirt," said Harvey, grinning from ear to ear.

"He is," said Chloe and I, making our own tuneful duet.

Another, brusquer knock came at Chloe's door, and Mother marched in, looking amazingly like a giant stuffed pouter pigeon.

"Have you come to see the baby, Mother?" Chloe asked sweetly.

"I shall take a last glance at the dear child," said Mother in a frosty voice. "But I know when I'm not wanted. I shall be leaving for Boston on the first train."

"Oh," said Harvey. "There's no need for that, Mother Allcutt."

Mother absolutely *hated* being called Mother Allcutt.

"There is. I have been made to feel unwelcome. Therefore, I shall leave."

"Have you already made arrangements?" I asked sweetly, knowing as I did so that Mother wouldn't know how to book a train ticket for herself if her life depended on it.

"Arrangements? Of course not, Mercedes Louise! That sort of thing is what *staff* is for."

"Ah," I said, still sweetly. "Is Father's secretary making arrangements for you?"

"Your father's secretary? Why, no. I don't think so."

Ha! I'd buffaloed the buffalo. I said, "That's too bad. Father has staff to do those sorts of things because he runs a bank. The servants here run a house."

"We didn't discuss arrangements," Mother said with something of a snarl.

"Oh dear," I said, shaking my head sadly.

After opening and shutting her mouth twice, Mother said, "I'm sure one of Harvey's minions will be able to arrange travel from here to Boston."

"Absolutely," said Harvey. "I'll be happy to have someone make arrangements for you."

"I knew you didn't want me here," said Mother with a loud sniff. "Family feeling is all but dead in this country."

"I don't think it's the whole country," I told her. "I think it's mostly in our family."

"Mercedes Louise Allcutt—"

"I'll be downstairs telephoning the train station!" I sang, and I pretty much bounced out of that room and to the telephone in the den. There I called the Union Pacific Railroad Company and booked Mother on a trip via the Los Angeles Limited to Chicago, and from there to Boston on the Boston and Albany/New York Central Line. Because she would expect it, I booked an entire train car for her so she wouldn't have to breathe the same air as those in a lower social station than she.

Social station. Good grief. You'd have thought we lived in India.

FIVE

Luckily for me, I didn't have to drive Mother to the train station the next morning. That task was relegated to Chloe's new chauffeur, Porter Methuselah Porter. I'm not making that up. It was his name, and he was a kind and gentle fellow who hadn't had a whole lot to do since he'd been hired.

Harvey had wanted Chloe to have a chauffeur to drive her and the baby around in the new Rolls-Royce Silver Ghost he'd bought for her, so he'd hired one. The poor fellow—Porter Porter, not Harvey—had been called upon by Mother to drive her to different places in Los Angeles when she felt a need, but he didn't seem to mind. That might have been because there was a glass panel separating the driver's seat from the passengers' seat.

Harvey, Chloe, the nameless baby, and I all stood on the gigantic front porch of the Nash palace, smiling, waving hankies and wishing her a speedy, safe trip. I might have been the only one there who hoped her car would somehow become detached from the rest of the train and plunge into a deep steep canyon, but I doubt it. I also didn't ask.

It wasn't until Wednesday of the week when things became

sticky again. Only this time the things weren't at the Nash residence, but rather on Harvey's set for the production of *Helen of Troy*.

Chloe and I had taken the baby outside to sit in the fragile sun on the Nashes' magnificent patio. The baby was still technically nameless, although Esther Rose, Helen Grace and Elizabeth Eve were top contenders so far. I preferred Esther Rose, but she wasn't my kid.

"If you name her Helen, everyone will think it's because of Harvey's movie," I pointed out.

"That's true," said Chloe, who was regaining her strength, such as it was, and who couldn't seem to stop staring at the baby's various body parts.

I had to admit they were wee and cute. I loved it when I held my hand to her and she grabbed one of my fingers. It wasn't as much fun when she drew the finger to her puckered mouth and started sucking on it. I wasn't a huge fan of baby spit, although Chloe didn't seem to mind. Heck, the kid even burped up on her shoulder a couple of times, and she only laughed. I could but stare in awe, as such behavior seemed so unlike my glamorous, delicate, ethereal sister. Speaking of which...

"What about Eleanor?" I asked. "Eleanor is a pretty name."

"It's not bad," said Chloe. "Eleanor Rose." She tilted her head, her blond hair gleaming in the sunlight and making me sigh.

"Ma'am?" Molly's voice came from the back door.

Chloe and I turned to look at the maid.

"What's up, Molly?" asked Chloe.

"It's Mr. Harvey, Mrs. Nash. He said he needs to speak with Miss Mercy."

After sharing a startled glance with Chloe, I rose from my chair and headed for the door. "Wonder what he wants with me," I muttered as I walked.

"He's been having trouble on that wretched set," said Chloe. "Maybe he wants you to investigate."

I laughed.

Silly me.

"Mercy," said Harvey as soon as I'd greeted him on the telephone, "can you call Ernie and ask him to get out here? I need to hire him. A door came unhinged today and nearly killed Francis Easthope. I think there's actual sabotage afoot here on the set."

"Good heavens! Is Francis all right?" As mentioned earlier, Mr. Francis Easthope was a costumer and a set designer and probably the most handsome man in California.

"He's all right, but it was a close call. These so-called accidents are happening all the time. There's something going on, and it's not natural. I've never had this kind of trouble on a set before. I only hire the best of the best, and they know their jobs and what they're supposed to be doing when. I can't imagine who would want to undermine my studio, but I fear it's happening."

"I'm so sorry, Harvey."

It was true he'd been coming home every day with tales of trouble on the set. Scaffolding fell; a wall collapsed nearly beaning two grips; a few tacks had "accidentally" been left on Mr. Ramon Novarro's chair; Miss Blanche Sweet's Helen-of-Troy wig had magically caught fire and might have seriously injured the actress had she not been quick enough to avert disaster by flipping it into a prop fountain. It did sound as if this string of goings-on weren't random.

"I'm sorry too, and I want to get to the bottom of it. So I'm hoping Ernie can come out here for a week or two and maybe you and he can pretend to be extras and snoop around. Bring that Lulu person who wants to be a star with you. The more people we have working on the problem the sooner we can solve it, I hope. I have to admit I'm worried, Mercy, and I don't want to worry. I want to leave everything to Sidney and be home with Chloe and the baby."

Sidney Lafayette was Harvey's second in command, and an able producer and director in his own right. But I understood Harvey's reluctance to turn the production over to him while everything seemed to be at sixes and sevens.

"I'll be happy to call him, Harvey. And Lulu too. She'd love it!"

"She might not love it so much after she lives it for a while. She'll be an extra, and they only stand around most of the time.

Also, most of the studios don't treat their actors as well as we do, you know."

"I know, Harvey. That's why everyone wants to work for you."

"Yeah, I know," he said sourly. "I paid a fortune to get Ramon Novarro and Blanche Sweet from another studio to work for me, but I'll be ruined if they both get killed on the bloody damned set."

As Harvey almost never swore, I knew he was truly desperate. "I'll telephone Ernie right now," I told him.

"Thanks, Mercy. Call me as soon as you can. I'm going to shut down production for the day. Every day we waste is money down the drain."

"Right." Everything revolved around money, and not just in Hollywood. It was a fact of life.

So I put a call through from Beverly Hills to the Figueroa Building in downtown Los Angeles.

"Templeton," Ernie snarled into the receiver on the second ring.

"Golly Ernie, you sound grumpy," I said.

"When are you coming the hell back here?" He barked. "You were supposed to stay until your mother left. Well, she left and you're still there."

"It's only been three or four days, Ernie," I said. "And you have Glennie answering the telephone for you."

"Huh," he grunted. I heard him rise from his chair and then heard his office door slam. "Glennie is about as capable as a warthog. She's fine filling in for Lulu, but anything else is above her level of competence."

"I'm sorry. I thought you'd only need her to answer the telephone for a while. She doesn't need to do anything else, does she?"

"Yes, dammit! I need someone I can talk to and who can take shorthand and type letters. Glennie's a nice girl, but she was born without a brain."

"That's not very nice," I chided.

"I don't care. It's the truth."

I forged ahead. "Anyhow, I'm calling because Harvey needs you. He wants to hire you. And maybe even Lulu and me."

"What? What the devil are you talking about? Soft soap won't work with me, Mercy Allcutt. You're my secretary, and I need you here, not there."

"It's not soft soap. All sorts of accidents are happening on the set of *Helen of Troy*. Harvey believes someone is deliberately sabotaging the production. He asked me to telephone you and maybe even Lulu as well. He wants all of us to pretend to be cast members and snoop. Ramon Novarro nearly sat on a seat full of tacks and Blanche Sweet's wig caught fire. If someone is interrupting the production on purpose, they're being vicious about it. Poor Francis Easthope nearly had a door fall on him today."

"Good God. Are you serious?"

"Yes, I'm serious! For crumb's sake, Ernest Templeton, do you think I'd joke about something like *this*? If anything truly catastrophic happens to this production, Harvey's studio might be ruined!"

"Shoot."

"So far, no shooting," I said, trying to be funny and not succeeding.

"But that'll mean we're both gone from the office. And who'll fill in for Lulu if Glennie's up here answering your 'phone?"

"I don't know. Can Junior answer telephones?"

Junior O'Fannin, Glynis's brother, was a young lad who worked for various people in various offices in the Figueroa Building doing odd jobs or carrying files for attorneys and what-not. I doubted if he'd want to be stuck at a desk, but I figured it was worth asking.

"Doubt it," said Ernie. "But I'll ask around. Either of your other tenants good with telephones?"

"Sue might be, but she already has a job working at a dentist's office. I don't think he'd allow her to be borrowed."

"Horsefeathers," muttered Ernie. "I'll ask around the building. Or maybe I'll call Rob Gabriel. He probably knows agencies who hire out temporary receptionists and so forth."

"Good idea," I said, thinking my education was still growing. I'd had no idea there were agencies that supplied temporary helpers to offices. "Is it all right if I telephone Harvey and tell him you'll take the job?"

"Yeah, I guess so. Want me to ask Lulu, or do you want to do that?"

"Maybe you'd better ask her. Harvey sounded pretty desperate. Then maybe you can find a trained secretary to do my job and Glennie can move to Lulu's desk."

"Excellent idea. What's today?" asked Ernie. He probably had a calendar sitting on his desk right in front of him, but never mind.

"It's Wednesday," I said patiently.

"Ask him if he can shut down production tomorrow and Friday. If I can work everything out so that all stations are covered here, Lulu and I can be there by the weekend. Then maybe we can figure out a plausible reason for you, Lulu, and me to suddenly appear on the set."

"I doubt that'll be a problem," I told him. "People come and go all the time on movie sets."

"Tell him anyway. I don't want you or Lulu—or me, for that matter—to get hurt because we're friends of Harvey. I don't want us to walk into a serious situation cold."

"Oh," I said. "Yes. That makes sense."

"Thank you," he said sarcastically.

"It will be good to see you again, Ernie," I said, probably too brightly. While we'd been "keeping company" with each other, to use an old-fashioned term, I didn't want to smother him. If anything might send Ernest Templeton, P.I. scurrying off into the sunset, I suspect it would be a clingy girlfriend.

"I miss you, too, Mercy," he said, surprising the heck out of me. "I'll call you tonight at the Nash place and let you know if I've figured out the job situation here."

"Thank you, Ernie. Harvey will appreciate it a lot. He wants to be home with Chloe and the baby, and all heck's breaking out on his latest project. He's not a happy movie mogul at the moment."

"The kid is still 'the baby'?" asked Ernie incredulously. "They haven't named her *yet*?"

"They're mulling over many names. I'll tell you all about them when you get here."

"Good Lord. Okay. See you soon."

"Thanks, Ernie." I hung up the receiver feeling kind of happy-ish. I mean, I was sorry about Harvey's troubles and everything, but Ernie'd said he missed me!

After basking for only a couple of seconds, I picked up the receiver once more and returned Harvey's telephone call.

"Thank God," he said after I'd relayed the news. He sounded relieved already.

"Thank Ernie," I told him.

"I'll thank him, all right," said Harvey. "I'll thank him with money."

With a chuckle I said, "He'll love that. He's still getting every-thing free from the Chinese population of Los Angeles."

"Good for him."

"He wants to know if you can shut down the production until Monday, so he can hire temporary staff and so forth."

"Shut down until *Monday*?" Harvey bellowed. "That's four days lost!"

"I know, but it's got to be better than losing Ramon Novarro or Francis Easthope. Or Blanche Sweet."

"I suppose you're right. So when is Ernie going to start?"

"He'll call here tonight," I said, "in order to tell me if he was able to maneuver people into temporary positions. If Lulu comes too, and I hope she will, the Figueroa Building will need a recep-tionist. Glennie O'Fannin can do that job. She's filled in for Lulu before. She's not especially helpful as Ernie's girl Friday. But if he loses Glennie, Ernie will need someone to answer his telephone and make appointments and so forth."

"Right. Of course," said Harvey, sounding distracted. "Oh, but wait," he said, cheering up some. "I can send Bev Hargroves. She's good with shorthand and typing and answering telephones. She might not mind filling in for you for a week or so."

"Who's Bev Hargroves?" I asked.

"She's in the secretarial pool here at the studio. She's probably the best of the lot, and if you allow her to stay at your place so she won't have to be driving back and forth from your house to hers every day, it might sweeten the pot. She lives with her parents, and they drive her nuts."

"You mean Chloe and I aren't the only ones?" I said. "That's almost comforting."

"Your parents sit on a pedestal high above anyone else's," said Harvey. I could hear his grin.

"Yeesh. How lucky for Chloe and me."

Chuckling, Harvey said, "Right. So I'll talk to Bev right now and let you know if she can fill in for you. You said you already have a stand-in for Miss LaBelle?"

"I'm not sure Dr. Clutter will let Glennie fill in for Lulu indefinitely. Ernie's going to check with a friend of his. Mr. Gabriel is a lawyer, and he knows about temporary agencies, according to Ernie."

"Hmm," said Harvey. "We might be able to use another good lawyer, but let's take care of urgent matters first."

"Sounds good to me," I said. "When do you want Ernie to arrive?"

"Tonight would be great, but he probably won't have temporary employees secured by then. Well, maybe he will if Bev agrees to stand in for you. Ernie and Miss LaBelle can stay at our place. We have rooms enough for an army or two."

"True. Thanks, Harvey."

"Thank you and Ernie," said Harvey almost reverently. "I'm *so* glad he agreed to investigate this mess."

"Providing we can find suitable replacements for Lulu and me," I reminded him.

"Yes. I'll ask Bev if she'd mind filling in for you for a week or two, and there may be another girl who can sit at the reception desk and file her nails." Harvey adored Lulu, but he knew her habits. Or he used to.

"She's buffing her nails now," I told him. "No more blood-red fingernails for her."

"Good Lord. That kerfuffle with the phony talent scout really scared her, didn't it?"

"It did indeed. She doesn't even wear ultra-bright colors any longer."

"I'm sorry she had to go through that ordeal," said Harvey. "But I'm also glad she doesn't dress so outrageously. If she, Ernie, and you work on the set, I don't want any one of you to stand out in the crowd."

"I think you'll be safe with Lulu now, Harvey."

"Good. Can you give me a minute? I'll talk to Bev and see what she says about living at your place while she fills in for you."

"Great. Thanks, Harvey."

"Thank *you*," said Harvey.

Sure enough, I didn't have to wait more than five minutes before the telephone rang again. Harvey didn't sound quite so desperate when he said, "Bev Hargroves said she'll be happy as a lark to fill in for you and live at your place for a week or two."

"I'm glad," I told him.

"So am I," said my brother-in-law.

"I'd better call Mrs. Buck at my house to tell her Miss Hargroves will be living at Mercy's Manor for a week or so."

"I hope it only takes a week, or we'll go broke."

"Ernie is a very good detective," I said. "I don't think you could find a better one."

"I'm sure you're right," said Harvey. "I'm just worried about the production, you know?"

"I know. But I'll telephone Mrs. Buck now, and I guess you can shut down production and tell everyone to come back to work on Monday."

"Lord, I hate losing so much time."

"You'll lose more than time if somebody manages to bump off Ramon Novarro or Blanche Sweet," I pointed out.

"Don't even *say* things like that!"

"Sorry, Harvey. Just making a point."

"An extremely sharp one," muttered Harvey. "But all right. It'll take me a while to wrap things up here, but I'll be home in time for dinner."

"Excellent," I said. We both hung up.

When I dialed my home number at Mercy's Manor, Mrs. Buck answered the telephone, sounding grim and professional.

"Allcutt residence." Actually she sounded as if she were throwing down a gauntlet and daring the caller to pick it up.

"Good morning, Mrs. Buck, it's Mercy."

"Oh laws, child, is everything good with the baby and Mrs. Nash?"

"Absolutely, but Ernie has had to hire a temporary person to fill in for me at the Figueroa Building, and I told Harvey—he's the one who found the temporary person—that she could stay in my home for the duration. I wanted to let you know."

"The *duration*? How long are you going to be gone?"

"Um...I'm not sure. Harvey—I think you've met him, haven't you?"

"Your sister's husband?" asked Mrs. Buck.

"Yes," I said.

"Yes, I've met him. Nice man."

"He's a very nice man, and he's hired Ernie to do some work for him, so he and I and...Oh dear. He's going to ask Lulu to help too. So you'll be cooking for Sue, Caroline and Miss Hargroves. I think. I'm not sure if Lulu will be able to help Harvey yet, but Miss Hargroves will be there for sure."

After a rather significant pause, during which I got fidgety, Mrs. Buck said, "Well, Miss Mercy, Mr. Buck and I work for you, so we'll do what you tell us to do."

"Thank you. I know this is kind of confusing, but I appreciate you and Mr. Buck very much for putting up with me."

"Miss Mercy, you're an angel. You're no trouble at all. I just hope you and Mr. Ernie won't be walking into danger because of him being a private eye. Plus, you never seem to stand behind him but bull on up to the front to get into the action. We worry about you, Mr. Buck and me."

I did that? *Me*? I had no idea.

Because I wasn't sure how to respond to that part of her statement, I just said, "Thank you very much, Mrs. Buck. I'll call you later if any of our plans change."

"It's all right, Miss Mercy, but we all miss you here."

"Thank you. I miss you too." It wasn't even much of a fib.

When I telephoned Ernie and told him a woman named Bev and whose last name I couldn't remember would be filling in for me, he growled and snapped, but he was too far away to do me any real damage.

SIX

W hen I went back outside to see how Chloe and the baby were doing, I found Buttercup and Pepper cuddled up napping together. They were awfully cute. To tell the truth, I thought the two fluffy dogs were more cunning than the infant, although I'd never tell Chloe or Harvey so.

Looking up from the baby, Chloe greeted me with a syrupy smile on her face. I'm sure the expression was for the baby and not me. "Is everything all right?" she asked.

"Not really. Harvey's worried about all the accidents on the set. He thinks they're deliberate, and he hired Ernie to detect who's responsible for what's going on."

"My goodness," said Chloe, turning back to her nameless baby. "Will Ernie stay here while he does his detecting?"

"If it's all right with you. And Lulu too, if you don't mind. Harvey wants as many people as he can get to help solve the problem."

"It's fine with me," said Chloe. She picked the pink bundle up from her lap and Baby's eyes opened.

"I can't tell what color her eyes are," I said after squinting hard for a second or two.

"No, they're kind of a bluish-black at the moment. According to all the books I read, most babies have blue eyes at first and then they'll change to whatever color they'll remain by the time they're one year old."

"Good heavens, it takes that long?"

With a delicate shrug—Chloe is the most delicate person I've ever known—she said, "That's what the books say."

"I had no idea," I said.

Very well, I seemed to be developing a negative attitude toward babies—the having of them, anyway. For one thing, it hurts like holy heck to give birth, and it's an exhausting process even if there are no complications and the mother is healthy.

Crumb, even during our enlightened times, giving birth can be dangerous. I read all the time about babies and mothers dying during the birthing process. Then, if the infant comes out alive and their mother survives the ordeal, the babies' faces are red and squinchy and they all look like dried apples for at least a couple of weeks.

And now I find out you had to wait a year to tell what color the baby's eyes are going to be! Whoever was supposed to be in charge when humans were invented did a lousy job of designing the female body and babies.

I hoped either my attitude or the newest little Nashlet's impression upon me would improve soon. I didn't like these feelings of aversion attacking me every time I thought about having a baby. After all, if I ever got married maybe my husband would want children.

Would Ernie want children?

For the love of Mike, how'd I get on *that* topic? I'm sorry. Back to the lavish patio of the Nash residence in Beverly Hills.

"Once Harvey gets here, I can call Ernie and ask him if Lulu can come too. I hope she can," I said.

"Who did Harvey get to sit in for you?"

"Yes. Somebody named Bev something or other."

"Hargroves. Yes. She's a very bright young woman, if a little dowdy."

"Everyone's dowdy compared to you, Chloe," I said, reaching out a hand to caress the baby's cheek. Cheeks were the one (oh very well, two) things in a baby's favor. They were soft as velvet; at least this one's were.

"You'll never forgive me for making you update your wardrobe, will you?" Chloe said upon a laugh.

"I've already forgiven you."

Just then the baby's face wrinkled up and she let out a bellow that frightened the dogs into jumping and yipping. Apparently the kid didn't appreciate the yips any more than the dogs appreciated the kid's screeches because she began howling even more loudly.

"Did you pinch my baby?" Chloe asked me severely.

"No! I'd never do anything to hurt your child! I can't even believe you asked me that!"

"I'm sorry, Mercy. Her yell just startled me I guess."

"Maybe she's hungry?" I posited. Personally, I never shrieked when I was hungry, but I wasn't a baby any longer.

"Maybe," said Chloe, sounding worried.

"And what do we have here?" came the welcome voice of Nanny Gibson. I looked up and saw her marching toward us, a smile on her face. "Sounds like a hungry baby. Or maybe she needs her nappies changed."

Ew. That's right. Babies peed and pooped in their diapers, too. Yet one more reason to think long and hard before I decided to have one.

"Thank you, Nanny Gibson," said Chloe sweetly, holding up the screaming pink bundle for the nanny to take. "You're a life saver."

"I love the daylights out of this little girl," said Nanny Gibson. "She's about the most beautiful baby I've ever seen."

"Really?" I didn't mean to sound so astonished.

"She truly is," said Nanny Gibson, snuggling the screaming child against her bosom and walking back to the house with her.

"You're not feeding the baby yourself?" I asked Chloe, having just recalled the two milk bottles on her chest that, according to anatomy charts, were put there to feed the children of one's loins.

"I thought about it, but I really don't want saggy breasts. The doctors and Nanny Gibson and the books I've read said that babies thrive on a formula featuring Karo syrup and canned milk."

"What's Karo syrup?"

With a shrug, Chloe said, "No idea."

"Well, for heaven's sake," I said in wonderment. "Is this a new invention?"

"Not really, no," said Chloe ending her sentence upon a yawn. "Infant formula, according to Harvey who had one of his assistants look it up, was invented by a German scientist in the eighteen-sixties."

"My goodness." Since the Great War, I'd looked upon anything the least bit Teutonic with grave suspicion. Still, I guess one can't stigmatize a country's entire population for the mistakes made by its leaders. Unless the people voted the villains into power, and Germany didn't. They had Kaiser Bill to blame for their crimes.

"Baby seems to be happy with her food," said Chloe, squinting at me. "What's wrong with that? Do you think I should feed her myself?"

"No!" Chloe must have thought I disapproved. "I'd just never heard of infant formula before. Plus, I don't trust Germans."

Chloe laughed her sweet laugh. "Oh, Mercy, you're too funny. Germany started a horrid war that killed thousands of our boys and even more of their own, not to mention the boys in England, France, Belgium and even Egypt and Palestine, but that was years ago. The German motion-picture industry is going great guns these days. Harvey says they're making outstanding, innovative films over there."

"I had no idea," I said. Then, having thought the matter over for a second, I asked, "What about maple syrup. Would that work as well as that other stuff?"

"Karo syrup?" said Chloe. "I doubt it."

"Might taste better," I said.

"I'm sure Nanny Gibson knows what's best for our bundle of joy," said Chloe with another yawn.

"Hope so," I said, pondering syrups. Whenever I hear the word "syrup," I automatically think of the maple syrup one puts on one's pancakes or waffles. The news that other syrups existed in the world made me feel like an ignoramus. Not a new feeling, but definitely not a good one.

Pushing herself up from her comfy lawn chair, Chloe said, "I'm going to lie down for a while. Having a baby saps one's energy."

"Yes, I can imagine," I said. I didn't mention how off-putting the notion of childbirth seemed to me. Every now and then I can hold my tongue. "I'll escort you. I hope Lulu can participate in our detective work. I miss her."

"I'll try not to take that personally," said Chloe with a not-quite-impish grin.

"I missed you all the time before I came to help here. And now I miss Lulu. I wish we all lived closer to each other."

"I understand," said Chloe. "Just joshing you."

As we approached the door to the house, the dogs raced ahead of us. Molly, after hurriedly stepping aside so as not to get upended, appeared and said, "Mr. Templeton is on the telephone for you, Miss Allcutt."

"Thanks, Molly." I smiled at the lass, whom I guessed to be in her late teens. "Wonder what he's calling about," I muttered as I left Chloe's dawdling self and hurried to the telephone.

"Probably the job Harvey hired him for," said Chloe, whose words followed me inside the house.

I took Ernie's call in the Italian marble foyer that looked liked whoever entered it was supposed to kneel at the feet of an emperor, only there was no emperor extant. As I strode to the gorgeous antique table with both a telephone and a magnificent flower arrangement on it, I glanced around. This house of Harvey and Chloe's was truly spectacular, although it was big enough for seven families. And their servants.

Molly left me at the entrance to the foyer, and I finished my walk to the telephone table, my shoes making a satisfying clicking noise on the fabulous floor. I'd been to Vaudeville shows where people tap-danced. I always left wishing I had some patent-leather shoes with taps on them. Maybe Lulu and I could take a tap-dancing class together when the mystery of Harvey's production problems was solved.

"Good afternoon, Ernie," I said into the mouthpiece.

"Not so's you'd notice," grumbled Ernie.

"What's that supposed to mean?" I snapped.

"Dr. Clutter said Glennie can fill in for Lulu for as long as it takes," he said.

"Why are you grumpy about that?" I asked him. "She's been annoying you, and this Bev Hargroves person is supposed to be competent."

"I know. And I appreciate Harvey hiring me. I just want to get the office back to normal again. It's been rough here without you, Mercy, but I'll deny it if you ever tell anyone I said so."

"I miss you too, Ernie," I said, trying not to sound cloying.

"Anyhow, Lulu and I can be at the Nash citadel tomorrow morning. Lulu's ecstatic. She almost fainted dead away when I told her what Harvey wants us to do."

"Bless Lulu's heart," I said, still inwardly holding Ernie's words to my bosom.

"Yeah. Well, I guess I'll have to wait until this Hargroves person arrives and I show her the ropes. Then I'll drive Lulu and myself to Beverly Hills. What's this movie Harvey's making that has him so flustered?"

"*Helen of Troy*," I said. "Blanche Sweet is Helen and Ramon Novarro is Paris. I think."

"Good God," said Ernie, and he hung up on me.

SEVEN

Ernie and Lulu arrived at the Nash palace a little after noon on Thursday. To say I was thrilled to see them both would be a major understatement. Even Lulu in a gray sweater and skirt and dull black shoes couldn't quell the joy in my heart as I ran to Ernie's more-or-less-new Packard Six.

And Ernie. Well, I didn't throw myself into his arms, but I wanted to. I was thwarted in the endeavor by the presence of Chloe, Harvey, Lulu, Molly the maid, and the Nashes' nameless baby. Also, Ernie carried two large suitcases. A hug from me would have been not merely superfluous but might well have knocked him over.

As I clattered down the vast staircase leading to the castle-worthy porch and ornately carved front door, I noticed Lulu standing still and glancing around, her mouth slightly open.

"It's amazing, isn't it?" I asked as I reached her and pulled her into a hug.

"I've never seen anything like it before," she whispered. "And Mr. and Mrs. Nash *own* this palace?" After we shared a hug, Lulu stepped back and continued to gawp.

"They do. If they rented out flats, they could probably house half of Los Angeles."

"Golly, Mercy," said a still awe-stricken Lulu, "I thought your place was the grandest I'd ever seen until Ernie drove us through Beverly Hills. Maybe I should revive my plans to become a star on the silver screen."

"You'll have time to do that," I told her. "I think Harvey wants you, Ernie, and me on the set starting Monday. We're supposed to snoop and find out who's undermining his production."

"Golly," whispered Lulu. "Golly."

"Here, Ernie, let me give you a hand with those suitcases," said Harvey, smiling hugely.

"I'll take care of them, Mr. Nash," said Porter M. Porter, appearing from somewhere behind the scenery and reaching for a suitcase.

"Thanks, Porter," said Harvey. "Do you think Miss Hargroves will work out for you, Ernie?"

"I think so. She's brisk and efficient, anyway. When I took her to Mercy's place to meet Mrs. Buck and show her where she'll be living for the foreseeable future, she seemed delighted."

Brisk and efficient, was she? Don't think for a second I was jealous of Miss Bev Hargroves. Until, however, Ernie showed up that day, I'd considered briskness and efficiency two of my more prominent workplace characteristics.

"She's no Mercy, though," said Lulu, snapping out of her grandeur-induced awe for a moment. "Everybody misses Mercy like fire."

See why I adored Lulu? She really was my best friend right after Chloe. "I miss you too, Lulu," I said. "The cook here is a French guy who throws tantrums or so Mrs. Biddle, the housekeeper, tells me. He's not kind and approachable like Mrs. Buck."

"But he cooks gourmet dishes for our many dinner parties," said Harvey, laughing at my description of Jacques Garnier, whom I'd met once. Once was enough, as he'd sneered at me. I mean, Chloe and Harvey's cook had *sneered* at me! Chloe's sister! What do you call a male prima donna? Whatever that word is was what Jacques Garnier was.

Chloe hadn't tramped down the long staircase to greet Ernie

and Lulu, but was holding No-Name and beaming from ear to ear when we all walked up the mile and three-quarters' worth of steps to her level.

"It's so good to see you again, Lulu!" said Chloe, who thought Lulu was the berries. "And you, Ernie. Thank you *so* much for helping us. Both of you!"

"May I see the baby?" asked Lulu, sounding uncharacteristically shy.

"Of course you may!" cried Chloe, pulling back the pink blankie to reveal the face of the newest Nash.

"Oh, she's beautiful!" said Lulu almost reverently. "I've never seen a more beautiful baby, and I've seen tons of them."

I squinted hard at Lulu, attempting to divine if she was playing nice for the new parents' sake or if she really meant her flattering words. I recognized not a whit of deception. Transferring my squint to the baby, I then attempted to divine if the baby had become gorgeous since I'd last seen her earlier in the day.

Couldn't do it.

Very well, so the fault in this case seemed to lie with me. Everyone else glimpsed beauty in the infant. I still saw a bulldog. Maybe she'd improved and now looked like a pug or a hairless Pekingese, but I discerned no loveliness.

As Chloe guided Lulu into the house, Harvey hovering behind them and Mr. Porter bringing up the rear, Ernie took my arm and whispered in my ear, "I don't see it, either, kiddo."

"Oh, thank God!" I whispered fervently back at him. I didn't even resent him calling me "kiddo."

Molly stood in the entryway, waiting for us all to pile our coats on her so she could take them to the cloakroom. Because in my parents' home in Boston all the servants were nameless, I made a point of introducing Molly to Lulu.

"Nice to meet you, Molly," said Lulu. "Here. Let me help you with those."

"There's no n-need for that," said Molly with something of a stammer. Guess nobody'd ever offered to help her before.

"Nertz," said Lulu. "Here, I'll take my coat and you can carry the other couple. Where's the closet?"

"Right over here," said Molly, giving up on not being helped by the helpful Lulu. The cloakroom sat just to the left as you walked into the marbled entryway of the Nash abode, so it didn't take long to deposit the coats in it.

As Molly drifted off to perform a duty elsewhere, Chloe said, "Mercy, will you please show Ernie and Lulu where their rooms are?"

"Happy to," I said, walking to the elevator.

"Golly, an elevator?" murmured Lulu.

"Nothing but the best for the head of Nash Studios," said Ernie.

"I usually take the stairs because I figure the exercise is good for me, but I thought you'd enjoy the elevator ride," I told Lulu. "Ernie's already seen it."

"I've never seen an elevator in a private home before," admitted Lulu.

"Amazing what money can buy, isn't it?" said Ernie drily.

"Yes," said Lulu. She didn't sound dry or sarcastic, only amazed.

When the elevator bumped to a stop on the second floor of the grand house, I pulled the cage door open and ushered Lulu and Ernie into the hallway. "I hope you guys don't get lost. I'll do my best to steer you in the right direction."

"Golly," said Lulu in a tiny voice.

"The first rooms off the hallway directly in front of the elevator and to the left are for Chloe, Harvey, the baby and the nanny and the two nurses," I told them, gesturing to the aforementioned hallway.

"They've got two nurses and a nanny for one kid?" asked Ernie, sounding amused.

"They have," I confirmed. "Harvey practically worships Chloe, and he didn't want her to get tired out tending to the infant."

"The baby's what?" said Ernie. "Eight pounds or something like that?"

"I'm not sure. She weighed six and a half pounds at birth, and birth was only ten or eleven days ago, so I don't know if she even weighs eight pounds yet."

"Two nurses and a nanny," whispered Lulu, stunned. "For one tiny baby."

"They're for the parents," said Ernie. "The baby only needs food and some kind of covering to keep it warm. But the two nurses and the nanny can clean up spilled milk and baby burps, change dirty diapers and wash the diapers when the kid soils them."

"My mother managed to do all of those things," said Lulu, "and she didn't have any nurses or nannies at all. And she had six kids. And a washtub."

"Most of the world is like your mother," I said, thinking of my own nanny, who had been a kind woman most of the time. Heck, I remember my childhood nanny better than I remember my mother from my earliest years. Mother'd had no use for dirty little babies back then.

"Yeah. My ma had four kids, and she had to do everything for herself, too," said Ernie. "My sister has two kids, and she has a lady who helps her clean the house, but Lizzy does all the baby-type chores."

I didn't speak except to say, "So the family rooms are on the right, and we turn right after leaving the elevator. See where this hall makes a turn to the left? That's where our rooms are. The set-up is kind of like in my house. Each apartment has a sitting room, a bedroom, a bathroom, and a closet. Every bedroom either has a bathroom to itself or a shared bathroom in between apartments."

"Golly," said Lulu. "In Oklahoma, we had to use an outhouse until about ten years ago, when Grandpa and Pa built a bathroom onto the house."

"An outhouse?" I asked faintly.

"An outhouse," said Lulu. "I was the first person ever to take a bath in the new bathroom."

"Yeah?" said Ernie. "Did you have hot and cold running water, or did you have to carry buckets?"

"Buckets before they built the bathroom. Then we got hooked

up to the city water and power company and got hot and cold water in the house. It was a blessing, believe me."

"I believe you," said Ernie.

Almost speechless after hearing about Lulu's deprived childhood, I said, "I believe you too."

"You never had to use an outhouse, did you, Mercy?" asked Ernie.

"No," I said. I hoped like anything he wouldn't bring up my bags of money.

"We didn't in Chicago either," he said, surprising me.

I didn't utter the *thank God* teetering on my tongue.

"Chicago's a pretty up-to-date city. In some ways, it's more modern than Los Angeles. But the bootleg gangs have taken it over, so it's not safe to live there any longer."

"All because of Prohibition?" I asked, not for the first time thinking Prohibition had been a really bad idea. People are people. As soon as you tell them they can't do something, they instantly go out and do it or gripe about not being able to do it. People are an odd and unsettling species.

"Mostly because of Prohibition," Ernie concurred. "My sister and her husband moved to Evanston. It's not all that far from Chicago, but it's a helluva lot safer."

"Still, it must be difficult to pick up your whole family and its belongings and move away from where you were born," I said. Then I noticed both Ernie and Lulu staring at me with incredulity writ large on their faces. "Oh, I forgot. The three of us did that, didn't we?"

"Yes, but all I had to haul was my own butt and a sack full of clothes," said Ernie. "That old Studebaker and I made the trip without breaking down more than three or four times."

"Yeah," said Lulu. "I took the train, and I had Rupert with me, so at least we could bolster each other's courage. It was a big step."

"It was easy for me," I said. "I'm only one person, and Chloe and Harvey had already offered me sanctuary in their home." I hesitated for a couple of seconds, then added grudgingly, "And I had money." Before Ernie could say something cutting, I said, "Was your brother-in-law able to find work in Evanston easily?"

"Oh, sure. He's a clerk in a bank. Evanston has lots of banks, and most people don't think to rob banks in Evanston because Chicago's much larger and has more banks. I worked as a cop in Chicago for a couple of years after high school, but I'm glad I came to L.A. when I did. Being an honest cop in Chicago must be even harder than it is here."

"Golly," whispered Lulu once more. "Everyone in my family farms. We grow food for ourselves and maybe a little extra to sell to other people, but that's it."

"Interesting," I said. "My father is a banker."

"He owns his own bank, doesn't he?" said Ernie.

"Yes," I admitted. "He owns his own bank, and he's attempting to establish a branch in Pasadena. That's why they bought the house in Pasadena. Or so they said. I think they just wanted to get me under their thumbs again."

With what sounded like a genuinely amused chuckle, Ernie said, "Hopeless cause if that's why they bought the house."

"Yes." I spoke firmly even though thoughts of my mother still made my insides wither up and cringe. "It was a hopeless cause."

"I'm glad," said Lulu. "Otherwise, I'd still be living in that dumpy boarding house right next to Angels Flight. Boy, was that place noisy."

"I can imagine," I said.

"I still live in a dumpy apartment right next to Angels Flight," said Ernie. "But I don't mind much. At least I get to dine at Mercy's house quite often." He gave me an angelic smile I didn't believe for a second.

Then something truly awful occurred to me. "Oh Lord, Father was expecting George to move to Pasadena and run the bank branch there. Now that George is entangled with a showgirl from Ziegfeld's Follies, Father will probably make him move out here sooner than I'd hoped."

"*Your* brother is involved with a showgirl from the Follies?" said

Ernie, laughing. "So you're not the only rebellious child in your family?"

"Wow," said Lulu. "That's what I wanted to do—be a showgirl for Ziegfeld—but it was cheaper for me to move to Los Angeles than New York City. Anyhow, Rupert wanted to move to Los Angeles because he said the job market here was booming. Besides, those Ziegfeld girls need ballet training according to everything I've read about them."

Tired of discussing my family because every time I thought about my family, my chest hurt, I said, "Here's your apartment, Lulu." I opened a door on the right side of the hallway. "Oh, look! Somebody's already brought up your suitcase and garment bag. How efficient of them."

"How'd they get up here?" asked Lulu. "Didn't they take that heavy bag up the elevator? I didn't hear it, but they were here first or my bag wouldn't be."

"Servants' staircase," said Ernie before I could.

"Yes. The servants have a staircase all their own," I agreed. "It's not as nice as the one we didn't walk up."

"Oh," said Lulu.

We traipsed into her room and Lulu let out another reverential, "Golly." She followed the word with, "This is swell."

"Chloe and Harvey believe in treating their guests well," I said.

"Even though they make their household staff take the servants' staircase," said Ernie.

Because he was correct and because I didn't want to fight, I only agreed. "Part of the bargain when you get a job as a servant in a rich person's house."

"You don't make the Bucks take the servants' staircase," Lulu reminded me. "And I'm pretty sure there is one, because when Lily Wu hid out as your place, she used the back stairs. Were those the servants' stairs?"

"Yes," I told her. "We didn't want any nosy policemen to get a peek at Lily Wu when she wasn't in her maid's costume. That's why she wore the uniform and took the back staircase."

"Worked great, too," said Ernie.

Giving him a disapproving frown, I said, "It's still working great for you."

"It is," said Ernie, complacent. "The Chinese community is appreciative when you rescue one of their own."

"They're grateful to some people more than others," I mumbled, still smarting. "I had to drag you kicking and screaming into solving the Chinatown murder. But do the Chinese merchants give *me* stacks of money or let me dine in their restaurants for free? Of course they don't. Only *men* receive *their* thank-you bounties."

"You're right," said Ernie. "Can't argue when you're right." He sounded so smug, I had to stop myself from doing violence to his person.

"Anyhow," I said, not quite hiding a tone of ill-usage and spite, "your rooms are right across the hallway from Lulu's. Want to see Ernie's rooms, Lulu, or do you want to unpack?"

"I'll go with you. I want to see this whole house. It's amazing."

"You're right," I said. "It's amazing. And huge."

They both agreed.

So, after first showing Ernie and Lulu Ernie's set of rooms, which were almost exactly like the suite Lulu had been given, I showed them the rest of the Nash home—although home to me connotes something warm and cozy. Chloe and Harvey's house, while spectacular in the way, say, Buckingham Palace is, it wasn't what I'd call warm and cozy. It was too huge and full of marble to be either of those things, although parts of it could be made comfy, if not precisely cozy.

Oh, never mind.

EIGHT

Once Lulu and Ernie were comfortable enough so as not to get lost when trekking to the dining room, I trod the mile and a half of hallway to Chloe and Harvey's suite of rooms. There I tapped lightly and walked in upon a scene that almost made me change my mind about their home not being warm and cozy.

The happy couple sat in front of the fireplace on a small sofa, Harvey's arm cradling Chloe's shoulder, worshiping the baby on Chloe's lap. I wished I had a camera with a flash attachment with me to capture the moment forever.

Chloe turned to smile at me. "Did you get Lulu and Ernie settled in?"

"Ernie's pretty well settled," I told her. "Lulu is too mesmerized by the grandeur of your mansion to settle in properly. It might take her a day or two."

"Grandeur?" said Chloe, as if everyone she knew lived in a palace like hers. I suppose it was possible they did.

"Your place is huge and full of expensive stuff," I said. "Lulu grew up having to use an outhouse in Oklahoma, and her family members are all farmers."

Chloe's ethereally gorgeous blue eyes grew wide, but all she said was, "Oh my."

"She got used to your house quickly, didn't she?" said Harvey.

"Yes, but I was there with her and it was my house. Also, my house isn't as magnificent as yours. I mean, it's big, but it's not seven acres of marble and stone. Plus, she doesn't know either of you very well yet."

"We'll make her comfortable," said Chloe with assurance borne of experience. She excelled when it came to calming a person's nerves.

"I'm sure you will," I agreed, walking over to observe the baby, hoping I'd catch a peek of what everyone except Ernie and I found beautiful. Narrowing my eyes and staring hard at the infant, I still couldn't do it. How disappointing.

"What's wrong, Mercy?" asked Harvey. I guess my expression alarmed him.

"Wrong? Nothing's wrong," I said. Then I compounded that lie with another one. "Just contemplating baby names."

"We'll think of the perfect name as soon as we know her better," said Chloe, again sounding sure of herself, although her experience with naming babies extended to this one alone as far as I knew.

"I like Rose as a middle name," said Harvey.

"So do I," I said.

"Emily Rose is nice," said Chloe, "but I'm not certain it fits *her*, you know?"

No. I didn't know. Rather than admit it, I said, "Right. I think I'll go see how Lulu's getting along."

"Jacques is preparing luncheon. It will be ready at two o'clock," said Harvey. "I doubt if Ernie and Lulu had time to get lunch, what with coming out here to help and all."

"That's nice of you, Harvey," I said, thinking I hadn't had lunch either and my stomach felt empty-ish. Perhaps it was hunger and not mere loathing that made my tummy twist when I thought about my family.

As I left Harvey and Chloe to ponder the many marvels of the being they'd created, I thought about hunger pangs versus family pangs. By the time I got to Lulu's room, I'd decided they were two different things and that I was definitely hungry.

I told Lulu about lunch as soon as I entered her room after a tiny tap.

"How nice of them," said Lulu, whom I found sitting on the small chair belonging to a vanity table and gazing around her. She still looked as if she didn't think she belonged where she found herself.

"I think so too," I said. "I'm hungry."

"Do I have to change clothes to go to lunch?" she asked in a small voice.

"No. Come as you are. And we don't change for dinner either. Unless the Nashes are throwing a big dinner party, we just wear the clothes we're already wearing."

"I'm glad of that. I don't have loads of clothes," said Lulu. "New clothes, I mean. I didn't bring my flashy clothes, not that I have many of them left."

"Is that consignment store in Chinatown able to sell your bright clothing?" I asked. I didn't want to use the word "flashy" although Lulu used to flash and sparkle all over the place. Her hideous experience with a horrible man changed her mind about extremely bright colors.

"Yeah," said Lulu. "They're selling like hotcakes."

"Good. That's extra money for you. You won't have to worry about what to wear here. I think we'll be dressed up like ancient Greek or Roman people on the set."

Another soft, "Golly" came from Lulu.

A tap sounded at her door and Lulu said, "Come in." Then she quickly looked at me, I presume to find out if she was supposed to have said something else. I only nodded and smiled, and she seemed relieved.

Ernie, as nonchalant as ever, walked into Lulu's room. "Any food in this place? My stomach's so empty it thinks somebody cut my throat."

"What a charming vision," I said, grinning at him. "Yes. The

Nashes' superior French chef is preparing a luncheon, of which we'll all partake at two o'clock."

"Good," said Ernie, rubbing his hands together. Glancing at the clock on the fireplace mantel, he said, "It's darned near two now. Where does one partake of luncheon in this place?"

"Generally in one of the smaller dining rooms," I said. "There are three dining rooms in all. A huge one for large gatherings, a middle-sized one for more intimate dinner parties, and a regular-sized one for family meals. You guys are family for the duration of our mission here."

"Got it," said Ernie, plopping himself onto a chair next to the one I occupied. Lulu still sat on the vanity chair, looking as if even now she felt out of place. Noticing her expression, Ernie said, "Relax, Lulu. Chloe and Harvey are nice folks. You know, just like you and me."

"They're rich," said Lulu, putting an end to Ernie's placating fantasy as soon as it hit the air.

"So's Mercy and you're not afraid of her, are you?"

"Well no, but I've known Mercy for months. And her house isn't as…as…as…I don't know what as this place is."

"This place is gigantic and full of expensive furnishings and art. It's intimidating," I said, knowing precisely how she felt.

"Yes," said Lulu.

See? Told you I knew how she felt.

"Bushwa," said Ernie. "Mercy and I will escort you to lunch so you won't have to enter the smallest of the three dining rooms by yourself."

"Thanks," said Lulu. Pensively, she added, "I hope I can get used to this place, but I'm not sure I'll be able to. I mean, who else do you know has three dining rooms?"

"Probably plenty of picture people," I said. "Why, Rudolph Valentino built his Falcon Lair just over the hill there." I gestured vaguely northwest. I think it was northwest. I get confused when using words like north and west and so forth. Tell me to turn right, and I'm fine. Or give me a landmark—"Turn left at the pet shop"—and everything's ginger-peachy.

"And don't Mary Pickford and Douglas Fairbanks have a huge estate somewhere close to this place?" asked Ernie.

"They do. It's called Pickfair, and it's just a little way in that direction." I pointed, but I'm not sure in which direction. "They don't merely have a swimming pool like Harvey and Chloe. They have an entire lake at their disposal. With boats and ducks."

"Good heavens," whispered Lulu, remaining all agog.

"They're just people, Lulu," I told her. "You should know that by this time. Heck, you went out to dinner with John Gilbert, and you saw Gary Cooper and What's His Name at Musso and Frank's a couple of months ago."

"John Gilbert was nice," said Lulu. "And Gary Cooper smiled at me. I thought I was going to faint."

"Cripes," said Ernie. "All they have that you don't is money."

"And fame," I added because it was the truth.

"Yeah," said Lulu. "That's what's making me so nervous. The money and the fame."

"You needn't be nervous now," I told her. "Save your nervousness for Monday, when you'll meet Ramon Novarro and Blanche Sweet."

"Ramon Novarro?" whispered Lulu, pressing a hand to her bosom. "I'm going to meet Ramon *Novarro*?"

"Yes. He's playing Paris and Blanche Sweet is playing Helen in the picture Harvey's making and someone seems to be sabotaging," I said. "*Helen of Troy*. That's the name of the picture."

"Wow," murmured Lulu.

A bell sounded. Lulu squealed and jumped in her chair.

"It's only the meal gong," I told her. "Molly rings it when meals are ready, so it must be two o'clock. Let's go get lunch. I'm starving."

"Sounds like a great idea to me," said Ernie, rising and holding out an arm each for Lulu and me.

We walked thus attached to each other out of Lulu's room and to the huge marble staircase. Our shoes made satisfying clicks as we descended the stairs, and I thought about tap dancing again.

"Say, Lulu, would you like to take tap-dancing lessons with me one of these days?" I asked her.

Lulu stiffened and said, "What?" She sounded alarmed.

"What brought that on?" asked Ernie. He sounded merely baffled.

"Clicking shoes on marble," I said. Then I heaved a sigh and added, "I love the sound of tap-dancing, and I thought maybe Lulu and I could take lessons somewhere. There must be dance studios where you can take lessons in Los Angeles."

"There are," said Ernie. "I'm surprised you don't remember Anthony's Palaise de Danse."

"Oh, Lord, I don't even want to *think* about that place," I said.

"Isn't that where we got arrested?" Lulu asked.

"Yes," I said.

"Yes," Ernie concurred. "And I had to bail you out because you'd been walking the streets like a couple of—"

"Don't say it," I interrupted.

"All right," said Ernie equably. "But when I got to the station and saw the two of you sitting there, I wasn't surprised you'd been arrested. You sure looked the part of a couple of—"

"Stop it!" I said, interrupting again.

"You're no fun," said Ernie as I led them across the fabulous marble foyer to yet another hallway. Delicious aromas would have led us to the correct dining room even if I hadn't known where it was.

"Sorry lunch is so late," said Harvey, greeting us at the door. "But I figured you two"—he gestured at Lulu and Ernie—"wouldn't have had time to eat before you got here."

"You figured correctly," said Ernie. "Any rules about seating?"

"Nope," said Harvey. "Chloe's taking the meal in her room so she can stay with the baby. Then she'll take a nap. Giving birth is exhausting work."

"It must be," I said, thinking that if Chloe, with a house full of servants and with nothing to do but watch her infant all day every day, was exhausted, normal women must *really* suffer after having babies.

"Here," said Ernie, standing behind a chair and pulling out a chair on either side of his, "why don't you and Lulu sit here?"

"Sounds good to me," I said.

"Thanks, Ernie," said Lulu, selecting the chair closest to the door.

"Thank you, Ernie," I said, walking a couple of steps farther and getting ready to sit in the other chair.

"Jacques said he had to pull together a quick luncheon," said Harvey, grinning. "And he wasn't happy about it, but I think we'll all survive until dinner.

Staring at the platters of food in front of Harvey, who sat across from us at the putative head of the table, I said, "I think we will." As the table was round, there wasn't truly a "head" of it, but I guess Harvey decided to sit where the food resided so he could start things off without any confusion on his guests' part.

He did it for Lulu, and I adored him for it.

The meal was great, and we chatted during it. It wasn't long before Lulu seemed to relax for the first time since she'd entered the house.

"So what's the picture you're making about?" she dared ask after we'd polished off a clear soup and started in on the fish course.

"*Helen of Troy*'s the name of the picture," said Harvey. "It's based on the Greek myth. You know, the one in which Paris, who's a prince in Troy, falls in love with Helen, who's married to the King of Sparta, Menelaus. Menelaus isn't happy about the affair, especially when Paris abducts Helen and takes her back to Troy."

"Somewhere in there, doesn't the Trojan Horse appear?" I asked.

"I've heard of that," said Lulu, surprised.

"Yes. We'll definitely build a horse. Not sure if it will be a big one or a small one that will just look big." Harvey paused with a bite of fish in a creamy sauce almost to his lips. "But I don't want to begin building anything until you three figure out who's sabotaging the production. There have been too many so-called accidents. I'm sure there's someone behind them, but I have no idea why. You need to discover and disarm the culprit before someone's seriously injured."

"We'll do our best," said Ernie.

"Yes, we will," I said.

"Sure," said Lulu.

"So what are we supposed to do on the set, Harvey?" I asked. "Are we going to be Spartan women and Ernie a Spartan man?"

"That's what I thought we'd do, yes," said Harvey with a shrug. "We'll put you in costume so you won't stand out as newcomers. In a way, it's lucky the picture has so large a cast. You'll be able to wander around and poke your noses into things without anyone thinking you're peculiar or snoopy. I hope."

"I hope so, too."

"Was Helen of Troy in the *Iliad* or the *Odyssey*?" asked Ernie. I'd been wondering the same thing, so I was glad he asked.

"I think Helen's mentioned in the *Iliad*," said Harvey. "But Helen's story was best told by Virgil in the *Aeneid*. Not that we're sticking to the plot. But it'll be a big extravaganza and I hope it makes tons of money."

"I hope so too," I told him. "This place must cost a fortune to keep up." I waved an arm in the air to indicate the whole of the Nash estate.

"Oh, it does, but that's not what worries me. If the picture's a flop, we'll survive. If someone is seriously hurt or killed on the set, however, things might be different." He shook his head. "I can see the screaming headlines now."

"Oh my, yes," I said. "The morality police are already calling motion pictures an evil influence on the youth of today."

"The youth of today will probably go to hell the same way the youth of yesterday did," said Ernie cynically. "The use of booze and drugs and simply behaving badly aren't reserved to any one generation."

Recalling history lessons of yore, I had to agree with him. "You're right. It's easier for people to get around these days, though, what with automobiles and so forth. In 1850, you couldn't get from

Los Angeles to Pasadena in an hour. You'd have to drive a wagon or get on a stage coach, and it would take days."

"I don't think Pasadena was a city in 1850," said Ernie.

"Probably not, but you know what I mean," I said.

"True. And what with moving pictures so popular, every girl in the United States who watches the flickers wants to become a star," said Lulu. "Believe me, I know all about it."

"True," said Ernie. "But you got lucky."

"If you think it's lucky to be suspected of murder, Ernest Templeton," I said, "you're a blooming idiot. Lulu went through heck after that evil man got his mitts on her."

"I don't think it's lucky, and I'm sorry it happened. Don't forget the cops fingered me as a murderer a few months back." He shook his head. "And then you *had* to go to that church and nearly get yourself killed."

Peeved, I snapped, "I was the only one who *knew* something or someone in that church was involved. And I was right!"

"And you almost got killed," repeated Ernie.

"Well yes, but if you weren't so stubborn, I wouldn't have had to approach that crazy woman alone."

"You shouldn't have approached her at all," grumbled Ernie.

"I had to because neither Phil nor you would listen to me when I told you about the church connection."

"Yeah, Ernie," said Lulu. "Don't rag on Mercy. I know how hard it is to get you to pay attention to Mercy when she gets ideas about crimes."

"Please don't throw Chinatown in my face again," pleaded Ernie. "I catch grief from Mercy all the time about the Chinatown affair."

"As is only seemly," I said and sniffed disapprovingly, which reminded me of my mother, thereby making me even grumpier. "I not only had to force you to look into the matter, but then all the Chinese folks named *you* as the champion of the piece and forgot all about me!"

"Are you still going on about how unfair life is?" came Chloe's voice from the door to the dining room. "Mercy, you know it's a man's world."

NINE

"I thought you were going to nap," I said. "And yes, I know it's a man's world. It's just that don't like it."

Harvey and Ernie laughed. Lulu, Chloe, and I didn't. I found nothing amusing about the disparities prevailing between the sexes. Or between the rich and the poor. Or between white people and pretty much everyone else in the world who isn't white. However, because I knew I couldn't change the world no matter how warped it was or how hard I tried, I let the matter drop.

Harvey rose from his place and went to Chloe. "Did you decide to dine with us, sweetheart?"

"No. I just felt lonely stuck away upstairs. I wanted to see how everyone's settling in."

"Great so far," said Ernie, who'd also risen when Chloe entered the room. He might be perennially casual, but he practiced good manners.

"Yes. Everything's swell," said Lulu, back to using her small, intimated voice.

"Good. Too bad it's winter or we could have a pool party," said Chloe, coming in and taking a chair next to Harvey.

"We have to solve the problems on the set before we throw a

party of any kind," said Harvey. "Don't ever forget about poor Fatty Arbuckle. He didn't even know the woman who died at his party, but her death ruined his career."

"Oh dear, yes. You're right," said Chloe.

"What a dismal thought," I said.

"So snoop hard, will you please?" said Harvey, sharing a speaking glance among Ernie, Lulu, and me.

"We'll do our best," said Ernie.

The rest of that weekend passed peacefully enough. On Saturday Harvey and Ernie closeted themselves in Harvey's home office—the den, in other words—probably to discuss strategy when Monday arrived. That's when Ernie, Lulu and I would appear on the set of *Helen of Troy* and use whatever detectival skills we possessed to finger the culprit trying to sabotage Harvey's production. With luck, we might even find out why he or she was doing it.

On Sunday, the two men consulted each other for another several hours. I don't know what Lulu thought because I didn't ask her, but I took umbrage that Harvey didn't include me in his and Ernie's conferences. I told Ernie about my resentment. "I'm your assistant, Ernest Templeton. I should be included in discussions about our work."

After heaving a large-sized sigh, Ernie said, "Last time I looked, you were my secretary. When did the title 'assistant' come into being?"

"Piffle! You know what I mean. Lulu and I need to know what we'll be doing tomorrow too, you know."

"I know. We'll have our own conference in my room."

I instantly thought such a meeting place to be scandalous and chalked up my reaction to my sheltered upbringing. It annoyed the heck out of me.

"Very well," I said, trying not to sound like my mother. "When do you want to have this conference?"

Ernie shook down the sleeve of his jacket and peered at his wristwatch. "About now would be good. Know where Lulu is?"

"Yes," I said upon a sigh of my own. "She's with Chloe and the baby. Lulu thinks the kid is the most beautiful baby she's ever seen."

"Yeah? Well, how about that."

"I know. The baby still looks...I don't know. Undercooked or something to me."

"Me too, but let's not tell the proud parents. Or Lulu."

"I'd never tell any of them. But I'll go get Lulu. Did you and Harvey come up with a plan?"

"Oddly enough, we did," said Ernie.

"Oh!" It was probably impolite of me to sound so surprised. At once I said, "I'll be right back with Lulu," in order to cover my astonishment. But honestly, my experience has been that men can sit and talk for hours, pretending to be in a meeting when they're really only gossiping and not coming up with solutions. I'd never tell them that, either.

When I tapped on the door and walked into Chloe's room, sure enough, Lulu sat on one of Chloe's lovely chairs holding a pink bundle on her lap and cooing at it as if it were her own, as Chloe looked on with an expression of rapture on her face. Attempting to hide my incredulity, I walked over to them, peered down at the baby and decided it looked slightly better today than it had the first time I saw it, a couple of hours after its birth.

"May I borrow Lulu for a little bit?" I asked.

Glancing up from the baby on her lap, Lulu said, "How come?"

"You may," said Chloe. "If you have a good reason. It's fun having Lulu here."

"Ernie wants to tell us what we'll be doing tomorrow on the set of *Helen of Troy*," I said.

"I guess I'd better go then," said Lulu, disappointed. "Your baby is beautiful, Chloe."

Smiling a beatific smile, Chloe said, "Thanks. I think so too."

So Lulu and I left Chloe with her child, two nurses and a nanny. "We're meeting in Ernie's room," I told Lulu.

"That's one lucky kid," said Lulu, perhaps not having heard my words. "She's not only gorgeous, but her parents are rich."

"Yes indeed," I said, having decided to take everyone else's word on the beautiful-baby thing. "You seem to have settled in better now," I added.

"Oh, I have," said Lulu. "Chloe's awfully nice, and so is Harvey. And everyone who works here is nice too, except nobody likes the cook."

"Jacques Garnier is a French fellow, and I think he prefers the title of *chef*," I said. "He's really mean and snobby, so I recommend staying away from the kitchen."

"That's what everybody's told me so far," said Lulu. "And that's fine by me. I'm no good in a kitchen anyway."

"Neither am I," I said, although with a hint of sorrow in my voice I hadn't heard in Lulu's. "But Mrs. Buck has told me she'll be happy to teach me to cook, so that's nice."

"Cooking isn't any fun," said Lulu. "Why do you want to learn to cook if you can afford to hire servants? And you can."

This question was difficult to answer. I knew in my heart that I not only wanted to live and function among the worker proletariat, but I wanted to be *of* them. Trust me when I tell you that traveling from the dizzying heights of Beacon Hill in Boston to the mean streets of Los Angeles is a darned difficult journey. Nevertheless, I attempted to answer Lulu's query.

"I want to be self-sufficient," I told her. "I want to be able to support myself and do everything for myself. You grew up in a family where you had to help each other in order to get food from the farm and onto the table. I grew up in a family where my mother ordered her servants to do everything from buying chickens to making bread and cleaning bedrooms. She demanded that *I* know the difference between a pickle fork and an olive fork."

"There's a difference?" asked Lulu. "Oh yeah, I think you told me you had to learn that stuff before."

"I'm sure I did. There isn't much difference between the two forks, but if I got them mixed up, my mother would scold me for hours. I mean, *why?* Is the world going to end if somebody sticks a spoon in the olive bowl and withdraws an olive? No, it won't. But if a rich person loses all of his or her money, he or she might die if all he or she has ever been taught is the names of the various pieces of silverware and precisely the order in which they're supposed to be set on the table for meals."

"He or she might be in for a world of hurt," said Lulu. "Anyhow, if he or she looked as rich as he or she used to be, he or she'd probably get mugged on the way to the pawn shop."

"Are you teasing me, Lulu LaBelle?" I asked ominously.

"Me? *Me?* Would *I* do a thing like that?"

"Yes. You and Ernie both would."

Laughing, Lulu threw an arm around my shoulder. "I'm glad I got to come here, Mercy. You're right about Chloe. Your sister could make a gorilla feel included and cozy."

"Told you so," I said smugly.

"You did. You do the same thing."

"I do? That's a surprise to me," I said, astonished.

"Pooh. You do, and you know it. You even made that escapee from the loony bin feel as if he was normal."

"I hate it when Ernie calls Mr. Brentwood crazy," I said, trying not to sound as disapproving as I felt. "Yes, the man's got problems, but he's not crazy."

"If you say so," said Lulu, unconvinced.

By that time, we'd made it the seventeen miles from the Nash suite of rooms to the guest rooms. I dropped the subject of Mr. Brentwood and tapped on Ernie's door.

"C'mon in," he hollered.

I turned the knob. "Can't. Door's locked."

"Aw, shi—oot," said Ernie. "Hold on. I'll let you in."

He did.

"Why'd you lock your door, Ernie?" Lulu wanted to know. "You afraid the servants will steal all your money?"

"All what money?" asked Ernie. "No. I just didn't want to be interrupted. I set up an easel and a tablet. I figured we could plot our activities on the paper. Harvey gave me a sketch of the *Helen of Troy* set. I put it here." He gestured to a drawing he'd set up on a table next to the easel.

"That's very organized of you," I said, wishing I'd come up with the concept before Ernie thought of it. Some kind of assistant I was, huh? Oh, well. Something to file in my brain for future cases.

"You're not the only person in the firm who can organize things," said Ernie.

"So I see." I tried not to sound disappointed.

"So this is what a motion-picture set looks like on paper, is it?" said Lulu, scrutinizing the sketch with fascination. "Gee, I never even thought about sets when I came here to break into Holly-woodland."

"Most folks don't," said Ernie.

"I've been on movie sets when they're filming. The process is boring as all get-out," I said, adding a truth I figured Lulu didn't want to know.

"Really?" said Lulu, surprised.

"Yes," I said.

"Yes," said Ernie.

"Oh. Well, it'll be interesting to watch something I've never seen before," said Lulu, making the most of a situation by which she had yet to be bored senseless.

"I'm sure it will be," I said, feeling charitable.

"Okay, let's look here," said Ernie. He tacked the sketch of the set at the top of the easel. "We'll drive to the set in my car. Harvey has a chauffeur, and he doesn't want people to know we're with him."

"That makes sense," I said.

"Thanks." Ernie sent me a sour smile. "Let me finish before you ask anything, all right?"

"I didn't ask anything," I said, stung. "I said the driving arrangements make sense."

"Thank you," said Ernie as his gaze paid a visit to the ceiling. "Anyway, try to get the set fixed in your mind. It's not going to look like this when we get to it. It will seem huge because it is, but if you get the different areas memorized, you'll at least know which direction to walk if somebody tells you to visit Menelaus's throne room, Helen's boudoir or the Trojan gate."

"Can Mercy and I stick together?" asked Lulu in a small voice. "I'm not too good with directions."

"I'm not either," I said.

"Sheesh," muttered Ernie. "Yes, you can stick together."

"Thank you," I said.

"The first thing we'll do when we arrive at the studio—Harvey gave me a pass so the gate attendant will let us in without a fuss—is visit the office of your pal, Francis Easthope."

"Oh, of course," I said. "For costumes!"

"Precisely," said Ernie.

"What kinds of costumes will we get?" asked Lulu, excitement overtaking her directional disability.

"Probably long robes." Ernie eyed Lulu's dyed locks. "Maybe a wig. I don't know if ancient Greeks had blondes among their citizens."

"Heck, Lulu and I will probably be slave girls or something," I said.

"Probably. Or Helen's servants. We've got to keep an eye on Blanche Sweet and Ramon Novarro. You two will be assigned to Miss Sweet, and I'll hang around with Mr. Novarro. We haven't met before."

"Too bad John Gilbert's not in the picture," I said. "We've all met Mr. Gilbert before. Has Harvey tipped Mr. Novarro or Miss Sweet off to our being there?"

"He will. Harvey said he'll talk to the two main stars tomorrow morning and let them know he's got people looking into the so-called accidents on the set."

"What are we supposed to do?" I asked him. "Tackle anyone who looks suspicious?"

"No. Tell Harvey or me if you see something suspicious. You two should definitely stick together, at least at first. Until you become accustomed to the set and all the people. Harvey's right when he said this is going to be an epic flicker with a cast of thousands."

"Thousands?" squeaked Lulu.

"Hundreds, anyway," said Ernie.

"Golly," said Lulu. "How keen is that? We're going to be in a movie!"

"In the crowd scenes maybe," said Ernie wryly.

"Will somebody drive a chariot? Like they did in *Ben Hur*?" asked Lulu.

Both Ernie and I turned our heads to look at Lulu.

She said, "What? Didn't they have chariots in wherever the Trojans lived?"

"They lived in Troy," said Ernie.

"Why do they call them Trojans then?" Lulu sounded a trifle miffed.

"I guess it sounds better than Troyans," said Ernie.

"I guess," she said.

"I don't remember a chariot race in *Helen of Troy*," I said. "But I haven't read the story for years."

"I don't think I've ever read it," said Ernie. "I think we learned about it in school, but I don't know what year or anything."

"Maybe we should read it again," I said. "Harvey must have a copy somewhere."

"I doubt it'll help in this case," Ernie said. "They're not sticking closely to the plot of the story. This is a flicker, remember?"

"The *real* story is a myth to begin with," I said.

"Good point," said Ernie.

"What difference does it make?" Pertinent question.

"None, I guess," said Ernie.

"You're right, Lulu. I think I'll read it again anyway if Harvey has a copy that isn't in Greek."

"Does Harvey have a lot of books written in Greek in his library?" asked Ernie.

"Maybe the Bible," I said.

"All right you guys, stop it," said Lulu, hands on hips and looking displeased. "You're making fun of me because you both went to school longer than I did, aren't you?"

"Huh?" Ernie.

"What?" Me.

Softening her pugilistic stance, Lulu said, "You mean you're not teasing me?"

"No," said Ernie and I in an unmusical duet.

That was kind of disappointing, actually. The unmusicality of our duet, I mean. I wanted us to sound good together. Ah well.

TEN

The next morning arrived entirely too early for me. But Harvey said he had to get to the set at six-thirty a.m., and we should arrive about an hour later. So we got up at five-thirty a.m. and stumbled around with bleary eyes.

"Crumb," said Lulu when we met in the upstairs hall on our way to the staircase. "If I'd known how early flicker people have to get up, I wouldn't have wanted to be an actress."

"I've never wanted to be an actress, and I hate getting up early," I muttered. "Private eye's assistant is the highest step on the ladder I ever wanted to climb."

"Hell," said Ernie, making me jump because I hadn't heard him approaching us from behind, "I thought your highest ambition was to be a published novelist."

"Well yes, that's true," I admitted. "But I don't think novelists have to get up early for anything."

"Maybe script-writers do," said Ernie.

"Are there such things?" I asked. "The flickers are silent."

"According to your brother-in-law, the viewing public has become sophisticated since the first motion pictures were distributed. Now they're even producing sound pictures, and actors have to learn lines and rehearse."

"Pooh. I don't want to be a script-writer," I grumbled. "I want to go back to bed."

"Tough luck, kiddo," said Ernie with a laugh, flinging an arm around my shoulder and giving me a squeeze.

The squeeze made me almost forget about being made to get up at an ungodly hour of the day.

"Golly, I'd love to see a picture with the actors talking," said Lulu.

"It's probably going to take a while before that happens," said Ernie. "Harvey told me they've got Vitaphone synchronized sound-tracks for some of them that have music and sound effects, but so far nobody can hear the actors speak. I'm sure brilliant people are working on the problem even as we stand here and whine about having to get up early."

"Phooey. If they're so brilliant, why don't they do something useful with their talents and cure horrible illnesses or prevent famines or something like that? Why waste their talents on moving pictures?"

"I suspect the flickers are easier," said Ernie. "And the actors in the flickers definitely make more money than do people who make big scientific discoveries."

With a sigh, I said, "True. Life is so unfair."

That morning I wasn't as enamored of the clicking of our shoes on the marble staircase as I had been a couple of days prior.

"Good morning," said Harvey as we straggled into the smallest dining room. "Jacques has prepared a lovely breakfast for us. The studio will provide lunch in the canteen for people working on *Helen of Troy*."

"I thought you'd be gone by now," I said.

"I'll leave soon," said Harvey.

"That's nice of the studio," I said. "Do you have a copy of the story of *Helen of Troy*, Harvey? I wanted to read it again."

"Oh, sure. I'll get it for you this evening. I spoke with Francis yesterday, and he's preparing two Grecian costumes for Lulu and you, Mercy. You'll probably have to wear wigs and headpieces too."

"What about Ernie?" I asked.

"He'll be in a more elaborate costume, because he's supposed to be a big shot in the Trojan army."

I squinted at my boss, trying to picture him as an ancient Trojan general. Or at least a colonel. Sergeant? Couldn't do it, but I said, "Great," anyway. "Are we supposed to be Trojans too, or are we Mycenaeans? What's a Mycenaean, anyhow?"

"An ancient Spartan," said Harvey promptly. "Sparta used to be called Mycenaea. It was part of ancient Greece."

"Ah," I said. "I didn't know that. I mean, I knew Sparta and Troy were Greek, but...never mind."

"Food's been set out on the sideboard here," said Harvey, gesturing at the sideboard, upon which had been placed a row of chafing dishes. Sometimes Mrs. Buck fed us breakfast from chafing dishes, but Mercy's Manor didn't have half as many of the dishes as the Nash household.

So we filled our plates at the sideboard. What a spread!

We then sat and began eating. After my first few hunger pangs were eased and after thinking about ancient Sparta—or Mycenaea, if you were Harvey—I said, "Those old Spartans were weird people."

"What makes them weird?" Lulu asked.

"They were bred to be tough and brutal, always warring. There's a story about a Spartan kid who captured a fox, and when he was being questioned by somebody or other, he allowed the fox to eat his guts and didn't flinch. I'm not sure why, except that Spartan kids were taught to be indifferent to pain. I guess if the kid cried, he'd have been spanked."

"He'd already be dead, thanks to the fox," said Ernie.

"Ick," said Lulu. "That's disgusting."

"You're right," I said. "And so's Ernie. Anyhow, I guess all those separate...what would you call them? Tribes? Anyhow, I guess they're now united into one country. Greece. I think. Maybe not."

Ernie shrugged. "Moot point at this stage," he said. "Last June a guy named Pangalos became a dictator until another coup under General Kondylis ousted him. I think Kondylis is still the dictator-in-charge, but Greek politics change every other week or so."

I gaped at my boss. "How come you know about Greek politics?"

"I read the newspaper," he said. Grinning at me he added, "I don't do much world traveling, so I have to read about these things."

"Sounds kind of boring to me," said Lulu.

Although I agreed with her, I didn't say so aloud for fear of coming across as a frivolous American who knew nothing of the greater world. In other words, I didn't want to reveal my massive ignorance to my pals.

"I'd like to travel someday, though," Lulu said dreamily.

"I went to England once," I said. "And we visited Scotland."

"That must have been interesting," said Lulu.

"It was cold, was what it was," I said. "Rained all the time. Sure is green and pretty though."

"I thought it was Ireland that's green," said Ernie.

"England and Scotland are green too," I said. "At least they were when I was there."

After a truly stupendous breakfast and two or three cups of coffee, I decided I might live through the day. "As much as I hate to admit it, Mr. Jacques Garnier fixes a top-notch meal," I said.

"He does," both Ernie and Lulu agreed.

Harvey only laughed. "I'm going upstairs to kiss my wife and daughter farewell. I might see you three at the studio, but I'd rather not announce to everyone that we're acquainted."

"We understand," Ernie said.

"Yup," said Lulu.

"Is it all right if we own up to knowing Francis Easthope?" I asked, thinking it might be a valid question.

"Huh. I hadn't thought about that," said Ernie while Harvey appeared startled.

"I'm sure Francis will acknowledge knowing you, so it doesn't matter," Harvey said. "The main reason I don't want to announce to everyone that we know each other is because you need to snoop, and if everyone knows you know me, they might clam up."

"That's fine," I said.

Ernie and Lulu nodded.

Harvey left for the studio in his chauffeur-driven Rolls-Royce Canterbury Landaulette. Nice car. Nice chauffeur. About a half-hour after Harvey's departure, we discovered how extremely nice the Nashes' chauffeur was. He'd washed and waxed Ernie's Packard-Six! Not that the Packard was an auto to sneer at, but none of us had expected Mr. Porter to wash and wax it.

"Mr. Porter sure does a bang-up job taking care of the cars in his custody," said Ernie, grinning as he ran a hand over the glossy surface of his car's hood. He opened the back passenger door, so I got in. Lulu followed me. I'd have sat in front with Ernie if Lulu wasn't there. Is that silly? Oh, who cares?

The studio wasn't far from the Nash mansion in distance, but boy, you could sure tell we were no longer where the rich folks lived when Ernie's car eased its way down the curvy streets of Beverly Hills and carried us through roads housing the "other half" of L.A.'s society.

A guard manned a gatehouse to the studio lot. He smiled at those of us in Ernie's car and, when Ernie flashed the pass he'd been given by Harvey, he nodded and told Ernie to drive on in. So he did.

After that things got a trifle confusing, at least for Lulu and me.

"Wow," said Lulu, glancing around at what looked a lot like another city within the City of Los Angeles. "Which way is Mr. Easthope's office?"

"To the left here," said Ernie, driving to the first street he saw. "Harvey said it's…Ah, yes, there it is."

"It is?" I said, glancing around in befuddlement. There were so many *people* everywhere. And they were garbed in costumes ranging from eighteenth-century European royalty to cowboys and Indians. I didn't see any ancient Greeks anywhere—to my knowledge. For all I knew ancient Greeks dressed like cowboys, but I didn't think so.

"Oh, there!" said Lulu, pointing at a building on the left.

Then I saw it too: a plaque nailed to a door read "Easthope. Costuming".

"Where can you park?" I asked Ernie.

"Anywhere I can find a spot according to Harvey," said Ernie. So he did, parking on the left side of the little studio street.

When the three of us stepped out of the Packard, I instantly lost track of where we were in the overall scheme of things. "This isn't part of the *Helen of Troy* set, is it?" I asked.

"No," said Ernie, looking at me as if I'd said something stupid. "The set is at the back of the lot. These buildings are where the people who have to work for a living have their offices."

"As opposed to whom?" I asked, not having been enlightened.

"The writers, runners, script girls, costumers, and set designers work here. The actors who only have to look good on a screen will be on the *Helen of Troy* set. If they're here yet."

"Oh," I said.

Lulu appeared totally captivated when I glanced her way. She darned near tripped up the curb in front of Mr. Easthope's office, which wasn't really an office. Rather, when Ernie opened the door and ushered Lulu and me inside, we saw a large warehouse-type room with racks all over the place. Many of the racks bore signs designating what types of costumes resided there. I didn't see Mr. Easthope.

I heard him, however, when he said, "Oh, good, there you are. I have your costumes ready. We'll need to measure the robes, and you'll have to try on sandals to make sure we get the fit right."

"Sandals?" I whispered, almost as overwhelmed as Lulu seemed to be.

"Yeah. The old Grecian folks wore sandals. They tie on, so they're pretty secure, but your feet will get dusty."

"My word," I said.

"Oh," said Lulu. She kind of shrank against me and clutched my arm.

I decided we were both being silly. Yes, this was a new world to us, but we could let it intimidate us or treat it as an adventure. I voted for adventure. I'm sure Lulu would have too if I'd asked her.

"Thank you," I said. I attempted to take a bold step toward Mr. Easthope, but after peering around the big room I still couldn't see him, so I put my foot down again. Then I saw the hard-to-miss sign hanging over a couple of costume racks. The sign said *Helen of Troy*. So I took my bold step and almost tripped over a fellow who was down on his knees peering under the hem of a garment. I hadn't noticed him. "Whoops! I beg your pardon," I said.

"It's okay," said the man, scooting back and sitting on the floor. He had a bunch of sewing pins in his mouth and spoke around them when he added, "Dropped a tiara." He held the item up and, sure enough, it looked like a tiara.

"Who wears that?" asked Lulu timidly.

"Dunno. One of the ladies in Helen's court, I think," the fellow said.

"Over here," said Mr. Easthope again, sounding the teeniest bit impatient. "I have to measure these robes to see if they need to be shortened or lengthened or whatever."

"We're here," said Ernie, striding to where Francis Easthope stood, big as life and twice as handsome in front of the *Helen of Troy* costume racks.

"I have no idea why I didn't see you there," I told him. "Sorry. Didn't mean to dawdle."

His smile eased my compunction about making him wait. "It's all right," he said. "You've never seen this place before, have you?"

"No," I said. "I've been on a couple of location shoots, but the studio and grounds are mysteries to me."

"You'll get used to them," said Mr. Easthope as if he honestly believed his words.

I wasn't so sure, but I was glad someone had confidence in us.

"Before we robe you, let me introduce you to my assistant. I think you nearly tripped over him," said Mr. Easthope. "He's always in the way." He sounded serious, and I felt sorry for the assistant.

Until his assistant said, "Yeah, I trip people up all the time. When Easthope isn't around, I then roast and eat them."

Both the assistant and Mr. Easthope burst out laughing. When I glanced at Lulu, I saw her face register horror until she realized the men were teasing. As I too thought the image a gruesome one, it took me a couple of seconds to overcome my own horror.

"Pay no mind to him. But if you want to talk to him, you can call him Greg. Greg Donner. Greg, please meet three more people who will be gracing the set of *Helen of Troy*. Miss Allcutt, Miss LaBelle, and Mr. Templeton."

"How do you do?" I said, extending my hand to Mr. Donner. He obliged and shook my proffered hand. "Oh!" I said suddenly. "I get it now! Donner. As in the Donner Party!"

"Hence the reference to roasting and eating people," said Mr. Easthope. "Don't pay attention to Greg. He has a sick sense of humor."

"I thought it was kind of funny," I said, smiling at Mr. Donner, who didn't look as if he'd be able to tackle and roast a day-old kitten, much less three sturdy individuals like Ernie, Lulu, and me.

"Yeah," said Lulu. I got the feeling she didn't know what we were talking about, but she shook Mr. Donner's hand anyway.

"Glad to meet you," said Ernie in a voice I didn't believe for a second. I think he'd pegged Mr. Donner as a fellow of Mr. East-hope's persuasion, which is the type of male who prefers to love males rather than females. I was kind of shocked when Chloe told me of Mr. Easthope's tendency, but I thought Ernie was silly to be grouchy about it.

At any rate, Mr. Easthope and Mr. Donner fitted the three of us in ancient Grecian costumes. "How do you know what the ancient Greeks wore anyhow?" I asked at one point. I didn't care which man answered.

"By looking at ancient Greek artifacts," said Mr. Easthope. "There are a lot of them available in museums. And there are illustrations in books. I have a stack of pictures under the mess on my desk over there."

He waved a hand, and I looked. He was right about the mess—costumes, fabric swatches, books, papers, and so forth littered a piece of furniture presumed to be his desk. "I'd love to see the illustrations someday," I told him.

"Any old time," he said. "But not until we're through for the day. Harvey runs to a tight ship."

"Fine with me," I said.

"Excellent," said Greg, waving pieces of fabric at me. "Now put this on and stand still while I measure you from shoulder to waist and waist to the floor."

So I donned the robe and stood still and he measured me from shoulder to waist and the waist to the floor. The robe was quite long, so Mr. Donner—I guess I should call him Greg from now on—stuck a couple of pins in the garment where the hem should be.

"Costuming is an interesting profession," said Greg, still speaking through a mouthful of sewing pins. "For instance, you probably think all the ancient folks like the Greeks and the Romans wore the same kinds of robes."

"They didn't?" said Ernie.

"No sirree," said Greg. "The Greeks used three main items of clothing. They're the peplos, the chiton, and the himation. We start with the peplos." He held up a rectangular piece of cloth. "This gets draped around your top half and pinned at the shoulders. He proceeded to drape and pin the peplos meant for me. "Then we have the tunic, which is called the chiton. It's draped over your shoulders too and held in place with different types of fasteners. Or, if you're poor, you'll just tie it on."

"Mercy can afford the fasteners," muttered Ernie who was being draped with his own peplos and chiton.

"Glad to hear it," said Greg. "After we get the peplos and the chiton in place, we'll drape the himation on you. It's a different color, generally bright red or blue. However, since the flickers are in black and white, yours will be black. It goes under the left arm and over the right shoulder and tucks into your girdle."

"My *girdle*?" I gasped. "I hate girdles!"

"Not those kinds of girdles," said Mr. Easthope—whom I should probably call Francis since I'm calling Mr. Donner Greg. "These are decorative girdles that wrap around the waist and hips and generally hold everything together with clasps or buttons. We'll use fancy fasteners. We'll also sew all the pieces together so you won't have to fight to put it on correctly."

"I'm glad of that," I said.

"Crumb," said Lulu. "I think the Greeks would have been better off just using a big sheet of cloth, cutting a hole for the head and holding everything together with a belt or another sash-type thing."

"That would definitely be easier," said Greg. "But Mr. Nash wants as much reality as can be had in these godforsaken times. The story's pure fiction, but he wants the costumes to look like the real thing."

"Kind of like *Ode on a Grecian Urn*?" I asked. "We'll end up looking like ladies painted on Grecian urns."

"I don't know what you're talking about," said Lulu.

"It's all right, Lulu," said Ernie. "Mercy's just flaunting her poetic education."

"Am not!" I cried indignantly.

"Don't fight, children," said Francis, laughing at the three of us.

After about an hour of having to turn this way and that and getting our peploses and chitons and himations constructed, we left Francis and Greg. The two costumers had sewn our costumes together so that they'd be easier to don and doff and wouldn't look different on different days should filming take more than one day, and both men were certain it would.

I made sure Greg gave me a pocket in mine. Although I wasn't going to be doing my normal secretarial duties for the next few days, I aimed to arm myself with a pad and some pencils in case I wanted to take notes.

When we left Francis's lair, we all looked like old-time Greeks, more or less. I liked Lulu's and my robes and wish they'd become fashionable. If a girl could throw on a robe and be considered chic and well-dressed, life would be a whole lot easier for most of us.

Ernie looked pretty good, too, although I don't think all men should wear robes. What prevented him from looking silly was the gilded laurel wreath on his head. For some reason, that wreath suited him. He looked quite masculine, perhaps even princely, and not as though he was merely a weird man wearing a dress.

I don't understand fashion.

ELEVEN

There was sure a lot of dust on the set. That's probably because the studio itself had been hacked out of a hill in California, and dirt was the prevailing cover on walking paths. People strolled here and there, some in costumes, some in regular dress. The ones in regular dress appeared to hurry more than the ones in costumes.

"I guess work is the same the world over," I muttered at one point.

"Eh?" said Ernie, eyeing a tall blonde decked out to look like a bar maid in the Old West. She had…Well, she had considerable cleavage, which I'm sure was what caught Ernie's eye. I swear. Men.

"I said," I said more loudly than I had the first time, "that work is the same the world over. See those people rushing around?"

"Yeah?" said Ernie, his gaze swiveling away from the blonde.

"The people in street clothes are the worker bees," I said. "The people in costumes are loitering because they don't have to work as hard as the un-costumed folks."

"How do you know that?" asked Lulu.

"Just a guess on my part based on my experience of life in Boston versus life in Los Angeles. The people who work the hardest are most often paid the least. Even Ernie's noticed it."

"Oh," said Lulu. She glanced around then said, "By golly. You're right, Mercy."

"She probably is," said Ernie. "We peons have to scramble for a buck. Actors just have to look good on-screen."

"I don't think Gloria Swanson is very pretty," said Lulu meditatively. "But she's in everything."

"She's got a rich millionaire on the hook," said Ernie.

"How many poor millionaires do you know?" I asked.

"Very funny, Mercy," said Ernie, not laughing. "Gloria's rich millionaire made his bucks from rum-running, or so I've heard."

"Are they married?" I asked, curious. I agreed with Lulu about Gloria Swanson. She might be a good actress but she wasn't my idea of a beauty. She couldn't hold a candle to, for instance, Dolores Costello, Mae Bush or Marion Davies. According to me. Since Gloria Swanson was everywhere in the flickers, as Lulu said, I was probably wrong.

"No," said Ernie. "He's married and he's a Roman Catholic, and Catholics aren't allowed to divorce. I guess adultery is the next best thing and even Catholics do it."

"That's terrible," I said, sounding prissy and prim.

"I agree," said Lulu.

"I expect he goes to confession every day and twice on Sundays."

"That's a cynical view of the world, Ernest Templeton," I said.

"You're right," He said back. "And you agree or you wouldn't have brought up the subject of worker bees and actors."

"I suppose so," I muttered.

The three of us almost jumped out of our laced-up sandals when a huge crash followed by an even huger shriek rent the air.

"Good heavens, what was that?" I said, hoping the noise wasn't produced by a lethal, or even semi-lethal, accident on the set. "Where did it come from?"

As Lulu and I swiveled our heads right and left, Ernie took off running straight ahead of us. I contemplated hollering at him to slow down but didn't. Ernie wouldn't have obeyed even if he'd heard me.

As almost everyone else traveling on our road had come to a screeching halt, Lulu and I sped up. The sandals made fast walking difficult, but we persevered. I attempted to keep my gaze on Ernie.

"Crumb," I said as I saw him gallop around an upcoming corner. "I hope we can find him."

"Me too," said Lulu, hurrying at my side.

When we approached the corner Ernie had rounded, I attempted to visualize the set design in my mind's eye. No luck. My directional antennae don't work well.

However, when Lulu and I rounded the same corner, we saw Ernie pushing his way into a small mob of costumed spectators about half a block away. We hurried up a little more, attempting as we did so to keep our sandals on. Both of us lifted our robes to our knees. Realizing my mother would be scandalized if she saw me thus, I lifted it higher.

When we got to the moblet, Lulu and I also pushed people out of our way. Many of them glared and swore at us, but we didn't stop. That is, we didn't stop until we saw the body of a man, his limbs at odd angles, tangled up in some fallen scaffolding. When we got close, I saw a puddle of blood spreading from under the mess of scaffolding and downed man. Ew.

"Shoot, Ernie, what happened?" I asked when I panted to a stop beside him. He knelt at the foot of the wooden and human pile and frowned at me when he turned his head.

"Dammit, you shouldn't see this," he snarled.

"Don't swear at me," I said. "What happened? Did the scaffolding fall on top of him, or was he on it when it fell?"

"Don't know yet. I sent a kid running for a doctor, but we'd better move all these people away from the scene." He stood, holding up his arms and looking almost like a by-gum ancient Greek official of some sort. "Get back," he bellowed. "Go back! This is a police matter!"

"Are you supposed to say that?" I whispered when the mob's titillated noises ceased and it shuffled back a few feet.

"Don't care at this point. This poor guy is dead, and it

happened on the set." Lowering his voice, he said, "Harvey's not going to be happy about this."

"Guess he won't," said Lulu.

"The dead guy's family most likely won't be happy either," I said, thinking Ernie's priorities were out of whack.

"Yeah, I know," he growled. "This is what we were supposed to prevent."

"You're right," I said.

"Yeah," said Lulu. "We didn't do too good, did we?"

"To be fair," said Ernie, "we weren't hired to do anything except memorize the set until today."

Crumb, Ernie was right. We were supposed to have memorized the schematic drawing. I'd already failed miserably. I didn't tell Ernie or Lulu so.

"How can you memorize the set from a picture?" asked Lulu, thereby making me feel a tiny bit better. "It was small and on paper. This set"—she waved her arms—"is gigantic."

"Maybe we should have come here over the weekend," I said. "We might have gained a better understanding of what scenes take place where."

"Maybe," agreed Ernie distractedly.

An automobile skidded around the corner we'd recently rounded and sounded its horn. And kept sounding its horn. Lordy that thing was loud. A man leaned out of a window on the passenger side of the vehicle holding a loudspeaker and hollering, "Everyone off the set! Get going now!"

Between his yelling and the horn beeping, the noise level was piercing enough to deafen a normal human being. Therefore, we three plugged our ears with our fingers. The car screeched to a stop a few feet away from the catastrophe, flinging up enough dust to coat the entire City of Los Angeles.

It might have been the dust storm that finally convinced people to obey the fellow with the loudspeaker. Or maybe they knew who the guy was and didn't want to get on his bad side. Whatever the crowd's reasoning, everyone in it backed away several more yards. Ernie, Lulu, and I stayed where we were.

The guy with the bullhorn jumped out of the car before it had stopped completely and ran over to the scaffolding, the dead guy and us.

"Who the hell are you?" he demanded, sharing a glower among Ernie, Lulu, and me.

"I'm Ernest Templeton, and I'm a private investigator." He glanced around and lowered his voice, although I don't believe many spectators were close enough to hear him. "This is a suspicious death."

"What the hell do you mean, 'it's a suspicious death'?"

"Just what I said, and who are you? Do you work for the Nash Studio?"

"Yes," said the foul-mouthed man. "I'm Vic Bedini. Why's a P.I. here on the set?"

Another car roared around the corner and stopped behind the first car. I didn't recognize the driver, but darned if Harvey Nash himself didn't step out of the automobile. He didn't look happy.

"What happened here?" he demanded of Ernie. "What are you doing here, Vic?" he asked of the man with the bullhorn.

"Heard the noise and thought I'd better check it out," said Mr. Bedini, or Vic if you were Harvey.

"Go back to the stables," Harvey ordered. "I'll take over here." Turning back to Ernie, he said, "The doctor is on his way. Good Lord, is that poor man dead?"

"Haven't checked for a pulse yet, but I don't think he could be alive and look like that," said Ernie.

Lulu and I nodded. "Do you want us to go away, Mr. Nash?" I asked. I called him Mr. Nash because we weren't supposed to know each other.

"No. There's no need at this point," said Harvey. He shook his head sadly, "That's Mel Flynn. He's been with the studio since it started. This is horrible."

Two more automobiles, these marked SECURITY, came to a halt nearby. A fellow carrying a black bag stepped out of one of the cars.

"Where's the...Oh. I see," said the man I presumed to be the doctor.

"I think he's dead," Ernie told the doc.

Not stopping, the doctor walked right past Ernie and up to the mess of human limbs and wood. "I think you're right," said the doctor. He opened his bag and put it on the ground as close to the mangled man as possible. Then he knelt after pulling up his trousers a bit, I guess so they wouldn't pinch when he bent his legs.

"Ernie Templeton, this is Dr. Elbert Sherman. He's one of the doctors for the studio," said Harvey.

"Sorry to meet under these circumstances," said Ernie.

The doctor grunted something I didn't catch.

"Do you know how this happened?" asked Harvey, of anyone nearby. The only people still nearby were Harvey himself, Dr. Sherman, Ernie, Lulu, and me.

Ernie answered for all of us. "No. We heard a crash and a loud holler, and we ran here. We were at the costuming place before."

"Does someone have a camera?" asked Dr. Sherman. "We need to get a photo of the accident scene before we extricate this poor fellow."

"This is a motion-picture set," Harvey reminded Dr. Sherman. He pointed at a fellow with a gigantic camera. "Pete, please take some still shots of this mess."

"Will do," said the man named Pete. He unlocked the big camera from its stand, walked forward and pointed his camera's lens at the bloody mess.

Glancing up at Ernie, Dr. Sherman said, "You are correct, Mr. Templeton. This poor man is definitely dead."

"Do you think the crash of that scaffolding is what killed him?" asked Harvey.

"I suppose so. I wasn't here," said the doctor. "I doubt Mr. Flynn would be in this position on purpose."

"I didn't see it happen either," said Ernie. "Just heard the crash and some yelling."

Harvey turned around and, with his hands cupped to his mouth, shouted, "Anyone who saw this accident happen, please come here."

The far-off crowd peered at each other. Some nodded, some didn't. Finally, three or four of them, all clad in Grecian robes, took some tentative steps toward Harvey.

"I was here, Mr. Nash," said a Greek peasant. I could tell he was a peasant because he had the hem of his robe drawn up and tucked under his belt. He had knobby knees, not that it matters.

"What happened?" asked Harvey.

"Well, we were just getting ready to film a crowd scene—I'm a grain-grinder—when the entire wooden frame collapsed. That poor guy"—he pointed to the dead Mr. Flynn—"was at the top of a ladder on the other side. Not sure what he was doing there, but I remember hearing some hammering."

"Were there any creaks or groans before the whole thing collapsed?" asked Ernie. Harvey looked at him with his brows lowered until he realized the significance of Ernie's question, and he lifted them again and nodded to the fellow who was giving information.

"Didn't hear any," said the man.

"What's your name?" asked Ernie. Then he looked at me. "I don't suppose you brought anything to write with, did you?"

Aha! Attempting not to look smug, I put my hand in the pocket of my peplos—or maybe it was my chiton or himation—and withdrew a secretarial pad and a pencil. I didn't have extra pencils with me, so I hoped the witnesses wouldn't talk a lot.

With a grin for me, Ernie said, "Good thinking, Mercy."

"Yes, Miss Allcutt," said Harvey, giving Ernie the stink-eye, I guess for calling me Mercy. "Thank you."

"How come you've got a pad and pencil with you?" asked the witness.

"Not important," growled Ernie. "What's your name?"

"William Crowder," the witness said.

"Thank you, Mr. Crowder. And you said you're an extra for a crowd scene in this film?"

"Well, yes, but I'm hoping for bigger things," admitted Mr. Crowder.

Weren't they all? Apparently it wasn't merely young women who flocked to Hollywood in search of fame and fortune. Young men did, too.

"Can you ride a horse?" Harvey asked him.

Appearing startled, Mr. Crowder said, "No, but I'm taking lessons."

"Maybe we'll be able to use you in another picture," said Harvey.

"But I'm still in this one, right?" Mr. Crowder sounded anxious.

"Yes, unless we discover you sabotaged this set," said Harvey.

"Me? *Me?*" said Mr. Crowder pointing at himself as if outraged.

"Yes," said Harvey. He glanced at a young woman standing a few steps away from Mr. Crowder. "Did you see what happened, miss?" he asked the woman.

"I...I think so," she answered uncertainly.

"You don't know if you saw the accident?" asked Ernie.

"Well, I was here talking to a friend when we heard a big crash and a scream. We turned and saw the mess and that poor man." She pointed to the deceased fellow. "But I didn't *see* it fall. All I saw was all that tangled scaffolding and a huge cloud of dust."

"I see," said Harvey. "And what is your name?"

"Lucy Fowler," said the lass, who was probably no more than seventeen or eighteen years old.

"We'd better leave the doctor to his business," said Ernie. "We should go somewhere else and question the witnesses."

"Good idea," said Harvey. "Anyone who saw the accident, please come with Mr. Templeton and me"—he hesitated for a few seconds—"and these two ladies should come with me too." He nodded at Lulu and me. "This young woman can take notes."

"Where will you be?" asked the doctor.

"In Helen's boudoir."

"Where's that?" The doctor again.

"Down this street and turn right. You'll see Mount Ida, and then you'll see what looks like a Grecian temple and a bathing pool. We'll be in the temple."

"Good. I'll find you and report as soon as I deal with this poor fellow. You should call the police and an ambulance," said Dr. Sherman. "He's not going anywhere on his own again."

Poor fellow indeed. Almost wishing I weren't there, I tapped Lulu on the shoulder, and the two of us walked to Harvey's car along with Ernie. A driver sat in the front seat. I guess he was hired to drive and not poke around crime scenes, because he hadn't budged since Harvey arrived on the scene.

TWELVE

M y goodness, but Helen of Troy's boudoir was fancy. It even had a gigantic tiled bathtub in it, which is what Harvey had called a pool. Someone had scattered rose petals in the water and Blanche Sweet, in an unburned wig and very little else, had her toe stuck in the water. I shot a glance at Ernie, but his gaze was paying a visit to the surrounding columns and so forth.

"Harvey!" Blanche Sweet said, removing her toe from the water. "Did you find out what happened?"

"Yes. It's worse now. Whoever the saboteur is, he's claimed a life."

"Good Lord," said Miss Sweet. "Who was killed?"

Ernie, Lulu, and I looked at each other. We three so-called investigators could only shake our heads.

Therefore, Harvey answered her question. "Mel Flynn. He's been a carpenter for the studio for years. He was tangled up in the fallen scaffolding when we left to come here. The doctor is still at the scene." Harvey looked around. "Where's Sidney? He's supposed to be directing this scene."

"Yes. He was here a minute ago," said Miss Sweet. "May I put on a robe now? The day's chilly. Unless we're going to go ahead and shoot this scene."

"No, we'll have to stop filming for the day. This is now a police matter." Harvey sounded gloomy, primarily because the death would delay filming. That's not because Harvey has a cold heart; he doesn't. But *Helen of Troy* was going to go way over budget if these "accidents" kept happening.

"Good. I'm cold," said Miss Sweet. As she wore pretty much nothing at all, I understood.

"Harvey!" a voice roared from behind a couple of Ionic columns on the far side of the set. "I heard someone died."

And there was Sidney Lafayette, Harvey's second-in-command. He hurried from behind the columns and aimed himself at us.

"Where were you, Sid?" asked Harvey.

"Back there." Sidney pointed to the columns. I saw a desk cluttered with papers a few feet away from the last column on the left. "I heard the racket, but I was trying to figure out the Mount Ida scene. This"—he waved an arm around Helen's boudoir—"is just a bathing scene. Blanche and her handmaidens can do it blindfolded."

"Thanks, Sid," said Miss Sweet sarcastically. "What if you were at your desk when some evil person decided to drown *me*? People would pay a heck of a lot more attention to a dead Blanche Sweet than a dead carpenter."

"She's right, Sid," said Harvey. "We need to protect everyone, and especially the stars, or the Nash Studio will be toast."

"Kind of like my wig," said Miss Sweet.

"Cripes. You're right," said a distracted Sid. "Maybe I can get Vic to direct this scene. Is he still at the stables?"

"Precisely who is this Vic character?" Ernie asked. "He was the first one to show up at the accident scene."

"Yes," said Harvey. "I don't understand that. The stables are in the far back lot."

"I don't care for Vic," said Miss Sweet, taking a robe from a girl I presumed to be a wardrobe assistant. "I'd rather do the scene alone than have Vic direct it."

"Why don't you care for Vic?" I asked, forgetting I was a nobody.

After glancing at me as if she wondered why a nobody was speaking to her, Miss Sweet said, "I don't know. I just don't. He kind of gives me the willies."

"Interesting," said Ernie.

"I guess," said Harvey. "Ernie, will you please…Oh, my God, I forgot to introduce you!" He pressed a hand to his forehead. "This picture is giving me a headache. I think it's already given me an ulcer."

"Who are you introducing to whom?" asked Miss Sweet.

Harvey took Ernie by an arm and guided him to the chair in which Blanche Sweet sat. I was glad she'd put on her robe. "Blanche, please allow me to introduce you to Ernest Templeton. Ernie is a private investigator who has agreed to look into the problems we've been having on the set."

Ernie executed a perfect bow and said, "Delighted to meet you, Miss Sweet."

Sticking out a hand for Ernie to shake, Miss Sweet said, "Glad to meet you too. A shame you weren't here earlier this morning. Or a week or so ago."

Harvey spoke before Ernie could respond. "Yes, I should have called you in earlier, Ernie. Too late for that now."

With his hand still holding Ernie's arm, Harvey came back to Lulu and me.

I saw Miss Sweet blinking after Harvey and Ernie, both of whom were polite men as a rule. Harvey was definitely distracted by the death on the set, as well as a wife and a new baby at home. I knew he'd rather be with Chloe and No-Name than here on a troubled picture locale.

He said, "Ernie, I'm going to talk to these people." He gestured at Mr. Crowder and Miss Fowler. "Can you question Vic Bedini? Miss Allcutt can take notes, if you don't mind, Miss Allcutt."

"Don't mind at all," I said.

"Need me?" asked Lulu as if she felt left out.

"Um," said Harvey. "Maybe you could stand behind that column and make sure it doesn't wobble during filming."

A wobbling column? I scooted over to the nearest column and knocked lightly on it.

"Be careful!" Harvey said. "I don't need any columns falling apart. Or over, for that matter."

"I didn't knock very hard," I said. "Are these things made of papier-mâché?"

"They are indeed," said Sid.

"So, Miss…" Harvey looked blankly at Lulu, whom he knew as Lulu.

"Miss LaBelle," I prompted.

"Oh yes. Yes, I apologize for forgetting your name, Miss LaBelle."

"It's okay," said Lulu. "I'm pretty much nobody."

"You can be of immense help here today if you can make sure the columns closest to the scene of the action don't lean or fall over."

"I thought you were going to shut down for the day," said Miss Sweet from her chair.

"Oh, yes. Of course we should. Lord, I forgot that too. I *know* I'm losing my mind," said a flustered Harvey. "The doctor needs to talk to me anyway. Crumb. Guess I'll have to take my own notes, because Ernie is the one who should question Vic, and Miss Allcutt needs to take notes."

"Have you called the police and an ambulance yet?" I asked.

Harvey seemed to deflate. "No, I haven't called the police. I'm sure the doctor has called an ambulance." He glanced at Ernie. "Don't you know a police detective, Ernie?"

"Yeah. Phil Bigelow, but he works out of Station One in downtown L.A. I'm not sure where we are as far as the L.A.P.D. goes, but I'm sure Phil isn't stationed anywhere near here."

As I'd recently had a little trouble with Detective Phil Bigelow, the only honest copper in the entire L.A.P.D. according to Ernie, I wasn't filled with remorse to hear this. I heard Lulu offer up a soft snort. She entertained even more doubts about the L.A.P.D. and Phil Bigelow than I.

"Rats," said Harvey. "Well, there's nothing I can do about anything at the moment, it seems. I definitely need to talk to the doctor. The studio will make arrangements for Mel Flynn's funeral. I hope to God he doesn't have a wife and six kids."

"Me too," said Sid, who still stood in the loose clump of people consisting of Lulu, me, Mr. Crowder, and Miss Fowler. "We'd better send runners to tell everyone that business is closed for the day."

His shoulders slumping, Harvey said, "You're right. You're right." He shook his head. "This is awful."

"If you want me to talk to that Bedini guy, I can tell him you're shutting down for the day," suggested Ernie. I got the feeling he felt as much sympathy for Harvey as I did.

"Thanks, Ernie. Sorry for all the confusion," said Harvey, heaving an enormous sigh.

"But will you tell me precisely who Bedini is first?"

"Good Lord, haven't I done that yet?" Harvey shook his head.

Patting him on the shoulder, Sid said, "Try to calm down, Harvey. We should be here for the doctor and the police when Mr. Templeton and..." He glanced at me. "I'm sorry. I know I've met you before, but I don't recall your name."

"This is Miss Allcutt," said Ernie, taking over for Harvey. "She's good at taking notes."

"Yes. Right," said Harvey. "And Vic Bedini is assistant to the second-unit director." His lips flattened into a straight line. "Although he's not been doing a sterling job on this picture."

"That's the truth," muttered Sid.

"He's at the stables?" said Ernie.

"He's *supposed* to be at the stables," said Harvey. "I don't know how he got to the accident site before I did. Sid, you're right. Ernie and Miss Allcutt can handle Bedini. I'd rather you stay here and talk to the doctor and the crew. Ernie is good at questioning people."

"Good point. Mr. Templeton is a professional." Sid turned a troubled face to Ernie. "Right?"

"Right," said Ernie.

A forlorn Lulu again asked, "What about me?"

"Can you take shorthand?" asked Harvey, sounding almost excited.

"No," said Lulu. "I'm useless."

"We've got an entire secretarial pool at our beck and call," Sid reminded Harvey. "We can use one of the stenographers."

"True. Thanks, Sid. Okay, Ernie, go on to the stables. You remember where they are?"

"Yup," said Ernie. "Come along, Mercy."

"What about me?" Lulu looked as if she might begin crying.

"Come with us," said Ernie. "I'm sure you'll be useful."

"Gee, thanks," said Lulu.

"I need you, Lulu," I told her.

"What for?" she asked, sounding glum.

"Moral support," I replied promptly.

"Good. Now we have that figured out. Do you have a car we can borrow, Harvey, or do we have to take shank's mare to the stables in the back forty?"

"Crumb," muttered Lulu.

"Take my car. The driver—his name is Lewis King—knows his way around the set."

"Thanks," said Ernie.

Lulu and I added a duet of "Thanks" too.

Lewis King was napping when Ernie, Lulu, and I reached his automobile. Ernie cleared his throat loudly, and Mr. King awoke with a start. He cast an alarmed glance at Ernie, who stood at his elbow appearing a little less like ancient Greek royalty than he had when we all left Francis and Greg's wardrobe rooms. I suspect dust played a major role in his current look. The fact that his laurel leaf wreath had slipped, and it now looked as if he were wearing a petrified snake on his head and almost over his left ear also dimmed some of his prior glamour.

"Lewis King?" asked Ernie politely as he attempted to straighten his laurel wreath.

Rubbing his eyes, Mr. King said, "Yeah, I'm Lewis King. Who are you?"

"Ernie Templeton, Private Detective. These two ladies are Miss Allcutt and Miss LaBelle. Mr. Nash wants you to drive us to wherever Mr. Vic Bedini is supposed to be."

Mr. Lewis, after producing a gigantic yawn, said, "Sorry about that. Sure, I'll be happy to drive you to the stables. That's where Bedini's supposed to be. He usually isn't where he's supposed to be."

"Yeah?" said Ernie. "So far no one who's mentioned him seems to like him much. What's up with Mr. Bedini?"

"I honestly don't know," said Mr. King, pressing the starter button of the dusty automobile. I think it was a Chevrolet but couldn't tell for sure. "He used to be okay, but for the past few weeks, it's like he's mad at the world." With a shrug, Mr. King then said, "Hop in."

So Ernie opened the back door for Lulu and me. We didn't precisely hop in, being encumbered by floppy tie-on sandals and long robes, but we managed. Ernie got into the front passenger seat.

"Everyone all set?" asked Mr. King as the engine roared to life.

"I think so," I said.

Ernie turned and grinned at Lulu and me over the seat back. "The ladies look set and I'm set, so let's go find Mr. Bedini."

Mr. King's automobile took off, creating a dust storm that seemed to follow us as he maneuvered his way past different settings. It was an interesting trip, especially since he acted as a tour guide.

"This is Mount Ida. That's where Paris tends his sheep. The sheep aren't there yet. The picture's behind schedule, so there's a herd of sheep being tended about a mile away where we can't smell them unless the wind turns."

"I thought Paris was the hero," muttered Lulu. "How come he's a shepherd?"

"He was a shepherd first," I said. "He was quietly tending his flock of sheep when several Greek goddesses made him judge a beauty contest."

"A *what?*"

"A beauty contest. Zeus dropped a golden apple among the goddesses. The apple was engraved 'To the Fairest.' Well, the jealous goddesses argued over the apple, each of them claiming to be the fairest of them all. So Zeus chose Paris to pick the one he favored most. Have you ever heard of the judgment of Paris?" I lifted a couple of eyebrows at Lulu.

"Yeah, it rings a faint bell," she said.

"Very well, so all the goddesses—I can't remember all of their names—tried to bribe Paris. Paris chose Aphrodite because she said she'd make sure he'd get to marry the most beautiful human woman—as opposed to the most beautiful goddess—in the world."

"Sounds just like a man," muttered Lulu. "What if that woman couldn't cook or was a nasty piece of goods?"

"Hey," Ernie chimed in from the front seat. "This happened in the olden days."

"Yeah. Women were worth even less then than they are now," I said.

"Well, that stinks," said Lulu. "So he picks Aphro...Whatever her name was."

"Aphrodite, right," I said. "So Paris, who was from Troy, then visited Sparta where Helen lived. She was married to Menelaus at the time."

"She was *married?*" Lulu sounded shocked.

"Yes," I said, trying to remember the convoluted myth. "I think Menelaus was the king of Sparta, but Paris abducted Helen and carried her to Troy."

"This is one of the stupidest stories I've ever heard," said Lulu.

"I agree," I said. "But there's more."

"Crumb," said Lulu.

"Here we are at the stables," said Mr. King. He sounded faintly relieved. Guess he didn't care for Helen's story either.

"Tell me the rest later, okay?" said Lulu.

"Sure."

Mr. King opened my door, Ernie opened Lulu's, and we both exited the car and found ourselves in the stable area. Being a city girl, I don't think I'd ever seen so many horses in one place.

"Golly!" said Lulu. "This looks like my Uncle Ralph's farm, only with horses instead of cows."

Interesting.

THIRTEEN

The three of us—Ernie, Lulu, and I—stood gawping at a big herd of horses in a...I guess you call them pastures. Anyway, they were beautiful creatures—the horses, not the pastures. We also saw people clad as cowboys walking around. Cowboys in ancient Greece? I decided I'd ask later. One of them, a bowlegged fellow, spotted our car and strode our way.

"Mr. King!" he said when he was still several yards away. Mr. King hadn't exited the automobile. He was probably used to seeing a herd of horses on the set.

"Greetings, Arnie," said Mr. King. "These folks are here to talk to Vic. Is he around somewhere?"

"Vic?" Arnie said. "I think so." I felt my eyes widen. The fellow, Arnie, had just said what sounded like "Ah thank sew." I figured it out without too much trouble. "I think he's in his office," Arnie continued. My brain translated this piece of chat into English right away.

"Thanks, Arnie. There's been a fatal accident on the set, so Mr. Nash is shutting down production for the day."

"Well, shucks," said Arnie. "That's a durned shame. Aw'll let the boys know." He turned and walked back to the horse enclosure.

122

Whispering to Lulu, I said, "I didn't know people really talked like that."

"Like what?"

"Like...like...I don't know. Like cowboys, I suppose."

"They talk like that where I come from," she said. "I had to study hard to learn to talk like you."

"They don't talk like that in Chicago," said Ernie. "Most of the slaughterhouses are run by Germans and Poles. There aren't a whole lot of live horses in Chicago these days. Most folks drive automobiles."

"Ugh," I said, not meaning to. "I mean, slaughterhouses? Really? In Chicago?"

"Yup," said Ernie with an ironic grin for me. "Cowboys like Arnie drive cattle herds from Texas, New Mexico, and other western states to Kansas City, where the bovines are put on a train and chugged to Chicago and slaughtered. You probably eat beef from Chicago at home, Mercy."

"I had no idea," I said.

"Me neither," said Lulu. "Uncle Frank and some other farmers generally got together and slaughtered their own beef. They sold it or salted it. If there was enough ice, they'd chop ice and freeze the carcasses. Not sure how they kept it from going bad if there wasn't enough ice. Salted it, I reckon. Mainly, we ate chicken and pork. The cows, we mostly sold."

"I don't think I want to talk about this any longer," I said, my tummy beginning to rebel. I hoped Harvey and Chloe's fussy chef would feed us chicken or fish this evening. But wait. He'd have to kill chickens or fish too, wouldn't he? Clearly, I was doomed. Or a naive idiot. Perhaps both.

"Yeah," said Ernie, still grinning. "It's best not to think about where your food comes from."

"Mrs. Buck gets ours from the Grand Central Market most of the time," said Lulu. "Not sure where the market gets it."

"Let's pretend we don't know, okay? I feel queasy," I said.

"Okay by me," said Ernie.

"Me too," said Lulu, her nose wrinkling.

We walked away from the horse enclosure toward a tent set up just far enough away from the horses to miss most of the dust. The tent sat a few steps from the auto in which Mr. King drove us.

When we reached the tent, Ernie said, "Knock, knock. Mr. Bedini, are you in there? I'm a representative of Harvey Nash."

I'd heard a low conversation taking place behind the tent flap. It stopped as soon as Ernie voiced his first "knock."

"Yeah, I'm here. What do you want?" said a person I assumed to be Vic Bedini. His question seemed impolite, although the tone of his voice was friendly enough.

"Ernest Templeton, Mr. Bedini. I have a couple of other people with me."

I heard a grunt, and then Mr. Bedini said, "Sure. Be there in a minute."

"The studio's stopping production for today because of a fatality on the set. As you were one of the first people there, I need to speak to you," said Ernie.

Mutterings sifted from inside the tent, and then Mr. Bedini pulled the tent flap aside and blinked at us. "I've seen you before," he said to Ernie. "You were there too, weren't you? What do you need me for?" Again, although the words sounded rude, his voice was pleasant.

Strange. Or maybe it wasn't. This entire I-don't-know-how-many square miles of Southern California soil were being devoted to creating fantasy stories for gullible people to feast their eyes upon. If Harvey was to be believed, and he was, they'd be hearing them as well as seeing them soon.

Ernie walked right up to Mr. Bedini, who took a step backward and seemed alarmed. "Name's Templeton. I'm a private investigator." He stuck out a hand.

After looking at Ernie's hand for a couple of seconds, Mr. Bedini shook it. "Not sure why you have to talk to me," he said.

"Orders from headquarters," Lulu said in a placating voice.

"Ah, jeez," said Mr. Bedini. "Come inside. I guess we can talk. Who are they?" He pointed at Lulu and me.

Now *that* was rude!

Then he said, "Sorry. I'm just frustrated about getting the right number of horses in the right places. Didn't mean to sound impolite."

Very well then.

"Secretarial staff," said Ernie. "Move over. We're coming in."

"No place for you all to sit," said Mr. Bedini, who was a softish person of medium height. He had extremely black hair, and I wondered if he dyed it.

"Have fun," hollered the amiable Mr. King. "I'll stay here and drive you back." I got the feeling he wanted to resume his nap.

"Thank you," I hollered in response.

"Tent looks plenty big enough to me," said Ernie, surveying the insides of the tent.

It looked big enough to me, too. There were even sufficient chairs if the darkish man sitting on one of them rose from it, and if the stacks of papers were removed from three of the others. Because I couldn't seem to help myself, I went to one of the paper-covered chairs and lifted a stack therefrom.

"Be careful," Mr. Bedini barked at me. "Those are in order!"

"They're still in order," I barked back. "Miss LaBelle and I need to sit in order to take notes. I'll place these right here." I set my stack of papers on the floor next to the chair I'd chosen. The tent had a canvas floor, so it wasn't as if the papers would get dirty or anything.

"Cripes," muttered Mr. Bedini. He turned to the man with whom he'd been conversing when we arrived. "We'll have to talk about the matter later, Frank."

"Not much later," said Frank who had a voice that might have been ricocheting around a rock quarry before it landed in his throat. His short statement sounded like a threat to me, although I might have been wrong. Wouldn't have been the first time.

"Yeah, yeah," said Mr. Bedini. "Don't worry about it."

"Oh," said Frank, "*I'm* not worried." He gave Mr. Bedini a smile that would have sent me running had it been aimed at me.

Then the man named Frank turned to us doffed his hat and bowed. "How do, folks?"

After a short hesitation, during which no one else seemed inclined to answer Frank, I said, "We're fine, thanks."

Plopping his hat on his slicked-back black hair, Frank said, "That's good. That's real good." He turned back to Mr. Bedini. "See you soon, Vic."

"Yes. Yes. Soon," said Mr. Bedini. I got the impression he wasn't looking forward to more visits from Frank.

Couldn't blame him. Frank reminded me of photographs and sketches I'd seen in newspapers of Italian gangsters in Chicago and New York. My brain instantly began spinning a tale of bootlegging criminals moving into Los Angeles and trying to take over the motion-picture industry. My story, which only took a mere second or three to create, suffered a blow when Ernie said, "All right, Mercy, get out your pencil and pad. You'll have to take notes for us."

Piffle. Well, I'd attempt to remember the story I'd started after I got home again.

Either Ernie or Lulu must have removed the two stacks of papers from the other two chairs, because they were both seated when I managed to jolt myself back into reality. Mentally, I mean.

Mr. Bedini sat in his desk chair once more, folded his hands and placed them on his desk blotter. "So what do you want to know?"

"Why were you the first person to the scene after that piece of scaffolding collapsed?"

Mr. Bedini opened his brown eyes wide. "What do you mean?"

"You roared up in an automobile about three seconds after I'd made it to the accident site. It took much longer for Mr. Nash and the security team to get there."

"Oh," said Mr. Bedini. "I was close by when my driver and I heard the crash."

"Why?" said Ernie.

"What do you mean, why?"

"Sounds like an easy question to me," Ernie said with a smile that might have looked pleasant if one didn't know him.

I'd kept my head bowed over my secretarial pad. I glanced up at Mr. Bedini to see his reaction this time, mainly because I also thought Ernie's query an easy one to answer.

Unlocking his fingers, Mr. Bedini waved an arm in the air. "I'd been to the costuming room to find more peasant costumes for a couple of the cowboys to wear in the picture. They're real cowboys, you know, but they can't appear in an ancient Greek picture wearing cowboy garb from this century."

Why, the blatant fibber! He was nowhere near the costume room when Ernie, Lulu, and I left it. I'd opened my mouth to say so, but Ernie jogged my elbow. Darned near dropped my pad. Did drop my pencil.

Ernie picked up the pencil for me and, leaning over so that his back was to Mr. Bedini and his face was almost in mine, he mouthed, "Don't say a word, dammit!"

Oh. Well then, I guess I wouldn't speak until given official permission. After contemplating getting sniffy at Ernie, I decided his order had been a correct one. We didn't want to let on that we thought Mr. Bedini might be a suspect. Maybe.

Whoa. I was getting confused.

"True," said Ernie amiably. "Who'd you see in the wardrobe room?"

"One of those two Nancy boys," said Mr. Bedini. "Can't remember which one."

Darned near forgot myself and bellowed at Mr. Bedini. Pinching my lips together so tightly I'd probably have wrinkles by the end of the day, I sat still and wrote.

"So you don't recall if you saw Mr. Easthope or Mr. Donner?" asked Ernie.

"Those their names?" asked Mr. Bedini. "Naw. I just went in and said I needed two more Greek horseback-rider costumes and left. That's why I was close to the place where the scenery collapsed."

"I see," said Ernie. "Did you know Mr. Flynn, the fellow who died?"

Shaking his head, Mr. Bedini said, "Nope. This is a huge set. Most of us don't know each other. It's not like one-reelers in the old days, when you'd shoot a picture in a day, and everybody knew each other."

"You've been in the business for quite a while?" said Ernie.

"Twenty-one years. It's changed a *whole* lot since the early days."

"I'm sure. What's the name of your driver? Is he here too? I'd like to talk to him if he's nearby."

"Luca?" said Mr. Bedini. "His name is Luca Piccolo, and I don't know where he is at the moment. Probably at the canteen flirting with female extras."

His mouth turned up in a sneer. I know it did, because I glanced up at what seemed to me to be an odd last name.

"His name's Piccolo?" asked Ernie, saving me from doing so, which was a good thing because I wasn't supposed to talk. "I thought a piccolo was a musical instrument."

I'd thought it was too.

"It is. It's also an Italian name. Means small, which doesn't fit Luca very well, because he's maybe six-four and two hundred and fifty pounds."

Good grief. There were giants among us. I kept my mouth shut.

"And you don't know where he is right now?"

"Nope. Sorry," said Mr. Bedini.

"How long have you worked for the Nash Studio?" said Ernie.

"A few years," said Mr. Bedini.

"I've heard it's a good place to work compared to other studios. What do you think about that?"

Mr. Bedini sucked in a huge breath of air and appeared disconcerted for a moment. As I'd lifted my head to see him, I knew it was only for a moment.

"Yes," he said. "It's a good place to work. Better than most of them."

"It's a shame so many accidents seem to be occurring during the filming of this picture," said Ernie.

Mr. Bedini grunted.

"Do you have any thoughts as to why this one particular picture seems to be having such rotten luck with accidents and so forth?" asked Ernie.

"No." Mr. Bedini shook his head and seemed a little sad. "I don't. Freakish is what they are, all the problems."

"I've heard rumors that Italian gangs want to get into the picture business here on the West Coast," said Ernie. "You wouldn't know anything about that, would you?"

Mr. Bedini stood up from his chair and, bracing himself, he leaned toward Ernie, his face turning a mottled and fiery red. "Why are you asking *me* that? Because I have an Italian name? How should *I* know if Italian gangs are trying to get into the pictures? What about the Irish gangs? Or the Jewish gangs? That's insulting, damn you!"

"Calm down, Mr. Bedini. Just asking, was all," said Ernie.

"I don't think I can help you anymore today," growled Mr. Bedini. "I'm going outside to send everyone home. In case you didn't hear, the set is shutting down for the day."

"Yeah," said Ernie. "We'd probably better get going too, Mercy and Lulu." He stood and spoke to Mr. Bedini. "Please let me know if you think of anything you'd like to add to your statement."

"Yeah, yeah," said Mr. Bedini. "You know everything I know."

"I doubt that," said Ernie. "But we'll leave you to Frank now."

For a second, I thought Mr. Bedini was going to yell again. Or plead for help. I'd already risen and tucked my pad and pencil in my pocket. Ernie gestured for Lulu and me to precede him out of Mr. Bedini's tent.

FOURTEEN

When Ernie started driving us back to Chloe and Harvey's marble mansion that evening, I was tired.

"I'm bushed," I said. "Can't think why. We didn't do a whole lot today."

"I'm exhausted too," said Lulu. "I don't like having to get up before dawn cracks."

"That's right!" I said. "No wonder we're tired. We had to wake up too darned early."

"Better get used to it," said Ernie, who was at the wheel of his Packard Six. "We'll be getting up early until we figure out who's causing the problems on the set.

"Crumb," I said.

"Bet it's that Bedini character," said Lulu.

"I think so too," I agreed.

"Now girls, wait until we've collected more information before condemning the fellow, all right?"

"What fun is that?" I asked.

Ernie and Lulu both laughed.

"I'm tired of this costume, too," I said. "It's cumbersome. I think females should be allowed to wear trousers because it's easier to walk in them than in this stupid robe."

"Quit complaining," said Ernie with another laugh. "You're the one who asked me to come here and investigate the problems on the set."

"Only at Harvey's insistence," I told him.

We arrived at the Nash residence. The gatekeeper opened the huge wrought-iron gate, and Ernie steered the Packard up to the porch steps. Lulu and I climbed out. Mr. Porter dashed up to us and offered to park Ernie's automobile for him.

"Thanks, Porter," said Ernie, handing over his keys.

"Happy for something to do," said Mr. Porter as if he meant it. He'd probably be getting sick and tired of driving Chloe and No-Name all over Los Angeles in a few months. For now, his did appear to be a boring job.

Lulu, Ernie, and I trudged up the porch steps, where Chloe stood beaming at us and holding the baby. "You three look like you've put in a hard day," she said, smiling graciously at us.

"We have," I said.

"Yeah," said Lulu. "Can't imagine why I wanted to get into the flickers. They're really boring."

"According to Harvey, today wasn't boring," said Chloe.

Lulu and I exchanged a guilty glance. I said, "He's correct. A poor crew member was killed when some scaffolding collapsed with him on it."

"He told me, and I was so sorry. But come on in and get bathed and changed," said Chloe, looking askance at our dusty Greek costumes. "You look kind of silly in those," she added.

"I dunno," said Ernie, gazing down at his long, flowing robe. He stuck out a sandaled foot and wiggled a dusty toe. "I think we're adorable."

"If you say so," said Chloe.

We accompanied her to the front door, and Molly the maid let us in, smiling happily. "Good evening," she said.

"Good evening," we said in chorus.

"Is Harvey here yet?" I asked.

Poor Harvey had been talking to a squadron of police officers and doctors when we'd finally left the cursed set. I don't mean that. It wasn't cursed. It was hampered by people wishing the Nash Studio ill. Which, now that I think about it, might just as well make it cursed.

"Not yet," said Chloe.

"How's the darling baby?" asked Lulu, leaning over to peer inside the pink blanket.

"She's doing very well, thanks," said Chloe with satisfaction.

"Thought of a name yet?" I asked, perhaps not as courteously as I might have.

"Not yet. Harvey and I will have to agree on a name first," said Chloe, ignoring my peevish tone of voice, which made her a better person than I.

"Let's go wash up," Ernie suggested. "We're tired, and Mercy's cranky."

"I am not," I snarled, thereby proving his point.

By the time dinner was ready, I'd bathed, set my soiled Grecian robe aside on a bench in the closet, and had managed to fall asleep fully clothed on my bed. Lulu claimed she'd been pounding on my door for fifteen minutes before I surfaced. I think she was exaggerating.

After dinner, which was some kind of chicken dish that tasted delicious and had olives in it—which was a good thing, as the olives startled me so much that I forgot to ask who'd wrung the chicken's neck—we gathered in Harvey's office. It had been set to rights after Mother departed for Boston. The effrontery of my mother in taking it upon herself to redecorate a room in someone else's house without even asking first still almost shocked me, but didn't quite. Her children were all grown up now, and she couldn't boss us around like she used to. Therefore, she resorted to other methods to assert her authority. Her usurped authority.

At any rate, after dinner we gathered in Harvey's office.

Sitting with a huge sigh in the huge desk chair behind his huge desk, Harvey glanced at his three so-called detectives. "Any luck yet?" he asked hopelessly.

"Not yet," said Ernie. "For one thing, we heard the crash and all ran to the scene of the fatal accident. We didn't have a chance to follow anyone or talk to anybody but Vic Bedini."

"I was afraid of that," said Harvey.

As for me, I'd been thinking about sleuthing. Thinking probably isn't my most sparkling talent, but I believe my thoughts that evening might have been valid.

"I've been thinking," I said, and instantly wished I hadn't when Harvey and Lulu laughed and Ernie said, "God save us."

"Pooh on you," I told Ernie in my most grown-up sophisticated vocabulary and tone of voice. "I don't think we should be in costumes from now on."

"Why not?" asked Harvey. "I thought you wanted to blend in."

"We do," I said. "That's why we shouldn't be in costumes. I saw girls and young men running around all over the set today in street clothes, carrying books and what looked like scripts and so forth. Why can't Lulu and I be...whatever those people are called?"

"Script girls and office runners," said Harvey. He pinned his gaze on Ernie. "Ernie, you're the expert. What do you think about Mercy's suggestion?"

After mulling the idea over—at least I think his silence masked mulling—Ernie said, "You might be right, Mercy."

Well, hallelujah! "Are you afraid we'll be recognized?" I asked Harvey and Ernie. And Lulu, because she was there.

"It's a gigantic set," said Ernie. "I doubt anyone there knows you except for Harvey, Bedini, and the two costume fellows."

"And we could wear wigs and glasses!" said Lulu excitedly. Guess she hadn't completely forsaken her penchant for motion pictures. "We'd look like all the other females on the set who aren't in costumes."

"We could probably achieve the same effect without glasses and wigs," I suggested gently. "I mean, I don't wear glasses. I probably wouldn't be able to see if I put on someone else's."

"Clear lenses," said Harvey. "You could wear glasses with clear lenses. We do it all the time in the pictures."

"Yeah?" said Ernie. He squinted at Lulu and me. "That might work. Probably best if you wore a wig, Lulu. Your hair is pretty distinctive."

"Yeah," said Lulu upon a heartfelt sigh. "I want to let it grow out, but it looks stupid half blond and half brown."

"We can fix that in a snap," said Harvey. "We have an entire department devoted to makeup and hair."

"Oh, Lulu!" I said, having had yet another thought. "Maybe you can have them dye your hair the color it is naturally so when it grows out, you'll hardly notice."

"Excellent idea," said Ernie.

"Brilliant!" said Lulu, her hands clasped to her bosom.

Gee, and I hadn't believed the two thoughts I'd presented so far even came close to brilliant. Just goes to show…something. Not sure what.

The Nashes' doorbell chimed. Rather than waiting for Molly or someone else to get to the door, the silly person poking the bell pressed it and it chimed again. And again. And again.

"What the devil?" Harvey rose from his chair.

Ernie, Lulu, and I also rose from our chairs, making it unanimous. Suddenly a knock came at Harvey's office door, and Molly stuck her head in. She looked scared.

"I'm so sorry, Mr. Nash but—"

"Get out of my way!" came a loud male voice. Chloe wasn't with us, or we'd have been exchanging startled glances. "Where is she?" the voice demanded. "I know she's here somewhere! Dammit, you can't *do* this to me!"

Shoot. Shoot, shoot, shoot. Knowing I was the only one capable of recognizing and dealing with the menace who'd shoved Molly out of the way and now stood, swaying, in the doorway, I took a step toward the menace.

"George Monteith Allcutt, what are *you* doing here? How *dare* you force your way into Harvey's house and office?" I demanded back at him.

George blinked at me with bloodshot eyes. "What're you doing here?" he asked.

"George?" I heard Ernie say. "Who's George?"

"Go away, George," I said to my brother. "Go sleep it off on a park bench or something. Nobody wants you here."

"How *dare*—"

But the practice I'd recently had with my mother came in handy. I walked like a soldier up to my idiotic, inebriated brother and pushed him in the chest with my forefinger. Hard. He staggered backwards. "I'll dare more than that if you continue making a scene." Not willing to risk taking my gaze from him—I knew from childhood that George didn't play fair—I spoke to Ernie. "Ernie, will you please escort my brother off my sister and brother-in-law's property? I'll be happy to call the police if you need help."

"*What?*" squealed George. "Whattaya mean, eshcort me off the prop'ty?"

"Just what I said."

Ernie appeared at my side.

"Thanks, Ernie. Take him to a police station or something. Or dump him in a lake."

"Come with me, Georgie," said Ernie, taking one of George's arms and turning him around.

Lulu, Harvey, and I let the two of them get a few yards away from the office door before we followed. Molly had her back pressed against a wall and her hands covering her mouth. Her eyes looked like saucers as she watched the march of progress. That is to say as she watched Ernie march George to the front door.

"What in the world is going on down here?" said Chloe, posing on the glorious staircase in a pink Chinese robe with butterflies on it. I swear, Chloe would look beautiful in a mud puddle. These surroundings fitted her much better than mud, however. "Is that *George?*"

"It is." I said.

"Where *is* she?" bellowed George.

"Nobody knows where she is, George," said Ernie.

"Nobody knows *who* she is, for that matter," I said. Then I recalled eavesdropping on my parents a couple of weeks prior. "Oh! Your Ziegfeld floozy!"

"She'zh *not* a...what you called her!" slushed George.

"You can find a room in a hotel somewhere and look for her tomorrow," said Ernie more kindly than I'd spoken to my deplorable brother. "Sober up first, okay?"

"But-but...she's *gotta* be here!"

"No, she doesn't," I told him. "I expect Mother and Father paid her off, and she's having a vacation in Gibraltar or somewhere."

"*Noooooo!*" shrieked George. "She'zh *here!*"

Peering at me over his shoulder, Ernie said, "Gibraltar?"

I shrugged. I didn't know where people went when they were recovering from broken hearts or love affairs. Gibraltar sounded as good as anywhere else to me.

Harvey accompanied Ernie and George to the front door, and Mr. Porter joined them there. Ernie and Mr. Porter wrestled George into the taxicab, whose driver had exited, probably to pursue George who hadn't paid him. I didn't know that until he spoke, of course.

"He owes me two bucks and fifty cents," said the indignant driver. "I hate drunks."

"I do too," I said with sympathy. Heck, I loathed my brother even when he wasn't drunk.

"Here," said Harvey, reaching into a pocket and pulling out a wad of bills. He peeled off several and told the cabbie, "Can you take him to a hotel or something?"

"Thanks, Mister," the cabbie said, sounding pleased.

"Thank you for taking him away," said Harvey.

"I can take him anywhere you want me to, but I can't make him stay there," said the cabbie. "He seemed mighty anxious to get to this place."

"Take him to the local police station," I suggested. "Nobody here wants him, and he's clearly inebriated."

"Sounds like a great plan to me," said the cabbie, giving me a huge grin.

"Mercy," said Harvey doubtfully. "Do you really think that's a good idea?"

"Yes."

"I wouldn't argue with her, Harvey," said Ernie. "I've seen her in this mood before. It's best to do as she says."

"Somebody'll have to bail him out in the morning," said the cabbie.

With a big smile, I said, "He can telephone our mother and father in Boston for bail money."

"You know that's not going to happen, Mercy." Ernie.

"Then let him stay in the cell," Me.

"Mercy, he's your *brother*." Lulu. Shocked.

"Not my fault." Me.

"Fabulous idea, Mercy." Chloe.

"Well…" Harvey, sounding uncertain.

"He's a spoiled brat." Me.

"He is that," said the cabbie.

"Drive fast," said Ernie. "That way if he opens the door and tries to escape, he'll fall out and might kill himself."

"Ernie!" Lulu.

"Best idea I've heard all day," I said. "What a worthless glob of muddy soil you are, George."

"No!" George didn't sound as positive as he'd sounded a few minutes before.

"Don't come back, George," said Chloe, who'd followed us all outside. "And be sure the gatekeeper locks the gate when you leave, please," she added to the cabbie.

"I'll do that, Mrs. Nash," said Mr. Porter.

"Thank you," said Chloe sweetly. "You might as well turn on the electricity, too. That way, if he tries to climb over the fence, he'll electrocute himself."

"Wh-what?" slurred George.

"Go away, George," said Chloe. "And don't come back."

"But…"

"But nothing, Georgie-porgie. Your sisters don't want you here."

Ernie made sure all of George was inside the cab before he slammed the door.

The cabbie took off like a flash. Mr. Porter ambled after the cab. I presume if George managed to remove himself from the taxi before the cabbie cleared the gate, Mr. Porter would stuff him back into it.

"Sheesh, Mercy," said Ernie, watching the cab careen down the long drive. "Your brother is as bad as you said he was."

"He's probably worse, actually," I told him.

"Hard to imagine," said Lulu.

FIFTEEN

George's sudden intrusion into our lives was an interesting, if ugly, end to an exhausting day. Harvey took pity on us.

"Now that you know the layout of the location," he said (and I didn't set him straight), "you don't have to get up so early. I'll have to be there early. My own headquarters tomorrow will be Helen's boudoir, so meet me there. We can discuss plans for the day. I was hoping to do that tonight but I didn't anticipate my brother-in-law showing up and ruining the evening."

"I'm sorry, Harvey. I hope you don't regret marrying Chloe. We both come from a ghastly family," I said, feeling low and responsible. Which I wasn't, darn it!

"I will never regret marrying Chloe," Harvey said stoutly. "And now we have a beautiful daughter." He looked positively dreamy.

"Glad to hear it," I said. If I married into a family containing so many awful people, I might not appreciate my spouse as much as Harvey did Chloe.

"Not your fault, Mercy," said Ernie. "In fact, you got rid of him efficiently."

Surprised, I said, "Thank you."

"Is there a special place I should go in order to get my hair dyed brown?" asked Lulu, moving on to more important issues.

"Yes," said Harvey. "When you visit the costume building, either Francis or Greg can direct you to the makeup building. Then you can all come to Helen's boudoir. Ernie and I can discuss sorting out individual assignments. I guess you should probably stick close to the main stars of the production. And look out for anything you perceive as being strange at the same time." He put a palm to his forehead. "If you can do all of those things at once."

"Sure we can," said Ernie. He looked at Lulu and me. "Right, girls?"

"Right," I said.

"I guess," said Lulu. Incurably honest, Lulu.

With a chuckle, Ernie said, "Doing everything at once is in my job description."

"I hope we can figure out who's sabotaging the production soon, Harvey," I added. "Now poor Mr. Flynn is dead. And *George* is here!"

"We probably won't have to worry about your brother, Mercy," said Ernie.

"You don't know him," I said.

Unfortunately, I was correct and Ernie's blissful state of ignorance didn't last.

The next day, we arose at the more reasonable hour of seven-thirty a.m. More reasonable than five-thirty, that is. We had breakfast with Chloe and the sleeping baby in Chloe's upstairs sitting room.

"Boy, your chef might be a cranky old fusspot, but he sure fixes a great breakfast," I told my sister as I dug into my omelet.

"Yes, he's quite good," said Chloe happily, answering me but gazing at her sleeping infant.

"This is really good," said Lulu.

"Eat up, ladies," said Ernie. "I told Harvey Mercy and I'll get to

Helen's boudoir by nine o'clock. Lulu, you might be a little later because of the hair."

"Right," said Lulu.

So we ate up.

When we arrived at the Nash Studio lot, Lulu and I wore plain old regular clothes and sensible shoes. I dissuaded Lulu from wearing high heels, reminding her of the dust problem and also of the fact we would be called "runners" today. I wore my regular hair. Lulu was still a bottle blonde, but we anticipated this to change soon.

We popped into the costume hall to be fitted with clear eyeglasses before I headed to Helen of Troy's boudoir and Lulu headed to the hair salon.

"There," said Francis Easthope, stepping back a couple of paces to observe his handiwork. "You both look studious."

Ernie snickered in the background.

"Studious?" said Lulu skeptically.

"That's a good thing," I told her.

Taking off her eyewear and frowning at them, Lulu said, "If you say so. I'm not used to wearing stuff behind my ears."

"Gotta keep 'em on somehow," observed Ernie.

"I guess," said Lulu, replacing her cheaters. Only they weren't real cheaters, because the glass was clear. "But now I need to get my hair dyed. Mr. Nash said you fellows could direct me to the makeup building."

"Sure thing," said Greg. He proceeded to give Lulu directions. To the building directly next door to the costume hall.

"Come along, Mercy. We need to see Harvey," said Ernie.

So Ernie and I went along, leaving Lulu at the makeup place. She assured us she'd be able to find Helen's boudoir without a problem. As that was more than I could do, I was grateful I didn't have to get my brown hair dyed any other color.

We heard the commotion before we got to Helen's boudoir.

Speeding up, I said, "Good Lord, that sounds like George! How'd he get in here?"

"Your idiot brother?" asked Ernie. "I thought he was going to sober up and go home to Boston."

"How'd he get bail money?" I asked. "How'd he get onto the set?"

Ernie had no answer.

When we arrived at Helen's boudoir, there was George in furious converse with Harvey, Sid Lafayette, and a girl I'd never seen before. She was clad as one of Helen's handmaidens. She wasn't wearing much, in actual fact.

"Dammit, you were supposed to *marry* me!" bellowed George.

"Your parents wouldn't let me!" the girl bellowed back.

"Will you two please be quiet?" asked Sid in a hopeless voice.

"I've called security," said one of Harvey's minions.

"I need this job!" screeched the girl. "It's not fair if I get kicked out because of *him*!" The last word was loaded with what sounded like contempt if not downright loathing.

"But I *love* you!" shrieked George.

"You don't either!" the girl shrieked back.

Just then, two automobiles with SECURITY painted on their doors showed up. Two men jumped out of each car, making a total of four security people running up to a bedeviled Sid Lafayette and a browbeaten Harvey Nash.

Two of the newcomers grabbed George by one arm each. George tried to escape, but he was a spindly creature who had, according to my father, spent the past several months drinking himself into oblivion.

"C'mon, you," said the burlier of the two men holding George.

The other two men walked up to the formerly bellowing girl and grabbed her arms. She let out a hideous scream.

"Ernie, will you please take care of George?" I said as I walked up to the woman and smacked her across the face. I guess that wasn't nice, but I'd heard it was the best thing to do with a hysterical person unless one had a glass of water handy to splash in his or her face.

By golly, she shut up! Her eyes opened wide. She'd probably have lifted a hand to her burning cheek if she'd been able, and she stared at me as if I were the madwoman on the set instead of her. Unless that's supposed to be she. Oh, who knows? Who cares, is more to the point.

"Who the blazes are you?" I asked the now-silent girl. I call her a girl, but she was probably around my age, which was a middle-aged twenty-two.

"V-verna," she stammered. "Verna Borden. Who're you?"

"I am George Allcutt's sister. Are you the Ziegfeld dancer he took up with in Boston?"

"I don't know what you mean by—"

She didn't finish her sentence because I held up a hand and stuck it palm-first in her face. She jerked her head back, although I don't think I'd have smacked her again. I'm not sure, truth to tell. I was furious that George had managed to insert himself onto what was supposed to be a closely guarded location. And how the dickens had he found his lady-love?

"You be quiet," I told Verna. Then I muttered, "Something really weird is going on here. How'd George get in?"

"I have no idea," said Harvey. "He'll get out in that car." He pointed at one of the security vehicles.

"And what about the wench?" said Ernie, eyeing Verna Borden without approval. I was glad of that. His disapproval, I mean.

In fact, Verna Borden was a beautiful woman with glossy chestnut hair, dark and heavily lashed eyes, a rosebud mouth and a lovely figure, which one could see most of through her filmy and flimsy costume. Really, I think there ought to be standards of dress put into place for the motion-picture industry. No wonder people flocked to the flickers, what with everybody running around half-naked!

Her head whipped around, and she pinned Ernie with a death-stare. "Who're you calling a wench?" she snarled.

"You," said Ernie. "Are you an extra on this picture?"

"Me?" Miss Borden seemed confused. Didn't she know who she was?

"Yes. You," said Ernie.

"Miss Borden has been hired to be one of Helen's handmaidens," said Harvey. He'd told the first two security fellows to escort George off the lot, with the dire message for George to stay there or he'd be in *real* trouble. I doubted George would cooperate. He'd never been awfully cooperative. "But she can be un-hired in a snap."

Clutching her clasped hands to her bosom, Miss Borden said, "Oh, please, Mr. Nash! Don't fire me! I don't know how George found me. I was trying to get away from him when I came out here."

"Our parents paid you off, didn't they?" I said, still standing directly in front of her.

"P-paid me? What do you mean?"

"They paid you to leave Boston—"

"I'm not from Boston," Verna declared.

With a derisive roll of my eyes, I said, "New York and Ziegfeld then."

"What about New York and Ziegfeld?" she demanded.

"Stop acting stupid," Ernie growled at her. He walked up to us and I stepped aside, although my doing so gave him a perfect view of her bosom. Stupid girl. Woman. Ernie. Fiddlesticks. "The Allcutts paid you to leave town, and you decided to come to Los Angeles and try to get into the flickers, right?"

"I don't—"

Ernie held up a palm of his own. His was much larger than mine and seemed to have an intimidating effect on Verna. "It's a yes-or-no question, Miss Borden," he snarled. "Did they pay you to leave the East Coast?"

Her gaze faltered and dropped. "Y-yes," she whispered.

"Fine. How'd George find you?"

"I don't know!" she said.

"I don't believe you," said Ernie.

Oh my, good for him!

"We're not stupid, Miss Borden," Ernie continued. "You were involved with George Allcutt back East. His parents paid you to go away. You came to Los Angeles, got a role in this picture and all of a sudden, George shows up again. On a closed set. And he found *you* among a cast and crew of hundreds. I don't believe in coincidences, especially when they defy the laws of common sense."

"I don't know what you mean," muttered Miss Borden.

"I still don't believe you," Ernie said. "How'd George get on the set? How'd he find you?"

"I tell you, I don't know!" Miss Borden said, tears gathering in her eyes and spilling down her cheeks.

She appeared pathetic and innocent, but if Ernie didn't believe her, I decided I wouldn't believe her either. I trusted Ernie. Most of the time.

"Miss Borden," said Harvey, interrupting a seemingly futile interrogation, "I'm going to have you sit in the other security car for a few moments. Mr. Templeton and I need to discuss what to do with you."

"You're making me sit in a car? Mr. Who? What to do with *me*?"

Poor Miss Borden seemed to become more fuddled by the second.

"Come with us, miss," said one of the men holding one of her arms.

"No!" she screamed.

"It's them or the police," said Harvey, his voice harder than I'd ever heard it. In general, Harvey was a gentle soul. I have *no* idea why he'd decided to participate in the cut-throat motion-picture industry.

"It should probably be the police," said Ernie in a contemplative tone.

"No!" Miss Borden screamed again.

"In that case, take her to the car, gentlemen," Ernie told the two security fellows.

"You should probably stuff a gag in her mouth too," I said, feeling meaner than usual.

"Just take her to my office. Gag her if you need to," said Harvey.

After the security men took Miss Verna Borden to their automobile and the door was securely shut behind her, Harvey heaved a big sigh and looked at Ernie. "Have a seat, Ernie. You too, Mercy." He gestured to several Greek-inspired benches on the set.

"Where are the rest of the actors?" I asked. The morning thus far had produced merely George Allcutt and Verna Borden. I'd seen no Blanche Sweet, no Ramon Novarro, no fake Greek cowboys, nobody at all except Harvey, Sid, Miss Borden and George.

"I sent them all away for a while," said Harvey. "When George showed up on the set, I decided we *really* need to get to the bottom of the problems here. There's no earthly excuse for George to be able to get onto a closed set. There must be a leak somewhere." He palmed his forehead, closed his eyes and sighed deeply. "We *have* to solve these problems! And soon. My God, someone has been killed on the set!"

"Yeah," said Ernie soberly. "You've got a serious leak or serious sabotage going on. Both, probably."

"What's happening?" came Lulu's voice from a few feet away.

When I turned, eager to greet her and tell her the latest catastrophe to befall the shooting (so to speak) of *Helen of Troy*, I couldn't find her. "Lulu?" I asked, puzzled.

Suddenly a young woman appeared before me from behind one of the papier-mâché columns. She wore a plain black dress, had on black-framed glasses and her hair was a pretty brown bob.

She threw her arms wide and said, "Surprise!"

SIXTEEN

"It's me!" the strange person continued.

I gaped in awe at my second-best friend in the whole wide world. "Good golly, Lulu! You don't even look like you!"

Smiling hugely, Lulu said, "I asked Greg if he could find me a dowdy dress to wear. I wondered if you'd recognize me."

"I didn't at first," I admitted.

"Nor did I," said Ernie. "But this is great. You can help us snoop without being recognized as a spy. Mercy's brother showed up on the set, which is supposed to be impossible to do, so we need to figure that out too." He squinted at me.

"What?" I asked, suddenly worried.

"Do you suppose the costume fellows might do a make-over for you as they did for Lulu? The two of you could then prowl around on the set, and no one would think anything of it. There are girls all over the place running errands for people."

"Let's not waste a lot of time on this," said Harvey. "Sid, we set up that hut during the recent rains. Isn't there some makeup in there? And a couple of different-colored wigs?" Harvey eyed me up and down as if he were trying to decide if I'd fit into the cook-pot. The sensation was most uncomfortable.

"We do," said Sid in a contemplative voice. Turning to me he said, "Miss Allcutt? Would you mind coming with me for a few minutes?"

Yes I'd mind! I didn't say so, realizing this was just another part of show-biz. I'd hate to have to depend on my looks in order to earn a living. And I'd *never* say that aloud in front of Ernie. He'd probably laugh and say I didn't have anything to worry about in that regard.

"I'll come with you too, Mercy."

Approximately ten pounds of anxiety slid from my shoulders. "Thanks, Lulu," I said, perhaps too fervently.

"He's not leading you to your death, Mercy," said Ernie. "Just to get a wig and some makeup."

"I know," I told him sounding grouchy. That's because I was.

"Are all flicker extras temperamental?" Ernie said to Harvey, who grinned.

"Most of them, yes."

"I'm *not* temperamental," I declared. "I just don't appreciate being looked at as if I were a horse at an auction."

"Do horses participate in auctions?" Ernie asked innocently.

"Bother you, Ernest Templeton," I snarled.

It had already become clear to me that I wasn't cut out for the silver screen.

Laughing, Lulu took my arm. "C'mon, Mercy. I'll save you from the bad man. I'll help with your makeup too."

"Sorry, Lulu," I told her softly. "This is just so…new to me. And I don't like it. Everything they do here seems so…I don't know. Insubstantial. Frivolous. I can't figure out how Harvey stands it and stays a nice person."

"He's got Chloe and the baby," said Lulu.

I turned my head to stare at her and almost tripped over a rope attached to one of the papier-mâché columns. The column in question teetered ominously. Fortunately, Lulu caught me before I could fall. Also, fortunately, Harvey, Ernie, and Sid were watching. All three of the men rushed to the column and kept it from crashing to the ground, taking Lulu and me with it. Lulu and I stared at the men and the column and then at each other.

"That was rigged," I said, pointing at the…I don't know what it was. A piece of clothesline? Whatever it was, it had been tied around the column towards its bottom and strung across what was pretty much everyone's walking path if they were going from Helen's boudoir to Mount Ida. "Somebody deliberately tried to trip someone with that cord."

"Yeah," said Ernie. "Somebody deliberately did that."

"This is insane," said Harvey.

"Is Georgie-porgie already off the set?" asked Ernie.

"I don't know. I can use the intercom system and call the front gate. Why?"

"It's all too convenient," said Ernie. "George shows up, instantly finds his lady-love, and right where they stood attracting attention, another effort at sabotage takes place. There's got to be a connection."

"Talk to Miss Borden some more," I suggested.

"Dammit," said Sid. "I'll have to get someone in to repair this column. It's dented where we all grabbed it so it wouldn't fall."

"You're right," said Harvey. "And so is Mercy. We should have another conversation with Miss Borden."

"How heavy are these columns?" asked Ernie.

"Not sure," said Sid. "They weigh a whole lot less than marble or cement, but a ten-foot papier-mâché column would sure hurt if it fell on someone."

"It almost fell on two someones," I said, unnerved as well as angry. "I wish it had fallen on George."

Ernie held up his arms. "All right. We thwarted this attempt at interference. Mercy and Lulu, go along with Sid and fix up Mercy so she's unrecognizable. I'm going to have another little chat with Miss Borden." Turning to Harvey, he added, "Might be a good time to call in the L.A.P.D. I don't know if they'll help, but it can't hurt to talk to them."

"Right. I'll give Rod Crowhurst a ring. He'll know the names of any police officials who are on our payroll."

On his *payroll?* Shocked, I whirled around and said, "Harvey?

Do you mean to say you've *paid* Los Angeles policemen to do your bidding? Is *that* what you mean?"

Ernie, Harvey, and Sid shared a three-way eye-roll. "Don't worry about it, Mercy," said Ernie. "It'll be all right. Go ahead and get your wig and makeup on. I have plans for you and Lulu."

"Might as well do as he says," said Lulu. "Nothing we can do standing here staring at a dented column."

I sucked in a breath, prepared to protest. Then I realized there was nothing I could do about the corruption rife in the Los Angeles Police Department, the motion picture industry, the government, the world, or anywhere else. How…depressing. "Very well, Lulu. You're right. Let's go make me into someone else."

"Turn her into someone who isn't outraged by the injustices of the world if you can!" Ernie called after us. "I'm tired of her lectures."

I lifted a hand, considered making a rude gesture and didn't. None of this nonsense was Ernie's fault.

"Here, Mercy and Miss LaBelle," said Sid, his tone of voice indicating his attempt to soothe ruffled nerves. Didn't work on me.

"Thanks, Sid," said Lulu. "And call me Lulu, okay? We don't care about the formalities do we, Mercy?"

"No," I said. I think I'd just fibbed.

"Here's the building. We just had this one room built during those massive rainstorms we had a few weeks back," said Sid, withdrawing a big loop of keys from his jacket pocket. "That's when we had the canopy erected over the boudoir and the Mount Ida locations too. I'm not sure, but I think all that rain would have damaged those papier-mâché columns."

"Guess you didn't need the rain to do that," I muttered.

After heaving a gusty sigh, Sid said, "Too true. Anyway"—he unlocked the door and shoved it open for us—"I'll show you where the wigs and makeup are stored."

"Thanks," said Lulu.

"Yes, thank you," I said.

"Good Lord!" said Sid, dismayed as he peered around the

insides of the small building. It was only one large room, and it appeared to have been ransacked. "Not this too!"

"Oh my," I said, sharing his surprise and consternation. "What a mess."

"Wow, somebody sure hates this movie, huh?" said Lulu.

"Yes," said Sid. "I believe somebody does."

"Well," I said, looking at the clothes, hair pieces and makeup containers that had been thrown everywhere, "Lulu and I can clean up this mess, salvage what we can, and pile the damaged merchandise in a corner or something. Then we'll find me a wig, and Lulu will fix my makeup."

"I can't believe this," said Sid mournfully, pulling at his side locks. They weren't awfully long. "The padlock was still locked. I don't know who could have made a duplicate key."

"I don't either, but you'd probably better report this newest problem to Harvey and Ernie and the police when they get here," I told him.

"Oh look!" said Lulu happily, picking up a Clara-Bow red wig and waving it at me. "We can use this one!"

"You've got the right attitude, Lulu. I should take lessons from you and not let bad things get me down." I stared more closely at the wig. "But do you really think I should become a redhead?"

"Sure! You'll give Clara Bow a run for the money."

Shaking my brown, shingled head, I said, "I don't want to do that."

"Well then, you'll just look like somebody who was born with red hair."

"You really think so?" I asked doubtfully, taking the wig from Lulu's fingers. The style was rather cunning: a wavy bob that wasn't unlike the style in which my own personal boring brown hair was brushed on a daily basis.

"Yes, I think so!" cried Lulu. "Just you wait."

"Guess I'll have to," I said, still doubtful.

"I'll go back to Harvey and Ernie now," said Sid, who sounded not simply doubtful, but very nearly defeated.

"Help me pick up this table and mirror first please," Lulu said.

"Sure."

The table to which Lulu had referred was a dressing table. The mirror attached to it was cracked, but we could still see ourselves in it. I went over and helped, figuring I'd sulked enough by then.

"What a mess," I said, gazing at the boxes, tins and bottles of makeup that had spilled to the floor when the table and mirror had been overturned.

"Huh. Might be a helpful mess," said Lulu, bending to see what was on offer on the floor.

"I'll leave you two for a bit," said Sid. "I'm going to send the police to this area too."

"We probably should try not to leave many of our own finger-prints," I said, having suddenly remembered an important investiga-tive clue. Some private-eye's assistant *I* was, huh?

"Botheration," said Sid. "We should have worn gloves to set that dressing table to rights, shouldn't we?"

"I suppose so," said Lulu. "But we'll be careful from now on."

To prove it, she grabbed a piece of fabric from a pile of clothing and shook it out. The fabric turned out to be part of a Grecian costume, although I wasn't sure if it was a peplos, a chiton, or a himation. It didn't matter to Lulu. She draped it over the chair she set upright, using the fabric as gloves so as not to leave one of her fingerprints on it. She might be rubbing out already-there prints, but I didn't care.

"Will you two be all right if I leave you and go back to Helen's boudoir?" asked Sid, as if he feared Tommy-gun-toting gangsters to appear and shoot up the place.

"We'll be fine," I fibbed.

"We'll be great," said Lulu, sounding much more positive than I had.

"I'll get Roger to stand at the door and keep other people out of the cabin," said Sid.

"Who's Roger?" asked Lulu.

"One of the grips."

"Thanks, Sid," I said.

"Okay," said Lulu, smiling at me. She looked *so* different from the Lulu I was used to seeing, I almost hesitated to put myself in her hands.

Then I scolded myself for being an idiot and a coward, threw away my remaining reservations, sat on the chair and said, "Do your worst, Lulu. I hope I *do* look like Clara Bow. I think she's darling."

"Everyone thinks she's darling," said Lulu. "What's a grip?"

"I think the grips are the folks who set up and rig equipment used in the production of a flicker. You know, like the lights and other stuff."

"Why do they call them grips?"

"I have no idea. You should probably ask Harvey these technical questions."

"All right now. Sit still. I'm going to brush back your hair first. Then I'm going to do your face."

"Do what with my face?" I don't think I sounded as alarmed as I felt.

"Give you the complexion of a redhead. Only you won't have freckles. Most of the redheads I've known have had a ton of freckles." She selected a tin of pancake makeup from the mess on the table and picked up a sponge-type thing. She dipped the thing in the tin and gazed at me in the mirror. "This is gonna be fun."

"Great," I said, thinking I was going to look like a circus clown after Lulu was through with me.

SEVENTEEN

But by golly, I didn't!

"Lulu, you're a genius with makeup," I said as I stared at my new face in the cracked mirror of the dressing table. "I wouldn't recognize me if I saw me on the street."

"You look great as a redhead," she said, stepping back a pace and smiling at her handiwork.

"Maybe you could get a job as a makeup artist in the flickers. I'm pretty sure all those actors and actresses don't put on their own makeup for movies."

Lulu wrinkled her brow. "I never thought about doing something like makeup," she admitted. "All I ever thought about was being an actress."

"If you got a job as a makeup artist, you wouldn't be fired when you got old," I pointed out. "If an actress gets too old, they don't let her appear in the flickers any longer. It's *such* a hellish business." I stopped myself before I got carried away again.

"Interesting. How can I find out about being a makeup artist?"

"Show me to Harvey, Sid, and Ernie," I said. "We've got to go back to Helen's boudoir anyway to get our assignments. Harvey and Sid will probably want to hire you on the spot."

"Golly, you really think so?"

"Don't know, but so far in this one morning, you've done a spectacular job on yourself and me. I think you'd make more money as a makeup artist than a receptionist, too, although don't take my word for it. I guess it depends on how many pictures you get hired to do makeup for. Did that make any sense?"

"Yeah," said Lulu, losing some of her earlier enthusiasm. "It made sense."

"I'm truly impressed, Lulu," I told her, rising from the dressing-table chair. I wanted to keep looking at my reflection. I looked better as a redhead than I looked as a normal, brown-haired, blue-eyed female.

Hmmm. Perhaps I could ask Lulu to give me tips on my own makeup habits. I don't suppose it was entirely frivolous to want to look good—as well as professional and efficient—at the office.

"*Eeek!*"

The eeking came from Lulu and me at the same time. We'd been so occupied changing me from myself into a glamorous redhead, we'd neglected to remember Sid had told us he was sending a grip—Roger? I couldn't remember—to guard our little room.

"Cripes!" said the poor grip, leaping about a yard in the air.

Lulu planted a hand over her no-doubt thundering heart. "Who're *you*?"

Then I remembered "Oh, I'm so sorry we frightened you," I said, laying a hand on the poor lad's shoulder. "Are you Roger?"

"Uh, yes. I'm Roger Hollis. Mr. Lafayette sent me to stand outside the door and make sure nobody else could get in." He held up a padlock. "I've gotta lock the door before I take you back to the set."

"Thanks, Roger," said Lulu, allowing her hand to drop to her side. Her heart was probably still beating hard. I know mine was. "We didn't mean to scare you. We forgot you were going to be there."

"Yeah," said Roger. "I figured as much." He stuck the new

padlock into its place and clicked it shut. He showed us the key before he thrust it into his trouser pocket.

"Thank you for guarding us," I said, my voice weak. "Will you remain here or come back to Helen of Troy's boudoir with Lulu and me?"

"Mr. Lafayette said to stick with the two of you because he's afraid something might happen to you."

"Thank you," said Lulu.

"Yes," I said. "Thank you."

The notion that Sid and Harvey (and probably Ernie) didn't want Lulu and me even to walk on the set unescorted didn't make me feel any safer, but I didn't tell Roger so. What a stupid business, this motion-picture stuff. Because it was so profitable, *everyone* wanted to get in on it. According to Harvey, even gangsters were leaving Chicago and New York City in order to get in on the flicker action. *Not* a comforting thought.

My next thought, which was of Vic Bedini, wasn't a comforting one either. And that big threatening fellow called Frank didn't make me feel any better. They were both Italians, I thought. Were they…*gangsters*?

I heaved a sigh when the three of us approached Helen's boudoir. Harvey, Ernie, and Sid were in deep conversation with a couple of fellows in uniform. Guess the police had arrived. I wondered where Miss Borden was.

"Roger!" said Sid, leaping to his feet and staring at poor Roger in dismay. "I told you to stay with— Oh. Is that you, Lulu and Mercy?"

"Ha," said Lulu in a satisfied voice.

"It's us," I confirmed. "Roger performed his duties admirably."

"Good God, is that *you* Mercy? My capable secretary? As a ravishing redhead?" Ernie goggled at me.

I didn't appreciate his scrutiny. Or his words. So I was a ravishing redhead, was I? What was I the rest of the time? Horse meat?

"Yes," I snapped. "It is I."

"Okay, now I know it's you. Nobody else would say, 'It is I'.

You're a peach, Mercy. I hope you know that." He grinned as he spoke.

"But I'm only ravishing as a redhead?" I said, snarling a bit.

"You're always ravishing. Did Lulu fix your makeup and hair? You look ravishing in a different way, is all," said Ernie, trying to back-pedal.

"Yes, she did." I turned to Harvey. "What do you need to do to get hired as a makeup artist by a studio, Harvey? Or do the studios hire makeup artists?"

Harvey seemed taken aback by my question. He said, "Makeup artists? I can't hire anybody until we get our current set of problems solved, Mercy." Squinting at me, he added, "Although, if Lulu did your makeup and hair today, she'd definitely be good at it."

"Gee, thanks, Harvey," said Lulu, blushing even through her layers of pancake and powder.

"Okay, enough of the rah-rah," said Ernie in a getting-down-to-business tone. "Mercy and Lulu, I have assignments for you. Remember to stay together at all times. We don't know who's responsible for the trouble on this set, but you might be recognized by whoever's causing it. He or she has already killed once. I don't want to lose either of you."

"Gee thanks, Ernie," I said.

"Dammit, I mean it, Mercy!" he barked back at me. "Snooping can be dangerous. You should know that by this time!"

"He's right you know, Mercy," said Lulu.

After heaving one of my larger sighs, I said, "I suppose so." I *knew* so, but this whole business was unnerving me and aggravating the heck out of me. And my face itched. I feared I might be getting a rash from the makeup. Bother!

"Suppose nothing," said Ernie. "You and Lulu *must* stay together. Do you understand?"

"Yes," I said grudgingly. "I understand. Sorry for snapping, Ernie."

"It's all right," he said giving me a little hug. I appreciated the hug more than I could express, especially after his "ravishing redhead" remark. "Did you talk with that woman again? Miss Borden?"

Ernie, Harvey, and Sid exchanged a sheepish glance.

"You didn't!" I accused them.

"We tried," said Ernie. "She'd already managed to elude her captors."

"How the heck did she do that?" I asked, seriously irked. "She was in a car in between two burly men! How'd she get out?"

"Unfortunately," said Ernie, sounding aggrieved, "the two body-guards acted like gentlemen. When Miss Borden said she needed to visit the powder room, they let her."

"How *stupid* of them!" I said. "She's a lying piece of goods!"

"Yeah, I think so too, but she managed to elude her guards, so she's loose on the set somewhere," said Ernie.

"I'm about to throw in the towel on this production," said Harvey, sounding defeated. "It'll cost a bundle, but—"

His words so shocked me that I burst out in a roar: "Don't you *dare* shut down this production, Harvey Nash! You can't let the criminals get away with the damage they've done. And a *murder*!"

One of the uniformed police people cleared his throat and said, "It might be wise to stop production, Miss...uh, miss. It's difficult to investigate a crime in such a crowded venue."

"Nuts to that!" I bellowed at the uniform. "The City of Los Angeles is a crowded venue and you catch crooks there, don't you? This is supposed to be a closed set, but people who shouldn't be here manage to get in. Do your job and find the creatures who are causing the problems."

A couple of glances were exchanged between the uniformed police people. "Ma'am, I understand your concern—"

"Boloney! Do you think you're dealing with a pack of idiots?" I barked. "Lulu and I—and Ernie—have had ample experience with the Los Angeles Police Department. I wouldn't trust you to find a lost elephant. *And* I don't trust you any more than I trust the crooks on this set who are causing the problems."

The first Mr. Uniform stood up straighter and looked offended. Piddle on him.

"Mercy!" said Harvey, shocked.

"Don't Mercy me, Harvey. Or Lulu. We both know how useless the L.A.P.D. is unless a person lives in Hancock Park, Beverly Hills, Holmby Hills, or other upper echelons of society."

"Ma'am," said the second Mr. Uniform, who was becoming snarly, "we take the troubles on Mr. Nash's set *very* seriously. We will do our utmost to solve them."

Still feeling ferocious, I said, "Maybe you will. After all, Harvey's rich enough for you to take his problems seriously."

"Mercy!" said Ernie. When I swiveled to get a quick look at him, I saw he was attempting to smother a grin. "Stop scolding the nice policeman. Harvey's not going to end production on this flicker." He turned to Harvey. "Are you, Harvey?"

Harvey had both hands on his head. The poor guy looked as though he were being besieged on all sides which, in a way, he was. "If you're still willing to help out, Ernie and Mercy and Lulu, I guess we'll continue. But we *have* to find the culprit. Culprits. However many there are of them."

"Yes, sir," said the policeman.

I gave him a *look*. "Unless your name is Ernie, Mercy, or Lulu, I believe you're presuming a bit too much."

"Mercy," said Ernie again, only this time he sounded stern.

I humphed. "Very well, I suppose the cops *might* be of help. For once."

Lulu grabbed an arm and said, "Let's get going, Mercy. Leave the coppers to yak with Mr. Nash and Ernie. Yakking is what they do best."

"That's for sure," I grumbled. Turning to Ernie, I said, "Want us to start anywhere in particular?"

"I was thinking of the stable area. Here. Carry these with you so you look official." He handed each of us a few papers and a folder or two. "And *stay together*. Don't take any chances!"

"We won't," I told him. "And I have pencils and a pad in my pocket."

"Great," said Ernie.

"Would you like me to send Roger with them?" asked Harvey.

Roger jumped slightly at the sound of his name. He'd been listening intently to the conversation.

"No thank you." I spoke for Ernie. But really, I didn't want a guy who started so easily getting in Lulu's and my way.

"That's not up to you, Mercy," said Ernie, still stern. Then he tilted his head to one side, gave Roger a good looking over (which made Roger blush) and said, "But no. Thanks, I don't think they'll need Roger." Whipping his head around to stare at Lulu and me he added, "As long as you *stay together*."

"Got it," I said.

"Sure, Ernie," said Lulu.

I was about to take a bold step forward on my investigative journey when I thought of something important.

"Which way are the stables?"

Shaking his head, Ernie pointed to his right. "They're that-a-way," he said.

"Thank you." I attempted to appear confident, intelligent and independent.

So Lulu and I started out on our way, heading to the right. Lulu still held my arm. That was okay with me, because I suddenly felt as nervous as a rabbit being pursued by a pack of wild hyenas.

"Thanks for asking the way," Lulu whispered as we walked forward. "I didn't know which way the stables were either."

"You're welcome," I whispered back. "Do hyenas run in packs?"

Lulu turned to look at me strangely. "I have no idea."

"I don't either. Just wondered, was all."

EIGHTEEN

I t was a long hike to the stables. By the time they were in sight, I was tired of wearing the stupid red wig and decided the discomfort of wearing a wig and a ton of makeup, even to look ravishing, wasn't worth the bother. I told Lulu so.

"Crumb, I forgot you had to wear that wig, Mercy. I'm wearing my own hair, so at least my head's not uncomfortable."

"Glad the weather isn't hot," I muttered.

"Oh, me too!" said Lulu. "That wig would be torture in the heat."

It felt like torture anyway but I didn't say so. Nor did I mention my itchy cheeks. Big of me, huh?

"What should we do when we get to the stables?" I asked. "Should we talk to Mr. Bedini?"

"Not sure," said Lulu. "Let's just walk around for a bit and maybe listen outside his tent. We can pretend we're looking for someone. Ernie gave us props so we'll seem official." She lifted the pile of papers in her hands.

"Yes, Ernie knows his job," I said, even though I was about as tired of carrying stuff around as I was of wearing the red wig.

Then I scolded myself for being a spoiled brat. I'd defied my parents and about seven dozen other relations in order to move to Los Angeles and be a private eye's secretary. Very well, so my first ambition was just to get paid employment. The fact I managed to find my first job with a P.I. was a bonus. *So stop whining and start looking, Mercedes Louise Allcutt*, I lectured myself.

It took all my willpower not to tell myself that being this uncomfortable wasn't part of my job and to shut the heck up. Maybe there was no hope for me.

"Isn't that a girl?" Lulu whispered as we got closer to the stables and the herd of beautiful horses. She tilted her head tent-wards so as not to have to point a finger.

Squinting, I thought I discerned a female figure near Mr. Bedini's tent. She lifted the flap and went inside. I didn't hear any hollers or screams, so I figured she wasn't unwelcome. Unless Mr. Bedini was away from the tent and she aimed to burgle it.

"Could she be Miss Borden?" I asked. "I couldn't see well enough from this far away. It didn't look like whoever it was had on a handmaiden's costume. It looked like she was wearing regular clothes."

"I can't see that far either. These cheaters I'm wearing may have clear lenses, but they're still in the way if you know what I mean."

"Yes. I do." As I was suffering from terminal face-itch and wighead rot, I understood even though I wasn't wearing specs.

"Let's get closer," whispered Lulu. "Maybe we can figure out what's going on in there. I hope that Frank character isn't with Mr. Bedini again today."

"So do I," I said, having only that second entertained the same thought.

"Howdy, ladies. Hep you?" came from a few yards away from us.

Both Lulu and I whirled around. Darned if it wasn't Arnie the cowboy! He seemed like a nice lad, even if he did speak in a strange dialect.

"Thank you," I said, since Lulu appeared incapable of speech. "We have some papers for Mr. Bedini. Is he in his tent?"

"Garn, I dunno," said Arnie. "Wah me tah check?"

"No thank you," I said, ready to tackle him if he headed for the tent in spite of my words. "We'll just drop these off."

"Yes," said Lulu. "We're just bringing some papers to him." She held out the papers in her hand. When she noticed the doodle of a monkey climbing a Greek column on the top page, she drew them all to her chest.

"Owl Rawt," said Arnie. "Lemme know if ya need somepin."

"We will," I assured him, having taken only a second or three to decipher his offer. "Thank you."

"Welcome." Arnie tipped his big cowboy hat—are those hats called Stetsons?—at us and ambled back to the horses.

I noticed people seemed to be doing something to a few of the horses today. Squinting, I couldn't tell precisely what it was they were doing. "Um, sir?" I called after Arnie.

Arnie turned and again tipped his hat. Polite fellow. "Yas'm?"

"What are those men doing to those horses?"

With a broad grin, Arnie said, "They's makin' 'em ready fer ridin', ma'am."

"Oh," I said, flummoxed. I'd seen horses being ridden, and their accoutrements didn't look like those on the pasture horses, although I couldn't decide what the difference was.

"Didn't the Greeks use saddles and bridles?" Lulu asked. Gee, I'd never have thought to ask such a pertinent question. I reminded myself that Lulu had grown up in a farming community and didn't feel too stupid.

"Not accordin' ta the scree-upt," said Arnie.

"My goodness," I said.

"Oh," said Lulu. Squinting through her cheaters, she said, "Are they putting leather reins on them? And are those saddle cloths? It looks as if the cloths have straps that attach under the horses' heads."

"Yas'm."

"Must be hard to ride like that," I opined.

"Not iff'n ya git used to it," said Arnie.

"The rider has to use a leather rein and the tie is supposed to keep the saddle cloth on?" asked Lulu.

"Yas'm," said Arnie

"And there aren't any stirrups or anything?" I asked, thinking horses were a heck of a lot bigger than people. "How do people climb onto their backs?"

With a grin, Arnie said, "We use that thar fence, ma'am."

"Ah. I see. Thank you."

He tipped his hat again and strode off.

"You know," said Lulu in a musing tone, "I've seen pictures of ancient people riding horses, and the people are wearing skirts."

"Skirts?" I said in astonishment.

"Well, you know. Not pants. Short togas or something. Wonder if they wore underwear. It would be really uncomfortable to ride a horse without long pants and a saddle, even with a saddle blanket or some kind of cloth covering the horse's back."

"Good Lord, I never even thought about that," I said, realizing precisely how correct Lulu's observation was. "My mother didn't make Chloe and me take riding lessons when we were little, although she thought about it. A whole lot of rich kids in Boston had horses and learned to ride. Some of them even played polo."

"Polo?" Lulu seemed puzzled for around ten seconds before she said, "Oh, yeah! That's the game where you hit a ball with a stick while you're riding a horse, right?"

"Right," I said.

My mind reverted to people having to ride horses astride without underwear or the horses wearing saddles. Especially men, who had those peculiar dangly bits. Then the same mind boggled. "I've got to read more about ancient Greece. I haven't even finished *Helen of Troy* yet."

"So far, from what you've told me, the story is kind of stupid," said Lulu.

"It's quite stupid," I agreed. "But let's be quiet as we approach the tent. You were right. We should listen outside for a while."

"Yeah, we might be able to figure out who that girl was," whispered Lulu.

So we tippy-toed up to the back of Mr. Bedini's tent and listened.

"Dammit, Vicky, what are you doing here?"

Lifting my eyebrows at Lulu, I mouthed, *Mr. Bedini?*

Lulu nodded vigorously.

But who the heck was Vicky?

"Don't you swear at me, Victor Bedini," came the loud, angry voice of the woman we'd been introduced to as Verna Borden.

Lulu and I exchanged another surprised glance. So Verna Borden's first name was actually Victoria? Who knew? With a duet of shrugs, Lulu and I went back to eavesdropping.

"Dammit. It didn't work out with George," said Vicky/Verna. "Somebody was supposed to rig more than one column."

"Not my job," snarled Vic Bedini. "Anyhow, this is all your fault. If you hadn't fallen in with the Salvatore mob and their gambling dens, we wouldn't be in this mess."

Lulu and I heard a huff of angry breath, and then Vicky/Verna said, "I know, I know. But dammit, George was supposed to wire me the money from Boston. I didn't know he'd follow me to Los Angeles without the money!"

"Well, *that* didn't work out too well, did it?" snapped Mr. Bedini. "Why couldn't you have just milked your pigeon back East?"

"Dammit Vic, I *did*! And his parents gave me tons of money to leave him!"

"Which you promptly threw away at the gambling tables," said Mr. Bedini.

"Oh, *God*," said Vicky/Verna. "What are we supposed to do *now*? I'm sorry about gambling away the money. I think the speaks rig the tables."

"No, really?" said a supremely sarcastic Mr. Bedini. "How shocking."

"Oh, be quiet," Vicky/Verna's voice was shaky. "Did Frank say when he was going to come back here?"

"No. He said he'd see me 'soon.' I don't know what that means, but I don't like it."

"Maybe we can run away?" suggested Vicky/Verna. Sounded to me as if she were suggesting a plan she didn't believe would be viable.

"You tried that," snarled Mr. Bedini. "It didn't work."

"It's because of George," said the woman. "It would have worked if he'd just sent the money and hadn't followed me. I thought he was too scared of his parents to defy them."

Me too, although George's lapses had begun after Mother left Boston. She was the iron hand in the velvet glove in our family. Well, she didn't usually bother with the velvet glove.

"How'd he get on to the set?" asked Mr. Bedini.

"Same way everybody else does," said Vicky/Verna. "On the floor of somebody's car."

Lulu and I exchanged another wide-eyed look. So. That meant there was a traitor, or perhaps even traitors, somewhere in the Nash Studio sneaking bad people onto the set. While I could definitely see the sniveling George hiding on the floor of someone's automobile, I found it difficult to imagine the large man named Frank whom we'd met the day before agreeing to do so in order to gain access to the set. Still, I couldn't think of another way he could get in.

"Well, what are we supposed to do now?" asked Mr. Bedini in a hopeless-sounding voice.

"I don't *know!*" said Vicky/Verna. Then I guess she broke down, because Lulu and I heard loud sobs issue from the tent.

I jerked my head at Lulu, indicating she should join me in walking away from the tent for a bit. I wanted to chat with her. Maybe we'd discovered something important. Or maybe we hadn't. Just because George was having woman trouble, and the woman was addicted to gambling, it didn't necessarily follow that they were responsible for the problems on the set. Although Vicky/Verna *had* said something about rigging more columns in Helen's boudoir.

Nertz. This was too complicated for me.

We walked to a nearby boulder conveniently situated ten or so paces from the tent. "What?" asked Lulu. "Wow, I wonder if that woman is married to Mr. Bedini."

After considering the thought for a couple of heartbeats, I said, "She's probably his sister, not his wife. Or maybe a cousin or something. They don't sound like a married couple."

"I've known a few married couples who sounded a lot worse than those two," muttered Lulu.

"I don't doubt it. But I'd wager her name is Victoria Bedini and not Verna Borden."

"Oh," said Lulu.

We were whispering, by the way.

"He called her Vicky, and his name is Victor. At least I suppose it is. They're Italian, and that guy named Frank was Italian. And Mr. Bedini said something about a Salvatore mob. I wonder if that's where Frank fits into the picture."

"Lordy, I don't know," said Lulu, "but it makes sense if they're siblings. She looks kind of Italian."

"Yeah, she does," I agreed.

After standing behind the boulder for a few silent moments, Lulu said, "Should we go back and tell Ernie about this? It might be important."

"One of us should stay here and continue to listen," I said.

"Ernie told us to stay together. He was pretty definite about it, Mercy."

Darn. Lulu was right. "You're right."

"I almost wish he'd sent Roger with us," muttered Lulu.

"I don't. Roger's a scaredy-cat. He jumps when anything startles him."

"Can't hardly blame him," said Lulu.

"You have a point," I admitted.

We both stared at the pasture of horses for a couple of seconds. Then I thought of something. It wasn't brilliant or anything, but it might get us to Ernie quicker than walking.

"Say, Lulu, can you ride a horse?"

Lulu reared back as if *she* were a startled equine. "Ride a horse? I learned when I was a kid, yeah, but I haven't ridden in years."

"Do you think it's a skill that will come back to you if you try it again?"

"Are you trying to get me onto one of those horses with no saddles or stirrups or bridles, Mercy Allcutt? I'm not eager to fall off a horse and break my neck, you know."

"I thought maybe we could get Arnie to saddle and bridle a horse for us," I said.

"*One* horse for the both of us?" demanded Lulu.

"Well, I don't know how to ride very well," I admitted.

"I thought you said you *couldn't* ride a horse. You said your mommy wouldn't give you lessons."

"My *mommy*?" I asked, nearly bursting into laughter. But I didn't dare laugh. Mr. Bedini or Vicky/Verna might hear me.

"Your battleaxe of a mother then," amended Lulu.

"Better description. You're right, though. I can't really ride, but even if I'm not good at it, taking horses back to where Ernie and Harvey are will be quicker than walking. If we had a horse or two, we could eavesdrop some more."

"You know, Mercy," said Lulu. "Harvey can give you a studio pass so the gate guard will allow you to enter the set. We could take your little roadster anywhere we need to go."

"True, but my roadster currently on Bunker Hill. I don't have it today, and today's when we might need speed."

"We might not need speed," said Lulu.

"You're right," I said. "But let's go eavesdrop some more."

"Good," said Lulu. "I'm ready."

So we tiptoed back to the tent and stood close enough to hear what was going on inside. When we arrived, the only thing we heard was Vicky/Verna still crying and Mr. Bedini occasionally slipping in an unsympathetic, "Oh, shut up. This is all your fault."

Not precisely gentlemanly. Then again, I don't suppose Vicky/Verna was particularly ladylike. I probably should have liked her for that because she was so different from my mother, but I didn't.

NINETEEN

S uddenly a new voice spoke. Unfortunately, it didn't come from the tent but from directly behind Lulu and me.

"Well, well, well, what do we have here?" The voice was gravelly and coarse and sounded as if it had ricocheted around a rock quarry several times before landing its owner's throat.

Frank Sabatini!

Lulu and I both leaped back, Lulu to the left, I to the right.

"Us?" Lulu squeaked.

"You," growled Frank.

"Nothing!" I said, not quite as squeakily as Lulu.

"Looks to me as though you're snooping. That's not a nice thing to do," said Frank.

"Oh, but we have a good reason!" I said. Then I wondered how to continue upon my theme. What reason could we possibly have to eavesdropping outside a tent on a picture set?

Bless Lulu, who was quick on the pick-up. "Yeah! There's a lady in there, and she was involved in an incident this morning! We think she's in danger!"

Honestly, Lulu was wonderful. I'd never have thought of such an excellent excuse.

"Is that so?" said Frank.

"Yes," said Lulu.

Because she said no more, I improvised. "Yes! She was involved in sabotaging Helen of Troy's boudoir! So the police came and were supposed to take her away, but she escaped!" Remembering what Lulu'd just said, I added, "And now we think that man in there is going to hurt her!"

Frank's heavy features changed slightly, from sly to possibly a teensy bit interested. "Zat so?"

Lulu nodded. So did I.

"That's a real corker, that is," said Frank.

And then a miracle occurred. Perhaps it wasn't a huge one, but it was big enough for Lulu and me. From inside the tent came a shriek of terror and then Vicky/Verna said, "Oh my God! Is that Frank talking outside?"

"Shut up," ordered Vic Bedini.

But it was too late. Frank's hearing was at least as good as Lulu's and mine. In fact, I said, "See? We were telling the... Ugh!"

I grunted when Frank grabbed one of my arms and my papers went flying. He tried to grab one of Lulu's arms, but she slipped smartly away from him and darted off toward the pasture full of horses.

"Arnie!" Lulu shrieked. "Arnie, help us!"

"Shit," snapped Frank. "Well, you can come with me, girlie. You ain't no everyday eavesdropper." He yanked the wig from my head, scattering the pins Lulu had used to secure it and eliciting a cry of anguish from me. "And you ain't a redhead neither. You're one of the gals who was talkin' to Vic yestidday."

Frank dragged me, my eyes watering from pain, to the front of the tent. There he and I both saw Vic Bedini and Vicky/Verna exit the front of the tent and attempt an escape *a la* Lulu. Didn't work. Frank roared, "Stop, you two!" To emphasize his point, he hauled out a handgun from somewhere on his person and shot a bullet into the ground only inches from Mr. Bedini and Vicky/Verna's feet. Both of them froze in their tracks.

"Let *go* of me!" I shouted.

In answer, he shook me. Then I recalled that I, while not precisely armed, did have a couple of weapons at my disposal. So I gave him a huge kick in the back of one of his knees (don't know which one), grabbed a pencil from my pocket and stabbed him in his big fat neck.

I think the kick buckled whichever knee I'd whacked. I know the pencil hurt going in because he roared. Have I mentioned that I always keep my pencils sharp in order to be ready to take dictation? Well, I do.

And then came the galloping of horses' hooves. I don't know if ancient Greeks shod their horses, but Arnie apparently shod some of the ones he was paid to watch. Frank let my arm go in time for me to whirl around and witness a gigantic brown horse smack right into Vic Bedini and Vicky/Verna. As the two of them fell to the ground, the horse then whipped his head around—it happened so fast, I couldn't tell for sure, but I'm sure Arnie pulled on its reins—and walloped Frank so fiercely, he wobbled back about a pace and half and fell, hard, on his butt.

"Mercy! Mercy, are you all right?"

"Lulu, you saved my life!" As soon as she got close enough to me, I staggered to her and threw my arms around her. "That man had a *gun!*"

"I was so scared!" said Lulu. "But he doesn't have his gun any longer." To prove it, she shook off my arms and ran the few paces to where Frank still sat, stunned and bleeding from the pencil stuck in his neck, and scooped up the gun. It must have been heavy because Lulu said, "Uff!"

"Yew ladies owl rawt?" A concerned Arnie slipped from the big brown horse and ran to Lulu and me.

"Yes, but don't let those people get away," I said panting. Lordy, I was glad I'd stopped Frank from kidnapping me, but I hoped he wouldn't get lead poisoning from that pencil tip.

What am I *saying?* I hoped he'd *die* of lead poisoning!

Cranky, wasn't I?

"Gimme that hawgleg," barked Arnie. He snatched the gun from Lulu's loose grip and pointed at the three people clustered at the flap of the tent. A couple of Arnie's colleagues had raced over to help him subdue the threat, one of them on horseback and the other on foot.

Hawgleg? I'd ask later. "Can you keep these three people subdued until we can get help here?" I asked Arnie. "Thank you *so* much for your assistance."

"Shore," said Arnie. "Lenny, kin yew take one o' these ladies to whar they kin find hep?"

"Sure thing, Arnie," said a freckled, good-looking fellow whom I presumed to be Lenny. He rode one of those golden-colored horses with the white manes. The horse's coat gleamed in the sunlight.

"Good. Git a couple more o' the guys from yonder to keep these here folks from runnin' away first."

"Will do," said the obliging Lenny.

"With hosses," added Arnie. "And rope. Might as well tie 'em up."

"Will do," Lenny said again.

I watched him trot to the fence, where all the horses and several other young men stood watching the excitement. As soon as Lenny gave the fellows Arnie's instructions, four or five of them leaped upon convenient mounts. I noticed that, while the horses had no saddles or proper reins, they did have...I don't know what to call them. Leading strings? I think those are for babies. Whatever they were, the cowboys handled the horses like champs, and a small herd of them soon surrounded our little group.

"Owl rawt," said Arnie once the three villains—I was only assuming they were all villains—were sitting together and not moving. "Lenny, you take one o' these ladies to whar they need t'go. Joe and Hank, tie these people up. The gal, too."

"No!" squealed Vicky/Verna.

"Hush up!" I told her, sounding so much like my mother, everyone standing around straightened. I think it was Hank who picked up some rope and saluted me. Crumb. Nobody to my knowledge had ever saluted my mother. I'd better watch it, or I might turn into somebody I wouldn't care for.

Lulu and I exchanged a glance. Then it was I remembered my

lost wig. My hands instantly went to my poor head. I couldn't see myself, but I must have cut an outlandish figure.

"You go, Lulu. I don't want to see anybody like this."

"What happened to the wig?" asked Lulu.

I pointed to Frank and hoped my mother in Boston would have a fit because of it.

"*He* happened to it. I think he pulled out half my hair at the same time."

"It's not that bad," said Lulu, although her expression revealed concern. "Here. Use this comb. Just comb it out, and it'll be okay. Good thing you had it bobbed recently."

"I guess." I took the comb. "Thanks, Lulu."

"Not a problem," said Lulu. She turned to Lenny. "I guess you'll have to take me to where the boss is."

"They's in Helen's bedroom," said Arnie.

"Boudoir," I corrected, pedant that I was.

"Her bood-war," said Arnie, giving me a look that asked what the difference was. I didn't bother telling him.

"Sure, ma'am. Will you please take my hand?" Lenny leaned over, took Lulu's extended hand, and helped her onto the horse's back. To my surprise, he lifted her in the air and plopped her in front of himself. I always thought people rode behind the folks holding the reins, although I have no idea why. I blame it on all the Western flickers I'd seen in my youth. Anyhow, the beautiful golden horse didn't have a saddle on him, if that makes any difference.

Lulu wasn't quite as unprepared for a horseback ride as I, but she dropped her stack of papers and uttered an indelicate, "Oof" when she landed on the horse's back. I think the horse would have "oofed" too, had it been able.

Then she realized her stocking-clad legs were showing and tried tugging her skirt down to cover her garters, at least. "Oh, Lord," she said, sending me a beseeching look. "Don't look, anybody!"

"You ready, ma'am?" asked Lenny politely.

"Y-yes," said Lulu. I feared she might cry. Lulu, formerly of the outrageously flamboyant colors and platinum-blond hair!

But Lenny gently kicked his golden horse, and it galloped off in what I expected was the direction of Helen's boudoir. My sense of geography is almost as bad as my ability with algebra. Mind you, I'd kind of liked geometry when we could draw pictures with our compasses and protractors and prove theorems. I worked better with pictures and words than I did with numbers.

Dang. I've strayed off the subject again, haven't I?

"Owl raht, ma'am," Arnie said to me, still holding the three criminals at bay with Frank's gun. "You want me just ta keep these owlhoots from movin'? They's all tied up, thanks to Hank and Joe."

Owlhoots? Hawglegs and owlhoots. Good heavens.

"Yes, please," I said. "Don't let any of them move an inch. They're responsible for lots of the trouble going on here, including a death, and we can't let them get away."

"Yas'm," said Arnie.

Boy, he meant his word too! When Frank lifted a hand, I presume to take the pencil out of his neck, Arnie barked, "Stahp it!" and fired another bullet into the ground, this one barely missing one of Frank's feet.

"But she stabbed me!" said Frank after executing a fairly good sitting high jump and sounding panicky. "With a *pencil*! Pencils got lead in them!"

"So do bullets," said Arnie, who was quickly becoming my hero. "We'll let the doc take kere o' yew, soon's he gits here."

"But I didn't do anything!" cried Vicky/Verna, sobbing. A whole lot of mascara dripped down her cheeks along with her tears.

"You did, too," I snapped. "You escaped from your guards, you got involved with my idiot brother, you took money from my parents under false pretenses and you're in league with *him*!" I pointed at Vic Bedini. "What's your name, anyhow?" I went on. "I already know it's not Verna Borden, because Mr. Bedini calls you Vicky."

"Oh, shit," muttered Vicky/Verna. My goodness. Until that moment, I don't believe I'd ever heard a young woman say such a word aloud.

"Now that jist ain't perlite," said Arnie, frowning fiercely at the woman.

"Your brother? Your *parents*?" Mr. Bedini said staring at me, agog.

Combing my hair (which hurt, curse it), I said, "Yes. My name is Mercedes Allcutt. George is my idiot brother, and my parents are the imbeciles who paid off that woman in an attempt to get George to behave himself. Which was stupid of all three of them. On the other hand, the woman is just as bad as they are if she's taken to gambling all her money away with gangsters and sabotaging the Nash Studio set. Now you've taken a man's life! You're all murderers, as far as I'm concerned."

"Z'at raht, ma'am? Why, you durned owlhoots," said Arnie. "You done kilt a man! We don't take kindly to that sort o' thang in my neck o' the woods."

"I didn't kill anyone!" shrieked Vicky/Verna.

Mr. Bedini and Frank then offered their own repudiations of the charge.

"Mr. Bedini, who is that woman?" I pointed again, and wished someone would take a photograph of me so I could send it to my mother. "What's her name?"

"What's it to you?" growled Mr. Bedini.

I withdrew another pencil from my pocket and wished I'd had more practice with darts in my youth. "A lot," I growled menacingly and held the pencil as I might hold a dart, ready to send it into Mr. Bedini's person. I'd probably miss, but he didn't need to know that.

"Ah kin jess shoot him, ma'am," said Arnie. "You don't need to waste another pencil on him."

"*No!*" bellowed Mr. Bedini.

"Don't you *dare*, Vic!" the woman screeched back at him.

"Aw, screw it. Who cares at this point?" asked Frank. I think he was worried about that pencil in his neck. I sure hoped so. "She's Vicky Bedini, Vic's sister, and she's a pain in the ass. She's in with some fellows in New York City. I'm here to help her. Some of the guys in New York think they need to get into the picture business. Like I said, she's a pain in the ass."

"Clean up yer lang-gwige in front o' the lady!" snapped Arnie.

Rustlings came from the other people on horseback. I glanced at them and saw them all staring daggers at Frank. For heaven's sake, I might well be witnessing some sort of Code of the West behavior. It was permitted to shoot an owlhoot with one's hawgleg, but it was forbidden to swear in front of a woman considered a lady. Interesting. I'd have to read up on the phenomenon, if it was one.

"But Vicky, that's not what you told me. You said you owed money to Sabatini!" whined Vic Bedini.

My brain stopped listening as soon as the name Sabatini left Mr. Bedini's mouth. I absolutely *loved* Mr. Rafael Sabatini's books. I couldn't imagine Mr. Sabatini, the author, having anything to do with Mr. Sabatini, the gangster. Then again, as ever, what did I know?

"She told me she got mixed up with that rich kid and blew all her money on the tables," said Mr. Bedini.

"You're her kin," said Frank. "Family's family. You owe one, you owe 'em all."

I wished to heck the police would show up. I'd managed to comb my hair, but I had no idea what I looked like. Probably a dusty female person with strange hair. Crumb. This wasn't what I envisioned when I thought about being a P.I.'s assistant.

Finally we heard the roar of engines! The horse pasture was at the far end of the set, so it took time for Lenny to ride Lulu to Helen's boudoir and explain things. Glad it didn't take any longer. I'd begun to feel frazzled. And really, *really* itchy.

And there they were! Two cars marked SECURITY on their sides screeched to a stop on the road, creating a dust storm I tried to bat away from my eyes. And there were three police cars! Oh, yay. And there was Ernie's Packard-Six! And Lenny rode the fabulous golden horse at a gallop several yards behind the automobiles. Lulu must have grabbed a ride in a car, because she no longer sat in front of Lenny on the horse.

The dust flung up by the automobile tires was so thick, it was difficult to see anything. Because I feared a villain attempting escape, I edged toward where the three scoundrels were. Darned near bumped into Arnie.

"Beg pardon," I said. "I can't see."

"S'all right, ma'am," said the amiable Arnie. "They ain't moved none."

"Ah, good."

"*Mercy!*" I heard Ernie roar.

Squinting, I could barely make out his driver's side door opening and him leaping out of the Packard. Because Lulu raced around the back of Ernie's machine, I figured she'd ridden with him.

"I'm here!" I called. Then I spat out dust. They really ought to pave this place. Or at least water it so the dust wouldn't blow up into people's faces all the stupid time.

Lulu careened into me, and we hugged each other hard. Then Ernie barreled into both of us and we all three shared an embrace.

"Cripes, Mercy, Lulu said you stabbed that Frank fellow with a pencil," said Ernie. "Are you out of your mind?"

Well, of all the nerve!

"He was manhandling me, Mr. Ernest Templeton! I kneecapped him from behind and made him fall. I stabbed him in the neck with a pencil, because a pencil was the only weapon I had with me, and his neck was the only thing I could reach."

Lulu backed out of our threesome and attempted to get her own windblown hair out of her face. That left me alone in Ernie's arms. I wouldn't have minded if he hadn't continued to scold.

"Lulu told us he had a *gun*! And you conquered him with a *pencil?*"

"And a kick to the back of one of his knees. I don't know which one. Why are you yelling at *me*? I'm not the bad guy here!"

"No. You're not a bad guy," said Ernie, no longer bellowing at me. "I'm not convinced of your sanity, though."

"Stop berating my sister-in-law, Ernie," said Harvey, looming toward us through the rapidly falling dust. "She's a heroine."

"She's an idiot," grumbled Ernie.

So I kicked the back of one of his knees, too, just to show him. He crumpled to the ground and hollered, "Hey!"

I didn't care.

TWENTY

After what seemed like forever, the police put handcuffs on Mr. Vic Bedini, Miss Vicky Bedini, and Mr. Frank Sabatini. I don't know if he belonged to the same family of gangsters that owned the speakeasies and gambling establishments in which Miss Bedini claimed she had lost all her money. I also didn't care at that point.

"Mr. Nash," said a portly policeman in a gray uniform with an L.A.P.D. badge pinned to his chest. "Would you like us to take these three to the station, or would you prefer we question them in your office. I expect you have many questions you need answers to."

How come he was asking *Harvey* where he wanted the police to question the crooks? This didn't seem proper to me. As usual, I had to open my mouth and say so. I swear, I just can't seem to keep mum sometimes.

After squinting at the policeman's badge, I saw it had "Sergeant" engraved on it. "Do you always question suspected criminals in the places where they've committed their crimes, Sergeant? I thought you had to haul them down to a police station and question them there."

Everybody in the group turned to look at me, even Ernie, who had risen and was dusting off his trousers. He didn't appear pleased with me. It was embarrassing. On the other hand, my question was a serious one and I wanted clarification. "I only wondered. When Ernie was suspected of a crime, the L.A.P.D. didn't hesitate to haul him down to a police station. They sure didn't interview him in the deceased woman's home."

"Yeah," said Lulu. "And when you arrested my brother Rupert, you didn't bother questioning him at Mr. Easthope's house. You just handcuffed him and drove him away as if you'd already tried and convicted him."

"And then there was Charley Wu," I said. "You popped him in a cell and didn't even *try* to find other possible suspects."

"True," said Lulu. "And you pinned a murder on poor Calvin Buck, who wasn't even at the scene of the crime when it was committed."

"That's right," I said, "And—"

"Cut it out you two," said Ernie, raising his voice, I presume in an attempt to drown out Lulu and me. "If you haven't figured out by this time that the L.A.P.D. works in different ways for different people, you're both stupider than I thought. Don't rile the coppers, okay? You're not helping."

My lip curled all by itself.

Lulu said, "Phooey."

I noticed she'd removed her stockings. Didn't blame her. I'm sure my own stockings had ladders long enough to climb a wall with. I don't think that makes any sense. Oh, who cares?

"You don't want these guys to get away with ruining Harvey's studio, do you?" Ernie's voice remained louder than usual.

After heaving a sigh and regretting it—dust still lingered in a fuzzy pall around us—I decided this probably wasn't the time to air my grievances against the L.A.P.D. It riled me that they treated poor people and people of color differently from those with heaps of money; however, as I'd already learned to my sorrow, I couldn't change the world.

"Ahem," said the sergeant. "Mr. Nash?"

Harvey gave me a tight grin and answered the copper. "Please take them to my office. I'll get a few of the people who have been affected by the disturbances to join us. Thank you for your consideration."

The sergeant didn't even bother with a grin. He scowled at me and said, "Thanks, Mr. Nash. We'll drive these folks to your office."

"Thank you," said Harvey.

"Nertz," I muttered as they stuffed the two men into the back of one police car and the woman in the back of the other. The latter scenario bothered me. "Somebody else had better go with the female Bedini creature. Men can't be trusted around her."

Ernie turned to Harvey. "She's got a point, Harvey."

"Yes," said Harvey. "She does." Guess he'd forgiven me for abducting his conversation with the sergeant. "Will you go with her, Ernie?"

"I've got to drive my own car," said Ernie.

"Lulu and I can sit in the backseat of the police car," I suggested. Darned if I wanted him to be on his own with that evil siren. "She'll be in the middle, and there's no way she can sweet talk us into letting her go for any reason at all. Ever."

"Good idea," said Harvey, giving me a real smile this time. "Thanks, Mercy and Lulu. You sure you don't mind, Ernie?"

"Naw. It's fine with me," said Ernie, giving me a squint that told me he knew the motivation behind my suggestion and would tease me about it later. Huh.

So with the sergeant—whose name I couldn't read on his badge—barking orders to his subordinates, Lulu and I walked to the police car in which Victoria Bedini sat. She gave us each a hideous scowl. Well, as hideous as she could manage which wasn't very. The ghastly woman was a true beauty even with her face smeared with mascara. Looking at her gorgeous face made me want to pat my hair to feel how much of it I'd lost, but I didn't.

"What are you two doing here?" she snarled at Lulu and me. "They arresting you, too? I hope so."

"Nope," I said, trying to sound breezy. "We didn't think you should be left alone with a couple of men whom you might twist to do your will as you did earlier today. You can't charm Lulu or me." I gave her a smile that was meant to be breezy too, but I doubt it succeeded well. I was filthy, exhausted, half my hair had been pulled out by the roots, and my face itched even more now that the makeup Lulu had smeared on it had dust stuck to it.

"That's the truth," said Lulu. "You're one of those…what do you call them, Mercy? A temptation?"

"A temptress. More like a succubus, I'd say, but apparently she's not very good at her job. If she were *really* good at it, she'd have saved all the money she stole from stupid people like my brother and my parents and would be living in luxury in some foreign country."

"Shut up," snarled Miss Bedini. "You're only jealous."

"*Jealous!*" screeched Lulu. "Why, you stuck-up witch! Who'd want to be like *you?*"

"Really," I said. "You must not have any talent, because you *do* have looks. But if you need to pander to people like my idiot brother, I'd rather be plain old me."

"Yeah," said Lulu. "Mercy may not be gorgeous, but she's real nice and she has Ernie."

I could have lived happily for the rest of my life without hearing Lulu tell this vamp how un-gorgeous I was, but I'd never let on. Besides, she was right about Ernie. At least I hoped she was. After today's events, I was no longer certain.

Stupid day.

"Huh," said Miss Bedini. "You don't know what you're talking about."

"Unless your brother and Mr. Sabatini were both lying, we know precisely what we're talking about," I growled.

"Yeah," said Lulu,

Miss Bedini's hands were cuffed behind her back, but she had free use of her feet. She used her right foot to stamp on Lulu's nearest foot and her left to stamp on mine.

"Ow!" I yelled.

"Yow!" Lulu yelled.

As neither Lulu's nor my hands were encumbered with cuffs, we took the opportunity to use them to trap Miss Bedini's feet by confiscating and using one of Lulu's stockings, which she'd cleverly stuck in a pocket of her ugly black dress. Miss Bedini tried to struggle, but I threatened her with a pencil and she calmed down.

The policeman behind the wheel said, "What's going on back there?"

"Not a thing, Officer," I told him.

Miss Bedini opened her mouth to say something, but Lulu snapped her arm with one of her garter clips and I held a pencil in front of her face as if I aimed to stab her, so she didn't say it. I think the awful girl was afraid of Lulu and me! Fancy that. I was proud of us.

It didn't take long for the police car to arrive at Harvey's studio office. The other police car was already there, and we saw several policemen escorting Bedini and Sabatini ungently to the door. I noticed my pencil still sticking out of Sabatini's neck. Gosh, I hadn't realized I'd shoved it in so far.

Miss Bedini couldn't walk because Lulu and I had tied her feet together. I didn't care. "Lulu," I said. "Will you please take Miss Bedini's right shoulder? I'll go around the automobile and take the other one. She can hop to Harvey's office with us holding her up."

"Sure," said Lulu. She sounded pleased with my suggestion.

"Dammit, you can't do that!" screeched Miss Bedini.

"Watch us," said Lulu in a deadlier tone than I'd heard from her in a long time.

"Officer!" hollered Miss Bedini. "Officer, they can't *do* this to me!"

Ernie pulled up in his Packard-Six as Lulu and I were dragging Miss Bedini out of the police car. He bolted from behind the driver's seat and ran over to us.

"What's going on here?" he demanded. He saw Miss Bedini's bound feet and said, "How'd she get her legs tied up?"

"She attempted to inflict bodily harm on Lulu and me," I said, only then realizing she'd done more than attempt. "In fact, she hurt us! My foot is probably broken." I glanced at Lulu. "What about you, Lulu?"

"Hurts, but I don't think she broke anything," said Lulu, looking and sounding grim.

"How'd she do that?" asked a puzzled Ernie.

"She stomped on our feet," I said.

Ernie took a good look at the undoubtedly strange picture we three females presented, tilted his head to one side and said, "That wasn't very nice, Miss Bedini. But you don't have to help her, Mercy and Lulu. I'll take care of the lady."

"She's not a lady!" I barked.

"I know," said Ernie, picking Miss Bedini up from the police car's backseat and flinging her over his shoulder in what I believe is called a "fireman's hold."

"*No!*" Miss Bedini shrieked.

"Oh, shut up," I told her. "At least this way you don't have to hop."

Lulu and I followed Ernie and his captive into Harvey's building.

"Mercy Allcutt and Lulu LaBelle, you two slay me," said Ernie as he entered the building. Two uniforms had kindly opened the door for him.

Lulu and I hurried after him before the officers could shut us out. I was pleased to see Ernie dump Miss Bedini—roughly—onto a wooden chair in front of Harvey's gigantic desk.

"Ow," said Miss Bedini. "Damn you."

"You have an ugly mouth, Miss Bedini," said Ernie. He turned around, saw Lulu and me, came over and led us to a sofa at a far end of the room. He sat in the middle and took my hand, which I appreciated.

Two police officers sat in chairs on either side of Miss Bedini. Mr. Bedini sat next to one of the officers. Another stood behind him. Mr. Sabatini was in another corner of the room—which was huge—and it looked to me as if a medical professional had been called in to take care of Mr. Sabatini's pencil wound.

"Too bad," said Ernie, giving my hand a squeeze. "Guess we won't get rid of him as easily as we did Mr. Septicemia in Chinatown last year."

"Who is this 'we' of whom you speak, Ernie Templeton," I grumbled. "I had to haul you into that case, and it was one of those poor captive Chinese women who shot the son of a b-gun." Good Lord, I'd almost used a bad word. Being around Miss Bedini was clearly unhealthy for me.

Squeezing my hand a little too tightly, Ernie grinned and said, "Yeah, yeah. I know, but let's not fight about it now. We need to listen to what those three have to say for themselves."

I huffed, but I shut up. I felt awful. My head hurt, and I was sure I was getting at least a rash if not hives from all the greasepaint and dust on my face.

Harvey sat in his big chair behind his desk, the sergeant stood to attention beside the desk, and Sidney Lafayette sat on an edge of the desk. After the medic had attended to Mr. Sabatini, wrapping a bandage around his neck, he was escorted to another chair a couple of coppers dragged over. All three crooks were still handcuffed, which was as it should have been.

After clearing his throat, Harvey said, "Sergeant, will you please question these people? We need to know if we have a traitor on the set. They've somehow been able to gain access to what is supposed to be a closely guarded production."

"Well?" growled the sergeant, giving all three criminals a sharp stare. "Who'd you bribe to get onto the set here?"

"Nobody!" said Vic Bedini. "I didn't even know Frank and Vicky were here until they showed up in my tent out by the horse pasture."

"Is that the truth?" the sergeant demanded of Miss Bedini.

"I didn't bribe anybody," she said.

"No comment," snarled Mr. Sabatini.

"You'd better cooperate with us," said the sergeant. "A man's dead, and we'll charge the three of you with murder in the first if none of you will spill the beans."

"Don't forget George," I said from my seat on the sofa. Ernie squeezed my hand again, hard. I glared at him.

"That's right. I forgot about George," said Harvey. "How did *he* get onto the set?"

"I don't know," said Vicky Bedini. "I was trying to get away from him, but this morning he showed up where we were going to shoot the scene in Helen's boudoir."

"How convenient for you," said Ernie. He let go of my hand, ambled over to the desk and sat on the opposite edge from Sid Lafayette. "You'd be smart to tell the coppers what you know, Miss Bedini. Coppers tend to go easy on ladies," he said, then added, "Not that the noun fits you."

"What's he mean?" Vicky asked, frowning at her brother.

"He means you're a slut," said Frank Sabatini. "Which makes you no lady."

"Why you—" Vicky tried to rise from her chair, but her escorts didn't allow her to do so. She finally settled for saying to Ernie, "You bastard!"

Ernie tutted. "Such language."

"Oh, go chase yourself," muttered Vicky.

"Be quiet, Vicky," advised her brother. "If you don't tell them the truth, I'll tell them as much of it as I know. I don't know everything, but you and Frank do."

"Maybe we'd better hear more from you, Vic," said Harvey, looking sad. "I never expected treachery from someone I trusted."

"I'm sorry, Mr. Nash," said a plainly miserable Vic Bedini. "But she's my *sister*."

"She not a very nice one," observed Ernie. "She's got looks, but she doesn't seem to have much of anything else except a dirty tongue."

"I hate you," growled Vicky.

Her words made me smile. Guess I didn't have to worry about her when it came to Ernie.

A nudge from Lulu made me turn and look at her. She appeared concerned. "What's the matter, Lulu?" I whispered, not wanting to interrupt the questioning.

"I think you have a rash, Mercy. Your skin is all red. Well, what I can see of it."

"Crumb. I itch too," I muttered.

Lulu rose from her chair. "Mr. Nash, Ernie, Mercy's not well. I think we'd better get her home."

"What?" Ernie slid off the edge of the desk and rushed over to the sofa, where he knelt before me and stared at my face. "Good God, what's the matter with you?"

Scowling, I said, "I think it's the makeup and dust. And he"—I pointed at Frank Sabatini—"pulled most of my hair out when he yanked off my wig. I hope he dies of lead poisoning!"

And then I humiliated myself by bursting into tears.

TWENTY-ONE

Ernie decided to leave questioning the three villains to the police and Harvey. He hauled out a hankie and tried to dry my tears. As his handkerchief was quite dusty, he didn't have much success. In actual fact, the dust made my condition worse. As I'd already made a fool of myself, I didn't say so. Not that I could have spoken, what with crying and all.

"Let's get you back to the Nash place," he said. And darned if he didn't scoop me up from the sofa and head for the door of Harvey's office. Turning, he told Harvey, "You should get a secretary or stenographer in here to take notes before you ask any more questions."

Although the sergeant frowned at him, Harvey said, "You're right, Ernie. Thank you."

Before we headed out of his office, I saw him press a button on his desk. Guess he was summoning secretarial help. I'd ask him later.

When we returned to Chloe and Harvey's place, it turned out that Lulu and I were correct about the state of my face. According to reports from Molly and Chloe, it was a brighter red than they'd ever seen on a human, even No-Name Nash when she was screaming.

"Good Lord, Mercy, what happened to you?" Chloe asked, staring at me in horror after Molly opened the door and Ernie carried me into the house. Lulu made it on her own two feet.

"The motion-picture industry," I said, my words still thickish because I was finding it difficult to stop crying. That's because gunk kept finding its way to my poor swollen eyes. "I swear, I'll never wear makeup again."

"You don't need to go that far," said Lulu. "But gee, I'm sorry you had a reaction to the stuff I used on you."

"It's all right," I said, snuffling.

"Want me to take you up to your room?" Ernie asked. "You'll probably need a bubble bath or something."

"Good heavens, yes!" said Chloe. "I'll have Molly bring you some soothing creams and lotions. I've got some Pond's vanishing cream and some Woodbury's cold cream.

And you probably need calamine lotion for the rash. Oh, Mercy, I'm so sorry!"

"It's all right," I said, not sniffling quite so much.

"Let's take the elevator," suggested Ernie, still carrying me.

I appreciated him a whole lot just then. Yes, I could have walked up the stairs, and I could have ridden the elevator on my own, but it felt *so* good to have him carry me.

The elevator clunked to a stop on the second floor, and Ernie carried me to my room. I decided I'd milked my discomfort long enough. "You can just leave me at the door, Ernie. Thank you for c-c-carrying me." Stupid tears came again.

"Don't be an idiot," he said in an un-lover-like tone. "You look like you've crawled through a field of poison ivy."

"You really do, Mercy. I'm so sorry! I shouldn't have used the stuff that was on the floor," said Lulu, who sounded as if she too might begin crying any minute.

"Stuff from the floor?" asked Chloe, sounding horrified some more.

"We'll tell you about it later," I said."

Chloe swerved from Ernie, Lulu, and me. "Molly, please help me get a basket of skin-care products for Mercy to use. I've never seen anything like that in my life."

"Yes, ma'am. And maybe Nurse Hall will have a suggestion. She's really good at caring for people's skin."

"Wonderful idea," said Chloe.

Lulu turned the knob on my bedroom door and Ernie carried me inside. He plunked me down on a chair in front of the fireplace, not in use on this pleasant day. Well, it was pleasant except for my own personal misery.

"You and Lulu go on into the bathroom, Mercy," Ernie ordered. "I'll send in whoever comes to rescue you when she gets here."

"Thanks, Ernie," said Lulu. "Come on, Mercy."

By then, my eyes were so swollen, I could hardly see, so I appreciated Lulu's gentle hand on my arm.

"Sit down here," she said, guiding me to a chintz-covered bench in front of the vanity table's mirror. The bathrooms in the Nash residence weren't your typical convenience chambers. The bathtub itself was in a tiled recess and had a step one had to climb to get into it. The vanity table already boasted an array of creams, lotions and talcum powders on it for the benefit of guests. The tiles were cold, but they were a soft blue color that didn't *look* especially cold. Anyway, there were pretty mats to stand on here and there.

"Thanks, Lulu," I said.

"Don't thank me," she said. "I'm the one who did this to you! I'm *so* sorry, Mercy!"

"It's not your fault," I whimpered. "It's whatever was in that makeup."

"It might have been contaminated when the hut was ransacked."

What a delightful thought. I didn't say so.

"But here," said Lulu. "Let me get the top of your dress unbuttoned. You don't want to get cold cream on it."

She proceeded to unbutton my dress, although I didn't really care what happened to the stupid dress. Nevertheless, Lulu unbuttoned it from the back and drew it down from my shoulders so that it puddled at my waist. I wore a satin bandeau with straps, so at least I wasn't totally naked, although I'd begun feeling frightfully exposed. I scolded myself as a prig and then told myself I already had enough problems without inventing more. Lulu was my friend.

A couple of sets of running feet preceded Molly and Nurse Hall's entrance to the bathroom.

"Oh, good heavens," said Nurse Hall. "Here. Miss LaBelle, please let me take your place next to Miss Allcutt."

"Sure," said Lulu, popping up from the other end of the bench. I couldn't see much because of my eye situation, but Lulu seemed distressed.

"Very well," said Nurse Hall, efficient as ever. "The first thing I'm going to do is scrape a little of this makeup off your face using this tongue depressor. I'll analyze it and try to find out what's causing your rash."

I made a whimper of consent.

Nurse Hall continued, "Then I'm going to drape a towel over your shoulders. The next thing we need to do is clean your face. Soap and water might be too harsh, so I'm going to use a mixture I made myself."

"You *made* it?" I asked, wishing she'd just use the Pond's Cold Cream Chloe had mentioned. I used that and knew it to be soothing. I wasn't sure about any homemade concoctions.

"There's no need to worry." Nurse Hall chuckled. "It's benign and *very* good for damaged skin."

Damaged Skin? Oh Lord, I didn't want damaged skin!

"I make it myself with water, beeswax, and a little almond oil—I prefer the almond scent to rosewater, although you can use rosewater if you decide to make it yourself."

As if I'd ever make it myself!

She went on, "Oh, and you need a teensy bit of borax for the cleansing effect."

I think I squeaked something like, "Oh," but I'm not sure. I was petrified in terror, fearing I'd come out of this adventure looking like a wicked witch from one of Grimm's grimmer fairy tales.

"This is very gentle, but it will get that awful dusty makeup off in no time," said the nurse in a soothing voice. I think she knew she'd be working on a craven coward.

So she stuck a couple of fingers in the jar she held. I couldn't see anything about the jar, not even its color.

"Close your eyes, please," said Nurse Hall.

Not a problem. They were pretty much swollen shut already.

The two fingers she stuck in the jar evidently came out covered with her homemade cleansing cream. With great delicacy, she began smoothing it onto my cheeks, moving up to my closed eyes and to my forehead in a gentle circular motion. Before she began her efforts, my skin felt as if it were on fire, but darned if her home-made cream didn't feel good as she smoothed it on.

I almost relaxed but decided to wait until she was through with me. If I came out of this experience with a bright red bowling ball for a head, I'd probably die of an apoplectic fit and then I'd be relaxed forever without even trying.

"And now I'll dampen this cloth and gently rub away the cleansing cream," the nurse said in a comforting tone. I winced a tiny bit when she touched the cloth to my face. "There's nothing to worry about, Miss Allcutt," she said. "After we get that junk off your face, I'll put some soothing aloe on it."

My lips were pressed tightly together so I couldn't ask her what the heck aloe was.

"Can I help?" asked Lulu, her voice coming from behind me.

"Will you please fill this bowl with cool water?" Nurse Hall asked. "After we get the cream off, I want to splash some water on her face."

I could hardly wait.

"Sure," said Lulu. I heard her turn the tap on the sink next to the vanity table and figured she was doing the nurse's bidding. "Here you go." I felt Lulu place the bowl on the dressing table. Well, I heard the bowl make a gentle clunk too.

"Thank you. Now, Miss Allcutt, will you please bend over a little? I'll direct you so that your face is right above the bowl. Then I'll rinse your face. Please don't open your eyes yet. I want to go through the procedure without getting anything in your eyes. That way we'll be sure to get all the contaminants washed off."

Contaminants? Aw, crumb.

So I moved at her tender touch and, sure enough, she splashed water in my face. Not a whole lot all at once. She splashed a little here and a little there and blotted the places with a soft towel.

"There. Now sit back again, and we'll cleanse your face one more time. After we do that, I'll put some calming aloe juice on your face." I felt her turn away for a second. "Molly, will you please bring that aloe vera plant here and place it on the vanity table?"

"Yes, ma'am," I heard Molly say. I heard her walk away, and a few minutes later, return.

"That looks spiky," said Lulu, making me twitch again. "You're not going to stab her, are you? She already looks kind of like a ripe tomato."

As I was a prisoner and could open neither my eyes nor my mouth, all I could do was squeak in alarm.

Nurse Hall laughed merrily. And why not? It wasn't *her* face turning into a mutant tomato.

"Heavens no," she said. "I'm going to cut off one of those spikes, run a little knife down it and use the juice I gather to spread on Miss Allcutt's face. Aloe is an amazing plant. It's been used for centuries. Why, according to history books, Cleopatra herself used aloe on her face." After another chuckle or two, she said, "I imagine even Helen of Troy used it."

"Golly," said Lulu. "Really?"

"Really," said the nurse, and she began smoothing her home-made cleansing cream onto my face again.

I almost hate to admit this because I've already proved myself to be a spineless weakling, but that stuff felt good on my face. My poor cheeks had been itching and burning for hours, and the itch had traveled down to my neck and up to my brows. However, when she began her second session with her lightly almond-scented cream, I think I might have purred if I were a cat.

"Miss LaBelle?" said Nurse Hall after cleaning the second bout of cream from my face, "will you please refill the water in the bowl?"

"Sure," said Lulu. "Boy, that stuff you made must really work. Poor Mercy doesn't look as if she's going to catch fire anymore."

Thanks a lot, I didn't say because I couldn't. I did find Lulu's words slightly comforting though.

"There," said a satisfied-sounding Nurse Hall. "Now keep your eyes shut. I'm going to slather aloe juice on your poor face."

So I kept my eyes shut. Not sure I ever wanted to open them again although, according to Lulu, I no longer looked as awful as I had when we'd come home. I heard a snap, a happy sigh from the nurse, and then felt a cool moist liquid being smeared over my tortured countenance.

"Wow," said Molly. "I didn't know you could break those spikes and they'd have juice in them."

"Me neither," said Lulu, sounding very nearly awestruck. Or should that be awestricken? Bother.

"You have to scrape the juice from them a little," said the nurse, "but it has amazing power to heal burned flesh."

Burned flesh?

"Did I really burn her?" asked Lulu whose voice now sounded merely stricken.

"No, you didn't," Nurse Hall assured her. "But she had an allergic reaction to something in whatever was on her face, and it was also covered with dust. Dust isn't good for anyone."

"I'm really sorry," said Lulu for the umpteenth time. "I should have used my own makeup instead of the stuff we found in that shack."

"I think Miss Allcutt will be as good as new soon," said the nurse.

"Really?" asked Lulu.

"Indeed."

"That cold cream you made must be really good," Molly said.

"I'll be happy to give you the recipe," said the nurse.

"Thanks," said Molly. "And I didn't know that spiky plant was good for anything at all, much less healing people."

"It's good for some things," Nurse Hall temporized. "It won't heal a broken bone or anything of that nature, but it's excellent for this sort of thing."

Jeepers, I'd always wanted to be *this sort of thing*. Again, I spoke not. Couldn't. I was still being smeared with some kind of plant nectar. Juice. Whatever plants have in them.

"There," said the nurse with satisfaction. "We'll just sit for a minute or two and let the aloe dry. Then I'll gently wash it off and rub some of my special cold cream on your face, Miss Allcutt. You'll be as good as new soon."

I finally dared open my mouth. Nothing nasty dripped into it. "How soon?"

All the ladies in the bathroom except yours truly laughed. I didn't think anything that had happened that day was the least bit funny, darn it!

TWENTY-TWO

Perhaps fifteen minutes after Nurse Hall had begun working on my abused skin, the ordeal was over. The very last thing she did before allowing me to open my eyes—I wasn't yet sure I could even do that—was to wash off the dried aloe-vera juice, pat my face dry with a soft cloth, and then rub some of her special cold cream on all the parts of me that had felt burn-y. She took special care around my eyes.

"We need to be sure nothing gets into your eyes," she said. She was approximately eight hours too late with her warning, but I didn't say so. "I'm sure a boric-acid rinse will help them along, but you should wait until tomorrow for that."

"How are things going in here?" came Chloe's voice from afar. Well, it wasn't all that afar. I suspect she was standing in the doorway to the bathroom.

"Pretty well," said Lulu.

"*Very* well," said Nurse Hall. "Poor Miss Allcutt had a terrible reaction to something she had on her face."

"It was my fault," said Lulu. "I'm the one who smeared that stuff on her."

"You didn't know she'd have a reaction to it," said Nurse Hall.

I heard a baby burp and realized Chloe'd brought No-Name with her. "Don't be silly, Lulu," Chloe said in her musical voice. "We all know you'd never do anything to hurt Mercy on purpose."

"I guess," whimpered Lulu. She sounded close to tears again. "I just feel so *guilty*."

"Aw, it's all right," said Chloe. "Here, why don't you hold the baby for a little while? That might calm you."

"Oh, thank you, Chloe."

I heard relief and gratitude in Lulu's voice. I contemplated asking what she'd do to calm me but didn't for fear she'd take the baby from Lulu and hand it over to me. I'd already come to the conclusion that I was an unnatural female human being. No-Name baby—probably any baby—would be more likely to drive me insane than calm me. If I needed calming, I'd take a comfy chair before the fireplace, Buttercup on my lap, a rip-roaring book to read and a cup of Darjeeling tea to sip. Ernie could be there too, as long as he didn't talk.

"Here you go," I heard Chloe say.

"Oh, you sweet thing," cooed Lulu. I heard her walk from the bathroom to the sitting room in my suite.

"I'm going to dab just a little bit of this eye salve on your eyelids and under your eyes, Miss Allcutt. Then I recommend you take a bath to get the rest of the dust off you. After your bath, I recommend using some of the powder I made for the baby." She laughed. I have no idea why. "It's totally pure. I make it from cornstarch, arrowroot powder, rice flower, and several drops of lavender oil. Then you need to lie down for a while. I'm going to send Molly up with some cucumber slices to put over your poor swollen eyes. Cucumbers are excellent when it comes to soothing swollen eyes."

"Yes, I read about cucumber slices in a magazine," said Chloe. She walked over until I felt her stand beside me. "Oh, Mercy, you poor thing."

Bravely daring, I opened my mouth and spoke. "Do I still look awful?"

"Not as awful as you did, but I think you'd be wise to follow Nurse Hall's advice."

"I will," I said.

"What's going on in here?" came Ernie's voice from my sitting room. "Is Chloe in the bathroom with Mercy? Why are you holding the baby, Lulu?"

"Chloe said I could," Lulu answered, sounding defensive. "I was upset because I hurt Mercy. The baby is helping settle my nerves."

"Yeah? Interesting."

His footsteps came closer, and I used my voice again. "Don't look at me! Stay out there!"

"Cripes, Mercy, I'm not the big bad wolf, you know."

"I don't want you to see me like this," I told him.

Both Nurse Hall and Chloe misunderstood what I meant. Chloe said, "I'll get you a shawl, Mercy. Then you won't be the least little bit indecent."

"I don't *care* about being indecent!" I wailed. "I don't want Ernie to see me looking all red and *ugly*!"

After uttering a soft chuckle, Ernie said, "That bad, is it?" I could tell he now stood at the door of the bathroom.

"Mercy is modest," said Chloe in the same voice she used to use on me when she'd call me dowdy.

"Nertz," said Ernie. "I'm really sorry, Mercy. I didn't think you'd actually be in danger when we accepted this job."

"May I open my eyes now?" I asked the nurse.

"Yes, you may. But you still will need to rest them for an hour or so."

"Holy cow," said Ernie. "You really did have a reaction to that makeup, didn't you?"

"Go away," I said.

Ernie, as I should have expected he would, chuckled. "You're going to be as good as new in a few hours, kiddo. Don't fret. We all have problems sometimes."

"I bet you'll never get a rash from wearing makeup," I said bitterly.

"Don't be too sure about that. If I aim to be an ancient Greek nobleman in the flicker, I'll have to wear makeup."

"Not the kind we found in that stupid hut," I said.

"Undoubtedly true," said Ernie. Then he bent and kissed the top of my head. I thought the gesture a sweet one until he added, "Shoot, what happened to your hair? Looks like some of it was pulled out by the roots."

"It was," I said through gritted teeth. "That Sabatini creature ripped the red wig off my head and took half my hair with it."

"It's not all *that* bad," said Ernie uncertainly.

"Ernie," said Chloe. "Come with me. Mercy still needs to bathe and rest. You two can catch up later."

I silently blessed my sister six ways from Sunday. I'm not quite sure what that expression means, but I appreciated her as much in that moment as I'd ever appreciated anyone in my life thus far.

"All right," said Ernie. "Buck up, Mercy. You're going to be fine soon."

"Yes, you will," Chloe confirmed. "You just rest for the afternoon, and maybe Harvey will be able to tell us how things turned out on the set today."

Good heavens, that was right! I'd forgotten all about *Helen of Troy*. In my heart, which seemed to have developed scabs during my day's ordeal, I hoped Miss Victoria Bedini would be hanged as a murderess. Right next to Frank Sabatini.

Not very sweet and kindhearted, was I?

"I'll start your bath for you, Miss Allcutt," said Nurse Hall. "Molly will be up soon to bring you cucumber slices. Would you like me to set out a robe for you or anything?"

"Yes, please. My nightgowns and robes are in the second drawer in the bureau." My stomach growled and I thought of another imperative. "Oh, and will you please have Molly bring me something to eat? I don't know what's available, but crackers and cheese will do if there's nothing else. And some cold water too, please."

"I'll do that right away," said Molly.

"Of course. It *is* late," said Nurse Hall.

"What time is it?" I asked.

"Two-thirty," said Nurse Hall. "I'm sorry you haven't had luncheon yet."

Luncheon. One of my mother's words. I'd struggled for months to shorten the word to *lunch* whenever I said it, but I didn't fault the nurse. She probably had to sound upper-crusty in order to get hired by people like Chloe and Harvey. I caught myself sneering and stopped. Nurse Hall was one of those women who actually had to live on what she earned; none of this was her fault.

"Would you like some bath salts?" she asked next. "We have some sandalwood and some lavender. Mrs. Nash is very generous with her guests, isn't she?"

"Yes," I said. "She is. She's even generous with her sister."

Stop it, Mercy!

"You all right in there?"

I turned on my bench to see Lulu, still carrying the nameless baby in her arms. I couldn't see well yet. My eyes had suffered attacks by makeup and dust and who knew what else that day. She was blurry, but I saw the pink bundle in her arms and knew it to contain No-Name.

"We're fine," I said, trying to curtail my grumpiness. "Will you get out my Chinese pajamas and robe, Lulu? Middle drawer in the dresser."

"I can do that," said the nurse.

Reminding myself that none of this was Nurse Hall's fault, I said sweetly, "That's all right. You're getting my bath ready for me. I feel so pampered." And if that wasn't a big fat lie, I didn't know a lie when I told one.

"Here you go," said Lulu. I saw her waving some gorgeous blue fabric at me.

"Those are the very ones I wanted," I said, feeling grateful for once. "Thanks, Lulu. Would you mind putting them on the bed?"

"Sure," said Lulu, and I heard her walk across the carpeted floor of my sitting room and the rustling of silk as she laid out my afternoon's resting garments.

I turned and tried to focus on the nurse. Couldn't. "And thank you too, Nurse Hall. I wouldn't have known what to do on my own."

"I'm happy to help," said the nurse. "Would you prefer sandalwood or lavender bath salts?"

She'd asked me that before. This time I attempted to sound gracious when I answered her. "Why don't you use the sandalwood? I like the sandalwood soap I buy in Chinatown."

"Sounds lovely," said the nurse. I smelled the soothing scent of sandalwood as she poured the crystals into the tub.

"Would you like to try the bath, Miss Allcutt? Just to see if the temperature is to your liking?"

"Sure," I said. Then I realized I didn't want to take off my bandeau and the rest of my ugly dress and underpinnings and stand naked in front of the nurse or Lulu. "It's all right though. You go on about your duties. I'll fix the bath. Thank you very much, both of you." My brain shrieked, "Prude, prude, prude!" but I didn't care much. I was still suffering, curse it.

"Are you sure?" asked the nurse.

Rather than holler at her, I said politely, "Yes. Thank you." I ungritted my teeth to say, "Please close the door as you leave."

"See you, Mercy," said Lulu. "And I'm still sorry I put that gunk on your face."

"You didn't know I'd have a bad reaction," I said through re-gritted teeth.

"Take as long as you need, Miss Allcutt," said the nurse. "I'll have Molly set the bowl of cucumber slices and your luncheon on your bedside table."

"Better not set it there," I said. "Buttercup might eat my lunch." Then something awful occurred to me. *Buttercup!* I squealed. "Where's my dog? If any of those villains did anything to Butter—"

"It's all right," Lulu said, interrupting me mid-rant. "Buttercup is fine. She was outside playing with Pepper when we came home. I'll have Molly put your lunch on the dresser. You want Buttercup to rest with you, right?"

God bless Lulu LaBelle. "Yes. Thank you, Lulu."

Then finally I was alone in the bathroom, my eyes still burning, but my face feeling a little better. Deciding I didn't really want to scrutinize myself in the mirror before I'd bathed, I disrobed, threw my dirty clothes on the bench upon which I'd been sitting and stuck my toe into the fragrant water in the tub. The temperature was perfect. First time anything perfect had happened all day.

The water felt great on my achy body. My wonderful sister, who truly *did* treat her guests and even her sometimes-troublesome sister like gold, didn't merely stock the bathrooms in her home with a variety of bath salts, she also provided a variety of soaps and shampoos. At home, I generally used plain old Palmolive shampoo, but this day I decided to experiment.

Deciding Canthrox sounded too much like a disease cattle got, I reached for the Gouraud's Oriental Cocoanut Oil Shampoo. What the heck. I was bathing in sandalwood and planned to use some lavender-scented dusting powder. Why not use cocoanut on my poor nearly-bald head? Maybe I'd smell like a spring bouquet if I was lucky and the day ever ended.

I'm not certain how much time I wallowed in that glorious bathtub, but I finally decided I'd dithered enough and climbed out again, pruney all over. Chloe also stocked the softest towels in the universe, so I used one to dry my body and head. Then I wrapped another dry towel around my clean body and nearly suffered a spasm when a light knock came at the bathroom door.

"Yes?" I managed not to scream through sheer luck.

"It's Molly, Miss Allcutt," said Molly. "I just wanted you to know that your lunch is on top of the dresser along with a bowl of cucumber slices, and your sweet Buttercup is waiting for you."

"Bless you, Molly," I said. "Thank you *so* much. I'll be right out."

"Take your time, Miss Allcutt. I hope you're feeling better."

"Thank you. I am," I said after taking a silent inventory of my body.

"Nurse Hall said the makeup on your face looked as if someone had mixed dried stinging nettle leaves into it," Molly said then. "That was a mean thing to do, and I'm sorry."

"Stinging nettles?" I said. What were stinging nettles? I knew what poison oak and poison ivy were.

"Yes. Stinging nettles."

"Do they grow around here?" I asked the maid.

"Oh, yes, they grow everywhere there's water," said Molly.

"My goodness," I said, wondering why anybody would bother tampering with a lowly tin of pancake makeup. Maybe they'd had other plans for it, although I couldn't imagine what they might be. "Thanks, Molly."

"You're more than welcome, Miss Allcutt. I'll leave you to your lunch and your precious pooch now," said Molly.

"Thank you!" I called one last time as I heard her footfalls retreating from the bathroom and to the door to the hallway.

Actually, except for my eyes, which were still sore and swollen and could probably, as the nurse suggested, benefit from some boric-acid eye wash, I did feel better. My head didn't hurt so much, except when I touched the places where my hair had been yanked out, but I hoped I'd be able to brush my bob so that the bald patches, should there be any, didn't show.

Picking up the box of dusting powder Nurse Hall said she'd created with her own hands, I opened it and sniffed carefully. It smelled faintly of lavender! Why I was surprised, I don't know. Standing dead-center on the bath mat, I dusted myself with the stuff. It was silky and soothing, and I decided to ask Nurse Hall if she'd relinquish the recipes of some of her potions and powders.

After liberally powdering myself and stamping on the mat to make any excess powder fall from my body, I sucked in a deep breath. Then, bravely daring, I tiptoed from the bath mat to the vanity table, frowned at my dirty clothes lying there and rubbed at the fog on the mirror with my fisted hand. Squinting as well as I could under the steamy circumstances, I tried to see myself.

Big mistake. Not only were my eyes still swollen, but they were also bloodshot. My hair stood on end, although when I picked up the hairbrush and gently ran it over my head, it lay down again as usual. I figured I'd ask Lulu or Chloe if I was bald anywhere. My face no longer looked like a ripe tomato, but I was sure one pink lady. I smoothed some Pond's Cold Cream over my face and neck. Didn't make me look any better, but it was definitely soothing.

Stupid day.

However, I could do nothing about what had already happened. I *could* hang up the towels, throw my dirty clothes in the hamper, enter my sitting room, put on some clothing, pet my darling dog, eat lunch and lie on the bed with cucumber slices on my eyes. So that's what I did.

Buttercup was delighted to see me, and I was delighted to see her. I picked her up and hugged her until she yipped. Then I apologized, gently set her down and climbed stiffly into my pajamas. I didn't bother with the robe. Then I went to the dresser, lifted the cloche from my luncheon tray, and saw it contained a bowl of soup and a sandwich on a plate. A glass of lemonade accompanied the meal and I suspected Molly—because Chef Garnier would consider it beneath him—had made the entire pitcher of lemonade and then placed it on a trivet next to my meal.

"I love my sister, Buttercup," I told my precious poodle. "And I think I was awfully bratty today. Can you imagine what a normal person would have done under circumstances similar to mine?"

Buttercup tilted her head, and I decided to clarify my comment as I carried the tray of edibles to the vanity table across the room. "I mean, someone who'd had a terrible reaction to something and had her hair pulled out and whose eyes were red and swollen, what would *she* do if she didn't have money?" I remembered something that made me feel even guiltier for my earlier behavior. "Buttercup, did you know that when Lulu had pneumonia a year or so ago, before I moved to Los Angeles, she was laid up in her crummy boarding-house room and she didn't have *anyone* to help her? Well, Ernie and Junior brought her soup sometimes. If Chloe and I weren't from a wealthy family, I might be blind right now. And still bright red."

I set the tray on the vanity table, lifted the bread-lid from half of the sandwich and saw that somebody—probably Molly again—had fixed me a toasted cheese-and-tomato sandwich. Along with the sandwich was some tomato soup. I suspected it was Campbell's soup, but that was okay by me. I dunked an edge of my sandwich into my tomato soup, took a bite and decided I'd survive to live another day, whether I wanted to or not.

When I'd finished off the sandwich, soup and a couple of glasses of lemonade, I took the lunch tray back to the dresser, covered it with the cloche again and picked up the small bowl containing cucumber slices.

Nurse Hall sure knew her onions. Well, she knew her soothing potions and cucumbers, anyhow.

TWENTY-THREE

Not precisely sure how long I slept, but when somebody knocked on my bedroom door, I didn't want to wake up. "Buttercup," I muttered, "make it stop."

Poor Buttercup didn't know what I was talking about of course. Boy, I was sore. Being yanked around by a great big gangster hurt. Then I recalled my eyes. They still felt gritty but, greatly daring, I removed the now-warm cucumber slices from each eye and attempted to open them.

A knock came again, this time accompanied by a voice. "Mercy, are you okay?" Lulu asked. I heard her turn the door knob and knew she aimed to walk in and assess my fitness.

I could actually see! Mind you, my eyes felt as if somebody had thrown sand in them and my eyelids were still swollen, but I could open my eyes more than I'd been able to before I ate lunch.

"Hey, Lulu," I said groggily. I managed to scoot over and sit on the edge of the bed. "I think I'm going to be okay."

"Crumb, I thought I had it rough when I had to ride on a horse in front of that cowboy."

"You did," I assured her. "How embarrassing. I mean, in a dress and all."

"Yeah. But at least I didn't get jerked around and have my hair pulled out."

"Botheration, I forgot my hair," I said, my mood sinking again. "Can you tell if I'll have to do anything crazy with it? I mean, do I have any big bald patches I'll have to comb hair over?"

"Lemme see here," said Lulu, pressing my head down and scrutinizing it. She turned it to the right and to the left. "Naw. I can see where that stinker pulled out a few hairs—but I think I'll be able to help you fix it."

"Phooey," I muttered. Lifting my head and affixing my gritty gaze on Lulu, I said, "You got cleaned up too. I had no idea we'd both get battered and filthy when we went onto the set. I thought we'd just be looking around for anything strange."

"Me, too. But I guess we succeeded. Harvey just got home about a half-hour ago, and Ernie and him have been jawing in his office ever since."

"And they didn't let you in?" Indignation made me forget about some of my bodily woes until I stood up abruptly. Then I sat again, also abruptly. "Crumb, everything hurts."

"Yeah, I know. Me too. Those men treated us both like rag dolls. Even that cowboy, who was a nice guy, hurt my arm when he yanked me up onto his horse. And riding bareback didn't do my butt any good either."

"I can imagine."

Lulu plunked down beside me on the bed. "But it's going to be dinner time pretty soon. Want me to help you get dressed?"

Did I? I glanced down at my pretty blue silk pajamas with embroidered butterflies all over them. "Do you think anyone would faint dead away if I wore my pajamas to dinner? I can put on a bandeau so my... Well, you know, so I won't be bouncy."

Checking out her own raiment, which consisted of a white blouse and a gray skirt, Lulu said, "I think that's the best idea I've heard all day. Put on your bandeau and some shoes and meet me in my room. I'll wear my green pajamas. If anyone objects, we can be scolded together."

"You're a true pal, Lulu," I said, the words coming from my heart.

As it turned out, there were a total of three ladies—well, women—wearing pretty Chinese pajamas to dinner that evening. Chloe wore her own set of pink silk embroidered pajamas. Heck, not even Harvey or Ernie wore approved dinner jackets, etc. They just had on trousers and shirts. Ernie wore a vest over his shirt, which made him more formally dressed than Harvey.

How about that?

As was customary, the family plus Lulu and Ernie gathered in the front parlor directly off the marbled entryway. Lulu and I walked in together to give each other moral support. Chloe sat on the arm of Harvey's easy chair and both of them gazed adoringly at the nameless girl-child on Harvey's lap.

Nanny Gibson stood behind the chair in her white uniform and cap, her hands folded at her bosom, beaming like an angel upon the trio.

"Wish I had a camera," I said. "You guys would make a charming photograph, especially if we could get someone to colorize it."

The new parents both looked up from their treasured child and smiled at me. It was then that I was amazed and delighted to see Chloe in her own Chinese silk pajamas. And we hadn't even coordinated our outfits beforehand! I mean, not all three of us. Lulu and I had.

"Boy," said Ernie from a sofa across the room. It looked as if he'd been perusing some papers. "You sure look better than you did a few hours ago, Mercy."

"Thanks," I said, attempting to sound chipper. "I feel better too, except for my eyes. Lulu and I ache where those men manhandled us."

"The cowboy fellow didn't mean to hurt me," said Lulu. "I just think he didn't realize how hard he was pulling on my arm."

Chalk up another demotion for Mercy and another gold star for Lulu. I managed not to sigh aloud. "I'm sure you're right," I said. "But Ernie and Harvey, you have to tell us what happened! All we know is that the coppers were letting you interrogate all the suspects in your office when we had to leave."

"Let's have a peaceful dinner," said Harvey. "After we dine, we can retire to our sitting room upstairs, and Ernie and I will tell you all about it."

"How come Ernie knows?" I asked sharply. Then I recalled what Lulu had said to me. "Oh yeah, that's right. You and Ernie already discussed everything, didn't you?"

"Yes we did," said Ernie. "And don't get huffy about it. Neither you nor Lulu was in any condition to sit through that conversation. You might, if you're fair, be glad to learn we finally figured out most of what happened and how and why it did."

"I'm not huffy," I fibbed, but Ernie was right. "I'm glad you figured out everything."

"I am too," said Harvey in a heartfelt voice. More somberly he added, "I'm sorely disappointed in a few of the people I'd trusted though."

"If you're thinking about Mr. Bedini," I said, "I got the feeling he was only trying to help his sister. If he knew what a villainess she truly was, he probably wouldn't have. Helped her, I mean."

"You may well be right," said Harvey. "But he's not going to work for Nash Studios again."

"He deserves worse than that," said Lulu. She sounded neither heartfelt nor somber. Vengeful might be the correct adjective to describe her tone of voice.

"He'll get more," said Ernie. "Harvey's too nice for his own good sometimes." He gave Harvey a jolly smile to take the sting out of his words.

"No, I'm not," said Harvey. "It's only that if someone has earned my trust over five or ten years, I tend not to believe he could be a traitor."

"Lesson learned," I said. I sounded downright belligerent. "What happened to his sister?"

"Harvey's going to tell us all about it after dinner, Mercy. Remember?" said Ernie.

"I remember," I said upon an aggrieved sigh. I wanted to know *now*.

Just then I nearly jumped out of my skin, pajamas and all, when the dinner gong sounded. Molly or one of the kitchen maids, I presumed.

"Oh, good," said Chloe, delicately prying herself from the arm of Harvey's chair. "I'm quite hungry."

"Let me take the wee one," said Nanny Gibson, expertly relieving Harvey of No-Name.

Chloe, Lulu, and I preceded the two men into the smallest dining room. Ernie politely held a chair out for Lulu and me, and Harvey did likewise for Chloe, giving her a kiss first. Ernie didn't bother with a kiss.

The chef might have been a temperamental bloke, but he could sure cook! He—well, the forever-timid kitchen maid—first served us bowls of a clear consommé, which we all managed to sip without slurping. Following the consommé came a plate of anchovy toast (not my favorite, but I did my portion justice). Then came the main course, a gorgeous rib roast served with asparagus and roasted pota-toes. He even managed to make gravy, which I'd heard from rumors was impossible. According to my sources, if you roasted potatoes in the same pot in which you roasted the meat, the roast wouldn't release enough drippings and fat to cook the potatoes and also make gravy. Maybe he boiled other beef bones and made the gravy with the stock thus created. But I was no cook, as mentioned before, so take my words with a grain (even several grains) of salt. Chef Garnier served the roast and potatoes with—ta-da!—Yorkshire pudding! A French chef serving Yorkshire pudding. I was astounded. And happy.

Oh, and the only reason I knew about roasting potatoes and what "stock" was in reference to food is because Mrs. Buck told me. What a basically useless human being I was. But I was learning, darn it! "Wow, how'd you get your stuffy French chef to make York-shire pudding?" I asked as I gazed at my plate in awe.

"I asked him politely," said Chloe.

"He already had the recipe?" I asked, still in awe.

"No," said Chloe. "I provided him with the recipe and some popover irons. He didn't use them this evening, but used a baking pan for the pudding."

Never having thought about my beautiful sister as having a plethora of homemaking skills, I said, "I didn't know you could cook! Maybe *you* can give me lessons. Mrs. Buck said she would, but she's always busy."

"I?" said Chloe. Then she charmed us with one of her musical laughs. "Good Lord, Mercy, where would *I* have learned to cook? I asked Charlie Chaplin's cook."

"Charlie Chaplin's cook is British?" I said.

"Charlie Chaplin was born in London," said Harvey.

"Yeah," said Lulu. "I read about it in *Photoplay*."

"I didn't know that!" I said, again feeling useless.

"Well, you can't hear him talk in the flickers," said Ernie. He sounded as if he were attempting to make me feel less foolish. Kind man, although he didn't want people to know it most of the time.

Harvey added, "He likes Yorkshire pudding, Scotch eggs, sausage rolls, and other British fare. Fish and chips, I expect."

"Yes," said Chloe. "Harvey and I went to a dinner party at his place where he served a roasted leg of lamb along with popovers. So I asked him if his cook would share the recipe, and he was delighted. Mrs. McKinney, his cook, wrote down the recipe. She told me where to purchase the proper cookware for it. She also told me that you have to pour grease in either the cast-iron popover irons or a cast-iron baking dish and heat either of them in the oven before you pour in the batter. I have no idea why, but I told Jacques he had to prepare Yorkshire pudding whenever I asked him to if he wanted to keep his job. Sometimes he uses the popover irons."

I stared at my sister whilst lifting a bite of beef, potato, Yorkshire pudding, and gravy to my mouth. Before I shoved it in, I said, "You're amazing, Chloe."

"She's my perfect bride," said Harvey, giving Chloe a smile that would have looked silly on anyone else.

Harvey and Chloe adored each other, and you could see their love for miles. Almost gave me hope for...I don't know. The world?

Not a chance. Me? The latter would have been laughable if I weren't chewing.

"Anyhow, I'll be sure I'll give you the recipe and get the proper cookware for Yorkshire pudding before you have to leave for home," said Chloe, eating as delicately as she did everything else.

After I swallowed, I said, "Thank you. This is delicious."

"Jacques can be touchy at times," said Harvey. "But we pay him well."

"We also pay the kitchen staff who have to work with him well," said Chloe. "It's only fair."

"I should say so," said Lulu. "I wandered down to the kitchen a couple of days ago, and he was having a tantrum at one of his helpers."

"We have two kitchen maids," said Harvey. "Do you know the name of the one he was yelling at?"

"No," said Lulu. "But I'll bet Molly or Nanny Gibson or Nurse Hall would know. Is he ever nasty with Nanny Gibson or Nurse Hall?"

"Not that I've heard about," said Chloe with another one of her tuneful laughs. "I expect either one of those iron ladies would bean him with a skillet if he had a tantrum with one of them."

Thinking about Nurse Hall, whom I knew slightly better than Nanny Gibson, I said, "I expect you're right."

Out of curiosity and because I personally hated mint sauce with lamb, I asked, "Did Charlie Chaplin's lady chef serve mint jelly with his leg of lamb?"

"No," said Chloe, this time sounding about as dry as she could sound, given her sunny personality. "And I was exceptionally happy about that. I hate mint jelly with lamb or mutton."

"So do I," I said, happy to have at least one thing in common with my spectacularly gorgeous sister. "Mother *forced* us to put mint jelly on our meat every time she had the cook prepare lamb or mutton."

"One more good reason not to serve it at your table," said Ernie with a chuckle. "Back in Chicago, nobody served mint jelly with anything. At least none of us in the lower classes did. I suspect some of the millionaires gave themselves airs. The best sheep meat I've ever eaten was in the Greek part of town. Chicago is made up of lots of different ethnic neighborhoods."

"Really?" I said, thinking I'd like to visit Chicago one day.

"Yup. You've got your Germans and your Poles who fix all kinds of sausages, sauerkraut, and rolls. There are Jewish enclaves where you can get excellent bread and chopped liver—"

"Ew," said Lulu. Then she said, "Sorry, Ern. I just don't like liver."

"You don't have to like liver. The Jewish neighborhood has great matzo ball soup and the best chicken soup I've eaten in my life. Then you've got Little Italy, where you can get delicious Italian food. Then there's Chinatown and Greektown. Greektown was my favorite."

"I didn't know that about Chicago, Ernie," I said, feeling kind of left out. After all, we were kind of a pair. You'd think he'd tell me about the wonders of his hometown. Then again, having been born and bred on Beacon Hill in Boston and only spending boring winters at some cape in Maine, I didn't know much about my *own* hometown.

"I'll tell you about Chi-town later," he assured me. "You don't want to go there now, because the bootlegging gangs are shooting up the city. A shame, that. The Germans had the best beer in town too." I heard him heave a little sigh.

"I doubt Prohibition will last much longer," said Harvey in a judicious tone. "I think there are more drunks and winos on the streets these days than when buying booze was legal."

"I think you're right," said Ernie.

"Golly, in Enid we mostly ate chicken and pork. We sold the cattle, so we didn't eat beef very often, unless we had salted beef in the smoke shed." She turned and looked at me, which required her bending over and peering over Ernie's dinner plate and flatware. "You really like *liver?*"

"I do. I know it's not everyone's favorite," I told her. "But every now and then I could persuade our cook in Boston to fix some chicken livers and onions for me. Neither Mother nor Father knew or they'd have raised the roof."

"Why?" asked Ernie. "Lots of people like liver and onions."

"Liver and onions as a main course is considered poor people's food," I told them. "You've met them, and you ask anyway?"

After hearing my answer, Lulu nodded, sat up and cut herself another bite of beef.

"Yeah," said Ernie. "That was a stupid question, wasn't it? Did you dine on pheasant occasionally?"

"Yes," I said. "They're little birds with a billion bones and you have to pick shot out of them. Give me a good old chicken any day. Or a duck or a goose, for that matter."

Chloe laughed. "I swear, Mercy, do you remember when Great-Aunt Agatha was alive and she took you to Maine for a week? You couldn't talk about anything but fried clams for months. Except, of course, if we were in front of Mother or Father."

"Fried clams are food for the gods," said Ernie.

"I think so too." I considered my history with food. "You know, I think I can remember every good meal I've ever eaten in my life. Guess food is really important to me, but I don't weigh six hundred pounds. Is that odd?"

"Sounds odd to me," said Lulu. "I ate soup and crackers for weeks on end until I went to live at Mercy's Manor. Mrs. Buck cooks great meals, but I try not to eat too much at any one of them."

"She does, doesn't she?" I said wistfully. "So does Chef Garnier, but he's mean. Mrs. Buck is never mean, even when I ask her stupid questions."

"When do you ask her stupid questions?" Lulu said.

"Well, I asked her to teach me to cook. That was kind of stupid."

"Why?" asked Ernie. "Cooking is a useful skill."

"I guess it is," agreed Lulu.

"I agree," Harvey and Chloe chorused.

I didn't feel so bad after that. My good mood increased substantially when Molly carried in a tray upon which sat a magnificent Charlotte Russe.

Oddly enough, although I believed the decadent dessert to be beautiful, I wasn't a huge fan of Charlotte Russe. That's because people put whiskey or sherry in it, and I didn't care for the taste of the liquor. It's a good thing I didn't aspire to be a flapper. I'd never be able to follow the rules.

I heard a soft, "Ooh" from Lulu, followed by, "That's beautiful. What is it?"

"It's a Charlotte Russe," said Chloe. Then she smiled at me. "And don't worry, Mercy. I forced Chef Garnier to use vanilla extract rather than sherry."

"You're a saint, Chloe. I'm *so* glad you're my sister."

I don't think Chloe heard Ernie's soft, "Damn," but I did. As I'd never seen him drink anything more outrageous than apple cider from a flask he carried, I think he was kidding.

TWENTY-FOUR

W hen dinner concluded—and I hoped Chef Garnier would create something spectacular with the leftover beef, of which there was plenty—we all retired to Harvey and Chloe's upstairs sitting room. I think Nurse Hall was off duty, because it was Nanny Gibson I saw through the open door to the baby's nursery. She rocked the baby's cradle and sang softly to No-Name.

"Would you like me to close the door to the nursery?" I asked when I witnessed the touching tableau in the other room.

With a sigh, Chloe said, "Yes, I suppose it would be best. We don't want to wake up the baby."

So before I sat on one of the cozy chairs in the sitting room, I went to the nursery door and smiled at Nanny Gibson, who smiled back. On my way to our detectival group, I said, "You know, Chloe, you've had that baby for…what? A month now?"

"Yes," said Chloe. "She was a month old today. Or yesterday. It's difficult to tell with February."

"Oh, yeah," I said. She was born on January 29, wasn't she? And there isn't a February 29."

"Every four years there is," said Ernie.

"But this isn't one of them," said Lulu.

215

"No, it isn't. Don't you think the poor child deserves a name? You don't know her well enough by now?"

"No," said Chloe, softly and sweetly. "*I've* come to know her very well, but poor Harvey has been tied up with that production of his, and he deserves some getting-to-know-you time with her before we bestow a name upon her. The decision has to be made by the both of us. You and I, of all people, should know the value of a name given at birth." she said, reaching for Harvey's hand. She didn't have to reach far, as he sat in the very next chair to her and had already held out a hand to her.

"Why we of all people?" I said.

"I do not like the name Clovilla," said Chloe whose first name was actually Clovilla. "Nor do I care for Adelaide." Adelaide was her middle name.

"You have a point," I admitted. "I've never been overly fond of Mercedes Louise, either."

"It's better than Clovilla Adelaide," said Chloe.

"You're right," I said. "So after this film nonsense is solved, you and Harvey and you will care for little No-Name together and give her a good name, right?"

"Correct," said Harvey. "That's one of the reasons I'm glad we finally got to the bottom of the sabotage on the set today. Most of it, anyway."

"Wonderful," I said. "So tell us. We're all dying to know."

"I'm not," said Lulu. "I thought we were dead already. I thought you were going to die of makeup rash, and I was going to fall off that horse and crush my skull. But maybe I'll leave dying to someone else today."

"Oh dear," said Harvey. "I'm sorry to have put the two of you in so much danger. I honestly didn't believe the saboteurs would kill anyone. I don't think they meant to kill Mel Flynn, but they're still guilty of his murder."

"Do you have a way to prove it?" I asked, curious.

"I believe we do," said Harvey.

"Really? That's wonderful!" I said.

"It's over except for a couple of nasty details we need to sweep up," said Ernie.

"Is George one of those nasty details?" I asked.

Harvey and Ernie gazed at each other for a moment or two and my heart, which hadn't been acting strangely for at least a couple of hours, took the opportunity to give a big twinge. "You haven't even considered how to get rid of George, have you?" My voice sounded more accusatory than I'd intended it to.

"Well," said Ernie. "No. We haven't, although we'll have to get rid of him somehow."

"Call Mother and Father and tell *them* what he's been up to," I suggested. "They even paid the Bedini woman a substantial sum to leave George alone, but he followed her here. She must have told him where she was going. He wouldn't have been able to figure it out on his own. He's not awfully bright, you know."

"I know," said Chloe.

"As do I," said Harvey.

"Me too," said Ernie. "The guy's an idiot."

"Told you so," I said with some satisfaction.

"Does anybody know where he is now?" asked Lulu.

This time a quintet of glances sped from person to person to… well, you know, until we'd all five given each other worried looks.

"The police hauled him off this morning," said Ernie. "Could he still be in jail?"

"That would be a good place for him," I said. Suddenly, as often happens with me, a perhaps-brilliant idea occurred to me. I think I've already mentioned how difficult it is to know if an idea is actually brilliant. "Somebody should telephone Mother and Father in Boston and tell them he's in jail and that if they want him back, they'll have to bail him out and get him on a train to Boston."

"I'm not going to call them," said Chloe, her voice firmer than normal.

"Don't look at me," said Harvey. "I'm sorry, Mercy, but I want nothing to do with your parents."

"Understandable," I said.

"You're the only one who's ever been able to deal with Mother,

Mercy," said Chloe. "You're doubtless the only person who *can* call her and get your point across."

And then I had a thought which, while not brilliant, was at least decisive. "I will *not* put in a trunk call to Boston. I had to handle Mother for the short time she was here, and I don't aim to do it again. Ever. Period."

"But Mercy." Chloe began.

"No," I said, adamant.

"Wait a minute," said Ernie, butting in, for which I was grateful. "What's the name of that attorney of yours? Crowfoot? Croyden?"

"Roddy Crowhurst!" Chloe burst out. "Why didn't we think of him before?"

"I don't know," said Harvey. "But that's a brilliant idea, Ernie, especially if George is still behind bars, and I suspect he is. Haven't heard from him or anyone connected with his arrest today."

I was peeved because Harvey had called Ernie's suggestion brilliant and hadn't said anything about mine, and mine was the one that started the conversation. It was ever thus. Women get short shrift in this old world. However, I didn't quibble, which I think was magnanimous of me.

"Was he arrested?" I asked, because I didn't yet have a clear picture of the day's events before Ernie, Lulu, and I arrived at Helen's boudoir.

"Yes," said Harvey. "He balked at being removed from that woman, so I told the officers he was trespassing, had likely broken and entered and had no business being on the set. I told them I didn't know how he'd managed to get onto what is supposed to be a closed production but, however he'd done it, it was a criminal offense. I don't know if he's still residing in a cell. We have gate guards and give people passes when we want them to be on-set, but George managed to elude everyone and show up anyhow. And then he found that girl of his! I'd like to know who abetted him."

"I suspect a Bedini or Frank Sabatini," I said. "Well I'm not sure about Vic, but he seems to be putty in his evil sister's hands, so he might have done it. And what about that Sabatini character?"

"Both Bedinis and Sabatini were arrested," said Harvey. "And they won't be getting out any time soon. We still have to figure out who was responsible for Mel Flynn's murder. Even if those three didn't mean to kill him, their devious plans did it anyway." Suddenly Harvey pinned his gaze on me. "And poor Mercy was injured today! I don't know what was in that junk Lulu put on you, but you looked like a boiled lobster the last time I saw you."

"Nurse Hall thinks it was stinging nettles," I told them.

"Yeah, and that Sabatini guy pulled out some of her hair, too," said Lulu. Giving me a guilty glance, she added, "I'm still sorry about that, Mercy."

"Wasn't your fault," I told her. Well, she wasn't responsible for contaminating the makeup, but she'd smeared it all over my face. "Why didn't you get a rash, if that tin was contaminated with stinging nettles?"

"I used a makeup sponge on you," said Lulu. "I never actually touched the makeup."

"Ah," I said, not wholly enlightened. Lulu knew a lot more about makeup than did I.

"I got the impression Sabatini was in the Salvatore mob back East," said Ernie meditatively. "It's more than likely the mob got to one or more of your employees, Harvey. They have ways of getting even good people to do their bidding. Guy down the street from me in Chi-town had an uncle who owned a bakery in New York City. He already paid graft to the New York City P.D., and he refused to pay the Salvatore representative more. They said it was for the guy's own protection. When he kept refusing to pay them, they bombed his bakery."

"How terrible!" I cried, horrified. "How'd they know it was the Salvatore people who did it?"

"According to my source, it was an open-and-shut conclusion. Do you know of any legitimate businesses that bomb other businesses because they don't give them 'security' money?"

"Well, no, but I've lived a pretty sheltered life so far, you know."

With a wide grin, Ernie said, "I know."

"So how are you going to sweep up the loose ends?" I asked.

"Do you know any gangsters who'll spill the beans on the Salvatore people?"

"I think our best bet," said Ernie, "is Vic Bedini. He might have cooperated with his sister, Sabatini, and the mob, but I don't think he wanted to. If we persuade him, I think he'll rat out the whole organization."

"Even his sister?" I asked, thinking she'd got him into the mess in the first place. "If she wields so much moral power over him, he might not want to turn on her."

"Ernie doesn't think Vic knows the extent of his sister's criminal acts," said Harvey. "He said he's going to make some telephone calls to folks he knows in Chicago and New York City who might know more about the mobs than I do. What was the name she was using? It wasn't Italian."

"Verna Borden," I said, the name having stuck in my head like some disgusting substance not unlike the day's makeup. "She kept her initials but changed Vicky to Verna and Bedini to Borden."

"It's a funny thing, but people tend to do that when they give themselves fake names," said Ernie.

"Really? How come?" I asked.

With a shrug, Ernie said, "Beats me. Maybe it's easier to remember a name with your real initials at the beginnings of the two words."

I contemplated his sentence until I'd parsed it properly, then said, "I can't see how it would make any difference unless they had their initials embroidered on their hankies."

"Maybe Vicky has a drawer full of embroidered hankies," proffered Ernie.

I decided to drop that topic and bring up another. "How are you going to talk to Vic Bedini long enough to get him to spill the goods on his sister and Sabatini and the Salvatore gang?" I asked.

A huff preceded Ernie's, "Don't know yet."

And *then* I had an idea I *knew* to be brilliant. "Ernie! *You* call our parents! Pretend to be a lawyer or a police chief." After thinking about it for a second and three-fifths, I said, "No. Be a lawyer. Our parents have friends who are lawyers. I'm sure they consider police persons to be beneath them. Anyhow, you can tell them George broke several laws after he came to California. Talk to Father. He'll be more likely to tell the truth than Mother, who will pretend her sweet little boy can do no harm. I mean, our father's a skunk, but at least he's not criminal or delusional. You can even talk to a real attorney, and he can tell you what to say, how to say it, and come up with some hideous punishments that will not only nail George to a penitentiary wall but will cause a huge scandal! If there's anything more frightening to my parents than scandal, I don't know what it is. Heck, they consider *me* a scandal, and all I did was take a couple of classes at the Boston Y.W.C.A. and move to California." I sat back in my chair and smiled.

Silence filled the room for maybe sixteen seconds before Chloe, giving me an almost incandescent smile said, "What our parents *should* be afraid of is you, Mercy. I'd never have thought of so perfect a scheme."

"Wow, Mercy," said Lulu. "You're good at this."

"Excellent idea, Mercy," said Harvey. "Ernie, would you like me to call Rod Crowhurst and see if he can give you pointers?"

After a short spate of thought Ernie said, "No. No, I think I have an even better option."

"What is it?" I asked, perplexed.

Clasping her hands to her bosom, Lulu said in an almost-whisper, "Rob. It's Rob, isn't it, Ernie?"

"You got it in one, Lulu," said Ernie, grinning at her.

Have I yet mentioned that Mr. Robert Gabriel, Esq. and Lulu had been seeing each other recently? Well, they had been.

"Of course!" I cried. "He'd be *much* better than Mr. Crowhurst, because not even my parents can think of a reason to connect Mr. Gabriel to your studio, Harvey. If they find out Crowhurst is on the Nash payroll, they might find him suspicious. If an attorney with absolutely no connection to the studio or anyone in the picture calls them about George, it'll scare them."

"He's also a defense attorney, and he knows the laws of California and Los Angeles like the back of his hand," said Ernie,

221

reaching for my personal hand. "We make a darned good team don't we, Mercy?"

"You bet we do," I said, basking.

Ernie placed a call to Robert Gabriel, Esq., that very evening. Because Chloe told him to, Ernie invited Rob to the Nash residence in order to learn the whole story. Rob would need to know everything in order to relate the details to our parents. He could also be sitting right next to Ernie when Ernie placed the trunk call to Boston. That way, when Mr. Gabriel took the receiver and spoke to our parents, Ernie could pass him suggestions if they were deemed advisable.

We discussed the case for a while longer, but when the baby began fussing, Chloe insisted we all retire for the day.

"Good idea," said Ernie. "We'll get more information about our criminals and their crimes before Rob calls your parents. I want to be sure we can nail their hides to the wall and get your brother back to Boston."

"Perfect," I said with a sigh. Then I remembered I probably still looked like raw meat that had gone bad, my eyes still hurt and I truly didn't want Ernie to see me like this for much longer. So I said, "Want to go upstairs to bed, Lulu? You must be exhausted too."

"Thanks, Mercy. Yeah, I am."

"I'll walk the two of you," said Ernie gallantly. As I didn't want him to see me for much longer, his gallantry was wasted on me.

However, he escorted Lulu and me to the elevator. "You've exercised enough today," he said. And he walked Lulu to her bedroom first and then walked me to mine.

He even gave me a chaste kiss on the lips and said, "You did a great job today, Mercy. I'm sure your rash will go away soon. And your eyes will get back to normal. And hair always grows back."

I smiled sweetly and resisted the urge to kick him in the shin. I did, however, use a boric-acid wash on my eyes and smeared some more of Nurse Hall's cream and some more Pond's on my face before I went to bed.

TWENTY-FIVE

The next morning I looked nearly human again. A slight pink cast to my cheeks was the only remnant of the horrible rash. Even my eyes were normal-ish. Perhaps a little bloodshot, but not very. For the first time since my skin began itching the prior day, I believed I might one day be myself again.

Also the next morning, uniformed policemen and more uniformed private agents hired by Harvey guarded every possible entryway to the Nash Studio set for *Helen of Troy*. Not a vehicle was allowed into the lot until a uniform of one sort or another grilled the driver, and the vehicle and all passengers were searched.

The searching turned out to be a good idea, because various examined automobiles, trucks and vans netted not only George Allcutt (hiding behind a pickle barrel in the grocery van), but also four thugs from the Salvatore gang and a couple of other people who refused to tell the coppers their names. Didn't matter. They were breaking the law of trespass, so they'd get locked up anyhow.

The police identified the mobsters because they had been in touch with their fellow officers in the New York City Police Department. According to Harvey, the cops sent telegrams rather than using telephones, as trunk calls were expensive and iffy if placed from one coast of the country to the other. From the Pacific Ocean to the Atlantic Ocean (and vice-versa), the United States of America is really big, isn't it?

So now all we had to do was figure out who did what to whom and, perhaps more importantly, why. Harvey, Sidney Lafayette, Rodney Crowhurst, Ernie, Lulu, and I were allowed to attend an inquisition in Harvey's office at the studio. The only outsider was Vic Bedini, because most of us believed him to be the least guilty of crime and more troubled by it than the other conspirators.

After we, the good guys, were all settled in Harvey's office along with several public and private police people, a heavy knock sounded on Harvey's door.

"Enter," said Harvey in an executive-sounding voice.

The door opened revealing two uniformed members of the L.A.P.D. They had a handcuffed Vic Bedini between them. Mr. Bedini didn't want to be there. As soon as he realized what awaited him in Harvey's office, his knees buckled. He straightened them before he fell over, but he looked frightened and uncomfortable. I guess the participants of this inquiry had either practiced or been well coached because, without being told what to do, the two uniforms led Mr. Bedini to a chair beside Harvey's enormous desk and made him sit by pushing down on his shoulders. Then one bull stood behind him and the other stood to attention beside him. Mr. Bedini didn't stand a chance of escape.

Oh, and both Ernie and Harvey had asked me to take notes. I appreciated this for several reasons. First, because I liked being useful and second, this way of being useful was a heck of a lot more to my liking than pretending to be an ancient Greek or a studio employee. As a secretary, I was on solid ground.

The only other person who aimed to help us was Rob Gabriel, but he'd had to rearrange his schedule before driving to Beverly Hills and joining us. Lulu was happier than I'd seen her in days. She missed her man. I understood.

Mr. Bedini looked miserable, as he should. His hands were cuffed behind his back, so when he sniffled, he couldn't grab a hankie. "H-harvey? Mr. Nash?"

"I'm here, Vic," said Harvey. His brows lowered. "Do you have to have him handcuffed in here? He can't go anywhere without being tackled. Ernie?" He glanced at Ernie.

"I suppose he doesn't have to have the cuffs on," said Ernie.

The bull standing next to Mr. Bedini's chair unlocked the handcuffs, and Mr. Bedini heaved a sigh of relief and flapped his hands, probably to get his circulation going.

"You need anything to drink, Vic?" asked Harvey. "Miss LaBelle, would you mind visiting my secretary and getting a glass of water or a cup of tea for Vic?"

Lulu's expression turned mulish, but then she heaved a sigh and said, "Oh, why not?" She left us and went to the room usually occupied by Mrs. Lamb, Harvey's secretary. She came back a few seconds later carrying a glass. "Mrs. Lamb wasn't there, but I poured some"—she peered into the glass—"it looks like lemonade, from the pitcher on her desk. It'll have to do."

"That's just lemonade?" Mr. Bedini asked, sounding worried.

"It's just lemonade," said Lulu. She walked over and handed the glass to Mr. Bedini, who took a tiny sip. Then he set the glass on the corner of Harvey's desk.

"Thanks," said Mr. Bedini to Lulu. She didn't bother with a response, so he went on. "I had no idea Vicky and Frank were in cahoots. Or with the Salvatore gang. Honestly. I was trying to help my sister. We...we only have each other. We have no other relations."

Wish I could say the same. I didn't, because I knew talking wasn't my job. I just took down his words in Pitman Shorthand. I had extra pads and sharpened pencils available to me because I was an efficient secretary. Usually.

"That may well be true, Vic," said Harvey in a serious tone. "In fact, we'd already deduced you were involved only because of your sister. What we don't know is why. Why is there a concerted plot to sabotage *Helen of Troy*?"

"I...I don't know," whimpered Bedini.

"We don't believe you," said Ernie, rising from his chair to sit on a corner of Harvey's desk. Mr. Bedini, even with most of a desk between himself and Ernie, cast Ernie a frightened glance and tried scooting farther away from him. Didn't work. He sat in a chair, and its dimensions couldn't be altered.

"No, we don't," said Mr. Crowhurst. "We've had some trouble with bootlegging gangsters before. We're *not* going to allow them to sully the Nash Studio."

"Gangsters?" said Mr. Bedini, now trying to squish himself into the chair's upholstery. This ploy didn't work either. "I…I don't know any gangsters."

"That's applesauce and you know it," said Ernie. "We sat outside your tent and listened to you talking to Sabatini, who's a front man for the Salvatore gang. He was threatening to do something to you if you didn't do something for him. After spending more time with you and Sabatini, my two assistants"—he meant Lulu and me—"believe Frank Sabatini, as a member of the Salvatore gang, has some kind of hold over you that involves your sister."

"Aw, cripes," mumbled Mr. Bedini. "Vicky has a couple of problems. It's not really her fault."

"I don't believe that either," said Ernie. "From what we've learned so far, your sister lost a lot of money, probably to a gang-run outfit. The two of you being so close and all, I imagine she came to you to bail her out. I also imagine you couldn't afford to hand her a wad of cash."

"Oh God," whimpered Mr. Bedini.

"I doubt God has much to do with your problem," Ernie said in a tone so dry, it might have been made from Saharan sand. "I think your sister is a big-time loser. She came to you for help, and you decided to help her. Unfortunately, you've been unable to do so thus far. Is Sabatini the one behind the so-called accidents on the set?"

No answer came from Mr. Bedini, who now attempted to make himself smaller. Still didn't work.

"You'd be a lot better off talking to us than dealing with representatives of the Salvatore organization. For example, if you can't cover your sister's debts, we won't kill you. I'm pretty sure the Salvatores won't be so kind. They've already got one death chalked up against them, to which you're connected."

"I'm not!" cried Mr. Bedini. "I didn't have anything to do with that!"

"Indirectly you did," said Ernie.

"Why didn't you come to me, Vic? I might have been able to help you," said Harvey, sounding honestly grieved.

"I…couldn't," said Mr. Bedini.

"Why not?" asked Ernie in a reasonable voice.

"They… That is, my sister. Oh God." Mr. Bedini bowed his head and appeared about as defeated as a living man could appear.

"That's not much of an explanation," said Ernie, borrowing more sand from the Sahara. "Your sister what?"

No answer.

"Tell us, Bedini. The gangs have lots of their boys in prisons, don't forget. If you're arrested, as you should be, you probably won't last long."

"But I didn't *do* anything! Honestly!"

"Don't kid a kidder, Bedini," growled Ernie.

"But…but." Mr. Bedini stuttered.

"Your sister is a lot more on the ball than you are. Her problem seems to be an addiction to gambling. Hell, Miss Allcutt's family paid Vicky boocoo bucks to leave her brother, yet she seems to have gambled it all away. Gamblers are like drug fiends and boozers. They can't quit. You fouled up by making her problem *your* problem, and now this motion-picture production is suffering for it. And you'll suffer too. Don't believe for a minute the mob will forget about you. They have longer memories than elephants. And the L.A.P.D. isn't pleased with you either."

"Yes," I said, sticking in an oar, even though I knew Ernie didn't want one from me. "She not only spent all the money my family gave her to leave George alone, she must have told George to come to Los Angeles. He knew precisely where to find her. My brother isn't smart enough to figure out her whereabouts on his own."

"Exactly," said Ernie, giving me a look that spoke volumes and told me not to. Speak volumes, I mean. I suspect he didn't even want me to drop in a little word here or there.

I went back to my note-taking.

"I didn't know about any of that," whined Mr. Bedini. "All of a sudden, Vicky showed up at my door. She'd been roughed up, and she wouldn't say who'd hit her. She begged me to let her stay with me for a while, so I did. She's my *sister*, for God's sake!"

After studying Mr. Bedini's face for a few seconds—it wasn't a pleasant sight, being pudgy and pale—Ernie said, "So that explains why she came to Los Angeles. She didn't tell you who roughed her up?"

"No. She only said she was scared, and could I help her. So I helped her. She thought she'd be safe if she got a bit role in a flicker."

"Did she specify any particular motion picture?" said Ernie.

"She said she'd heard they were going to film *Helen of Troy*, and that they'd need a lot of extras to look like ancient Greeks." He took another slug of lemonade.

"Aha, so she already knew about *Helen of Troy*, did she?" said Ernie.

"Yeah. So I asked Carl—"

"Who's Carl," Ernie interrupted.

"Carl Hinkle. He's the casting director," said Harvey.

"Very well, so you talked to Carl, right?" said Ernie.

Mr. Bedini's mouth opened. When no words slid out of it, I glanced up from my note pad and saw he seemed to be having some sort of health crisis. His face had turned an even brighter red than mine had the day before, and he was having trouble breathing.

I jumped from my chair, still holding my pen and pad. "He's been poisoned!" I hollered.

The copper standing behind Mr. Bedini's chair whacked Mr. Bedini on the back, probably expecting something to pop from his throat. But I knew better. I'd had to visit the L.A. Public Library a few months back to do research about poisons.

"You can't help him," I said, being even more efficient than usual. "Pretty sure it's cyanide. He probably drank it from that glass."

"What?" shrieked Lulu. "You mean *I* poisoned him? No! I didn't!"

"It wasn't you," I assured her, heading next door, which was Mrs. Lamb's room. "But we'd better get the pitcher of lemonade away from Mrs. Lamb's desk." I turned my head and said over my shoulder, "And take that glass he drank from. The lemonade in it will have to be analyzed."

Lest you think Mr. Bedini was doing nothing while I was being efficient, he wasn't. Doing nothing, I mean. He not only turned red and seemed unable to breathe, he also began convulsing. I heard him fall out of his chair and turned to see him writhing on the floor. Shoot. I had a bitter feeling that Mr. Bedini was lost to us.

I should have been feeling sorry for Mr. Bedini, shouldn't I? Oh well. It had been a tough week so far, and I wasn't inclined to give people credit when it wasn't due to them. And Mr. Vic Bedini had been a dupe at best, and an out-and-out crook at worst. Even though I favored the dupe scenario, I couldn't work up much sympathy for him.

I also didn't find a pitcher or any other type of container on Mrs. Lamb's desk. I called, "Lulu? Did you say the pitcher was on Mrs. Lamb's desk?"

"Yeah," said Lulu, still sounding shaky.

"Well, it isn't here now."

"*What?*" I heard Lulu jump up, and she ran into Mrs. Lamb's room. "Oh, my gar!" she gasped and covered her mouth with her hands.

"Cripes," said Ernie. "Isn't Mrs. Lamb back yet?"

At that moment, Mrs. Lamb walked through the open front door of her room. She heard Ernie's question and said, "I'm here. I was only away from my desk for a minute or two to attend to... personal business."

She'd had to go to the bathroom. I understood.

"Did you leave a pitcher on your desk before you left?" I asked, keeping my voice calm.

"A pitcher. No. Why?"

Hideous noises indicative of human suffering emanated from Harvey's office.

"There was a pitcher on your desk a few minutes ago," I told her. "Along with a glass. You don't generally keep a pitcher and glasses on your desk?"

"No. We have an Arrowhead water cooler in the hall. We're very up-to-date here. What in the world is going on in Mr. Nash's office?"

"A man is dying of cyanide poisoning," I said, then wished I'd not been so candid when Mrs. Lamb tottered and kind of collapsed into her chair. Her mouth fell open but luckily, she could still breathe and her face had turned ashen rather than red.

"The studio doctor's on his way," Ernie said from the open doorway to Mrs. Lamb's office in which he stood. "No pitcher, eh?"

"No pitcher. No glasses," I concurred. I placed what was supposed to be a comforting hand on Mrs. Lamb's shoulder. She stiffened up like Lot's wife glancing back at where she came from, so I sweetened my voice. "Mrs. Lamb, there's been an accident."

"An-an accident?" she stuttered.

"Yes. Did you see anyone in the hallway when you were returning from the...where you'd gone for your personal business?"

"See anyone?" she said, clearly bent on repeating every question I asked her.

Rather than shake the shoulder with my hand that was meant to be comforting, I said, "Yes. Did you see anyone at all? Anyone you don't usually see, especially if the person carried a pitcher?" Turning to Lulu, I asked, "Was it a glass pitcher, Lulu?"

"No. It was ceramic. White with pink flowers on it. Like the kind we used in Oklahoma before we got indoor plumbing."

Where I grew up, in Boston, we had indoor plumbing when I was born, so I couldn't create a mental image of Lulu's pitcher.

But Mrs. Lamb seemed to gain some strength from Lulu's description, and she sat up straight in her chair. "Yes!" she said. "Yes, that large man with the funny name walked past me holding a flowered ewer and basin. I wondered about it because we aren't filming a western on this set."

"You recognized the man?" I asked, only realizing when she squeaked that I'd squeezed Mrs. Lamb's shoulder a bit too hard. "Sorry." I removed my hand.

Harvey, Sid, Mr. Crowhurst, and a goodly number of the police contingent streamed out of Harvey's office. When I glanced at the men, they all looked sick. Except for the coppers. They probably saw dead bodies all the time.

"He's dead," said Harvey. "The police are already here. The medical staff should be arriving soon."

"What's the name of the man you saw with the ewer and basin?" Ernie asked sharply, making poor Mrs. Lamb jerk in her chair. "You said he was a large man with a funny name?"

"Well, yes. He's well over six feet tall, and he looks rather like a bull. But his name is something odd. Something that reminds me of a musical instrument."

"*Piccolo!*" Ernie and I said together. We actually shouted the name together.

TWENTY-SIX

"Luca Piccolo?" asked Harvey in a small voice.

"Yes," said Mrs. Lamb, smiling at her boss. Her smile didn't last long. Harvey looked terrible. "What's the matter, Mr. Nash?" she asked, concerned.

"We'll tell you about it later," Ernie said brusquely.

I patted the poor woman's shoulder, this time softly and comfortingly. "It's a long story, Mrs. Lamb. We need to find Luca Piccolo now."

"Is that him?" Lulu asked, pointing at the door to the hall.

Sure enough, when we all glanced at the doorway, we saw a veritable giant standing there, looking panicky. He saw us staring, said, "Dammit," and threw the pitcher and bowl at us. Lemonade splashed everywhere, but the door was a long way from Mrs. Lamb's desk, and nobody got spattered. I hoped no one got spattered anyhow, because cyanide is potent stuff.

Then again, maybe it doesn't hurt you unless you drink it. I'd forgotten most of my library research on poisons. I should have taken notes. After all, when I resume writing my murder mystery, I might need to know about poisons. Again.

"After him!" Ernie yelled.

All the coppers in the room ran to do Ernie's bidding. Mr. Piccolo didn't look as if he aimed to go down without a fight. He flung the first policeman out of his way as easily as if he were flicking a fly off his coffee cup. Then he turned and ran like an enraged bison down the hall. Guess he didn't know the hallway in the direction he was headed stopped at a wall.

Which made me think of something. I tell you, in an emergency, one's thoughts land on the oddest notions. I hoped this one would work.

"Lulu, come with me!" I said.

Lulu said, "What?"

I grabbed her by the arm. "Come with me!" I all but dragged her through Mrs. Lamb's room and into Harvey's office.

The scenery in the office wasn't pretty. Mr. Bedini lay dead on the floor, but you could tell he hadn't released his hold on life easily. There was throw-up in a couple of spots, and his limbs were splayed at odd angles.

Lulu said, "Ew."

"I know, but come here."

Behind Harvey's desk was a gigantic window. Harvey said he liked to swivel his chair around and look at the set from time to time. Just then, I didn't care about the set. I cared about the tasseled ropes holding the draperies back. I ran to the left side of the window. "Aha!"

"Aha what?" asked Lulu, sounding more unhappy than curious.

"Get the sash holding back the drapery from that side of the window. I'll get this one."

"Sash?" After about five or six seconds, Lulu caught on. "Oh, yeah," she said. "That might work."

By crikey, it *did* work! Eventually.

Each of us got hold of a braided rope made of some kind of shiny gold-colored material which might have been satin or might not have been. Whatever it was made of, both pieces of rope were longer than the hallway was wide.

With ropes in hand, we raced out to the hallway again, just in time to see and hear Mr. Piccolo hit the wall at the far end of the hall. Flailing his arms and roaring like a maddened hippopotamus, he turned and started racing down the hallway toward us again. I shoved my piece of rope at Ernie. "Here! Take this. We'll trip him up when he tries to get past us."

It didn't even take Ernie five seconds to catch on. "You stay here," he ordered, and he dashed across the hall to stand in another doorway, holding his end of the rope. So I stayed there. He was my boss, after all.

Sprinting like a gigantic greyhound, Mr. Piccolo shoved past all of his pursuers and right into the rope Ernie and I held on either side of the hallway. He sounded like an elephant falling. Shook the whole building, by golly.

But he wasn't through yet. Heaving himself up and jerking my end of the rope from my hands, he roared. Didn't know what he roared. Whatever it was might have been in Italian, actually. At any rate, he was up and running again, flinging people here and there, when all of a sudden a golden lasso sailed over his head, slid to his shoulders, down to his upper arms, tightened and yanked him off his feet. He fell backwards with another building-rattling boom.

Unsure what had happened, I glanced around and darned if I didn't see Lulu, with Harvey and Mr. Crowhurst helping her, grasping the end of the rope. Even with the three of them pulling like mad, keeping Piccolo down was a struggle.

"Lulu!" I cried. "Did you make a lariat out of that curtain tie?"

She didn't seem to have enough breath to answer me, so she nodded. She, Harvey, and Mr. Crowhurst all three had to concentrate on keeping the lariat tight around Mr. Piccolo. Being lassoed didn't diminish Mr. Piccolo's fury. He kicked like a mule, swore like a muleskinner (I'm only assuming your typical muleskinner uses bad language) and it looked to me as if the police were going to have a hard time getting handcuffs on him.

I hurried, therefore, back into Mrs. Lamb's room, picked up a bronze statuette of Helen of Troy, nearly fell over because it was so heavy, but managed to get it out to the hall. There I thrust it at Ernie and Ernie, bless him, walked up to Mr. Piccolo, dodging his legs and curses and conked him over the head with poor Helen. He had to hit him twice, but eventually Piccolo lay still. I think Helen had a dent in her, but I doubted anyone would care.

By then the medical staff had arrived, although they remained clustered at the far end of the hallway as Mr. Piccolo and several other people clogged the area in front of Harvey's office. When Ernie finally managed to subdue Mr. Piccolo, the group of medics dared walk to the human roadblock.

"Um," said a woman who looked like a nurse as she wore a white uniform and cap. "We were told there might be a poison victim in Mr. Nash's office. Is this he?" She nodded down at Mr. Piccolo, her demeanor skeptical.

"No," said Ernie. "This guy's just out cold. If there's a doctor who can shoot him with some kind of sleeping medication or pour Veronal down his throat, the police can cart him off to a cell. The poisoned guy's in Mr. Nash's office." Ernie hooked a finger over his shoulder to show her the way.

"I'm a doctor for the studio," said a gray-haired man in a white coat. "You say the poisoned man is in that office?"

"Yes," said Ernie. "But this guy is a criminal, and he's huge. I managed to crack him over the head with Helen of Troy, but I don't know how long he'll be out. Do you have any barbital or morphine you can inject into him so the police can transport him to jail?"

"I can do no such thing," said the doctor huffily. "I can't just inject a person with a dangerous drug on your say-so."

"How about my say-so," said Harvey, nudging people aside and standing next to Ernie.

"Mr. Nash!" cried the doctor, straightening and looking as if he might execute a bow or kneel or something. "I... Well, I suppose if you can explain the matter to me, perhaps I can help without doing a complete physical examination of the fellow first."

"Happy to," said Harvey. "That man is Luca Piccolo, and he either murdered one of the set men, Melvin Flynn, or he abetted the murderer. He's also a member of the Salvatore crime family from New York City. He and other members of his gang have done thousands of dollars' worth of damage to this picture set. He's so big the police can't handle him if he's in full possession of his senses.

I would take it as a personal kindness if you could keep him asleep for a while."

"Ahem," said the doctor. "Yes, I believe I can accommodate you. You say he's a murderer?"

"He either did the deed himself or assisted in the crime," said Harvey. "He's definitely the one who poisoned Mr. Bedini. Mr. Bedini is the corpse on my office floor."

"Well, then, yes. I have morphine and a syringe in my bag."

Because there was no way around Mr. Piccolo and those standing with him ready to pounce if he awoke, the doc had to put his black bag on the floor. He didn't need to rummage hard, probably because he was an organized individual. He withdrew a small vial and a syringe. When he'd filled the syringe, he knelt beside Mr. Piccolo, who had begun to stir slightly. Ernie stood by with Helen of Troy in case Piccolo needed to be bashed again.

Thank the good Lord and Ernie, he didn't. The doc stuck the needle into Mr. Piccolo's arm, easily finding a patch of flesh to jab because he'd torn his shirt badly in his dash to escape. Mr. Piccolo's eyes flicked open once, and then he heaved a huge sigh and lay still once more.

"Thank you, Doctor," said Harvey. He glanced at the police contingent, some of whom looked as if they might benefit from medical care too. "Please see to the needs of these others as well."

The doctor didn't give the impression he was happy to be working on normal, everyday people, but he said, "Certainly."

Addressing the police contingent, Harvey said, "Will you be able to get him to the police station before he wakes up?"

"Dunno," said one of the coppers. This one had a big red splotch on one of his cheeks. I expected it would darken into a bruise later. "How long does that stuff last?"

The doctor said, "He should be out for at least an hour. He's a huge man, however, and although I gave him a large dose, I didn't dare give him anything more powerful lest the medication do more than merely subdue him."

"The world would be a better place if you euthanized him," I said. I mean, really! Mr. Piccolo and his gang of criminals had not merely killed an innocent man, but now they'd murdered one of their own! Or maybe merely the brother of one of their own. Either way, I doubted Mr. Luca Piccolo would be a major loss to the world. And then there was the traitor, Vic Bedini. Either a weak man or a bad one, he sure as heck wouldn't be much of a loss to the Nash Studio.

"True," said Lulu. "He's a real stinker."

"Now girls," said a grinning Ernie. "The police aren't in the business of executing people before they go to trial."

"Huh," I said.

"Huh," said Lulu.

"Can you please get that man off the hall runner and lug him away?" asked Harvey testily of the police. "The doctor needs to see Mr Bedini. He's the one we called about."

It took four uniformed policemen to haul Mr. Piccolo off the floor and to the exit. In fact, two other uniforms ran to help the first four when they began to flag and Mr. Piccolo started sagging in the middle. Mr. Piccolo was a true giant of a malignant human being. Those of us not directly involved in carrying him backed up against the hall's walls to be out of the way of the procession.

I recalled the ewer and pitcher of probably-poisoned lemonade as the medical personnel headed into Mrs. Lamb's room.

"*Wait!*" I hollered. "Wait! Don't go in there yet!"

Ernie, the doctor, the policemen, the nurse, Mr. Crowhurst, and Harvey all turned and frowned at me.

"What is it now?" barked Ernie.

"Mr. Piccolo threw lemonade with cyanide in it all over Mrs. Lamb's carpet," I said, panting slightly because I'd run to get ahead of the procession.

"You believe cyanide was used to poison the…poisoned fellow?" asked the doctor, whose name I later learned was Prendergast.

"Yes," I said. "And he threw the pitcher into the room. I'm sure some of it spilled onto the rug."

"Hmmm," said the doctor. "Has anyone inhaled the fumes?"

I glanced into the room and saw Mrs. Lamb, sitting in her chair, staring at the hallway and looking shocked.

"Do you feel all right, Mrs. Lamb?" I asked, walking into the room, this time being careful where I set my feet, and trying not to breathe. In all the excitement of subduing Mr. Piccolo, I hadn't recalled the cyanide-laced lemonade.

"My head is swimming a bit," she admitted. Then she crossed her arms on her desk and laid her head on them.

"Get this woman out of here!" snapped the doctor. "She may have inhaled cyanide!"

Ernie came to the rescue yet again. While all the motion-picture fellows stood still, looking vaguely like Stonehenge and staring at Mrs. Lamb, Ernie strode to the desk, plucked her from her chair and carried her out into the hallway. "Any way to open a window around here? I think fresh air will help her."

"Are the other offices along this hall like yours, Harvey?" I asked after a three- or four-second silence from those who knew.

"Yes. Yes, they are," Harvey said at last.

So I walked to the doorway on the other side of Harvey's, turned the knob and shoved the door open. The office was unoccupied, and there were two windows behind the big desk (not as big as Harvey's). I beckoned to Lulu, and the two of us opened the windows. Ernie carried Mrs. Lamb behind the desk, and I pulled out the chair. Ernie sat in the chair with Mrs. Lamb on his lap and moved the chair as close to the open window as he could get.

"Thanks, gals," said Ernie.

"Those movie folks don't think on their feet very fast, do they?" Lulu observed.

"No, they don't. I guess they make up stories, and their stories follow certain straight lines. When real life gets in the way, they don't know what to do," I said.

"Maybe not, but you two are tops," said Ernie.

"*Lulu* is tops," I said. "I didn't have any idea you knew how to fashion a lasso out of a piece of rope, Lulu. That was brilliant!"

"Thanks," said Lulu, blushing. "Rupert and I used to have to rope calves on the farm back home. Never tried to rope anything as big as that man before."

"You threw the lasso, Lulu?" asked Ernie. Mrs. Lamb had begun to stir in the cool breeze wafting through the open window. He carefully set her on the chair and eased out from under her, holding her shoulders so she couldn't slide from the chair.

"Yeah," said Lulu. "Didn't think I'd ever need to make a lasso after I left Oklahoma, but it came in handy today."

"It did indeed. And Mercy, thinking about tripping that brute and bringing me the bronze statue was also brilliant."

"Thanks, Ernie. You conked him really well, too."

"I was afraid he was going to kick me to death before I could reach his head," Ernie admitted.

We heard a commotion coming from the hall, and Lulu and I went to see what was going on. We discovered several things happening. First of all, a couple of medical men were carrying a sheet-covered body—I presumed it was that of Mr. Bedini—on a stretcher toward the exit. Second of all, several men carrying tool chests and with tool belts strapped to their waists strode into Mrs. Lamb's office. As they all wore work gloves and had scarves tied over their noses and mouths, I made another assumption: they would remove the soiled carpeting from Mrs. Lamb's room. They'd probably remove the carpeting from Harvey's room too, because it had yucky stains as well as cyanide on it.

Then a worried Harvey walked into the office Ernie, Lulu, Mrs. Lamb, and I occupied. "Is Mrs. Lamb well? I hope to heaven she wasn't poisoned too."

Mrs. Lamb used her feet to turn the swivel chair around and face her boss. "Oh, Mr. Nash, I'm so sorry I fainted. I guess everything was too exciting for me. I lead such a dull life as a rule."

"Nonsense," said Harvey in a reassuring tone. "I'm going to have Dr. Prendergast look at you. I don't know if there was enough poison in that lemonade to cause harm if it was inhaled, but I don't want to take any chances. I don't know what I'd do without you."

Wasn't Harvey a nice man?

TWENTY-SEVEN

S hortly after Dr. Prendergast conducted a brief physical examination of Mrs. Lamb and bandaged all other persons who had been injured during Mr. Piccolo's violent rampage, the medical personnel left the building. Most of the coppers did, too, but a man with a badge declaring his rank to be that of lieutenant remained behind.

Because of the carpet-removal—not to mention lethal poison—in Harvey and Mrs. Lamb's rooms, we stood in the corridor. I just stared at the almost-empty hall. You'd never know it had recently served as a venue for what might have passed as the running of the bulls in Pamplona, Spain, except there had been only one bull: Mr. Piccolo. Don't know what the annual casualty rate is in Pamplona, but I suspect Mr. Piccolo had matched it.

"What do you want to do with this, Harvey?" Ernie asked, holding the bronze Helen of Troy in both hands. "Sorry it got dented."

"It got dented in a good cause," said Harvey. "Just put it in the office where you took Mrs. Lamb."

"I think you should see another doctor and get a thorough check-up," I said to Mrs. Lamb. "Cyanide is horrible stuff. You might have inhaled more than was good for you." As if any inhalation of cyanide could be considered good.

"Thank you, dear," said she, "but I feel fine now. I was just a little lightheaded. I'm not accustomed to so much excitement."

Lulu whispered in my ear, "Her corset's too tight."

Startled by Lulu's keen observation, I glanced at Mrs. Lamb's office attire. Lulu was correct. Even if she'd wanted to be, Mrs. Lamb was too old to be a flapper. That, however, is beside the point. My personal opinion is that women shouldn't wear corsets so tight they cut off one's circulation. In order to be examined by the doctor, Mrs. Lamb had removed the jacket to the neat blue suit she wore, and I saw bulges where her corset started and stopped.

"You're right," I whispered back. Then I smiled at Mrs. Lamb and didn't tell her to loosen her stays, which would have been impolite if not downright brassy.

Oh Lordy, and then I almost giggled because the word "brassy" had flitted through my mind and instantly focused on poor dented Helen of Troy. Maybe *I* was the one who'd inhaled too much cyanide.

At any rate, we hallway-standers glanced at each other in silence some more, none of us sure what to do next. Finally Ernie broke the impasse.

"So, Bedini's dead and Piccolo's on his way to being locked up. We have Bedini's sister, Frank Sabatini, and several other gangsters in jail, and we still don't know who killed Melvin Flynn or why anyone was trying to ruin the making of *Helen of Troy*. So what do we do now?"

The man with the lieutenant's badge said, "We'll have to question them down at the station."

"I'd like to be there with my secretary. She's an ace at taking notes," said Ernie.

"We don't allow civilians to participate—"

Harvey of all people (because he's generally so polite), interrupted the lieutenant. "This fellow and his secretary aren't civilians. Ernie Templeton is a licensed private investigator and Miss Allcutt is his secretary." He glanced at Lulu. "And Miss LaBelle is an important assistant. I hired them to look into this problem."

"Which problem?" asked the lieutenant, who was short of stature as well as short on smarts. Not very nice of me, but nertz.

"To look into the sabotage of the picture, find whoever was doing it and attempt to stop him or her. Or them," said Harvey.

After frowning at Ernie, Lulu, and me, the lieutenant said, "Very well, Mr. Nash. I expect you'd like to be in on the interviews too."

"Yes," said Harvey. "I insist upon it."

My goodness! I didn't know if even my parents could insist upon being involved in a police interrogation and be obeyed. Harvey must pay the L.A.P.D. a fortune!

"All right," the lieutenant said. I'd give you his last name but I don't know what it was, so he'll always be "the lieutenant" to me. "Do you want to question them now or wait until tomorrow?"

"Piccolo won't be awake for another hour or more, according to Dr. Prendergast," said Harvey. "Ernie, do you have a preference?"

"I'd prefer to line them up against a wall and shoot them, but I doubt the L.A.P.D. will oblige."

The lieutenant huffed.

"You're planning to interview them separately, aren't you?" I asked, not giving a fig about his touchiness.

He gave me the same look he might have given a bug swimming in his soup. "We have rules to follow in the police department, ma'am."

"Don't call me ma'am," I snapped. "My name is Mercy Allcutt, and I've seen the L.A.P.D. in action more than once. In fact, 'inaction' should be in your name somewhere. If you question them all at the same time in the same room, they won't dare say anything that might incriminate another one of them for fear of being bumped off by a gang member."

The lieutenant stiffened at my jibe. He opened his mouth, probably to say something unkind, but Ernie took over.

"Listen, I used to be an L.A.P.D. police officer. I know the rules. Mercy's right. You'll have to question each of those bozos individually."

"Sounds logical to me," said Harvey.

After giving another huff, the lieutenant said, "Very well. When would you like to conduct these interviews?"

"About now would be good," said Ernie.

My stomach took that opportunity to growl. How embarrassing.

But then Harvey's stomach growled, and I didn't feel so silly. "Let's hit the studio canteen first, and then we'll meet at the police station. That all right with you, Ernie?"

"Definitely," said Ernie.

"Good," said Harvey. "I believe Sid should be there too because he's been involved in cleaning up the messes the crooks have made."

"Sounds good to me," said Ernie. He spoke to the lieutenant next. "So, make sure you get a room big enough to hold five or six inquisitors and one suspect. We'll talk to them separately at first."

"Listen, Mr. Templeton, you can't order me around like a lackey," said the now-intensely piqued lieutenant. "Why, I'm a sworn—"

"Stay here for a minute," said Harvey, again interrupting a person, which was astounding behavior on his part. "I'll call Chief Davis and get this sorted out."

Instantly, the lieutenant gave up. "There's no need for that," he said hastily. "We'll have a large room and several chairs for the questioners, along with a chair for a suspect."

"Thank you," said Harvey coolly. "That will be fine. We'll be at the station in an hour or an hour and a half."

"Yes sir," said the lieutenant. He lifted his hand as if to salute Harvey, realized what he was doing and let his arm drop.

"So you can go to the station and start getting ready now," said Ernie.

The lieutenant pinched his lips together but managed to say, "Yes." Then he turned and left us. Thank goodness.

"Want to lead the way to the canteen, Harvey?" asked Ernie.

"Sure," said Harvey. "Come with me."

He led us to what was, I guess, a private entrance and exit for the top executives in the organization. It opened onto a small lobby-type area. Then Harvey opened a door outside of which sat some of the cars used to drive important people around the set. As he beckoned us to walk down a small staircase, he said, "The canteen is quite far away from the *Helen of Troy* set. Its architecture doesn't suit ancient Greece."

As soon as Harvey appeared outside the building, several men in chauffeurs' caps slid from the fence upon which they sat. One of them raced over to a limousine, opened the back door and bowed to Harvey.

"Thanks, Glen," said Harvey, who was nice to all his employees and pretty much everyone else because he was...well, nice.

"Where to, Mr. Nash?" asked Glen.

"The canteen, please," said Harvey.

Glen glanced at our party and said, "You all going to the canteen?"

"Yes, we're all going," said Harvey.

So Glen hurried to the other side of the limousine and opened two more doors. We all managed to fit in quite comfortably, and Glen drove us in a slow and dignified manner to the canteen. Boy, it smelled good around there.

The food was good, too. Lulu and I each ordered a chicken sandwich, which came with something called French fries. I'd had fish and chips when I was in England once, and these potatoes were like those potatoes. I loved them.

"Boy, these are good," said Lulu, stabbing and waving one of her fries (or chips) on the end of her fork.

"Delicious," I said.

Harvey and Ernie both had the chopped beef patty with sautéed onions. I had a cup of tea with my meal, although the canteen provided lemonade. I was "off" lemonade for a while though, having recently witnessed the bright pink face and skewed limbs of the late Mr. Vic Bedini.

We chatted about not much of anything as we ate our lunches. Harvey had a special lunch room he used. "I don't want to stifle any conversations," he said. "People get nervous around me for some reason."

"Wouldn't have anything to do with the fact that you're their boss, would it?" asked Ernie, grinning at Harvey between bites.

With a shrug, Harvey said, "I expect so, although I'd like people to feel free to talk to me if they have anything useful to say. For instance, if anyone had noticed unusual goings-on at the various scenes of the mishaps on the set, we might have put a stop to them before anyone died."

"Hope the problem will be resolved soon," I said after swallowing a bite of my chicken sandwich.

"Me too," said Lulu. "I miss my home. Well," she amended, smiling at me, "I miss *your* home."

"And I miss my office," said Ernie. "This has been interesting, but I'd rather track a cheating spouse. More boring, but less hazardous to one's health."

"Unless you get entangled with people in the dog -show business," I said, reminiscing about a couple of recent cases.

"You have to admit the dogs weren't the problems in those cases," said Ernie. "It was the people who owned the dogs who were the problems."

"As always," I said with a sigh. "People can be *such* awful creatures, can't they?"

"Well," said Lulu. "Not all of them."

"True," I said, although I was beginning to have certain doubts on the worthiness of human beings to occupy the earth. I didn't say so to my tablemates, because I'd actually begun to fret about my dislike of the species to which I belonged.

"Not all of humanity is made up of people like the Salvatores or the L.A.P.D.," said Ernie.

"I guess. And not all Chinese people are slave traders and hatchet men either."

The silence following my comment prompted me to glance up at my dining companions. "What?" I said. "They aren't."

"No, they aren't," agreed Ernie. Lulu and Harvey nodded their heads.

"Of course, the slave trade isn't limited to the Chinese either," I said after musing on the subject for several seconds. "In fact, in this country slavery was supposed to have been abolished in 1864 or '65, wasn't it? But I've heard horror stories about non-white people trying to live in the southern states. White people just kill them for no reason."

A longer silence ensued this time. I finally realized the reason. "I guess this isn't a prime dinner-table conversation, is it?"

"Yeah," said Lulu. "Races generally don't like each other much, although you've opened my eyes a lot about that sort of thing."

"I have?"

"Yes. You have."

"Mercy's one of those people who hates you before you make an impression on her. If you make a *good* impression, she'll like you, but you have to earn her regard first," said Ernie.

"That's not true!" I said.

Ernie's eyes rolled so far back in his head, that I'm surprised they didn't get stuck.

"I wouldn't go *that* far," said Lulu judiciously. "But she has high standards."

"What's wrong with having high standards?" I said. I already regretted having aired my opinions at the table, mainly because my opinions were…I don't know. Radical? Maybe they were, but I grew up in an ivory tower and let me tell you, the so-called "real world" came as a shock to me.

"Not a single thing," said Harvey. I could tell he was trying not to laugh.

"Fiddlesticks," I said, and finished my lunch without speaking again.

I'm sure everyone else at the table was happy about my decision.

TWENTY-EIGHT

W
e arrived at the Los Angeles Police Department's headquarters approximately an hour and a quarter after the lieutenant had left the Nash Studio. A uniformed officer whose badge proclaimed him to be a "Policeman" had seemingly been placed in the station's lobby just for us. As soon as Harvey opened the front door so that Lulu and I could enter before he, Ernie and Sid did, the police fellow quick-stepped up to us.

"Mr. Nash?" he said, peering over Lulu's and my heads and addressing Harvey.

"Yes," said Harvey, startled because the guy hadn't been at the door three seconds earlier.

"The lieutenant asked me to escort you and your party to an interview room," said the policemen. Squinting at his badge, I saw his last was Bridges. He didn't seem as cranky as his lieutenant and actually smiled at us.

"Thank you," said Harvey. He turned and said, "Everyone ready to go to the interview room?"

"Yes, indeed," said Ernie. He glanced at me, "You loaded with tablets and pencils, Mercy?"

"Yes," I affirmed. I'd sharpened all my pencils in one of the offices near Harvey's before we went to the canteen for lunch.

"What should I do?" asked Lulu.

"Just sit and listen," said Ernie. "Harvey, Sid, and I will question the suspects." Recalling that he was at police headquarters, he added, "I suspect an L.A.P.D. representative will ask a few questions too.

"Here, Lulu." I handed Lulu a pad and a pencil so she wouldn't feel superfluous. "If anything catches your ear, write it down."

"I can't take shorthand," she whispered.

"It doesn't matter." I assured her. "You can hear and you're smart. If something someone says catches your attention and makes you think of something else, write that down too."

After staring at me as if I'd lost what little was left of my mind, Lulu said, "Okay."

We walked down a hall, and Officer Bridges opened a door for us. The room into which he led us looked a whole lot like a police conference room I'd been in a month or so earlier. Guess architects don't think it's necessary to be creative with police buildings.

As soon as Harvey's group had settled into various chairs, the lieutenant entered the room along with another uniformed police fellow whose badge declared him to be a detective. From the groveling exhibited by the lieutenant to the detective, I presumed a detective was of a higher rank in police circles than a lieutenant.

As soon as the two police fellows sat, the detective said, "Good afternoon, ladies and gentlemen. We're here to question several suspects about criminal activity during the filming of *Helen of Troy*."

"That is correct," said the lieutenant.

"Very well," said the detective. "Mr. Nash, will you please introduce your group? Just so we know who we're dealing with." My brain instantly corrected him but my mouth didn't, for which I'm sure everyone present would have been grateful had they but known.

"Well, I'm Harvey Nash," said Harvey. "Why don't the rest of you introduce yourselves?"

"That will be fine," said the detective.

So Ernie started. I was next, so I told the police my name. Lulu gave her name in a timid voice. Sid was louder.

"Very well," said the detective. "Mr. Nash, do you have a preference as to the first person we should interview?"

Good grief! And here I thought the police were the ones who kept the streets safe for normal citizens. Silly me. After almost a year of working for Ernie, corruption still surprised me, if this was corruption. It might not have been, but golly, shouldn't the police folks decide whom to interview first? Oh, never mind me. I think I belong in another century.

Even Harvey appeared slightly taken aback. He looked at Sid and then at Ernie, where his gaze stopped. "Ernie? Whom do you think should talk first?"

"Is Mercy's brother still here?" he asked.

"Mercy's brother?" The detective clearly didn't know Mercy's brother from a blot of smut on the sidewalk, which he pretty much was. George, not the detective.

After getting an eyebrow-lift from Ernie, I said in a firm and disapproving voice, "George Monteith Allcutt. He was picked up this morning when all vehicles were searched at the entrance to the set."

The detective looked at the lieutenant. The lieutenant looked confused.

"Unless someone's bailed him out, he should be here, held among the rest of the suspects who were detained at the studio this morning," said Ernie. "If he's not here, I want to know why. And so does Mr. Nash." I'm sure he added the last part because Harvey was the one who paid off the police department.

There I go, getting all offended by inequality again. I'll try to keep my notions to myself from now on, but I can't guarantee anything.

The lieutenant rose abruptly from his chair. "I'll ask the booking sergeant," he said and left the room with what I considered suspicious haste.

The detective frowned down at a pile of papers in front of him.

Flipping through them slowly, he said, "I see nothing here about an Allcutt."

"There should be several forms about him," said Ernie. "He's been picked up by the police twice or thrice in the last couple of days."

"Indeed there should be," I said.

Lulu patted my arm. "It's okay, kid," she whispered to me.

I whispered back, "No, it isn't."

"Mercy's right. It isn't okay," said Ernie, making my flinty heart soften a little. At least *he* knew right from wrong. Well, so did Lulu, but she was attempting to make me feel better so her fib didn't count.

Not sure how many minutes passed, the detective pretending to go through his pile of papers and the rest of us giving him unkind stares, but it seemed like forever. I began tapping my pencil on the table just because, and Ernie pushed his chair back and put his feet on the table. The chair in the conference room wasn't as easy to maneuver as the one in his office, but he got his point across admirably.

Finally Harvey broke the taut silence. "Detective Smithers, I'm disappointed in the Los Angeles Police Department's performance during these past few weeks. The fact that you don't seem to have written reports on George Allcutt only caps my disappointment. Not that I should *have* to bribe the L.A.P.D. to do its job, but the fact remains that I *do* bribe you folks, and I'll be speaking to Chief Davis about this debacle."

"Mr. Nash," the detective said, his face blazing, "I'm so sorry about this. You're correct. This case has been handled in a sloppy manner, and there will be repercussions. Heads will roll, in fact."

"We don't care about rolling heads," snapped Ernie. "What we want is for the police to do the jobs they're paid to do. Twice, if Harvey has to supplement what the taxpayers already pay for your services."

Shooting Ernie a hateful glance, Detective Smithers said, "I'm very sorry about this. I'll see what's going on with the lieutenant."

He pushed his chair back, prepared to rise from it and search for his inept cohort, but the door opened before he could.

And there, by golly, was George Monteith Allcutt in the flesh and being shoved around by the lieutenant. And he wore handcuffs! My antagonism towards the coppers lessened by perhaps an eighth of an inch.

"Huh. Had him all along, did you?" said Ernie.

The lieutenant cleared his throat. "Yes. Sorry for the delay. We didn't realize…" He stopped speaking before he finished his sentence, which was just as well. He'd been about to say something to the effect that George looked wealthy and, therefore, couldn't possibly be associated with any of the back-east thugs who'd infiltrated the movie set.

"Why am I here?" George demanded as if he were a member of royalty because that's the way people in Boston treated the Allcutts.

"Because you broke the law," said Ernie. "Now sit down and shut up. I'm going to ask you some questions, and I want honest answers."

"You can't talk to me—"

"Hush up, George. You're not in Boston any longer. Here you're a nobody," I said. "And a criminal nobody at that."

"Don't you—"

But Ernie had already risen from his chair and walked over to George, who was *fuming* with rage. When George realized Ernie stood beside him, he jumped like a frightened hare and opened his mouth again. So Ernie whapped him upside the head and said, "Clam up, George. You're in jail now and if you want to get out of jail, you'll cooperate with us. Your sweetie got her brother murdered. You want the same treatment?"

George snapped his mouth shut. He wasn't a pretty sight. His expensive suit was wrinkled, and he looked as if all the drinking and carousing he'd been doing had damaged his health some. I hoped it had.

"I don't know what—"

Another whap from Ernie shut George's mouth for him again.

"Don't say another word, George," said Ernie in a death-voice. "Don't say anything at all unless it's to answer a question put to you in this room by one of these people. Do you understand what I just said?"

"What? I don't—"

Another whap. "Not a quick learner are you, George?" said Ernie. "I'll be happy to stuff a rag in your mouth. The lieutenant can pull it out when it's time for you to answer our questions."

George finally caught on. He glanced wildly around the room but didn't speak. The lieutenant guided him to the chair at the end of the long table around which the rest of us sat. He then handed the detective three more sheets of paper. About George, I'm sure.

"Very well," said Harvey. "I'll ask George a few preliminary questions if you don't mind." His gaze traveled around the table. When no one objected he said, "George, why are you here in Los Angeles?"

George swallowed. "I...I...wanted to be with Verna. She told me she had to leave town because of some trouble."

"What town was it she had to leave?" asked Ernie after checking with Harvey to see if he minded. Harvey didn't mind.

"N-New York City," George stammered.

"And what trouble was she escaping from?" Ernie again.

"A...a...a gangster in New York was pestering her. She said she feared for her life if she didn't leave New York." He swallowed again. "She apologized to me and said she'd...she'd...always love me."

"I see," said Harvey, taking over from Ernie. "And you believed her name to be Verna Borden when you and she were seeing each other back east?"

"That *is* her name," said George. "Her name is Verna Borden, and she was a chorus girl with the Ziegfeld Follies! But she's really a ballerina. She'd gone to ballet school and everything. She was about to audition for a part in some ballet directed by a foreigner named Balanchine. She might have danced with Pavlova!"

"Right," said Harvey. "George, you've been duped."

"No!" cried George.

"George," said Harvey in a stern tone. "You must allow me to speak before you burst out yelling. Do you understand me, or would it help if Mr. Templeton stood beside you and tapped your shoulder when you're supposed to speak? Do you think you can regulate yourself, or do you need help?"

Clearly baffled, George said, "What? Regulate? But Verna is..." He shut up when Ernie rose from his chair and walked over to stand behind George's chair. George peered at Ernie with terror writ large on his countenance.

"Listen to me carefully, George," said Harvey in a slow, deliberate manner. "Don't talk. Just listen, because you need to understand some things. Nod if you understand me."

After a second's hesitation, a glimpse of Ernie's open right hand, poised as if to apply another whack to his skull, prompted George to nod and say a hasty, "Yes."

"Good. The name of the woman who worked in the Ziegfeld Follies as a chorus girl is actually Vicky Bedini. I have no doubt she was a talented dancer. A girl has to have talent to work for Flo Ziegfeld, but she wasn't your one true love, George. I'm sorry, but it's the truth."

"No!" cried George before shutting up once more at the appearance of Ernie's hand.

"Yes, George. Her name is Vicky Bedini. Her brother was Vic Bedini. Vic worked for me for quite a few years, and I thought I could trust him. Unfortunately, my trust was misplaced. Now Vic Bedini is dead because someone in the Salvatore gang from New York City murdered him with cyanide."

"Vic is dead?" whispered George, his eyes—still bloodshot—opening wide.

"Vic is dead. The cyanide was administered to him by Mr. Luca Piccolo. Someone must have directed Mr. Piccolo's actions. Do you know for whom Mr. Piccolo worked?"

"Piccolo?" asked George, sounding nearly as stupid as he looked. "I thought a piccolo was a little flute."

"According to what Miss Allcutt and Miss LaBelle heard outside Mr. Bedini's tent, Mr. Piccolo often worked with or for the Salvatore gang. Mr. Piccolo is an extremely large man," said Harvey. "An *extremely* large man."

"Oh, him," said George. "I think I saw him with Vic and Verna a couple of times."

"Her name isn't Verna, George," said Ernie. As he spoke from directly behind George's chair, George gave another violent start, but he was beginning to catch on to the rules and didn't speak.

"Mr. Luca Piccolo, the large man, poisoned Vic Bedini today in my office, George," said Harvey. "Vic is dead. Do you understand the finality of the word 'dead'?"

George nodded.

"He's dead because he was associated with your lady friend and her gangster buddies. I'm only sorry she persuaded her brother, Vic, to go along with their schemes."

"Verna wouldn't do that!" said George, although he didn't sound as positive as he had earlier.

"She did do that, George. And stop talking unless you're answering questions," said Ernie fiercely.

George froze in his chair, eyes wide open and searching for Ernie's hand. He didn't find it because Ernie didn't threaten him with it this time.

"Now George, what I want to know is precisely how you discovered where your lady friend was when she left New York and arrived in Los Angeles. How did you get the information?"

"What do you mean?" asked George, glancing back at Ernie and flinching for no reason. Well, not much reason anyhow.

"I'll speak more slowly this time, George, so pay attention," said Harvey. "How did you learn where your lady friend went after she left New York?"

After gulping audibly, George said, "She sent me a cable."

"I see. And did she also tell you about the picture Nash Studios is filming?"

"Y-yes. She told me she could get me onto the set."

"Did you ask her why *she* had to get you on the set, considering I'm your brother-in-law and have considerably more clout in the industry than she?"

"Sh-she said it was supposed to be a closed set," said George. "She said the rules were stupid."

"I see," said Harvey once more. "And she managed to sneak you onto the set even though it was supposed to be a closed set?"

"Yes. Yes, she…she did," said George, as if he was no longer quite sure what was happening in his own personal universe.

My brother George is exceptionally slow of thought. Wish I could divorce him, but I don't think siblings are allowed to divorce each other. A shame, that.

TWENTY-NINE

"I want you to listen to me carefully, George," said Harvey. "Are you listening? Just nod."

George followed instructions for once and nodded.

"Now, while I'm telling you these facts, I don't want you to burst out talking. Do you understand? Just nod."

George nodded.

"Good," said Harvey. "When your mother was staying with Chloe and me after our daughter was born, she received a trunk telephone call from your father in Boston. Your father told your mother that he was distressed about your behavior."

George opened his mouth but snapped it shut when Ernie bopped his fist lightly on his shoulder.

"Do you understand what I just told you, George?"

George nodded.

"Very well. Your father said you had fallen for a chorus girl in the Ziegfeld Follies. He also said you were spending a lot of money and time on the girl, and that you and she had been frequenting speakeasies and going to places like the Cotton Club in Harlem."

"Oh, God," whimpered George.

"Be quiet, George. I haven't finished the story yet. Nod if you understand."

George nodded.

"Your mother left Los Angeles for Boston almost instantly after receiving your father's telephone call," Harvey continued. "Before your mother left Los Angeles, she and your father decided to pay off your lady friend to get her to leave you alone and go away. They did. And she did. Do you understand?"

"No!" cried George. "They didn't! Verna would have told me."

Making a fist, Ernie bopped George on the head this time. Gently. I mean, he didn't sock him or anything, which I considered (and still consider) a rotten shame.

"Listen to me, George," said Ernie, back to using his death-voice. "Mr. and Mrs. Allcutt, your parents, paid Miss Bedini—or, as you knew her, Miss Borden—to leave New York City. They paid her a substantial sum of money to do so. That is the truth. Do you understand now?"

"I...I..." Tears gathered in George's eyes.

"A nod will do," Ernie said between clenched teeth. "Do you understand what Harvey and I just told you about your Ziegfeld chorus girl being paid to leave you and the state of New York? Just nod if you understand what we told you."

George nodded, but he didn't want to. He apparently didn't dare wipe his tears away, so they slid down his cheeks. If he weren't the piece of grotesquerie I'd known all my life, I might have felt sorry for him, but he was so I didn't.

"And then," Ernie continued, "your sweetheart cabled you. Is that correct?"

George nodded.

"And she told you where she was living and that she'd landed a role in *Helen of Troy*?"

Another nod from George.

"But when you got here, you couldn't find her so you went to Harvey and Chloe's house, asking for her. I know you did, because I was there when you were."

George executed one more miserable nod.

"But you managed to find her. How did you find her, George?"

After glancing at Ernie and Harvey, both of whom urged him to speak for once, George said, "I cabled her that I'd be staying at the Beverly Hills Hotel. But when I arrived, she didn't show up." He opened his mouth to say more, but Ernie held up his palm. I suspect most dogs are easier to train than my brother, but he seemed to have caught on at last. He snapped his mouth shut.

"So when you left the Nash home in your inebriated condition, you had the cabbie take you to the Beverly Hills Hotel?" asked Harvey. "You didn't seem awfully clear about your destination when we threw you out of our house."

After hesitating for several seconds, George said, "I told the cabbie to take me to the Beverly Hills Hotel. There was a little confusion at first."

"I'll just bet there was," I muttered. For the record, I was taking down the conversation verbatim and only glanced up occasionally to see if George was able to learn to follow directions.

"So she came to your hotel room eventually?" pressed Harvey.

"Yes. Yes, she did."

"And that's when she told you how to get on the set, right?"

George opened his mouth, but decided a nod was safer, so he nodded.

"And you followed her instructions on how to get on to the set, right?" asked Harvey.

George nodded.

"Had you met Mr. Bedini, Mr. Piccolo, or Mr. Sabatini before coming to Los Angeles?" Harvey wanted to know.

After a moment of confusion, George shook his head.

Glancing at Ernie, Harvey said, "Is there anything else you want to ask George, Ernie, or did we cover all the issues we need?"

"I have a couple of questions," I said. I know I'm not Ernie, but I butted in anyway.

"Sure, Mercy. Go ahead," said Ernie with a grin.

"George, did your lady friend ever mention to you that she was in trouble because of gambling debts?"

"Huh?" said George.

Good Lord.

"Did the woman you knew as Verna Borden tell you she was in debt to a gambling ring in New York or Boston?" I added Boston because George's imagination wouldn't stretch that far on its own. From New York to Boston, I mean.

"Huh? No! She never gambled. I don't believe it about our parents either."

"It's all right, George," I said. "You may speak to our parents tomorrow along with an attorney of our acquaintance. I have a feeling your conversation will be enlightening. At least to you. The rest of us, even our parents, already know the truth."

George gave me a hideous scowl, but I don't think he dared to say anything.

"Thank you, George," said Harvey. "Unless Ernie or Mercy have any further questions, I think you can be returned to your cell now."

"Cell? Why am I in a cell?" George demanded.

"You broke the law. You won't get out of that cell until somebody posts a bond for you, George," said Harvey. He went on to say, "It won't be me."

"But...but..."

"Shut up, George," said Ernie, showing George his open palm one last time.

George shut up. The lieutenant walked him back to wherever the police department was housing him.

Ernie returned to his seat next to me. "How'd you end up with a brother like that, Mercy? Neither you nor your sister is a brainless nitwit. Did the two of you get the allotment of brain power in your family?"

"I think they did," said Harvey with a chuckle.

As for me, I didn't feel much like laughing, but I appreciated Ernie's comment.

"Whom would you like to question next?" Harvey asked of Ernie.

"I think the lady is probably our next best bet. I'm curious to know if she knew her brother was going to be murdered if he didn't play along with the Salvatore gang. And I'd like to hear her take on the gambling issue. I'm beginning to think she made it up for her brother's sake, hoping he'd help her even if he disapproved of her associates."

"I expect you're right," said Harvey.

So the lieutenant left the room again. He returned shortly without Vicky Bedini. When he saw us all frowning at him, he said, "A policewoman will be bringing in Miss...the woman." Guess he wasn't certain of her name.

Sure enough, a few minutes later, a policewoman (she even had a badge with "Policewoman" etched on it) escorted Vicky Bedini into the room. Miss Bedini sent us all a hostile scowl but sat where the officer indicated she should sit. She too wore handcuffs.

"Who wants to start this interrogation?" asked Harvey.

Nobody spoke up at first, so I decided what the heck and said, "I would."

Harvey and Ernie exchanged a glance, and then Ernie shrugged. "Sure. Why not? Mercy's the one who first found out about this young woman, right?"

"Right," I answered for myself.

"Go ahead, Mercy," said Harvey. Then he folded his arms over his chest and sat back in his chair.

In case you were wondering, neither the detective nor the lieutenant said a single word but allowed Harvey's party to conduct the interviews. They didn't even have a stenographer in the room taking notes. It would have been unbelievable except it happened. Shoot, even Phil Bigelow, Ernie's best friend and an L.A.P.D. detective, wasn't *this* lax in his duties as a copper.

"Very well," I said. "Miss Bedini, how are you today?"

"How the hell do you think I am?" she snarled.

"I have no idea," I said.

"Huh."

"Have you been told about your brother's death by cyanide poisoning?"

Miss Bedini jerked in her chair and looked at me as if I'd lost my mind. "What're you talking about? There's nothing wrong with Vic!"

"Vic is dead, Miss Bedini," I said stonily. "He drank poisoned lemonade delivered to him by a fellow named Luca Piccolo."

"No! You're lying!" Miss Bedini stood from her chair and hurled herself at the big table as if she wanted to get to me and scratch my eyes out. Not sure how she figured she'd do that with her hands cuffed behind her back. Perhaps she wasn't thinking clearly.

"Get back here," the policewoman growled, grabbing Miss Bedini by the cuffs and hauling her back into her chair.

"You're lying!" Miss Bedini yelled at me. "Vic didn't have anything to do with anything! Luca wouldn't poison him!"

"Wrong on at least one of those counts," I said. "Vic may or may not have known what you and your Salvatore cohorts had planned for the movie set of *Helen of Troy*, but he is definitely dead. Killed by Luca Piccolo. I suspect Mr. Piccolo didn't come up with the idea all by himself. Did you encourage him? Did you think, as your associates plainly did, that your brother posed a threat to them?"

Miss Bedini's mouth had begun to tremble. Her gaze went from person to person around the table, but she found no solace from anyone's expression. "V-Vic's really dead?" she said in a tiny voice.

"Vic is really dead," I said. "Mr. Nash, Mr. Templeton, Mr. Lafayette, Miss LaBelle, and I watched him die. It wasn't pleasant."

"Oh, God," whimpered Miss Bedini. She laid her head on the table and shook with sobs.

"Does anybody have a clean hankie?" I asked the assemblage.

"Yeah. She can use mine," said Lulu.

"Actually, I don't think she can," I said. "Her hands are cuffed behind her back."

"Shall I unlock the handcuffs?" the police lady asked, sounding tentative.

"*No!*" we all said in chorus. Well, the police people didn't speak.

"Ernie, just wipe her face, all right?" I asked my boss.

"Sure, if she lifts it."

He had a point. Miss Bedini didn't appear to be in a head-lifting mood. She was still adding to the puddle of tears on the table.

"Lift her head and blot her face. Then she can put her head down again if she wants to," suggested Lulu, who sounded as if she were feeling approximately as cold-blooded as I.

"Good idea." Ernie pulled on Miss Bedini's pretty black hair, giving her cause to screech a little, mopped up her tears, and then let go. She didn't replace her head on the table.

"Now. Are you up to answering a few more questions, Miss Bedini?" I said.

"N-no," she said.

"Too bad," I said. "If you don't answer my questions, the Los Angeles Police Department will have no other option than to charge you as an accomplice in your brother's murder. If you *are* complicit in his death, fine. If you aren't, you might tell us the truth and get a lesser sentence."

"What do you mean?"

"Luca Piccolo murdered your brother using lemonade laced with cyanide. Did you know he was going to do that?"

Her lips still trembling, Miss Bedini shook her head.

"We need an audible answer," I said. Wow, I didn't know I had it in me to be so cold and hard.

"N-no," she whispered.

"You did not know Luca Piccolo was going to poison your brother with cyanide. Is that correct?"

She nodded, but I made a gesture with my hand on the order of beckoning someone to come hither. She got the point and said, "Yes. That's correct." She sniffled hard and burst out, "I don't believe you! Luca and I love each other! He wouldn't hurt Vic!"

Some more sobbing from her and total silence from the rest of us eventually nudged her to stop crying. Ernie wiped her face again.

"So you and Mr. Luca Piccolo were lovers, correct?" I said.

Looking totally miserable, she nodded. "Yes."

"And did you know that Mr. George Monteith Allcutt believed you and he were in love?"

She breathed heavily for a second or two in order to get her emotions under control before she said, "Yes."

"Very well," I said. "So in effect, you lured Mr. Allcutt into an affair with you?"

"I-I wouldn't put it like that," said Miss Bedini, her voice hoarse.

"I'm sure you wouldn't. However, the rest of the world would think you and Mr. Allcutt were in love based on your behavior. Is that correct?"

"I can't help what other people think." She tried to sound defiant, but grief made her words wobble.

"Oh, I think you can," I said. "You wanted George. That is to say, you wanted Mr. Allcutt to fall in love with you, and you wanted other people to believe you two were an item. Is that correct?"

After a longish silence, she whispered, "Y-yes."

"Was it Mr. Piccolo who first introduced you to the members of the Salvatore crime gang in New York City?"

Her face more or less crumpled up into an ugly mask of woe, but she managed to eke out a tiny, "Yes."

"I see. How much money did Mr. Allcutt's parents pay you to throw over Mr. George Allcutt and leave New York City?"

She gave us the woeful mask-face again then muttered an almost inaudible, "Ten thousand dollars."

Wow! That was a big bundle of mazuma.

"Very well. You and your New York acquaintances knew Mr. Allcutt was not only under thrall to you, but that he had a wealthy brother-in-law in the motion-picture industry. They also believed the latest Nash production might become a lucrative opportunity for the Salvatores if you played your cards right. Is that correct?"

"I-I-I...don't know what you mean," said Miss Bedini.

"I don't believe you," I said. Miss Bedini gasped, but I didn't care. "Why were members of the Salvatore gang creating havoc on the set of *Helen of Troy*? Leaving you out of the equation for a second, what did they aim to achieve by their mischief on the set?"

"I...I. Oh, hell."

She was interrupted, supposing she'd aimed to spill her guts—boy, that's a disgusting expression—by a hard knock at the door.

Without waiting for a response from those of us at the table, a uniformed policeman carrying several pieces of paper opened the door and walked directly to the detective.

"Sorry to interrupt, sir, but we thought these might be important."

Frowning, the detective took the messages—they looked like cablegrams—from the policeman. He scanned them briefly, lifted his eyebrows then his head and said, "Thank you," to the uniform. "You needn't wait."

The uniform saluted and left the room. As soon as he was gone, Detective Smithers held up the cablegrams. "News. News that might make a big difference in this case."

We waited for Smithers to go on, but he must have decided to create a dramatic effect and sat silent. Actually, he waited a trifle too long, because Harvey finally said, "Well, what is it?"

Ernie piped up, "If you can't read, I'll be happy to read it for you."

The detective dared frown at both men, but he didn't let his gaze linger on either one. "According to these cablegrams just received at the front desk from the New York City Police Department, Carmine Salvatore along with two of his head henchmen were gunned down in the Bronx this morning. The head of the gang is dead. His organization is in disarray. It is thought the hit was perpetrated by Arnold Rothstein or by his associate, Jack 'Legs' Diamond." The detective looked up from the papers. "So it looks as if Rothstein and maybe Capone will wage a war over Salvatore's leaderless pack and the neighborhoods it terrorized."

"Well, isn't that just the pip," said Ernie. It wasn't a question.

Her eyes wide and nearly bugging out of her head, Vicky Bedini said, "What? Did you say Carmine is *dead*?"

Detective Smithers waved the cablegrams in the air. "That's what it says here. I have no reason to doubt it."

And by golly, she broke down and told us the whole story. It was an ugly story and full of wretched deceit, criminality, and ghastliness, but she told it.

Eventually Miss Bedini was escorted out of the conference room.

A few seconds after she left, Harvey stood. "I think we'll leave the rest of the leaderless gang to you police folk," he said. Frowning with meaning, he added, "I expect convictions on all the counts of sabotage we've related to you as well as the murder of Mr. Melvin Flynn and Mr. Vic Bedini. Do you think the L.A.P.D. can handle that much?"

After first pressing his lips together in anger, the detective said, "Yes. We can and will handle the case from here."

"Thank God," I muttered. I'd taken notes through the entire ordeal. I'd taken notes until my fingers cramped.

I'm honestly not sure if I'd ever been so happy to leave a place as I was to leave that conference room. Harvey's chauffeur drove all of us, including Mr. Lafayette, to the Nash residence. Silence filled the limousine the whole way home.

It was only later that we learned Luca Piccolo had not only murdered Vic Bedini, but he was behind the scaffolding failure that killed the carpenter, Mel Flynn.

From Miss Bedini, we also learned that Carmine Salvatore had wanted to worm his way into the picture business because pictures made a lot of money. Too bad for him and several of his gang members, his dream died with him. At least six of his pals also died in the few days following Carmine Salvatore's own demise.

Harvey, Ernie, Lulu, Chloe, and the rest of the people involved in the filming of *Helen of Troy*, didn't grieve for any of them.

THIRTY

W hen we chauffeured up the drive to the Nash residence, I felt like an overcooked noodle. From the appearance of my companions, they felt likewise droopy.

A gasp from Lulu startled me into an upright posture. "What is it, Lulu?" Lord, I hoped it wasn't George again. Or—heaven help us all—one or both of my parents.

"I-I think that's Mr. Gabriel's machine," Lulu said softly. I heard the longing in her whisper.

"I think you're right," said Ernie, peering out a window of Harvey's Rolls-Royce Limousine. "It looks like a Flint E-55, and Rob's the only person I know who drives one of those."

"Oh good," I said, feeling a teensy bit more sprightly. "We can all talk tonight and figure out how to approach my parents tomorrow."

"Yeah," said Lulu dreamily. I think Lulu was head over heels for Mr. Gabriel. I wasn't sure about Mr. Gabriel, but if he broke Lulu's heart I'd break his head.

It was definitely Mr. Gabriel. He hurried from the Flint E-55 to the backdoor of Harvey's limo. He went to the door closest to Lulu, which I took as a good sign. When he opened the door and Lulu all but fell into his arms, I figured it was another good sign.

"Glad you got here, Rob," said Ernie. He helped me exit my side of the car.

No answer from Mr. Gabriel, who was occupied in embracing Lulu.

"Oh, I'm so glad you finally made it home!" came Chloe's voice from the top of the porch stairs. "Harvey telephoned and told me what happened today. I'm so sorry you had to go through all of that nasty business. It's difficult to imagine real New York gangsters trying to take over the studio."

"It's not all that hard to believe for some of us," said Ernie, his tone ironic.

Lulu and Mr. Gabriel finally released each other. Lulu's face flamed in the fading light of the day. Mr. Gabriel appeared happy as a lark ascending. He'd better stay that way.

Hmm. Evidently, I had a prolonged case of the surlies. It had been a rough week so far, and it was only...Tuesday? Crumb. No, it was Wednesday. Unless it was...nertz, I didn't even know what day it was.

"Come on up. Is that Mr. Gabriel?" asked Chloe in her musical voice.

I honestly adored Chloe, who was my best friend as well as my sister, but it did seem a little unfair that she got all the beauty in the family. I mean she had a beautiful face, hair, voice, and gait. You'd never find Chloe suffering from an allergy to stinging nettles in her makeup. As I trudged up the porch steps, I managed a smile for her. And the pink bundle in her arms.

"If you never put that baby down, it'll never learn to walk you know," I said, trying to make my voice sound teasing and not merely cantankerous. Don't think I succeeded very well.

"Don't be silly, Mercy," said Chloe, who smiled even though she'd heard my touchy tone.

"Sorry," I said, peeking at the cherub in the pink blankie. Still looked like a hairless pug dog to me. I'd almost decided motherhood was a definite "no" for me, although one never knows what the future will bring, does one?

"Oh, you have the baby!" cried Lulu, who didn't share my opinion about babies, as already noted. "Rob, come here and look at this beautiful child! I've never seen a prettier baby." Lulu hurried up the stairs behind me and bumped me aside. I don't think she meant to. She was excited.

"A baby!" said Mr. Gabriel, sounding as if he'd expected to see a nest full of ducklings. "That's a cutie-pie, all right," he said, peering over Lulu's shoulder at the baby.

Ernie joined me and we shared a significant glance. It signified that neither Ernie nor I could detect beauty in that newish human being. It was good to have a pal in an opinion other people would consider strange at the least.

Those of us who had been at the studio all day, except Harvey and Mr. Gabriel who stayed downstairs and chatted, took the elevator to the second floor. Lulu's step was light when she took off for her room. She didn't even wait for me. I didn't mind.

"Glad she's happy," Ernie said, taking my arm.

"Yeah." I sighed. "I am too, but I'm bushed."

"So am I. I'll walk you to your room. I think Lulu's flying."

"Yeah," I said again. Then I shook my head hard, which hurt. Guess I hadn't fully recovered from the day before. Well, and that day too. Neither ranked among the top days of my life.

"It'll be all right now, Mercy," said Ernie. "Now that the Salvatore gang has lost its head and a couple of its arms and a leg or two, it will take a long time for some other gang to shoot its way to the top of the pile again."

"Why do people do that?" I asked.

"What?" Ernie sounded surprised.

"Kill people and threaten people and deliberately lead people astray. I've always considered George an imbecile, but I know his heart is broken. Until this escapade, I didn't think he had a heart."

"Don't know," said Ernie. "For some kids, I think joining gangs is a way to feel safe. In some cities like Chicago and New York, there are neighborhoods full of wretchedly poor people who live miserable lives. Lots of kids in those neighborhoods join gangs in order to feel safe. Hell, they'll join gangs in order to get enough food to eat."

"Golly," I said. "I know I'm innocent, but that sounds…incredible."

"It's true though," said Ernie. "I was lucky to grow up in a neighborhood not quite as bad as some of those run by the gangs. Hell, there have been gangs in New York City since the last century. Probably in Chicago, too, but I managed to miss out."

"I'm glad." I said.

We'd made it to my bedroom door, where Ernie took me into his arms and gave me a very comforting squeeze. Then he kissed me, and I decided I might be able to live another day. We just stood there with our arms around each other for a few minutes.

"Sorry you've had such a rough few days, Mercy. I honestly didn't think the problems on that set were gang-related. Don't know why. Just about everything has been gang-related since Prohibition was made the law of the land."

"But you think the problems are over now? For sure?" I asked.

"I do, at least for the studio. And after we fill Rob in on the state of your idiot brother, tomorrow will probably see the end of him too."

"I'm so glad," I said, my eyes filling with tears. Stupid emotions.

"But let's get cleaned up now. It's almost dinnertime."

"It's past dinnertime," I said, swallowing the lump in my throat. I looked at the clock in the foyer and found I was correct. It was already past dinnertime. "I expect Mr. Garnier is throwing a tantrum in the kitchen right now."

"I'm sure Chloe will feed us something," said Ernie soothingly. "You all right? I need to get cleaned up too."

Reluctantly, I allowed my arms to drop from around Ernie's person. "Yes, I'm all right. I'll be ready in fifteen minutes or so."

"Take your time," said Ernie. "There's no hurry."

"That's good," I said. Then I turned the knob to my door and entered the room Chloe had allotted to me. The one room was big enough for a family of four to live in. Would there ever be anything even close to equality in the world? I decided I was too melancholy and exhausted to think about it, so I went to the bathroom and took a bath. It took me longer than fifteen minutes to prepare myself to meet everyone again.

When I'd dusted the last of the powder on my face and fluffed off the excess, I heard a timid tap on my door. Lulu said, "Mercy? C'n I come in?"

"Sure, Lulu." I attempted to sound chipper for her.

Lulu looked as if she'd been touched by a fairy's wand when she entered my room. "I didn't want to walk downstairs alone," she said. "Are you ready?"

"I'm ready," I said with a sigh. "I'd almost rather have a sandwich sent up and go to bed."

"Oh no, you can't do that!" Lulu said. "Rob...I mean, Mr. Gabriel is here! We have to talk about how he's going to get your parents to bail your brother out of the pokey and get him back to Boston."

"Of course. Sorry, Lulu. I forgot about that for a second." I hadn't forgotten; I was in a disillusioned mood and didn't feel like thinking about the real world for a while.

Huh. Listen to me. All I'd wanted when I'd first come to Los Angeles was to see for myself how "real" people lived. Right then, I believed I'd seen about enough of them to last me another year or twenty. I attempted to buck myself up. It wasn't Lulu's fault my family was filthy rich and most of the rest of the people in the world were merely filthy.

Ernie walked to my room shortly after Lulu arrived in it, and I perked up some. For all the differences in our backgrounds, Ernie actually seemed to understand why humanity's many disparities bothered me.

It's a good thing Chloe was a perfect person, because even though he had to make special arrangements, Chef Garnier served a spectacular meal. He'd never have done such a thing if anyone but Chloe had asked him to do so.

"He whined a bit about having to tear the chicken apart and serve it up in an Italian sauce," she told us as we sat at the table sipping a delicious vegetable soup. "He had to make minestrone with his vegetables too. That's the soup you're eating."

"It's delicious," I said. "I'm impressed. I don't even know how to roast a chicken, much less tear it up and fix another dish entirely. And the soup has noodles in it."

"We used to get good Italian grub in Chicago," Ernie said. "This is as good as any minestrone I ate in Chi-Town."

With one of her tinkling laughs, Chloe said, "I'll be sure to tell Mr. Garnier you said so."

Ernie and I sat across from Mr. Gabriel and Lulu, and I was pleased to note that he seemed as eager to be with her as she was to be with him. Sidney Lafayette sat beside me on one side, and Ernie sat on the other.

Perhaps I was merely hungry, or perhaps it was more than that, but I didn't feel as discouraged and crabby as I had when we'd come home. That is to say when we'd returned to Chloe and Harvey's home.

We gathered in the Nashes' upstairs sitting room next door to the nursery and discussed how to get rid of my idiot brother on the morrow. The Salvatore crew members were all going to be locked up for decades, if they didn't have a short sit in the electric chair. But my brother wasn't actually guilty of anything except stupidity, and, while I thought he deserved a long prison sentence for it, the state of California wouldn't.

By the time we all went to bed, I was ready to go home to Bunker Hill and to my job at the Figueroa Building. The motion-picture business held no appeal whatsoever.

Rob Gabriel, Esq. spent the night in the Nash mansion. Chloe had Molly or another maid fix one of the guest suites for him. His room was right down the hall from Lulu's, Ernie's, and my rooms. When he stepped inside the first room, he blinked, looked around and said, "This is bigger than my apartment in Los Angeles."

"Yeah," said Ernie. "The Nashes are rolling in it."

"I guess so," said Mr. Gabriel. Then he glanced at Lulu.

"We'll leave you here," said Ernie quickly. "I'm for bed."

"Me too," I said.

"Me three," said Lulu. "I'll be right there." Her cheeks were bright pink when she glanced at Ernie and me.

As Ernie and I returned to our rooms, I whispered, "He'd better not try to do anything with Lulu."

"He won't. Unlike some of his friends, Rob is a gentleman."

"You mean you're not a gentleman?"

"Not much of one. But neither Rob nor I think seducing young women is a good idea."

"Good. Remember all those Mrs. Smedleys we met a few weeks back? Mr. Smedley sure didn't mind seducing young women. And it's always the woman who pays the price."

"Yes," said Ernie. "I know. We've had this discussion before."

"Are you laughing at me?"

"Nope."

We'd reached my door and Ernie took me in his arms. "I'll be glad to get back to the Figueroa Building," he said after he'd given me a satisfying kiss. "These places in Beverly Hills, Hancock Park, and Holmby Hills make me think of all the starving kids in Chicago, New York, and other places."

"Really?" I was shocked.

"Really. You're bad for me, Mercy. Because of you, I now have a conscience. It's a real pain in the neck sometimes."

That was probably the nicest thing anyone had ever said to me.

THIRTY-ONE

The following morning, Ernie and Harvey made arrangements for a trunk telephone call to be placed to my parents' home in Boston early in the evening. When it was early on the California coast, it was three hours later in Boston, so my parents would surely be home.

After making those arrangements, Harvey and Sid Lafayette—who had also spent the night in the Nash castle—discussed the resumption of *Helen of Troy*. They decided Sid could take over direction of the production from now on. All the disrupters were locked up (or dead). Harvey was delighted because he wanted to stay home with Chloe and No-Name for a couple of weeks or months or whatever.

The next order of business was for Mr. Gabriel to telephone the jail where George languished behind bars. He discovered the price to bail George out of the clink was five-thousand dollars. That seemed high to me. I told Ernie so.

"It is high," he told me. "I made sure of it yesterday when we were at the P.D. I wanted it high enough so that your parents will feel a small pinch and your idiot brother will be ashamed of himself.

With any luck, he'll also straighten up and stop messing around with chorus girls."

"You really think so?" I wasn't so sure of my brother's future uprightness.

"If he's threatened with disinheritance, I expect he'll toe the line."

"How will you be sure Father will threaten him with disinheritance?"

"Rob sent your daddy a cablegram this morning telling him about George's recent career as a criminal and a patsy for the Salvatore crime organization. I expect the newspapers are filled to the brim with the murders of Carmine Salvatore and his top henchmen. I have a feeling Daddy will hop to it to get Georgie back home and under his thumb again."

"Crumb, when you put it like that, I'm afraid Father will disinherit him anyway. Then we might be stuck with him forever."

"You got any more brothers hanging around back in Boston? Any close male cousins?"

"No," I said.

"Then I have a feeling George will be hauled back to Boston immediately if not sooner."

"I hope you're right."

Ernie was absolutely correct. When the operator called at five p.m. that day and said the trunk call to Boston had been placed, Harvey and Mr. Gabriel sat at the table in the marble foyer. The rest of us gathered in Harvey's office and lifted the receiver from the hook. We wanted to hear as much of the conversation as possible. Ernie held the receiver and we all huddled around it like a bunch of kids pulling a prank.

Rob Gabriel sounded legal and official (maybe even a little officious) when he related George's recent antics to Father. He emphasized the two murders on the set and told Father that George might be charged as an accessory after the fact for at least one of the deaths. He really slathered it on thick. I was impressed.

Father and Mother conferred out of our hearing for several moments. Then Mother got on the wire.

"What *is* this nonsense?" Mother said in her best overbearing, rich-lady voice.

"If you consider your son's involvement with the Salvatore mob nonsense, ma'am, we have nothing left to talk about. We'll just leave him locked up. You might be called upon to provide him with a defense attorney when his case comes to trial."

"What? *What?*"

Wow, I'd never heard my mother screech before. Almost made the last few days worthwhile, but didn't quite.

"I don't believe I need to repeat my last statement, Mrs. Allcutt. All you and Mr. Allcutt need do is tell me if you plan to post bond for your son. If you do, I'll see that he is out of his cell today. I can even put him on a train to Boston, but that courtesy will add to the bond that has already been levied. I will be able to negotiate with the Los Angeles Police Department to allow him to leave the state, but I won't represent him henceforth. You will need to hire another attorney for his trial."

"His-his *trial?*"

I'd also never heard my mother nearly speechless before. I was about ready to begin calling Mr. Gabriel Rob.

"If he is charged as an accessory to murder after the fact, he will face a trial for the crime. My duties as his attorney for today's negotiations have been paid for by Mr. Harvey Nash, but will not be representing your son after today. Therefore, I believe you and your husband would be best served by giving me an answer now. Will you post his bond, or will you not post his bond?"

"H-how do we post his bond?" asked Mother, her voice still small.

We heard what sounded like a scuffle filter its way through the telephone wire from Boston to Beverly Hills, and the next person to speak was Father.

"I will make arrangements to cable you the bond money for George," said Father. "I'm not sure I can get you the money tonight. And did you say his bond might be higher if you can get him on the train to Boston?"

"Yes, it will be higher. Because I believe your son is guiltier of gullibility and stupidity than criminality, I am willing to remain his attorney until noon California time tomorrow. This will add another fifteen-hundred dollars to the total cost."

"So I'll need to wire you six thousand five hundred dollars, is that correct?"

"Yes," said Rob. "That is correct."

After a few seconds of silence, Father said, "Very well. I shall cable the money to you. Where shall I send it?"

Rob gave him his office address on Flower and Eighth Streets in downtown Los Angeles. His office was far, far away from Beverly Hills, but neither of my parents needed to know it.

"Very well," said Father in a tone I knew boded ill for George. I couldn't think of a more deserving recipient of our parents' wrath.

After another, shorter conversation, Rob put the receiver on the hook in the foyer. Ernie did the same to the telephone in Harvey's office. Then those of us in the office skedaddled out to the foyer, where a lot of hugging and congratulations ensued.

Not sure about anyone else, but I would be extremely glad when my idiot brother was out of Los Angeles and on his way to Boston. I hoped, with some justification, that our parents would give him heck and keep him on a short leash from now on.

On the following day, Sid went to his own home. He assured Harvey that he was prepared to resume work on *Helen of Troy*.

Also on the following morning, Ernie, Lulu, and I waited until Rob received a telephone call from his secretary in downtown Los Angeles, telling him my parents had come through with the dough.

As soon as the news was received, Rob and Ernie went to the Los Angeles County Jail to bail out George. Because his bail money had been received but was in downtown Los Angeles, Harvey paid for George's bail and his train ticket to Boston. Although Harvey said he didn't need to, Rob told him he'd pay him back as soon as he could.

For the record, Rob was as good as his word. He sent Harvey a check as soon as he got back to his office and got the money Mother and Father cabled to his office. Harvey refused to cash it, telling Rob he deserved the money. I thought both men were extremely kind.

On Friday, it was a relieved party of six (seven if you count No-Name) that gathered in the downstairs parlor while the Nashes' household staff packed our bags. I actually felt as if I'd lost maybe ten or twelve pounds of worry. I'm sure that's silly, but it's true.

"I'm so glad they sent the moola," I said to Chloe and Harvey. "I feared our parents would wash their hands of George. Then he might be in your hair for the rest of his life."

"No, he wouldn't," said Harvey. "I know people who handle people like George."

"People?" I said, alarmed.

"People," said Harvey.

"Good," said Ernie. "If your people need help my people can assist, but I think George will be a good boy from now on."

"I wouldn't bet on it," I muttered.

"Thank you for negotiating with our parents, Mr. Gabriel," said Chloe.

"Not a problem. And call me Rob."

"Very well. Rob," said Chloe, adding a beautiful smile.

"I'm so glad we don't have to go back to that set," said Lulu. Then she shot a scared glance at Harvey. "We *don't* have to go back to the set, do we?"

"Nope," said Harvey, smiling broadly. "You've fulfilled your duties well. I'm only sorry they turned out to be hazardous. I hadn't anticipated the violence."

"You hadn't anticipated New York gangsters showing up," said Ernie.

"True," said Harvey.

"Oh, but we have some good news for you!" said Chloe. "Mercy will be particularly happy to hear this."

"I will?" Puzzled was I.

"We've named the baby!" Chloe announced.

"Hoorah!" I shouted. My shout was unwise, as it woke the child.

Fortunately, she only let out a little jump and squeak and then settled into her pink blankie in her beautiful mother's arms. Harvey gazed upon this scene with a sentimental expression.

Oh, very well. Maybe all new fathers look like that. I doubt it, though, or there wouldn't be so many unwed mothers running around loose. Not to mention orphans.

Somebody stop me! I'm climbing on my soapbox again!

Whew. Sorry.

"So what have you decided to name her?" asked Lulu, who got up and walked to Chloe's other side.

Chloe and Harvey exchanged a loving glance. It was so sweet, it nearly made me sick.

Mercy! Stop it!

"Our precious daughter will be known forevermore as Heather Rose," said Chloe.

"Heather Rose Nash," Harvey confirmed. "Until she gets married."

"I love it!" I said, not quite as loudly as I'd spoken earlier. But I spoke the truth. I thought it was a beautiful name.

"I do too," said Lulu, clasping her hands over her bosom and appearing enraptured. "She's *such* a gorgeous baby. And now she has a gorgeous name to go with her looks."

"Indeed," said Rob, not quite as ecstatically as Lulu, but doing a good job of sounding happy.

"Great name," said Ernie. "I like it."

Rob and Lulu shared Rob's auto on the way home. Ernie and I went in Ernie's Packard-Six. Buttercup sat on my lap.

Ernie and I didn't speak for several miles. Then Ernie said, "I like Heather Rose. It's a nice name."

"I agree," I agreed.

"A helluva lot prettier than that baby," said Ernie.

I hesitated for a few seconds, agreeing with Ernie but thinking it wouldn't be nice to say so aloud. Finally I said, "I expect she'll grow into her name."

Ernie only laughed. So I laughed with him.

DANCING ANGELS

A MERCY ALLCUTT MYSTERY, BOOK TEN

"If you ever go back to that place, I'll kidnap you and lock you in a closet!"

My boss, Ernie Templeton, P.I., had never hollered at me like this before. I didn't like it one bit. He was mad as heck. His startlingly blue eyes practically shot flames, his fists were clenched and his face wore the colors of a fiery sunset.

"You have no right to tell me what to do!" I hollered back, my own fists clenched and planted on my hips. I suspect my cheeks were also red and my own eyes blazed. "You're my boss, not my father!"

"Cripes," said Ernie, his voice lowering slightly. "Not even your father could tell you what to do and be obeyed. But that dancing studio is off limits! If you think I'm spewing applesauce, go back one more time. I'll fire you!"

"You can't fire me for something I do out of the office!"

"Try me!"

Very well, so this wasn't getting either of us anywhere. I made an effort to unclench my fists and calm down but didn't succeed. Nevertheless, I tried to sound reasonable when I said, "Ernie, it wasn't my fault that somebody killed Marian Murray."

"I never said it was!" he roared. "But you're not hanging around another murder scene, dammit! Can't you *ever* stay away from trouble?"

"I'm not *in* trouble! It was poor Marian Murray who was murdered, Ernie! I should think you'd want to find out who did it and *why*!"

"I'll look into what happened and why when somebody hires me to do it!" He was still roaring.

"Good!" I snapped. Then I marched out of Ernie's office and into my own. There I opened the right bottom drawer of my desk and plucked out my handbag. The drawer should have held dozens of file folders, but business had been slack of late. I opened the purse in my handbag, and withdrew three twenty-dollar bills. I know, I know. It's not my fault I was born with a silver spoon in my mouth. Ever since I'd moved from Boston to Los Angeles, I'd been attempting to fit in amongst the worker proletariat with mixed success.

Stomping back to Ernie's office, I held out the tree twenties and snapped, "Here! *I'm* hiring you to bring Marian Murray's killer to justice!"

"*I'm not going to take your money!*" Ernie went so far as to stamp his foot. He'd also resumed bellowing.

"Whoa," came a voice from my office. "I could hear you two from the elevator." This time it was I who stamped my foot.

The voice belonged to Phil Bigelow, detective with the Los Angeles Police Department and Ernie's best friend. According to Ernie, Phil was the only incorruptible copper in the entire department. I'd begun to wonder about this assessment after slightly more than a year's exposure to Detective Bigelow.

"Phil," I said in a colorless tone.

"Dammit, Phil, tell this woman it isn't safe to look into murders by herself!"

"Who said anything about doing it myself?" I barked in a no-longer-colorless tone. I pointed at Ernie and whirled around to face Phil, who most likely wouldn't be on my side, but what the heck. "I asked *him* to find the murderer! I never said I'd do it on my own."

"You did too!" hollered Ernie. "You said you were going back to that damned dance studio!"

"So what?" I bellowed back. "Why shouldn't I? Lulu and I are taking *lessons!*"

"Because people get *murdered* there, you idiot!"

"I'm *not* an idiot!"

Raising his hands as if to ward off a blow, Phil said loudly, "Hey, kids. Take a powder and calm down."

I was about to tell him to mind his own business when Ernie, upon whom I'd turned my back—big mistake, that—clamped his hands on my shoulders. "Shut up, Mercy. I think Phil has some information for us."

"Who precisely is this *us* of whom you speak?" I said, trying and failing to free myself from his hands. "And now you're using physical *restraint* on me? Officer, arrest this man! He's abusing me," I shrieked at Phil.

Another voice joined the chorus, this one high and piping. "Holy cow! What's goin' on in there?"

Junior. I sagged under Ernie's hands. Perhaps we had been a bit noisy. Junior was only a lad who did odd jobs in our workplace, the Figueroa Building. I didn't want to set a bad example no matter how furious I got with my boss.

"You better now?" asked Ernie in his normal speaking voice.

I flared up again and almost shouted that I hadn't been unwell and therefore couldn't get *better*, but I didn't. In fact, I didn't speak at all. I was still irate.

"If you two have finished your...disagreement," said Phil, "you might be interested in the case we just got. Involves a murder at a dance studio."

"Oooh, a *murder?*" Junior sounded delighted. Then he must have seen the bills in my hand. "Criminy! Are those *twenties?*" He spoke as if he'd never seen a twenty-dollar bill before in his life.

I sagged a little more when I realized he probably hadn't.

Unhanding me, Ernie said tentatively, "You want to talk about the murder at the Murray Dance Studio, Phil?"

"Indeed I do," said Phil. He eyed Junior askance and said, "Better not to in front of the kid."

The inquisitive smile vanished from Junior's face, and he said, "Aw nertz."

"Say, Junior," said Ernie, reaching into his trouser pocket. "Will you please go across the street to the deli—or around the corner to the Chinese place—and get us some lunch?" He pulled out a ten-dollar bill.

Forestalling Ernie in his attempt to divert Junior's attention, I handed the kid one of my own twenty-dollar bills. I'd never seen a boy's eyes grow so wide. Good grief. This was how the "other half" lived, I guess. Only, since I'd left Boston for Los Angeles, it seemed to me that there were a lot more than half of the people in the USA who lived less pampered lives than mine had been.

Sometimes I got discouraged, thinking I'd never become comfortable living in the middle class. Upper middle class.

As Junior just said, nertz.

"Please go to the Canton Palace, Junior," I said. "Get enough for all four of us, including you."

Snatching the twenty as if he feared I might take it back, Junior turned and ran for the front office door. "Sure thing, Miss Mercy!" he hollered. His was a happy holler, unlike those Ernie and I had been flinging at each other.

Available in Paperback and eBook from Your Favorite Bookstore or Online Retailer

ABOUT THE AUTHOR

Award-winning author Alice Duncan lives with a herd of wild dachshunds (enriched from time to time with fosterees from New Mexico Dachshund Rescue) in Roswell, New Mexico. She's not a UFO enthusiast; she's in Roswell because her mother's family settled there fifty years before the aliens crashed (and living in Roswell, NM, is cheaper than living in Pasadena, CA, unfortunately). Alice would love to hear from you at alice@aliceduncan.net

www.aliceduncan.net